THE IRON TITHE

A catalogue record for this book is available from the National Library of Australia.

ISBN Paperback: 97806452353807
ISBN EPub: 9780645235814

First Printing, 2021
Hatta Press

The Iron Tithe

K. D. KIND

Hatta Press

The People of the Wave and the Wing

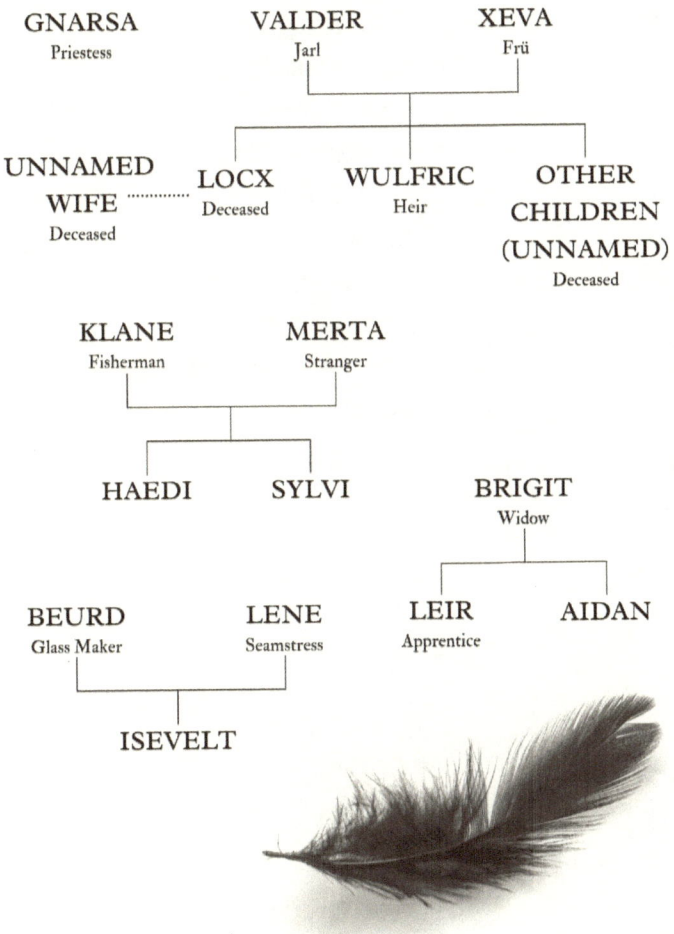

GNARSA
Priestess

VALDER
Jarl

XEVA
Frü

UNNAMED WIFE
Deceased

LOCX
Deceased

WULFRIC
Heir

OTHER CHILDREN (UNNAMED)
Deceased

KLANE
Fisherman

MERTA
Stranger

HAEDI

SYLVI

BRIGIT
Widow

BEURD
Glass Maker

LENE
Seamstress

LEIR
Apprentice

AIDAN

ISEVELT

They became sisters.
If sisters are women who are bonded in blood,
then that is what they became.
Bonded by being bathed in the blood of their mothers.
The bond was of little solace to them, that day,
as they crouched in the shallows,
silently sluicing the blood from each other's limbs.
It was of little solace to them, ever.
Simply knowing that another has endured the same trial
is not enough.
True comfort comes from knowing that another survived.
But these did not survive.

* * *

PART ONE

Before.

I

Hours before, when the day itself was so new-born that it hadn't yet drawn breath to cry.

The moon flew low on the horizon; so low that it was obscured by the ribbons of mist draping themselves over the length of the settlement. The village lay nestled in the crook of the coast; long, low lying houses and halls built almost exclusively of grey timber.

The timber was a comfort. Not only because it kept the wind (ferocious, incessant wind) outside, but also for the sound that it made in doing so. The quiet creak, like the subtle shifting of weight from foot to foot. Like the muttering made by the boats (equally as low, equally as long) housed in the little harbour. From the water, where the people drew their sustenance, found their security.

It was easy to see why the once wandering people had chosen to settle on that little stretch of coast. Why they'd turned their lashings to land, instead of just to spoils. The land called to their colouring (white wood on black sand/black hair on white skin).

Just behind the settlement, a bowshot behind the bay, grew a vast forest of silver birchwood. Left untouched for centuries, and densely packed where seeds had sown themselves year after year, the wood promised the people everything that they could require. That they could hope for. From the forest came the buildings, came the boats. Came the shields, and the bows, and the end.

And the end, and the end, and the end.

The settlement was secure on all sides. Indeed, so densely packed were the trees, that no enemy could get through the forest without first carving a path, either by furrow or by flame. The bay itself bottlenecked to the width of a single boat, built up on either side with rocky cairns that guaranteed the defenders the high ground.

There the people tilled the earth: small gardens a stone's throw from their front doors, where all hands toiled so that all mouths were fed. The children played and grew, the adults were industrious, and the elders were idly wise.

But perhaps...

Perhaps they would not have felt so safely nestled there, between wood and sea, if they saw the trap that they had built for themselves. Penned themselves in with scarcely a bark of a dog or a crack of a switch to serve as warning. Penned in and waiting to be overcome by the people with hair the colour of flames, the colour of the blood on their swords, flashing in the moonlight.

They were the danger crouching beneath the mist, in the hours before dawn.

It was an enmity that lived long before the people with the silver-white skin and the raven-dark hair made their lives in the birchwood bay. And although it lay dormant for generations, on that morning in the mist, it found them there.

No. Wait.
Further back... a moon or so.
Before they became sisters.

* * *

II

It seemed to Haedi that everything needed cleaning. The fish of their scales. The birds of their down. Her father's sword of its rust. The hearth of its ash. Her mind of its troublesome, wearisome thoughts.

Her mother, Merta, was exhaustingly exemplary; the determination with which she ordered the existence of her husband, Klane, and their two girls, Haedi and Sylvi, was bordering upon genius. And they all thanked her for it. But only *after* the scales, and the feathers, and the rust, and the ash, had been sluiced from their fingers by the water from the bay.

Her mother said it was a spiritual thing, the way she insisted that her family be drenched after a day of labour. Said that their bodies were born again: delivered by the water from all manner of injury and impurity. Haedi appreciated it once she was drying by the hearth fire, with the hearth already clean of its ash. But not before. Not while she was still shivering and blue from cold.

The fire burned dull and low that evening as she sat before it, turning her hair this way and that to the waves of heat. As she pulled, the strands separated and clung in turn, throwing thoughts of the nets the people used for fishing down in the bay through her mind, catching her thoughts like wriggling trout, demanding to be freed.

Haedi felt rather than heard her sister's presence. Sylvi dropped quietly down beside her — no, just behind her — absently twisting her own long, raven-dark hair into a simple plait that ended just below her ribcage. Sylvi never bothered to dry it before the fire. Said she didn't mind the water. Maybe she didn't.

Haedi turned to look at Sylvi. They were of a likeness. Could even be identical if they put some effort into it. But it took *trying* to change the very natures lurking just beneath the surface of their features; that differently coloured light that burst forth or dimmed in each expression and emotion. So, they seldom tried.

They'd spoken about it, at night, after the moon had set. When the darkness had stolen all need for faces. They'd talked about how there wasn't truly anyone they'd want to fool, even if they could. That, and the dormant terror of forgetting.

"I wonder sometimes," Sylvi murmured as she finished off her plait with a single strand of old thread, "If it's a good thing or a bad thing that we have to clean father's sword as often as we do."

Haedi separated another lock of hair and offered it to the embers. "The rust, you mean?"

"Yes." Sylvi frowned into the middle distance. It was a common practice for the younger sister; a safe place for her features to rest while her thoughts roamed unfettered.

"You mean, that we clean it as often as we do? Rust dulls the blade. It needs to stay silver if it's to stay sharp."

"No," Sylvi replied, as she shifted her weight on her long limbs, redistributing the load over interlocked arms and legs. "I understand that the salt from the air eats the metal. The air is always salty; and so, the metal always rusts."

Sylvi was always patient, despite Haedi being often abrupt. Immediate. Even though Haedi so often wanted to arrive at the end of an interaction the moment it began.

"What do you mean, then?" Haedi asked.

"I mean, the fact that it is *able* to rust. That father spends all of his time on the water throwing for fish, and that we are cleaning rust from the blade and not blood."

Haedi turned slowly to stare at her sister, aghast. "In what circumstance is that a bad thing?"

Sylvi shrugged simply. "I didn't say that I'd reached a conclusion," she said, "Just that I'd often wondered."

Well, why say it at all? Haedi thought. But she didn't give it voice. Sylvi's was a gentle spirit, with no malice in it. Any malevolence that Haedi drew from Sylvi's words was her own.

"Wulf spoke again of bonding," Haedi said quietly, in part to change the subject, and in part to ease the weight of the words from her tongue.

"When does the mere speaking stop?" Sylvi asked with mock exasperation.

"When he stops speaking to *me* and starts speaking to his father."

"How do you know that he hasn't already?"

Haedi gritted her teeth, fanning the last lock open to the heat of the hearth. "I somehow have the feeling that I would know."

"Mmm." Sylvi's acknowledgement was a resigned one. Wulf's father, a man by the name of Valder, was the Jarl – the King – of their people, and not a man to let plans sit idly by or go quietly unworked. Especially not in the wake of tragedy. "Well, he had better say something soon, or Valder will make arrangements of his own. Wulf needs to have children, especially now."

Haedi stood with a huff of breath. *We all need to have children*, she thought, *especially now*. She was already impatient for the bond between herself and Wulf to be established. It was not just that she loved him, no. She also loved their people. And as Wulf's wife, she would be able to serve them, too.

Sorry.
Further again.
For daughters often begin with their fathers.

* * *

III

It would not seem at a casual glance as though the paths through the village had any sort of planning to them. However, a day in observation of the dance performed by the people of the black sand bay revealed a clear set of steps known by all.

Beurd lumbered along the path that ran behind the hall, determinedly turning a piece of sea-coloured glass between his first three fingers. The long ribbon grass had been trampled into submission many years before, causing a deep parting that allowed for easy passage from the north end of the village to the south, where the bay lay.

The rate of the glass pebble spinning in Beurd's fingers matched the gallop of his heart. It was not from exertion, though; Beurd was a wall of a man, thickly muscled and with the lung capacity necessary for a glassblower of his skill. Rather, it was nervousness that aided the trip of his heart, the speed of his step, the spin of the sea-coloured glass.

At the end of the path, closer to the bay than any other house, lived the witch.

As far as he knew, Beurd was the only person who took issue with the witch. And it seemed that she knew it, too. Possibly Merta, the wife of Klane the fisherman, also had reservations, but that was on account of her being an outsider. Klane had fetched Merta back from some shipwreck decades before, and she still remembered the learning and spirituality from her life before. But Beurd was a raven man. The sorcery was part of his bones. It should not have disquieted him so.

Even more, his own daughter worked as a sort of apprentice to the witch. If his wife, Lene, would allow Isevelt that, then what threat could there really be in the place?

As he crested the little hill that hid the hut from the rest of the village, a dark bird started to shriek. Was it just a fancy, or were there more mists here than in any other part of the bay?

Roughly spun cloths snapped in the sudden wind, where they sat strung on lines suspended between the grey side of the house and a large, lone birchwood tree. *There were plenty of women in the village who would have done a better job on the cloth*, he thought. But Gnarsa would allow no fingers save her own to work the fabric that she used in her magics and in her healings.

Beurd stepped carefully through the overgrown garden to the front door. He hesitated before knocking; the last time that he had visited the witch, she had crept up through the garden and given him a fright. After minutes of what would have been silent stillness if not for the wind, Beurd lifted a heavy hand and banged his fist against the closed door. Footsteps from inside.

Rotten witch, he thought acidly. He was sure that this, too, was belligerent pageantry aimed at ensuring his discomfort.

The latch clicked and the door swung open, inwards, allowing a glimpse of the dimness within. The walls were the same grey inside as out. The age of the house had turned the birchwood from stark, moonbeam white to a dirt-washed silver. Little light was allowed in through the scant windows, as they were covered, like most of the surfaces, with drying and flowering plants. Not to mention the louvred wood which Gnarsa preferred over the glass that Beurd's family had made for most of the other buildings.

The witch herself appeared in the doorway. She and Beurd were of a height, and so would normally see eye-to-eye. As it was, the house was built upon a foundation that kept the flooring safe from tidal flooding, and so, Gnarsa was able to look down her broad, pointed nose at him for as long as she held the greeting in stasis.

"Gnarsa," he growled.

"Beurd. You're earlier than I expected. Why do you sound so displeased? Won't you come in?" She slid elegantly sideways, allowing him entry.

"This is the quality of my voice," Beurd replied as he followed her into the depths of the main room. "Think nothing of it."

As with nearly all of the houses in the birchwood bay, Gnarsa's doubled as her workshop. While most of her personal effects were mixed in with the flotsam of the workroom (here a dress, there a carved wooden comb), her bed was hidden from view by a screen of intricately worked ribbon grass. Beurd found that he was not at all intrigued by the mysteries lurking behind the ribbon grass screen.

He imagined the conversation were he to tell his wife of his lack of intrigue, and then allowed himself a single, small, wry smile. He looked up at the witch just in time to see her nod to herself in satisfaction, before extinguishing a guttering tallow candle in a single, sharp breath. The smoke curled toward him like a beckoning finger, and, as he tasted the deep, earthen scent on his tongue, the urge to smile again took over his features.

"Does something amuse you?" Gnarsa asked as she settled herself neatly onto a low stool.

"Much amuses me," Beurd replied. He remained standing near the threshold, where the straw was spread more thinly, and the cold was able to draught more freely. His boyish fear of the depths of the witch's lair had not been assuaged by mirthful thoughts of his wife, but merely held at bay. The pebble spun again in his hand, drawing Gnarsa's eye.

"You have it?" she asked. Her excitement was clear in both the shine of her eyes and the rush of her breath. As she reached out for the pebble, the draped outer layer of her clothing fell away, revealing the string of beads and bones around her neck. Beurd flinched, and the glass slipped from his hand. She did not mark his clumsiness. "And you made it the way we discussed?"

Beurd sheepishly scooped the glass from between the fingers of straw and dropped it into the palm that she still held aloft. "Yes. I took saltwater from the bay and burnt it back, then mixed the sand with black ash before I fired it."

"Good." She held the glass up to her eye, watching the light play through its centre. "And when the time comes, when I ask you, you will be able to turn this into vessels?"

Beurd swallowed, feeling his tongue catch on the roof of his mouth. He pictured the vessels in his mind, with their dangerously sharp points, like daggers. He had managed to blow three of them from clear glass, around simple seawater, to her satisfaction. "The *vaces* you showed me? Yes."

"Good," Gnarsa said again as she stood. She turned and pulled several more layers of draped cloth and fur from a hook attached to the wall. These she wound around her body so that finally, all that remained visible were her deep brown eyes set below impassive brows.

"What are you doing?" Beurd asked. Surely, she had further instructions for him? Their every interaction for weeks had been a to-and-fro of her demands and his attempts to meet them. Surely, she could not already be content?

When Gnarsa answered, her words were delivered in a muffled staccato that fell heavily in between each layer of warmth. She bestowed the pebble back into his waiting hand.

"I need to see something. Something irrepressible. Now that we have the glass, I can begin the next phase." She paused, midway through wrapping a shawl around her shoulders. "But it will make me late for an appointment that I have with Valder. Could I trouble you to deliver my apologies to him?"

"He'll be on my way home anyhow," Beurd shrugged, dropping the glass stone into his deep pocket. "What would you have me say?"

Gnarsa turned her deep-set eyes to him, and there was a sadness in her expression that had been absent in the fizz of the moment before. "My apologies. Just... give Valder my apologies."

Beurd swallowed hard against the sudden lump in his throat and nodded, once. That was all anyone could do now; tell Valder how sorry they were. Little good it did.

They left together, but parted ways at the lonely birchwood tree; him back up the way he'd come over the rise and through the village, the witch around the bend and into the depths of the grove proper. What issue she had to deal with that she could somehow find to be both pressing and irrepressible he knew not, and he little desired to ponder it.

The path seemed more overgrown on the way back up. Did his feet falter as he neared the outer buildings? Were his steps slower, his footings less and less sure?

He chided himself.

Valder was his Jarl, and never a man who would hold back his strength or leave a brother to flounder. Yes, his was a time of grief. *But Valder being generous with his sadness does not give me leave to be selfish with my comfort*, Beurd thought sternly. *What would Lene say if she saw this hesitation?*

His steps lengthened; his shoulders squared.

Most of the decisions that Beurd made were motivated by the thought of his wife, Lene. Whether she would be proud of him. Whether she thought that he could do better. Their daughter Isevelt was a lot like Lene. Sweet tempered, but fierce in her love for those dear to her. She had just reached her nineteenth birthday; a woman grown. With a pang that stung more even than the brine taste of the air, Beurd thought of Valder, and how he would never see his son reach his quarter-century. The younger son, Wulfric, remained. But whether watching the younger boy's lope turn into a stride, his shoulders broaden, the lines of his brow deepen... whether seeing that would ease or draw tight the anguish of losing the other one, Beurd knew not. He and Lene had only been gifted with one child.

Here the paths became more pronounced, the air lost some of its crystalline salt sting, and the heartbeat of the bay was drowned out by the many sounds of the menagerie that filled the village. Here and there a cow stood, loosely tied to an iron peg thrust deep into a yard. Or else, a gaggle of chickens or – if the family was brave enough – geese, strutted through the vegetables.

It was share and share alike in the village. The ones with eggs swapped them for milk; the ones with potatoes swapped them for beans. Once a month an animal was slaughtered, and its bones picked clean with relish at the ceremonial feast by those ravenous for red meat after weeks upon weeks of pink or white fish. The wine was always abundant, even if it was not of excellent quality.

Beurd wondered if Valder had taken to wine, this last week. He could imagine the longing for warm, wine-sodden oblivion in the wake of the icy-cold shock of seeing a son and heir, washed up on the sand, white, and water-logged, and dead.

Beurd stopped and shuddered, scraping his rough palms over the rise of his cheeks.

He walked on.

Death was next, or so said the witch.

She called herself priestess. As did everyone else.

But Beurd had always had within himself a scepticism when it came to the gods, to magic. A scepticism, and a voiceless fear. And while the gods had kept the people safe all these years, the truth was that the Jarl's own son had gone missing for half a moon, and then returned outside of his own power, drowned, and (rumour was among the women) full of holes.

Perhaps, Beurd thought quietly to himself as he unlatched the oiled gate outside the Ban, *it is the thought of the gods turned apathetic, rather than the gods themselves, that scares me now.*

The Ban – the longhouse belonging to the Jarl – was much the same as any other in the settlement. True, Valder could have furnished it more splendidly or decorated it more lavishly, but he had never seemed so inclined. The rich tapestries on the inner walls and the ornate scrollwork around the eaves still remained from his father's time, but that was the only evidence of the Ban's former opulence. Under Valder's stewardship, the floor was rushed, the wood was silver, and the gate was only latched – just like everyone else's.

Did Valder fear danger, now? Now that his son had been killed by an unnamed evil – be it drowning, or a failing of his body, or by some danger until now unknown?

Beurd's thoughts quieted as he reached the closed door of the Ban, as though his mind could hold either a great weight, or a fleeting emptiness, but not both. He knocked on the frame (a deep, echoing sound rather than a sharp rap) and then turned his ear to the quiet within.

While he listened for footsteps, Beurd's eyes came to rest on the symbol etched into the wood near his hand: a half-circle broken by a barely breaking wave. Or was it a raven's wing? The debate was an old one, despite it being pulled out, shined up, and argued anew at each moon's feast. Wave or wing? It truly didn't matter. For the people of the raven were the people of the waves. Beurd would often reach that it was both. The circle was the moon, and the line was both a wing and a wave. It was *them*.

Beurd squinted his eyes in an attempt to hear better with his ears. He shook his head minutely, then scratched it.

Knock again?

If Valder was expecting the witch, then surely Beurd's presence wouldn't be too much of an imposition. He raised his fist again, hesitating. Just as Beurd brought his hand down to knock once more, he heard a sharp wailing blow around the Ban on the back of the wind.

He halted mid-movement, his hand flung open from the fist that it had formed, so that he was standing before the closed door with his arm raised as though to strike it. His features hung unmoderated in a mask of bewildered disbelief.

A baby...? He thought, lowering his hand to press flat against his heart. There hadn't been a baby born to the village in twenty years. He knew this personally. Had pondered it, cursed it, wondered at its meaning in the desperate quiet of the silence of a grief-filled embrace. So, how was a baby crying, now, behind the Jarl's Ban?

He ran.

Horrid images of an abandoned infant, squalling in the salt air (blue with both cold and exhaustion) filled his mind, and then fuelled his steps. His fatherly instincts overtook all of the others battling for supremacy within him at any given moment: fear, thirst, affection, hunger.

But no need.

It became apparent, as Beurd laid eyes upon the Jarl, that paternal preoccupation was useless. Rather than a father, at that moment, what Valder needed was a brother... lacking as he was, now, the presence of his son.

Beurd hadn't known a grown man could make such a sound.

But as he drew level with the mouth of the big building that housed Valder's workshop, he had trouble ignoring the source of the wild keening. The Jarl was hunched over the ribs of a small boat, his shoulders bunched and shaking, and bereft of their usual broad strength.

As though in a dream played out before his very eyes, Beurd imagined himself turn to leave, to slink away unseen.

It was as clear a vision as if he were watching a stranger.

What would Lene say? His inner voice was a growl of guilt and shame. *To me, she would say "shame", and "courage". To Valder, she would say something soothing. And permissive. But I don't have a woman's words!* He felt caught in the beginnings of a panic which rose in intensity; a dissonant harmony as Valder's keen again built in his belly and eked out, unbidden, from between clenched teeth.

Beurd pursed his lips. He balled his fists, stepped forward, clapped a hand on his Jarl's shoulder. Valder turned towards him quickly, like a child caught in a quiet wrongdoing. His eyes were red-rimmed from either drink or despair. Beurd thought hard about Lene. About what she would say.

Soothing. Permissive.

"When..." Beurd began. His voice caught, and he cleared it with a cough. He spoke again. "When you cry out, it should be like the wolf in the moonlight, in defiance, and as an invitation to the rest of the pack. We keen with you, Valder. Be not ashamed. For we are few men here who know the misery that it is to burn a son half-grown."

Valder stared desperately, mouth agape within the confines of a soft black beard, hands pressed heavily against Beurd's where they rested on his own shoulder. It seemed as though the Jarl had many things that he might say as the moment stretched on, flicking across his features, and making his black eyes like the desperate dance of a starving flame.

"It is an agony to burn one's child, yes," Valder whispered, finally. "There is nothing more miserable than to know the waste of having to build that child's funeral boat."

Beurd's eyes darted to the long lines of the unfinished wooden craft and saw the care with which each whorl and groove had been planed and sanded smooth.

"Surely somebody else..." Beurd began to protest.

"No. Nobody else." Valder gathered himself and turned once more to the wretched work. "I will not say that it was an easy task, but I *do* know that it is mine."

Beurd had allowed his hand to fall from Valder's shoulder as the Jarl turned away. He took a long breath in through his nose, weighing the moment like wine on his tongue. It seemed to him as though the anguish in Valder had abated somewhat, whether from his words or through Valder's own sheer will. He waited for Valder to take up his plane once more before gathering his words together.

"I have just been to see the witch," Beurd began, addressing the other man's back.

"The priestess," Valder corrected firmly, and Beurd heard the significance in the admonishment. For a man about to burn his own son, it was of much more comfort to have a priestess performing the rites than a sorceress.

"Yes. She asked me to tell you that she would be delayed. Some pressing matter. She sent her apologies with me."

Valder sighed and rolled his shoulders, turning his gaze briefly to the pale orb of sun above the horizon.

"When is the ritual?" Beurd asked.

"Within the week, if I can get the boat finished in time."

Beurd squirmed inside. Of course. Any longer and Locx... The body would start to decompose. The witch could only hold death at bay for so long.

Valder dragged the plane across the skin of the wood again. The silence was uncomfortable. Beurd was uncomfortable. What should he say? People died all the time. Old age, sickness. Tragedy, even. Like that awful day with the little fletcher's girl and the longbow. But those deaths, even the tragic ones... None of them had left the pall of fear over the village that Locx's death had. The grey unease.

He clapped Valder on the shoulder once more and left.

As Beurd's heavy steps drifted away into quiet nothingness, Valder once again set down the plane. He lowered himself heavily onto the wooden support beam which held the ribs of the craft steady. Valder had been at the task for days and nights without end and would not stop for more than a moment or a bite of bread until the thing was done. It was a nebulous balance. For while he desperately wanted to be done with the thing, the end of the task meant the beginning of the ritual passage of his son from this world. The longer Valder took to make the boat, the longer Locx's soul would have to wait... caught, but not kept safe. It was his last duty as a father to set Locx free from this terrible stasis.

But once the thing was done... Once it was done, it was done.

Valder ground his teeth as feelings of shame surged up from the pit of his belly. A man was forgiven all manner of madness in his time of crafting. But he wished that Beurd had not seen...

No. It was not Beurd's fault. Valder wished that he *himself* had not. He was ashamed of his weakness.

The lines of the boat's big belly drew his eye, the way that his wife's body had once swelled and swung when the children had been growing inside. It was fitting. For while it was the woman's job to be the vessel that brought them into the world - with whatever wailing and weariness went with it – so, it was the man's job to build the vessel that would take them hence. Wailing and weariness included.

Xeva would be with the other women, now, preparing their son's body. Wulf would be gods-knew-where. If he was playing true to form then he'd be hiding someplace out amidst the sea cliffs, having spent all of his hours (and exhausted all of his stamina) to reach it.

Wulf didn't like to *feel*. That was one of the ways that he and his brother differed. Locx wasn't ashamed of his emotions. It was one of the things that had made Valder hopeful of the sort of Jarl the young man would one day be.

Not to say that Wulf would be any worse. Valder was just as proud of his second son. But the two were different in their souls. And Valder wasn't as sure that Wulf's style would lend itself to the people as well as Locx's would have.

Wulf would have to learn.

Time enough for that after the ritual, Valder told himself, and shuddered.

As yet another wave of loss rose up inside of him at the very word, Valder stood, determined to keep his lungs clear of the deluge.

Breathe.

Once more he picked up the plane, braced his shoulders against the coiling, rising wave of agony, and crested the sharp peak of it with a strangled sob that eased the aching rending of his body, simply by acknowledging that it existed.

That it had power.

Blunted it, just by letting it be heard.

IV

The people gathered in the hours before true dawn. They spilled from their houses in the quiet of the darkest hour, creeping towards the place where the beach met the bay like so many tearful rivers choked with mourning weed. They broke against each other, wave after wave of raven people, joining together to begin the ritual that would officially end the life of one of their own.

The Jarl and his wife would come after, once the sad little sun had peeked out from the rim of the water. She would join the women, to stand amongst them. He would pull the boat behind him on a long rope; he and his other son Wulfric. The Jarl's brother, too. And his clan brothers. The men would drag the craft so newly hewn that it had not yet been sealed, save for the thick lining of tar hidden under the body, under the layers of perfumed fur, that would help the fire to burn bright until it burned out, spent of all its fuel, lacking any more purpose.

They waited together, line after line, shuffling and craning their necks to see the top of the path, where the Jarl and the heir's bier would appear suddenly out of the half-light of dawn. The ritual would take most of the morning, and there would be a feast in the great hall at the end of it. None had eaten since the night before, for it was right that hunger would gnaw at their bellies, each pang mirroring the pangs of grief left in the wake of the death. Once Locx's soul had been safely sent on its way, then the hole could begin to be filled. Full stomachs like a promise of satisfaction that would one day come again.

The sun appeared like a whisper at the place where the sky met the sea, and with it came the ringing of a distant bell. Aidan (one of the younger girls, at twenty) started sharply at the sound, where she stood with her mother, Brigit. Aidan glanced around, trying to see who could be up at the tower ringing the bell. She couldn't see anyone conspicuously missing. Her brother, Leir, was not present, but that was because he was part of the procession that would even now be moving toward the water with the body.

Leir and Wulfric were old friends, and in the wake of the loss of his blood brother, Wulf had clung to Leir's presence all the more. The only people missing were the men who were designated to be part of the funeral procession. It was familiar pageantry. Her late father had departed the world from this very beach, when she had been a baby, carried by men of his own.

It must be Gnarsa, then, Aidan thought to herself as she rested her head on her mother's shoulder. *Some magic that is making the bell ring. If not just the priestess herself.*

Aidan caught the eye of another girl across the mass of people, where she was huddled half-behind her parents. Isevelt; quiet, impassive, slight. Perhaps her parents were so protective of her because *she* was the youngest of them all. In the wake of Locx's sudden and mysterious death, they had been even more so, for Isevelt was practically fixed by force to her mother's shadow, like a birth cord spun of sheer maternal will.

I wonder how that is affecting her, Aidan thought. A second glance at Isevelt, at the set of her shoulders (and the defiant angle of her head on her white neck) led Aidan to believe it was *not well.*

The people at the front of the gathering shuffled together; ruffled like the many flight feathers of an untamed bird. The procession was nearing the bay. Aidan could hear the low humming of the drums spurring the men on, calling to mind the thrum of a beating heart. She worried her thumbnail and glanced around as surreptitiously as she could.

Was Locx's spirit even now hovering over their heads? Watching his father drag his bier down to the bay? Or, perhaps, he was still among them, standing by someone's shoulder, grieving with them for the loss of his own life?

Aidan felt a chill travel up and down her spine like an unwanted caress. If someone could find Locx's spirit, could ask him how he had died... What would they learn?

She peeked at Isevelt again, who was still scowling behind her protective parents. Isevelt was practically the priestess' apprentice. Maybe *she* would know if there was a way to commune with the dead? Would know if Gnarsa had perhaps already tried? Aidan knew she'd never ask.

There they were.

It *was* sudden.

The Jarl at the front, straining at a length of rope wound carefully around his shoulder. The boat was the finest, whitest birchwood; neither the sea nor time itself had managed to turn the grain to silver, let alone its older, duller iteration of grey. Although Aidan tried to furtively peer into the belly of the vessel, she could see no figure through the rich piling of fur and birchwood branches.

The Jarl reached the lip of the water, where the rocky sand loosened and began to give way beneath his feet. He met the task stoically, wading waist-deep into the waves which gently jostled the craft now sitting easily atop the water.

Leir caught her eye and smiled warmly, before placing a firm and reassuring hand on the straight line of Wulf's shoulder. That's how it always was with Leir; blood sister taken care of first, clan brother attended to shortly after. The two young men stood at the front of the group of chief mourners. The women surrounded the Jarl's wife as she watched her husband's labour.

There was only so much Xeva could do. Support him, yes. Encourage him, of course. Praise him (after the fact) to all who would hear for his unflinching strength and bravery. But she couldn't truly understand. Not in the way that the other men could: the men who could truly empathise with a father sending his child, or his own sister, or brother, or parent, from the world.

Aidan attended the Jarl again. Here was a point in the ritual where one of two things could happen. Either a flaming arrow would be sent by bowshot from the beach to set fire to the boat, or else, the floating pyre would be lit intimately by the Jarl's own hand. She glanced at the beach, skimming the lines of people in search of an archer at the ready.

No.

There.

Gnarsa appeared behind Xeva, murmured a quick, comforting word. Slipped past and into the water, holding aloft a linen-wrapped, oil-soaked torch which flickered into life without a touch or a sound. She glided serenely into the water, matching the Jarl's depth, so that the waves lapped the fabric under her breasts. The Jarl took the torch, bent his head to hear a platitude, or an exhortation. Set his jaw, nodded once, and turned to face the body of his son, even now being drawn out by the current towards the unknown. Open, and empty.

Valder lowered the torch until the flame leaped onto the perfumed furs, then turned resolutely and waded back into the bay. Aidan had a fleeting and ridiculous vision of Locx's soul realising that the burning boat was floating out to sea without him and needing to splash after it into the waves and the peace of the afterlife. She managed to turn her giggle into a stricken cough without drawing her mother's ire.

The people moved as one back up through the reedy dunes to the main hall, following in the wake of their silent Jarl. In any other case Aidan was sure that the people would already be murmuring together, keen to fill their bellies with the rich, red, blood-running meat of the moon feast. But not yet. Not even a raven called, yet.

Aidan checked once more that her brother was occupied with Wulf but registered distantly the expression of stoic determination on her friend Haedi's face as the other girl skirted around the outside of the throng to intercept the Jarl's remaining son. Leir would not need to take charge of Wulf for long.

Isevelt remained behind near the water, with the priestess, while her anxious mother stood at the place where the tide licked the teeth of the beach, wringing her hands, and looking lost. Aidan's own mother was speaking with one of their neighbours, most likely to bargain over harvest, based on the snatches of meaningful signals being played out at waist level, accompanied by the occasional tut, or shake of the head.

It seemed to Aidan that death could silence, but it would not cease.

Even if it took longer than expected. In the presence of death, life carried on.

V

The bitterroot stung the soft pads of Isevelt's fingertips as she pulled it, curling tendrils and all, from the hoary earth atop the hill by the sea. It was an effort of will more than anything else to do the job properly, and indeed, when her resilience ran out, she pulled several plants away without their roots – like the cropping of a sheep, wasting the herb's arms and legs both.

She sat back on her haunches and tilted her head atop her shoulders, unbound hair whipping in the wind as she squinted against the paltry sunlight, judging the time. At this point in the year, it was impossible to gauge the day on the sun's height alone. Better to guess how far across it had travelled, than how high.

And wasn't that true of everything, she thought, working the rough wool of her heavy skirt across and between her fingers against the nettle-sting of the bitterroot. There was no merit in judging how high something managed to climb if it were only ever up there for an hour. Better to merit how far, than how high.

Isevelt herself had travelled both far and high that afternoon. The hills rose and fell, high and low for miles along the coast of the land. But the bitterroot only grew at the highest point. *Craving sunlight*, she guessed.

She empathised.

She valued the time that the priestess gave to her, and all of the learning, too. But Gnarsa's cottage in the grove was dim, and the air was thick. Isevelt spent the whole time she was inside silently screaming to get out. Hers was a position of privilege, serving the priestess. If only Gnarsa ever needed her. *She* seemed to spend more time concocting fool's errands than bestowing any real wisdom on Isevelt.

Thus, the excursion in search of bitterroot.

Isevelt had taken enough time. Even if the priestess had little use for an assistant, she had much use for the herb. Isevelt stood and scattered the useless leaves over the quietly dancing ribbon grass, feeling an odd sense of relief when they all but disappeared amongst the other plants. She gathered the expanse of her skirt in one hand, the woven basket in her other, and set off back towards the village by the bay.

She nodded silently to a girl about her age as they passed on the path leading out of the village. Or, into the village, from Isevelt's point of view. *One of the sisters... Haedi, by the set of her shoulders. Off to scout for the Jarl's son, most likely.*

Isevelt had heard talk of their romantic pairing. It was inevitable that she heard things, in the priestess' cottage. But she didn't speak of them. She couldn't confide in her mother, and she had no one else. No friends, no confidantes. Her father, perhaps... But his fear of the priestess was difficult enough, never mind Isevelt adding to his worry with what she had learned.

She had heard that, of the sisters, Haedi was the stronger one. That she had her heart set on the son of the Jarl, as his was on her. That she had a burning ambition, like molten glass, ready to be blown into shape with the drawing of a breath. Held breath. But Isevelt wouldn't speak of that to anyone. Not unless she heard word of it outside of the priestess' cottage.

When she returned, there was talk coming from inside the dim building. Isevelt heard the gentle rise and fall of Gnarsa's voice seeping through the slatted windows as she picked her way through the sprawling, overgrown garden. That was another reason that glass windows were better, even if they were novel and expensive; they offered more privacy.

Although, she thought to herself, *no one without proper business would dare to come near the cottage, anyway.* So, there was privacy enough.

Isevelt tapped gently on the doorframe before pushing her way softly into the cottage. One of the women – Sorrell, she thought – was laid out on the stone bench that doubled as a cot at times like these.

Gnarsa caught Isevelt's eye and gestured with her head for Isevelt to come stand beside her. In Isevelt's quiet obedience the only sound of her presence was the slow, sweeping hiss of the hem of her woollen skirt over the rushes.

Gnarsa carefully found the place where Sorrell's belt sat atop the soft cloth of her shirt and worked the ties loose. In a moment the woman's smooth belly was exposed, white and unmarked by either chore or child.

"How many moons is it you've been bonded to Ansel?" Gnarsa asked as her fingers walked across Sorrell's skin: digging here, pinching there.

"More than ten moons," Sorrell answered. She clearly didn't know where to put her hands; first, they formed fists by her side, then a steeple over her ribs, until finally, she rested them protectively over her breasts.

"And you say you've got tenderness?" Gnarsa asked, noticing the other woman's movements.

"Yes. Ansel says... he says fuller, too."

"Mmm, but that may just be on account of your age. How old are you?"

"Twenty-six."

"And no bleeding?"

"Not for two moons now. Do you think... could it be a baby?" The hope in her voice was a tangible thing, edged all around with golden awe and quiet fear, already fraying, both.

"It's not the time to tell," Gnarsa replied finally, drawing Sorrell's shirt back down over her skin. She helped to tie the skirt back in place, then braced Sorrell's arm against her own as the woman sat up. "For now, return to your husband. Enjoy him. And speak to me in another moon."

"We'll know by then?"

Gnarsa shepherded the woman to the door. "One way or the other."

The door was shut firmly, and Gnarsa stood for a moment with the tips of her fingers pushed against the bridge of her nose. They heard Sorrell's footsteps fall away to silence as she walked back to the centre of the village.

"Is there a baby?" Isevelt asked, finally.

"No."

"But you didn't say..."

"No." Gnarsa sighed and fixed Isevelt with a piercing stare. "There hasn't been a single baby in six years. Almost seven. One more month of the possibility of Sorrell carrying a child buys me one more month before the people start demanding I take action."

"Is there anything you can do?" Isevelt asked as she began to harvest the milk from the place where the bitterroot met its leaves, wiggling the very tip of a silver knife into the cavity, her tongue sticking out between her teeth. *Think of the task*, she told herself. *Think not of all the pale babes, dead and burned before their time.* She bit so hard she tasted blood.

"There's always something that I can do," Gnarsa murmured, her own lips bled of colour by the sting of her own thoughts. "But it always comes with a price to pay."

"What's the price for making life?" Isevelt looked up to see Gnarsa with her head bowed, her shoulders sagging under an unseen weight.

The sigh was the hiss of a failed cup, thrown back to melt again amidst the heat of the flames.

"What do you think, child?"

VI

Haedi nodded once as she passed Isevelt at the village mouth. She felt a pang, like salt on her tongue, at the thought of the loneliness and isolation inflicted upon the priestess' helper by Beurd and Lene; both in the way that they kept her so tightly leashed and by the fact that they hadn't given her a sister. At least Haedi had Sylvi, even if most of the time it meant simply one more hand to hold.

Not that Haedi begrudged the hesitation in Sylvi's steps as she wandered through life. Sylvi was careful, and guarded, and deep of thought. Haedi liked that. Admired it. Wulf was much the same. Careful, and halting, like a new puppy. But even the softest hound could be turned from nosing about shyly to leading a pack, if only someone took a firm enough charge.

But first: making sure that he stopped running away.

Haedi felt her breath coming with more urgency as she reached the peak of the second hill. The muscles in her legs ached in turn as she clambered up or down the side of the earth, and, despite the chill in the air, she felt beads of perspiration erupt on her upper lip. She paused, plucking a white-faced wildflower and breathing its scent, as her father had taught her, when she needed to catch her breath.

Slowly, in and out. Hold it there. No good to blow upon him in a rush and in a temper.

She wondered how far she would have to walk: how many hills she would have to traverse before she found Wulf. She plucked the petals counter-wise to the sun. One, two, three... seven hills.

He loves me.

His tendency to venture out over the hills to the wind ravaged cliffs was not something new. It hadn't begun as a way to cope with the awful loss of his brother and future Jarl. It was the old answer to a deep, untamed desire in him – to simply sit at the top of the world and be unaffected by its marching progress for even a few hours. The air was thinner on the roof of the world, he said. Less pressure. Like swimming.

Haedi understood that desire. To be removed, for a time, from the momentum. She often had dreams of losing consciousness, of being poured into bed and left to sleep, suspended in time, for days and days and days. The dreams came most often at the end of a salting day, or after a particularly energetic spar with Sylvi.

Their father seldom used his sword for anything, except for impressing upon his daughters the importance of being able to wield it. More than one person had passed quiet judgement on the folly of teaching them how to fight in combat, and not because they were daughters. The bigger boulder was the peace that they'd all known for so long; that neither Haedi nor Sylvi had any real recollection of being at war. The truce had held up. There was no need for them to learn to fight because the bargain with the distant enemy was sound: *"We can't both live in this place, so we will leave, and you will not follow us."*

Haedi was the stronger of the two sisters. Muscles wound more tightly over her bones. Teeth more rigidly set. Emotions more firmly in check. But Sylvi was elegant in her body, like a dancer, or an eel, and was always her sister's match.

That was how it had been with Wulf and his brother, Locx. Before. Locx was the warrior. Even the diplomat. But Wulf was elegant and, although he was quietly thoughtful rather than confidently thorough, he was a piece on the board in an advantageous position – if you were paying attention.

She almost missed him. Went a rise too far, in fact.

It was only because she squinted back the way she had come at just the right moment that Haedi happened to catch a glimpse of the lanky son of the Jarl curled up in a cave-like a leggy hart. He was nestled in the depths of a ragged cut worn into the face of a cliff by years of waves and wind too many to count.

Getting down into the cave was difficult for Haedi, mainly due to the voluminous folds of her skirt. On her own, she probably wouldn't have managed it. She would have slipped and plummeted the length of an abruptly gurgled scream into the churning sea below, had Wulf's strong hands not fastened around her waist at precisely the right moment. That was often the way of it. He helped, simply because she had started the thing, and could scarcely finish it on her own. Though they rarely started the thing together, it nearly always ended up safe between the clasping of their hands.

"I'm *not* hiding," Wulf corrected her, in the face of her accusation. "Not from *you*, anyway."

"What are you doing here, then? I know that you like quiet and scant, but why are you knotted up in this cave?"

"I was watching for someone. I didn't want to be seen."

That shocked her. Despite his wish, Haedi took the moment to truly *observe* him.

Like all of her people, he was fair-skinned to the point where he could be seen at three hundred paces just by the light of the moon. His hair was the black and silver of the sand that lined the edge of the water, the colour of the stone that they sat upon, just out of the reach of the biting wind. But after that, his face grew features.

The sweeping wing of his brow flicked up at the ends like a raven descending on the back of a breeze. Eyes like charred rock from the pits at the foot of the smoking mountain, where they buried their bread to bake it. His nose was long and straight, unbroken where his brother Locx's had been bent at an apologetic angle, as though the older brother's face were always sorry for losing the fight. High cheekbones, like all of the Jarls in the line of Valder, who had been Jarls for age upon age, in line with the will of the gods.

And gangling. Which made the way that he crouched and peeped past her now, hunched like a wary toddler moments after breaking a bowl of milk, all the more ridiculous.

Taken firmly in hand, she thought, and pushed her palm down atop his shoulder to add weight to her words. "This may have been a fine place for the second son of the Jarl to be found. But not the first."

"Do you think that?" Wulf's eyes flashed, calling to mind again the quiet heat of the mountain coal, and she checked, again, in surprise. "Perhaps I should tell you, then, that the reason I am here is that this was the place I saw my brother on the morning before he disappeared."

Despite her nudging, Wulf had not spoken at all of the circumstances surrounding Locx's disappearance, before now. He'd made suggestions, muttered suspicions, but never had he spoken so openly of the tragedy or what he knew of it. Certainly not with such bitter passion.

Haedi held her breath and waited. Nudging hadn't worked, but perhaps permission might. She turned her face impassive, kept her breath. Let him unspool his thoughts into weighted words.

"I saw him," Wulf confirmed, turning from her, and giving his face to the mist blowing up off the waves below. "I saw him rowing out along the cliffs, with no sword or shield, dressed for

journey and with provisions on his back, carrying nothing in
his hands but a single oar."

"Where could he have been going?" Haedi asked without
thought. Of course, Wulf wouldn't know, or else he would have
said something to his father. And then, as the thought struck
her, "Have you mentioned this to your father?"

He shook his head in negation, shoulders still pulled together and feet tucked underneath like a child. His lower lip
threatened to protrude; a habit that made him *seem* petulant
but was truly nothing more than an overspilling of emotion (of
which he had plenty).

"Why not?"

Wulf scowled at her. Past her.

"Because, if he left with permission and something went
awry, then my father has kept it quiet for a reason. I'll offer him
nothing by questioning him." The waves held his gaze, even as
Haedi held her breath. But then he turned his eyes full on her
face, open and pleading. His voice took on the tenor of a question. "But if he left of his own will, without consulting with
my father, then more can be gained by preserving his character
than questioning it, surely?"

Haedi heard the wisdom and the generosity of Wulf's
words, and she admired him for it. But he was putting the
needs of individuals above the needs of the people, and she
could not agree with that. She wrapped her arms around his
shoulders so that he could breathe the scent of her braided
hair and murmured words of comfort. Their closeness was a
balm to them both.

But her thoughts were miles away, chasing each other along
the rugged length of the cliffs, further than she had ever
walked herself – a field of flower petals at least – wondering,
searching for where Locx had gone... and how the perilously
mysterious journey had found him several days later, dead and
drowned. In that order.

VII

Aidan eased herself straight from the crouch that had held her bent over the earth for the past hour, dancing delicate fingers through the soil in search of gold. She had chosen to harvest the potatoes instead of cleaning the fish: a job that she hated and which had, instead, fallen to her brother, Leir.

He didn't seem to mind, squinting at the place where his sharp silver knife pierced the armour of the fish's scales, making sure that every link was lifted cleanly from the pink flesh underneath. He was on his third one; the other two specimens were split in two and neatly laid out, bare of bones on an earthen platter, ready to be pressed in salt.

"Why do you take so much care with the last?" Aidan asked. She ferreted around in the loose, rich soil that she had already worked, searching now for the two small potatoes that she had allowed her hands to leave, undiscovered, until this final, opportune moment.

"The last fish?"

"The last anything," she shrugged, finding one of the bulbs and flicking it into the pool that her skirt made where it fell between her knees. "You do it with the fish, and the salt, and the beer. I've seen you. You even do it with the bread, when you bake it. The last loaf always exactly the same size. The exact same amount of time spent kneading it. I don't understand you."

It was quiet for long enough that she looked up at him, where he sat on the porch beside the front door. He was frowning at her.

"I don't understand the question," he admitted, obviously perplexed. "The last of anything is always for the gods. For the *gods*, Aidi. What sort of person would leave them the least, or the worst?"

Aidan fought to hold her composure, even as her fingers closed upon the other tiny, misshapen potato that she had rejected earlier. Even as the blush crept from her lips up to her ears, and then down the length of her neck to fan across her chest. She weighed her skirt where the two sad vegetables butted up against one another amidst the other, finer, specimens: caked in dirt and lacking any real appeal. Rather than wonder at her own lack of obeisance to the gods, Aidan found herself questioning her brother's blind acceptance. What sort of person would sacrifice anything for something that didn't have any tangible bearing on their lives, where hunger, or weather, or sickness did?

Even so, she made sure to hide the sad little vegetables in the folds of her skirt as they moved quietly together into the house. It was no easy feat, considering how long it took her to stamp and blow the dusting of garden dirt from the fabric of her clothing and the soles of her shoes. Leir fared little better: Aidan spent a good five minutes plucking fish scales like seafoam snowflakes from myriad imaginable places: the back of his neck, the shell of his ear, even from the end of one long eyelash.

"I'll take the last," he offered, reaching out for the hidden vegetables.

"Nonsense. I'll do it." Was her voice too sharp? Would he guess?

He smiled, disbelief gently colouring his features. "Aidan, don't be ridiculous. You've just cleaned yourself off to go inside, and besides, you never do the offering. Hardly ever."

"Well then it's my turn, isn't it?" She wrapped the beautifully cleaned and butterflied fish in plain cloth, but still felt quietly unsettled by the way its flesh moved beneath her fingers. Granted, the thing was dry now, but the wetness of it was really less of a problem than the weight of it. The warmth.

She turned smartly away from her brother and strode purposefully through the village, towards the path that led down around Gnarsa's cottage, to the stone altar riven from rock long ago.

There was no one else there, and for that she was thankful. Evidence of their presence was all around, though, from the piles of fish flesh now beginning to smell, to a stretch of finely woven and perfectly finished cloth folded neatly at the foot of the stone table. The edges of the cloth were starting to colour from the layers of blood, human and animal, that ran over the face of the rock.

Not that they slaughtered humans here. Nor animals, for that matter. Aidan had heard talk that it had been done in ages past, to appease or appeal to the gods in times of dire need, or at the working of a particularly needful magic. But certainly not in living memory. Now, they collected and poured the blood of the last breath, human and animal, over the face of the stone: an offering due to the gods, as the last belonged to them.

She thought of the Jarl's son, and how some of the rust on the top of the altar had surely come from his veins. But who had collected it? Had there been enough of it not mixed with water? Was it pure brine that had been poured over stone? For surely that was the last of Locx. She admonished herself for her vile interest and hurriedly tipped the fish and potatoes out, flicking the edges of the cloth, like an impatient snap of her fingers.

There weren't particular rituals or words that needed to be offered along with the last. Just as well, as Aidan would most likely not have uttered them. But even she could not deny that there was something quietly powerful about the place.

As though the sound was cut off as one approached.

As though it was difficult to focus one's eyes on anything but the thirsty, stained stone.

Perhaps that was why she seldom went there.

VIII

"Don't stand with your back to the pot, child, your dress will catch under it and then you'll be nothing but flames."

Isevelt quickly made to turn around as her mother clucked and hopped like a frightened hen.

"No, not towards it! There's nothing protecting your face from the heat!" Isevelt hopped once herself, and then settled into an uncomfortable lean which found her somehow both turned away from, but still facing, the large metal pot that dangled above the fire in their hearth. "No, that's not it either. Gods, girl, just give me the spoon and I'll do it. There's no need for you to do it anyway, is there? I say it over and over."

When her mother took the spoon from her hand the movement was gentle, even if it was hurried. Lene prattled on, full of fuss, heedless of the way Isevelt's head drooped and her shoulders stooped, and the corners of her mouth drew together, tight against the threat of tears.

Her mother truly did mean well, she knew that. But Isevelt was suffocating.

It was a relief when her father got home. He, at least, would allow her to follow him into his workshop, even sometimes work the bellows, if it was a good day, and if her mother was otherwise occupied. But Beurd had been working on a secret project, like some kind of alchemy. Since he took it up, he'd scarcely even mentioned his trade in the house. He was working with Gnarsa, Isevelt knew it. But they were both doing everything they could to keep the truth of it from her.

"Isevelt, I thought you were going to make the soup tonight?" Beurd puzzled as he hung his heavy fur over the back of a smooth, wooden chair. He turned to his wife with gentle rebuke. "Lene, have you taken up all the threads again?"

Her mother tutted and crossed her arms defensively across her chest. "It's not needful for her to do it. I'm her *mother*. I *begged* the gods for her. I'm not going to sour that by not watching after her."

Beurd pulled Lene into a heavy hug, chuckling into her dark hair. "It might not be needful for her to do it, but it's needful for her to learn. How else will she find her feet?"

Isevelt hated her parents speaking as though she weren't there but, as their house comprised of one long room, it was often unavoidable. Where other families had separate areas for sleeping and living, Beurd's workshop took up the back part of the building, and as there were only the three of them, they made do all together.

"You know that Gnarsa trusts me beyond even the most basic tasks," Isevelt pointed out, smiling at the way her mother remained in Beurd's embrace, happily tucked under his chin. "I know how to make a soup. I even know how to pull a tooth. Gnarsa taught me."

Her mother looked horrified. Isevelt pressed on, sensing that she actually had Lene's attention.

"Next I'm going to learn how to pack a wound with bitterroot and sew it shut."

Her mother opened her mouth, speechless, then - and here was where Isevelt realised that she'd been too honest - grasped the front of Beurd's shirt in both hands. When Lene spoke, though, it was to her daughter.

"And we were debating what was needful! It's not needful for you to be... pulling teeth, or sewing wounds!"

"You agreed to let me be Gnarsa's assistant—"

"In serving the gods, not in dealings of blood and bone!"

Isevelt turned imploringly to her father.

Beurd was conflicted, turning his eyes from his wife to their daughter. On the one hand, he agreed with Lene, in that his stomach turned at the idea of Isevelt's dainty, white hands covered in blood. But the alternative was to encourage Isevelt into more dangerous dealings: the workings of the witch. He struggled for the right words.

"Is... do you... help? The wi— I mean, Gnarsa, much? With magic?" he managed.

Isevelt shook her head. A question that had long been settled within her threatened to make for the surface. "Gnarsa doesn't seem to do much of any magic at all," she said simply and turned away.

"Then why does she need you, child?" her mother wheedled. "Perhaps this is a sign that you should stop working with her, while it's not needful... and come back here, instead."

"You agreed!" Isevelt cried, rounding on her mother. "You agreed, and going to the cottage and actually being put to use? I'm needed, there. I'm useful. It gives me breath. You can't take that away from me, mother, you can't. Father, don't you let her take it back. I *breathe* there. *That's* what's needful. Breathing."

As Isevelt felt each word tumble from her lips like rocks down a cliff face, she dimly registered how much she sounded like her mother on a tirade. But fear made her speak. Lene made to take up, too, and match her daughter word for word, but Beurd held up a hand to quieten her.

"Hush, Lene," Beurd said kindly, his other hand still firmly around his wife's waist. "It will do no good to drive her away. But Isevelt," he turned to his daughter, kind eyes flashing with earnestness, "You know we'd rather you weren't involved in

such work. We initially agreed to let you give aid to the priestess, not to Gnarsa. By rights, that shouldn't be the same thing.
You *can* make this choice." The hand was proffered again, palm
out, as his wife bristled, threatening to make herself heard. His
voice remained gentle. "*You* can make this choice. But perhaps
you might ask Gnarsa why she does so little magic, or, perhaps,
why she so rarely finds you needful for it."

IX

Sylvi crouched in the shallows of the water, running hand-fuls of fine, black sand up and down the back of her arms. She stared, quietly transfixed, at the way the water made channels as it fled back to its body, leaving trails across her skin. She was cold. Wearing nothing but her light shift, and with her body being leeched of heat by the wind that blew by her, and with the sun nothing more than the promise of warmth to come, her body shook in rhythm with the breathy in and out of the little bay waves.

So enthralled was she by the tracks left by the water, Sylvi hardly registered the sound of her sister splashing out from the shore to where she crouched, shivering. Haedi kicked a spray of water at Sylvi's face to get her attention.

"How long have you been bathing?" Haedi asked when Sylvi glanced up from her own skin. "Your lips are blue. You look like death."

"Like Death, or like I'm dead?" Sylvi sat back on her haunches, dandling her fingertips on the face of the water.

Haedi shrugged. "What's the difference?"

"Is there a difference?" Sylvi mused, squinting away over the water, but not really searching for anything other than her own thoughts. "If there isn't a difference, then you could argue that the dead somehow draw you to them, in death. When you die, you become Death."

"If there *is* a difference?" Haedi prompted, patient with her sister's dancing mind, as always.

"Then Death doesn't necessarily *look* dead. Death could be beautiful *and* look full of life. Wouldn't that be a painful realisation? To be drawn into death by someone alive."

"Who do you think Death is, then?"

"Alive or dead Death?"

"Dead Death is you. Definitely. I wasn't exaggerating when I said your lips were blue."

"Alive Death, then," Sylvi said, taking Haedi's point and walking carefully back to the pile of her clothes at the water's edge. The shivering got immediately worse but quieted a little when Haedi draped her cloak over Sylvi's damp shoulders, as Sylvi had forgotten to bring her own.

"Definitely Gnarsa," Haedi declared.

"Really? No." Sylvi gasped as she misstepped and her ankle jolted to one side. She tried the foot tentatively, then put more weight on it. She was fine. "That's just superstition. Have you seen Gnarsa? She's definitely dead Death. The purple under her eyes, those sharp bones on her shoulders. No one's lips should be that pale. I think that alive Death is probably Isevelt."

"Impossible," Haedi said dismissively as she held their carved wooden door open. Sylvi set to the fire, working tinder and flint to start a spark under the carefully placed wood from earlier that morning. She had set the logs herself, once she had swept out the ash from the night before. "They can't be Gnarsa and Isevelt, because *those two* work together. Hmmm." Haedi rubbed her chin. "Wait there, I'll think on it."

Sylvi heard the door close softly behind her and relaxed at the sudden and complete warmth that came from the fire and the stillness of the air combined. She didn't think any more on the idea of death; the thought had passed from her mind.

Haedi returned moments later dripping wet and shivering. Her bath was always a quick affair – just long enough to rub sand over her limbs and shake out the dirt from her hair.

"Make room," she said, as she nudged Sylvi aside with her toe.

The fire crackled with the noise of quiet footfalls in a forest, moving through the thick air with a certain slowness that suited the sombre mood of the sisters.

"What do you think Isevelt and Gnarsa *do* together?" Haedi asked of the silence.

Sylvi shrugged. "I don't know."

"Why would the priestess want *Isevelt*, of all people?"

"I don't know. Perhaps you should ask her yourself."

Haedi scoffed. "And how could I expect her to answer me?"

"Ply her with wine. What does mother say? In vino, veritas."

Haedi turned her head to regard Sylvi where she sat just behind. She was so gentle. So unaffected by anything. Soft. Please gods she never had to change.

"Sylvi," she said after a time. She made sure to keep her eyes on the flames, her body still. "Can you think of any reason for Locx to have taken a boat out, all by himself, along the cliffs until the village disappeared?"

Sylvi separated the strands of her hair. The fire turned her skin and hair gold, giving her warmth and making her appear very much alive. "I can think of plenty of reasons."

"Can you think of any good reasons?"

"Do you mean good reasons, or reasons for good?"

"What do you mean?"

"Do you want me to think of reasons that make sense, or reasons that justify the thing?"

Haedi sighed. "Don't worry. You've answered my question."

"But I *didn't* answer your question."

"It's not one that needs to be answered, it just needs to be asked."

Sylvi nodded wisely, as though she thoroughly understood.

Perhaps she could lend Haedi some understanding.

Because although Haedi could accept that there was no clear, good reason for Locx's actions, she could not quieten her own need for one.

Perhaps there was a question that needed to be asked.

X

It was the kind of dark that begged for secrets.

Where the people lived, in the birchwood bay, there were four different types of dark. There was the dark of night, when it was truly night; but there was also the dark of day when the sun didn't quite manage to dip below the line of the horizon. Then, there was the night-and-day kind of dark when the sun never appeared at all, meaning that one could only discern the hours by the way their breath misted up in front of them under a weak sheet of moonlight.

Tonight, it was a true dark, where both sun and moon went away for a while, and the things that needed to remain unseen could be tended to.

Gnarsa moved along the length of the path to the stone altar, to do things that needed to be done but not known. Her role in the village had become little more than that of a healer – but that was not due to her own desires. It was the role that she had inherited from the woman before her, who had learned it from the woman before that. With every passing decade the need for magic, even the regard for it, waned, like a sorry moon, until it had chosen to hide its face entirely. Even the gods hid their face from them. But Gnarsa wasn't alarmed. She didn't mention it. Because it was better that the gods hide their face and fail to see how little they were regarded, than that they demand an audience with a people who had all but forgotten their names.

But Gnarsa knew their names.

In truth, she too had forgotten them, along with all of the other generations. But she had found them again – chanced upon them carved into the skin of a cave a day's journey along the sea cliffs, along with the beginnings of the true magic that she had managed to, bit by bit, claim back to her own.

But magic, and the full courtship of the gods, had waned for a reason. There was a cost, and the people were loath to pay it. But even though it was a costly courtship, ignoring the gods would incur their wrath – and that was a much higher price to pay.

"Priestess."

The word was soft, breaking upon her concentration like an eddy of wind. Gnarsa straightened from her place by the altar just as Isevelt stepped quietly from the shadows of the trees. It was uncommon for the girl to be out at such an hour. Gnarsa doubted very much that the girl had either of her parents' permission, and then wondered what nature of errand would draw her from the warm, golden closeness of her family.

"Yes, child?" Gnarsa replied lightly, purposefully using the term she had heard Lene use for her daughter when the woman felt the need to chastise. If Isevelt caught the intention, her face did not show it.

"I come to you with a question," Isevelt said.

Gnarsa sighed, turning back to the stone of the altar. "Like so many before you. Ask your question."

Isevelt continued to step forward, as though she wanted to see past Gnarsa's shoulder to the work of her hands. "Why do I assist you?"

Gnarsa frowned. It was the sort of query that required a certain answer. She tried to guess at the heart of Isevelt's intentions. Did the girl crave validation, not having received it from her parents? "Your help is useful," Gnarsa said finally.

"But what is it that we actually *do*?"

"We aid the people."

Isevelt scoffed and crossed her arms under the heavy fur mantle that she wore.

Not validation, then. What was her goal?

"Do you long to serve the gods?" Gnarsa asked slowly.

Isevelt shrugged, examined the tufts of fur where they twitched in the breeze. "I serve the people. Surely part of that is satisfying the gods."

Gnarsa felt her eyebrows shoot up in surprise. She was glad that her back was still turned. "Satisfying the gods?"

"Their wants eclipse our own. The people think only of themselves and their own needs. If they attend constantly to themselves, what need have they of me? Of my work? It is your duty, surely, and mine, to work on behalf of those blind people, for their good, in service to the gods?"

Gnarsa shifted and judged for a long time at the young woman, taking her measure. When she spoke, there was the ring of prophecy to her words: a sonorous sounding made all the more melancholy by the very nature of the air around the altar. She followed her instinct like a skulking fox, following the promise of eggs. Perhaps this gamble would pay, after all.

"What you have told me is of great importance," Gnarsa intoned. "You have told me much. Now I tell you that the time will come when the gods *do* require something of you, for the good of the people. May you be as willing on that day as you are now, by their stone, in the presence of blood not your own."

They were the sort of words that inspired a chill, but they left in Isevelt nothing less than a flame. Small and unimportant, but captivating, and full of promise. With the right fuel, even a tiny flame could be enough to turn a bier into a pyre.

"I understand you," Isevelt said simply. The glow of her words shone out through her eyes. "I do not know your meaning, but I understand you. And I will be ready."

Gnarsa regarded her assistant for a long time. The girl did not waiver. She made another small decision.

"You will assist me now," Gnarsa said, turning her body once more to the altar. "It is bloody work, and your hands will wear it. But the gods will thank you. Stand by me."

Isevelt moved to stand next to the priestess, copying her posture. She mirrored Gnarsa's pose, placing a hand atop the altar and running it firmly across the smooth surface. Words that she did not understand floated towards her through the empty space between them, but Isevelt was not troubled, so transfixed was she by the sight of blood and water welling up into the webbing between her fingers, as though she, herself, were the tide.

XI

The next day found Xeva, the wife of the Jarl, standing atop the hill at the edge of the village and staring out to sea. As always, the wind whipped around the edges of their little world, pulling at her clothes and hair the way that her children might have, long ago. When they were young. Had they survived.

Of the six that Xeva had borne, only two had outlasted childhood. Her second son, Locx, named for her father, and the baby, Wulfric – named *by* his father. She imagined for a moment a world in which all six clung to her, the sound of the wind like their cries, distant in her ears. A world in which she did not have only one child left to her.

While Valder was deep in his grief, Xeva was deep in her anger.

Merta, the mother of Sylvi and Haedi, found the Frü standing alone at the top of the hill. Xeva was tall and thin like nearly all of the Raven people, but in the turmoil of recent weeks, the lines across her shoulders and hips had been drawn out into a sharp relief where once there was softness. When the wind pulled her clothes just right, Merta could see how the bones pushed against her skin.

Merta herself looked nothing like the raven people. She looked like her own ancestors: people who had years ago sailed out in heavy ships, in search of a new home, only to be overcome by a vicious storm, and so, torn from the world. All except Merta. She had somehow floated atop a plank of wood into the birchwood bay, where Klane had found her, and cared for her, and eventually married her and made her into one of them.

But Merta remembered.

Her mother and father, with hair the colour of straw just like her own. The graves dug deep into the ground where they would lay their dead to sleep, rather than losing them to the marriage of sea and flame. Merta wondered as she gazed upon the wife of her Jarl, if Xeva might have gained more from looking upon a stone, and knowing that her son, whatever remained of him, lay peaceful beneath the ribbon grass: unseen, but still somewhere that she could find him.

The women stood in silent comfort, side by side, hand in hand.

XII

"I need an answer from you, Witch," Valder growled as he pushed into the cottage, unannounced.

"You will call me Priestess, Sire—"

"I will call you Priestess when you commune with the gods, yes, but when you do nothing but pull fingernails and fix blisters, I will call you Witch."

"A witch engages in magic, Sire, but the tasks you listed are n—"

"An answer from you, Witch."

Gnarsa paled and snapped her mouth shut. Valder was rarely so incensed. She had an answer, aye, but it was not one that she believed he wanted her to give. She squared her shoulders, pulling the shreds of her priestly mantle about herself.

"I have only the answer that I gave you when the last of your children died, Sire," she murmured. It was a slap, to state it so baldly. But although her voice was quiet, it was not weak or apologetic. "Will you listen to it this time?"

"You still stand by your foul indictment?" Valder snarled, his greying face crumpling with anger that was chasing fleet-footed fear.

"I did not call the wrath of the gods down upon you, my lord, I merely—"

56

"This is no answer." Valder slammed his hand down atop the polished wooden table, sending bunches of dried herbs and long, slender instruments scattering from their places. "This is no answer that I accept."

"You must. You must accept it, or else we will all pay the price." Gnarsa stepped towards him. He was *so* close. Closer than he'd ever been to this conclusion. She pushed a little more, leaning in, so that their hands and whispers formed a conspirator's knot. "How long do you think the gods will allow your people to go unnoticed? How long will *your transgression* hang over the heads of your people, without it ever occurring to them to look up?"

"My transgression?" She saw Valder struggling to keep his voice quiet. He glanced repeatedly at the louvred windows, suddenly stealthy in his contrition.

"Do you see any of the other children dying?"

Valder paled. Gnarsa pressed.

"You have a choice. Yours... or theirs, Sire."

"Theirs?"

Gnarsa swept her hands out and around in front of herself, palms up to the unseen sky. She gave him the answer that she had given him every time he had demanded it of her. Each time one of his children died. "The last belong to the gods," she said.

It was a prophecy, the word of the gods.

It was a promise of plague.

A price to pay.

A risk.

Valder left in the same manner in which he had come: loudly, and unannounced.

Isevelt remained where she had hidden, where she had crouched behind the rosemary bush in the moments of noise that had preceded Valder's arrival, her white knuckles trembling between clenched teeth.

XIII

Aidan was immune to the cold of the rain.

Although, in fairness, she may have just been numbed. The sky had pulled up a blanket of cloud some time while they slept, covering its expanse with a down like goose feathers that was somehow too dark a grey to be truly soft. A fine drizzle fell with such haphazardness that she didn't know at what point her clothes had become *completely* sodden, but the need for the knowledge of the precise moment did not bother her overmuch.

The people were used to rain. Whether it took the form of this swirling, chaotic mist, or else a driving tirade that beat at their exposed skin, there were many days passed under the weight of wet cloud. The rain, whichever way it arrived, did nothing to keep them indoors or out of its path.

Aidan rarely had trouble keeping up with Leir, except for when he was with Wulf. She'd debated whether or not to even try to find them, knowing that wherever they were, they were probably – hopefully – having the sort of conversation that might begin to address the hurt of Locx's death.

She had already tried the hill caves. She walked for an hour before giving up and heading back the way she had come, stopping by the drying shed (with her nostrils pinched shut) and even, much to her fear, Wulf's house, before his mother, Xeva, told her where she might find them.

Today the two boys were down at the water's edge, cleaning and repairing Locx's boat.

It was a task that needed two people. Not for the labour of it. Not for the *work*. For the burden, more like. For while it was a tragedy to retrieve the thing from the rocks where it had been found (wedged, pierced through, even splintered in places), it would have been more of a tragedy (for the people of the water) to not restore it.

Aidan dragged her feet, wondering right up to the moment that they noticed her if it was right or wrong for her to be there. She knew Wulf as Leir's friend, but he didn't know her. They had shared nothing beyond politeness. She stopped. No. This was not her place. It was not the place for her. And certainly not the time to insist upon herself.

Leir's words were spoken to her back, for she had already turned for home when he spied her. She offered him her face in return for his greeting.

"Aidi, come over. We could use another pair of arms."

Wulf's face was closed, but not uninviting. Like a house that was empty of kind people, rather than harbouring mean ones. Leir was waving emphatically. She let herself be drawn in.

"Can you brace your arms against the keel while we tip it over?" Leir asked, demonstrating what he needed.

"I can try, and if it doesn't work, I can run to fetch someone else," Aidan replied honestly.

"That's refreshing," Wulf said with a straight face. "I wasn't sure if you'd be much use, to be honest, on account of you being so small. But it seems you're of much value."

"Thank you, I think," Aidan said, moving to take Leir's place by the boat. It was an odd remark, and she didn't know how to respond to it.

Wulf shrugged. "I appreciate honesty. People who are willing to bow out if they're out of it."

Aidan simply nodded, aware that she was pressing her lips together in what aimed to be a smile but was just less than a grimace. She glanced back at the damaged craft. It was in a bad way.

Her mother, Brigit, had a small boat of her own, like this one, for short trips, or for fishing close to the bay. It was tiny compared to the longboats the village kept moored in the shelter of the cove, but it got far more use. The people never ventured out in the warships, anymore. They had left war behind them when they first landed in the bay, all those years ago. They were just for pride and memory, now.

Locx's boat must have hit the rocks with furious force. Aidan tried to resist the urge to analyse the damage, to try to glean clues as to what happened to Locx in those final moments. It was hard to ignore the splinters of birchwood that stuck out at dangerous angles, sharp and ragged, or the gouge in the front of the keel, torn through layers of wood like a newly skinned knee, but on a much more horrifying scale.

All three of them grunted with effort as they pushed and pulled from either side to get the boat over onto its face. The whole thing was about long enough for Leir and Aidan to lie head-to-toe along its seam. If it had been *Wulf* and Aidan who had tried, though, his whole head would have poked up over the top, so tall was he.

"How are you going to fix it?" Aidan asked, slyly eyeing the keel. She could see how far the damage crept along the length of the boat. She guessed that at least ten perfectly shaped planks of wood would need to be replaced, overlapping each other *just so*, to repair the gash.

"I think it'll need attention from here... to here," Wulf said, indicating with the stretch of his arms the place that she had identified herself. "I'm just going to look at it today, and then decide whether it's worth replacing the whole plank, or just a section of it."

"We're planning on talking to Klane, once we've worked out a plan of our own," Leir explained. "You know how the men despise it when we come to them with problems and no solutions – whether the solutions are viable or not."

He scratched the dark shadow across his jaw as he spoke. He tended to shave his beard clean when he was working with Klane, but he'd been granted time away in the wake of Locx's disappearance, for the sake of Wulf. And so, the growth.

"I do know that," Aidan agreed. "And it will float, then? Once you fix it? It will be back to seaworthy?"

"That's the hope." The boys bent down and squinted along the line of the wood, muttering to each other as they reasoned for and against each of Wulf's ideas.

"It's good practise, at least," Leir shrugged, clapping a hand on the flat part of the bottom of the boat. "Working with the ribs of it. Won't be long before we make our own boats."

"You won't just use this one?" Aidan asked, confused.

"I expect no one will use this one," Wulf said simply, and then clarified when Aidan seemed perplexed. "The point isn't to be able to *use* it. The point is to not waste it."

Aidan shook her head. "That doesn't make any sense to me."

Wulf took pity on her. "You know how each man makes his family faering, as a tribute for when he marries?"

"Yes." There was a moment of silence while no one spoke the name of Locx's young wife, who had been herself dead about two moons more than her husband. There was, to Aidan, the possibility that Locx's journey had been a mad quest in search of comfort over her passing. But it wasn't spoken of. Wulf pressed on, either ignoring or not noticing her wandering thoughts.

"Could you imagine laying your child down on a blanket not wrought by your own hands?"

Aidan shook her head mutely.

"Alright, but if your sister's blanket had a hole eaten in by moths, and for some reason, she couldn't mend it herself, would you leave it ruined?"

"No."

"You'd mend it, even if you were only ever going to tuck it away in a chest once the job was done."

Aidan nodded, accepting the sentiment. "Blankets don't take as much work as boats do," she protested.

Wulf laughed without humour. "That may be true, but show me a woman who stops to weave something start to finish, without having to work on the mending, and the cooking, and the animals, and the weather, and the crops, and the gods, too."

"Don't ask Aidan about the gods," Leir warned quickly, earning himself a glare from Aidan. "Or about the crops. She'll give you the smallest potato."

Aidan flushed red again and gave Leir a stout smack across his shoulder blade, while Wulf smiled bemusedly, looking politely confused. Leir laughed and poked her quickly in the ribs.

"No need to admonish me, Leir," Aidan said contritely, soothing her stinging fingers with the smoothing of her sleeve. Then she shook the rain out of her eyes, resolution in the down turning of her mouth; the weight of two small, misshapen potatoes in her palms. "I may be lacking in stature, but I'm not without ethics. Tell me how I can help."

XIV

Gnarsa had spoken of their impending doom while Isevelt had skulked, unseen, in the shadows, and so Isevelt had *some* small notion of what was on the horizon. But even that didn't prepare her. *Nothing* could have prepared her for the next day.

Or the days after.

Perhaps Merta alone understood. Merta, the golden-haired mother of Haedi and Sylvi. Isevelt heard her whispering to herself, muttering, as they stood amongst the crowd, reeling at the devastation before them.

"It's a plague," Merta had said. "A plague of blood, in the vessels of wood and stone."

The horror on the strange woman's face mirrored the turmoil that Isevelt felt in her own stomach. Merta's face was lined in the way of all women, but where skin over time was normally worn into rivers by the flow of worry and weariness, the effect of the sight of all ten of the warships torn to shreds by the thrashing, turbulent waves was a sort of *shattering*... a splintering of hope in a secret place behind her eyes.

The beach was filling with people. As each person came running to the water's edge, they invariably cried out at the sight of their history and their pride being smashed over and over against the black rocks by the turbulent water. Isevelt thought absurdly of a fox she had seen once, clutching a hen between its sharp teeth, whipping the poor feathered mess over and over and over against the corner post of a wooden fence, dashing its ruined bones to pieces and filling the air with whirling, feathered debris. She thought of the way her stomach had rolled within her, sending a plume of bile straight up to burn the back of her throat and bring tears to her eyes. The sight of it had been wrong, *so wrong*, and her very body had rallied against it.

Her body rallied against this destruction, now, as the normally soft and swaying water of the little black bay surged and tossed about, like a calf with a new ring through its nose. The water was angry.

No, Isevelt thought quietly. *Not the waves. The waves do not think for themselves. If they feel, that is another matter. If they feel anything at their hand in the demise of the people and their ships, their shame is apart from their responsibility.*

It was the gods who had done this. Taken what they were owed, and then ten times more.

As well they should.

XV

Gnarsa was ready for them to come. Ready for them to flood to her door, demanding answers to questions that they should have been asking for years.

Not because she knew of the salt-drenched wrath of the gods on the bay that morning. In truth, Gnarsa had not yet been told of the loss of every single one of the people's warships. Rather, she had been ready for such a rousing of the people every morning for nigh on six years. Since she had realised that they had stopped giving as was required of them.

The shouts from the bay were growing louder, trickling down through the wood where the silver ghosts were sparser like morning fog. Gnarsa guessed that the wrath had come, and as the people grew closer to her door, the truth of its form gathered like mist for mourning.

She clenched and unclenched her fists to keep from wringing her hands. It was essential that the people accepted her wisdom without question. She needed to present to them, immediately, a face of power. And consternation. They had done wrong in the eyes of the gods, and they were being punished for it. *She* was being punished for their iniquity.

Gnarsa quickly imagined the moment like a carving: she, imperious. They, imploring.

She squared her shoulders, and then carefully arranged her face: eyebrows furrowed, lips tight-set, chin raised.

She was ready for them to come.

XVI

The exodus of people from the beach looked, to the birds in the sky, like a riptide.

It was an unspoken decision that caused first one, and then another, and another (and another and another and another) to turn from the sight of their sinking ships and funnel back through the muttering masses in an unwavering flow, drawing those on its edges along with them.

The pull of the people away from the floundering ships and back towards the priestess' cottage was nothing short of tidal. A submission to the call.

Although the wave picked up speed as it gathered others into its swell, it was yet another unspoken understanding that none, no one but the Jarl, should approach the priestess' door. For wasn't it true that it was the Jarl being punished (first the son, then the ships), and only *them* by association?

The clouds seemed low; the whole day was grey, as though the clouds themselves had slipped down to dwell among the people, offering their very own rain to run as tears down their cheeks. There was a fear now that went beyond the mystery of the Jarl's son's death. For they had witnessed the threat of their own death that day in the bay. And just as much mystery surrounded it, for they had seen the end with their own eyes.

Where was the Jarl?

The words trickled back through the rustling crowd, accompanied either by furtive searching of eyes or shameless craning of necks.

Where is the Jarl?

Had he even been on the beach? Had he seen? Did he know?

The temperature was rising amongst the people. Klane and his women were there, towards the back of the throng. He could see over most of the shoulders, if not through all of the trees. By chance, he glanced behind him, and his vantage afforded him one of the first sights of the Jarl.

Like the rest of the world that morning, Valder was an ashen grey. Most wood, when it was burned, turned to a pewter sort of powder, leeched of all colour: a ghost of its original warmth emptied by a heat greater than its own. Silver birchwood fires, though, like those burned in the village, left behind an ash that could easily be lost in, or even mistaken for, the finest snow. That was the colour of Valder when Klane saw him. Such was the quality of his ash.

The Jarl was dressed for the weather in a heavy, homespun tunic, with his hart hide boots just visible beneath the swinging hem of the shirt. He wore a cloak of black feathers across his great shoulders like a mantle. These were not for the weather, but, perhaps, being the symbol of his sovereignty, were suitable for the climate.

He left in his wake a subtle shift from fraught fear to intense interest. Isevelt, standing with her mother and father, slipped the former's grip and fell in behind the Jarl, her way made easier by the slipstream of his massive bearing through the crowd. She had not been at the cottage that morning but, knowing now what she did, she would be with Gnarsa here. In the face of the people. In the eyes of the Jarl.

Valder reached Gnarsa's door without much of any difficulty. He hesitated for a moment, and then brought his knuckles sharply against the door. Isevelt thought there was much to know in the sound of those knuckles. Had his fist formed an assault on the door, or had his fingers tentatively tapped, they would have betrayed far different emotions. But the sharp, practised rap of knuckles meant business; everyday dealing that gave the days their shape and progress.

Isevelt quietly counted the seconds between the last ringing rap and the silent opening of the door.

Five.

Gnarsa would have known that the Jarl, let alone the crowd, had come to her door. Beyond the simple swelling of sound that accompanied such a procession, Gnarsa had other, more arcane methods of discerning a person's approach. So, it had been her choice to wait for the Jarl to knock, and then to wait to answer.

"How has the end come?" Gnarsa asked, loud enough for most to hear. To Isevelt's ears, it was a challenge. "How trumpetous our doom?"

The Jarl reddened. His eyes flicked once to the side, but he was disciplined enough to not turn his head to the people. His own shame and sadness might want them all gone from this conversation – out of hearing, out of sight – but the duty he owed far outweighed any vanity.

"Our doom is equal to the cries of the people. To the anguish of the guilty, and the ire of the gods." He paused, breathed deep through his nose, reassessed his approach. "Will you permit me within? There is much I would hear."

Gnarsa turned her body so that he could enter. A single black feather snagged and lodged in the door frame. Isevelt pushed forward, her eyes opened wide, asking for an audience, but Gnarsa frowned even deeper still, and, turning, closed the door quietly to the world.

The feather was no longer in the door frame.

XVII

The people of the black sand and white wood village relied on each other and provided for each other with a quiet kind of harmony. Where one person raised goats, another grew gourds, and swapped them for milk and wool – or else, already set cheese or spun shawls, depending on where their time and skills lay.

Once a moon, on the brightest night, the people came together in the biggest hall in the centre of the village; swapped stories and shared fires, ate and drank of the bounty of their peace. Such nights were often filled with music, laughter, friendly fists, and short-lived, explosive arguments whose wounds were swiftly doused with wine and ale.

That night, though, the meal was a sombre one. Not even the wake of the Jarl's son had seen such melancholic faces. It was of good fortune that the moon glared so balefully down upon them, as it gave them their only light.

No one dared strike tinder to kindling, seeing as half a forest's worth of birchwood lay ship-shaped and shattered at the bottom and along the shore of the bay. They did not yet know how to fix what had been broken, so they sat in cold air and silence as the food slid slowly to their bellies, leaving them taciturn and dissatisfied.

Haedi sat with her sister and their parents at the end of a long table. It was one of ten or so, scrubbed clean and then polished smooth by years of use, until it was so silken that Haedi felt her stomach turn at the touch of it on her fingertips. For as long as she could remember, there had been a connection between texture and the turn of her stomach. When they were small, Haedi had always coerced Sylvi to knead the dough and handle the bread, for the feel of the ground flour on her fingers made her hands shake and her eyes sting. Sylvi had asked once if it was only softness that offended her so.

If it were, the mere presence of the Jarl that night in the hall would have had her heaving. That morning, as the waves tossed the ships about, as the people gathered outside the priestess' house, the Jarl had been made of mountains. Hewn from stone, made solid by the many years he had spent at the helm of their people. Haedi had seen him and had believed that their loss was little more than a fleeting moment of ill luck.

Now, though, he seemed soft. Slipped sideways in his great silver chair. Skin sallow. His wife Xeva sat upright beside him, purse-lipped and perfectly still. If they had been neighbours rather than rulers, Haedi would have said that they'd quarrelled and that it had left its mark. She said as much to Sylvi.

"There isn't space enough for more marks," Sylvi replied, casually lifting a shoulder.

"How do you mean?"

Sylvi gestured loosely with the tip of her knife, squinting one eye shut to bridge the distance. "You see? Their parchment is all used up. Too many babies buried. A son and a fleet of ships sent to the sea in the space of a moon. There's no more room for marks on their piece."

Haedi hummed, giving neither a *yes* nor a *no*. Her hatred of being contradicted was warring with the patience she always felt for Sylvi.

"Mark or no, I still say they've quarrelled," Haedi muttered.

"My guess is the witch," Sylvi said simply, causing Haedi to quickly clap a palm fast over her sister's face.

"You can't call her that!" Haedi hissed. "Especially not here, in the hall, with the Jarl and Gnarsa herself within hearing or telling."

Sylvi spoke blithely, seemingly unaware or else unmoved by the muffling effect of her sister's hand.

Haedi sighed and uncovered her sister's mouth. "What?"

"I said *mother calls her a witch.*"

"Well, father doesn't," Haedi scowled, turning her shoulder between them. How quickly fear made her patience run thin. She narrowed her eyes, watching as the priestess rose carefully from her place and slid over to the Jarl. Haedi held her breath, expecting Gnarsa to at any moment look their way. The tall woman bent her head and whispered something to the Jarl. As she spoke, his head fell lower and lower, until finally, his chin rested on his chest, and his fingers pinched the bridge of his nose. He shook his head once, and Gnarsa rose to her full height. She scanned the room, her face falling to sternly set frustration.

The priestess' eyes rested heavily on Sylvi, and then slipped to Haedi, and at that moment, there flashed something in her eyes like triumph.

Haedi's shoulders curled tightly into her chest as she watched Gnarsa slip from the hall. Just as the tall woman reached the side door, her helper Isevelt emerged from a shadow and lightly clasped her arm. They spoke for only a moment, and although their words were unintelligible over the distance, Haedi knew that they were harsh and hurried. Gnarsa twisted easily free of Isevelt's grip and disappeared from the hall.

Haedi glanced across at Sylvi, who had turned her attention to the ends of her own braid. Watching Gnarsa speak to both the Jarl and Isevelt had left Haedi feeling unsettled. She placed the tip of her finger atop a bead of wine that had slipped down the side of her cup, deep in thought.

The wine allowed itself to be dragged apart, offering little resistance to the compulsion of Haedi's fingers. Perhaps the reason she felt so discomfited was the way that Gnarsa exerted her pull. Had the words between Gnarsa and the Jarl been the same as between Gnarsa and Isevelt? She had seemed annoyed by the Jarl, yet unmoved by Isevelt. Perhaps Isevelt would know? Perhaps Isevelt would tell Haedi if she asked?

Haedi rose from her place at the table, murmured a quiet excuse to Sylvi (who was not listening), and wove quietly through the people and the noise to the door at the back of the hall, hoping to meet Isevelt on the path outside. She walked with her head down avoiding the eyes of the people, for although the room was filled with a deafening lack of talk, it was also thick with stares and glances. She passed Aidan who was sitting with her brother and their mother in the darkest, coldest corner of the hall. Haedi wondered at the distance between Leir and Wulf, and if their reasons were the same as her own.

Aidan watched Haedi go, but not for long. She didn't have the energy, or the inclination, to worry about other people's faults and doings, considering how much time she had spent that day stewing on her own.

"You didn't eat the venison?" Leir asked, leaning close over her plate, and raising an eyebrow at the strip of pink meat lying in its own cooled juices.

Aidan had long been accused of having a predatory taste for red meat by her family, having pilfered and begged for their portions on more than one occasion. So, it was understandable that Leir would be surprised by the best of it being left at the end of the meal. Aidan shook her head quickly, dark hair shifting on her shoulders like sand in the wind, hoping that would be answer enough.

Leir shrugged and moved to skewer the venison with his own knife, but Aidan slapped his hand away childishly. He barked a laugh, surprised.

"I still want it," Aidan explained, telling half the truth, and hoping that it would suffice.

Their mother leaned in, over Leir, so that her face was even with theirs. A feat considering how broad his back was getting. "Enough, the two of you. Of all days."

They needed no more telling.

Aidan slowly moved the forlorn venison around, trying to divine the streaks like entrails. "Why are you still sitting with us?" she asked eventually. "You've normally gone to speak with Wulf by now."

Leir frowned and rubbed the rise of his collarbone. "*Of all days*, I suppose," he muttered, jutting his chin toward their mother's turned head. "I feel as though Wulf needs to remain in his own mind at the moment. If he needs my words, he'll seek them out. I do nothing for him and everything for myself if I force my wisdom upon a situation that I do not appreciate."

Aidan glanced up at the head of the hall to where Wulf sat by his mother. He seemed deep in thought, but not particularly troubled. She continued to look around. Sylvi sat by herself now, no more troubled than Wulf, but also obviously not deep in thought. She absently plaited her hair, an almost-smile on her face as she counted the rafters.

Back outside the hall, Haedi had not found Isevelt. The moon was indeed bright and gave light enough to reveal anyone not trying to hide from it. Haedi had dithered for a long time, too long a time, unsure of the best course. Should she return to the meal, and wait for Isevelt there? Was it better to seek her out at her house? Would she be with the priestess?

Haedi stood close to the wall of the hall, not wanting to be seen in the moonlight. There was a certain kind of quiet heat coming through the wall. She imagined that they were from the cookfires and the many bodies, in equal measure. There would have been more volunteers than usual, to make the meal, knowing that the only flames were for browning meat. But even they were long extinguished, and not terribly missed. It wasn't as though the cold had driven anyone home. There was something knowable about a room full of people. Even if they were silent, their warmth announced their presence. Even in the coldest of times.

Haedi worried at a sliver of nail, balanced precariously between tearing it loose and simply letting it be. She reasoned with herself. Isevelt wouldn't return home to her parents, not this early in the evening. The sun did not rise long at this time of year, but the people did, and there were still many hours before their beds began to beckon. So, she would most likely be at the priestess' house.

Even if I don't find Isevelt there, I can still demand answers of Gnarsa, Haedi thought, setting out toward the bay in a steady stride. It was false bravado.

She had left her heavy cloak atop the bench beside Sylvi, where it had been functioning as a cushion. Now, without it, her shoulders and neck smarted in the crisp, wintry air. It was not time for the streams to freeze or for the waves to turn from crashing to cracking as they worked the surface ice into seafoam, but it was still cold enough that her woven dress and knitted stockings were not protection enough.

She crossed her arms so tightly across her chest that her back was hunched. After a few minutes, she reached around and swiftly unworked the braid of her hair, deftly combing the strands apart with numbed fingers, feeling almost immediately across her back the relief brought on by the thick weight of it. Her breath puffed out like chimney smoke, more white and dense as the walk warmed her insides.

The altar swam into view like a tangle of weed under a turbulent wave. Haedi hadn't been meaning to come straight here and, in truth, the sight of the bloodstained stone filled her with instant regret. She never liked coming here. Underdressed, and on a fool's errand, she liked it even less.

A cursory glance told Haedi that she was alone at the stone. She would have liked to have known the colour of the rock under the many hundreds of years of blood that filled its pores. She wasn't about to clean it to find out, though. The gods liked to keep what was theirs.

The shiver as Haedi left that place had little to do with the cold.

She found Isevelt by the water, crouched atop a rock that was as black as the sand that it nestled upon, made darker in the moonlight where the water washed up, again and again. Haedi thought of the blood on the stone and wrinkled her nose.

"Isevelt," Haedi said quietly when she was close enough to be heard but not so close as to frighten her.

The other girl turned toward her. Her face was pale in the moonlight. She looked ill.

"What's the matter, Isevelt??" Haedi asked. She approached the rock slowly, as though Isevelt were a sea lion laid out in pain. She hitched her skirt high above her knees and stepped carefully onto the rock, making sure to sweep the folds firmly away from the waterline. They had not ever truly spoken before. In Haedi's mind's eye, under the cold moon, Isevelt took on some of Sylvi, and so Haedi couldn't help but tread softly, softly.

Isevelt sighed and gazed out over the sea. "I am faced with a conundrum."

"You alone?" Haedi hadn't meant for her words to sound challenging, but they did.

Isevelt weighed Haedi with her eyes. Haedi felt in the moment that Isevelt looked at her, that she was being found. Haedi would not accept being found wanting. She drew herself up to her fullest height; full as she could, perched sideways on a rock, and stared levelly back at Isevelt.

"You alone?" Haedi asked again.

"Yes, I alone," Isevelt murmured finally. She gazed out to sea again. "But not me alone. We are all charged alone."

Haedi's mind swept her consciousness along in its wake. She had never had the time for intrigue, and so, when it reared, Haedi would simply plunge ahead of it like a horse in the surf. "Isevelt, what do you know?"

Isevelt, it seemed, was equally as headstrong. "The people are charged by the gods, each to each."

"Yes, I know."

"The gods demand the last."

"Yes."

"They require that the last is both blessed, and freely given."

"...Yes."

Isevelt stared squarely at her again. "Haedi; why, then, have the gods begun to take?"

Haedi glared down at the black rock beneath her splayed hands. She remembered her mother once telling her that their rocks had all come from the belly of the earth, spewed out by a mountain in a fit of rage. The rage was cold now. How much worse was a cold anger? How much more terrifying was a cold god?

She left Isevelt; left her waiting for an answer that would not come. Haedi was still cold, but she no longer ached. Her body moved back along the path swiftly as a running doe. Her feet were just as sure, her limbs moved just as much by instinct. Her thoughts cantered out and away from her, unspooling on the edge of a panic like the doe that hears the hunter.

Her mother had told her stories of the man-god of her people, it was true. He produced wine where there was none. Rose his friends from the dead. But her mother's stories were not the only stories she had heard.

She and father had spent many an afternoon throwing nets from their boat; Haedi slumped happily in the bow, mending nets, and scaling fish, and listening while he told his stories of the gods. How they had breathed and spoke and sang and wept the world in turn. How they found the people hiding, cold and starving, in the forest, and had gathered them to themselves. How they had struck a bargain, sealed in blood. That if the last of everything was freely given, it would come back as a blessing. That if the people gave, then they would never again have to hide. What the people gave would be *returned* to them.

Haedi knew the stories. Better, perhaps, than Sylvi did. Sylvi had never seemed interested in listening. But Haedi had known from early on in her years that, as the wife of the Jarl's son, she would need to know the lore of the people. Haedi knew the lore of the people.

Haedi needed to find Wulf. Needed to find him before she found Gnarsa. He had to understand *why*, if her life were to be truly, freely given.

They were *all* charged, alone.

Not one was free of the charge to give freely.

The fires were still burning in the hall, but Haedi knew Wulf would not be in there. She'd find him at his father's house.

She'd find him.

He'd listen, and then he'd understand.

The day began, and ended, with blood.
Alas, here we are again.

* * *

XVIII

The moon flew low on the horizon; but not so low that it was obscured by the ribbons of mist draping themselves over the length of the settlement. The village lay nestled in the crook of the coast: long, low lying houses and halls built of timber.

The timber used to be a comfort. Before the people learned the sound that timber makes when it's twisted apart. Now, as the people slept, the timber was the last of their comfort, as it kept the mist and the moon out. Kept out the worst of the cold.

But it did not keep out the enemy.

They came pouring down the hillsides: running through the birchwood trees as silent and deadly as volcanic blood. Their hair flamed out behind them, like red flags where it flew free from braids under crudely worked metal and leather caps. But while lava goes where it wills, follows the path of least resistance, the enemy tribe followed a strict plan that their people had laid out in the days, in the hours, before they attacked. They were bloodthirsty, and they were enraged, but they were controlled.

Their silence was perhaps their most deadly quality. That, or the swords sharpened barber fine. They moved methodically through the village, teams of two, in and out. It wasn't until the screaming roused the raven-haired warriors that the invaders' method fell to madness.

Haedi and Sylvi's father, in particular, felled many with his own sword, before he, himself, was slain. It was a good death. A sword sideways through the shoulder cuff. Found the heart. Over in an instant.

For him, at least.

The girls saw it happen. Their mother, Merta, didn't make it past the threshold. She lived for a time, but she found she could not breathe, once her husband (her protector in this strange, strange place) was gathered onto a blade and then set free in an instant, with all the ceremony of a root vegetable bound for the coals. Merta watched as Haedi threw her body atop Klane's, and as Sylvi drew his sword (clean of rust) from his fist like it were a scabbard.

More than one fell to Sylvi's madness.

Across the village, but still near enough to hear Sylvi's cries, Aidan and Leir fought side by side.

Back to back, as occasion demanded. Without the precision of the sisters, perhaps, but certainly with all of their guttural fury.

Isevelt fled to the priestess' house; Beurd to the Jarl. He didn't make it.

Whoever the enemy was, with their fire hair, they must have had some knowledge of the gods, for when Gnarsa appeared in her robe and beads, with the Jarl by her side, they turned and ran.

They left their dead behind, beside the raven dead.

XIX

The people didn't know what to do.

The dead required birchwood biers to carry them beyond the waves and into the after.

The boats had all been broken.

It was the Jarl who told them the true problem, in the end.

The people gathered in the hall, in the hours after the slaughter, still bloodied and broken inside. Their grief was writ large on the face of the Jarl, but it was tempered by his own guilt. He had *not* lost another of his own; Wulf stood by his side; eyes open as empty shells. Yet as he spoke he sobbed, full of regret for his own stubbornness; for his own fear and failure that had led them into such sorrow.

He told them of his folly in the face of the gods' demand.

They demanded the last, and they had been denied.

"Haven't you realised what it means, that no baby has lived more than six years after birth, in twenty years?" Gnarsa said quietly, stepping smoothly in front of the Jarl. He gratefully sat down, resting his head in his hands. "*We* stopped giving, so *they* stopped giving. We owe a debt."

The people gaped back at her with death in their eyes.

"What's more blood?" One of them asked from the middle of the hall. "They can take mine, and be satisfied."

There were several murmured agreements as people shifted on the benches. Gnarsa nodded appreciatively but held her hands out, palms forward.

"That is admirable, Ansel, and I believe your offer. But *you* are not the last."

As though this was a signal, Haedi suddenly stood at the front of the hall where she was flanked by her sister. Her face was no longer streaked with blood, having been washed clean by Isevelt, or Aidan, perhaps, as they crouched in the shallows, but it was streaked again by tears. Her hair hung wild around her chin, where it had pulled loose from her night braid. "I am young. I am freely given. Let them have me, and give back freely in return."

Gnarsa pursed her lips, her eyes darting imperceptibly to the side, where Isevelt stood. "You know the power of the gods?"

Haedi nodded slowly, gripping Sylvi's hand. "I know the power. I know that our people need it now, more than ever before."

"More death won't even the account!" Leir shouted, standing in an explosion of limbs. "What gods would demand such as this?"

Aidan tugged him back down, shushing him furiously.

"It is not about evening the account," Haedi called back, before wheeling around to face Gnarsa again. "It's about giving what is owed. But they can give back, can't they? They will return us, won't they?"

Gnarsa pursed her lips, hesitating, counting the beats of her heart before counting the cursed cost and offering the blessed relief. "It will only work if those after you give themselves, too. But, yes. You will all be returned."

It was as though a great breath were drawn in by those filling the room. Those who had been spared (all of those older than

Haedi) drew back, drew tightly together like the cords on a purse full of jewels.

Isevelt was the youngest. Her parents had both been slaughtered. And she was the priestess' creature. She belonged to the gods.

Sylvi then – if Haedi gave herself, Sylvi would follow.

So, Aidan remained.

Unfaithful, irreverent, sceptical Aidan.

As those in the room desperately held their collective breath, all eyes fell on Aidan and Leir where their heads bent together, as Aidan whispered urgently in his ear, her gaze locked on the vice of his hand even as she tried to pry it from her own wrist.

"It's all my fault, Leir, don't you see?" Aidan whispered desperately. "It's all my fault. I never gave what was owed. Please, you *must* let me do this. For mother, and father, gods keep them. For *you*."

"No – *no* –" Leir's hiss was twisted into a strangled groan as Aidan stood straight before the gathering.

"The gods may have me," Aidan said, turning away from Leir, as she fought the lump in her throat back towards her belly. "And may they make good on the bargain."

"Then, come with me now," Gnarsa commanded, her sonorous voice carrying the length and depth of the hall.

Did she take their offer too quickly? Had she paused to breathe?

Would they guess?

No matter. She had them, now.

"We will make ready. And may the gods be satisfied."

PART TWO

Of Ash, Salt, and Blood.

Chapter 1

Ash

Ever this vace be pressed to my skin, let death be without and life be within, I thought between shallow breaths, and carefully pulled all of my limbs from the waves.

As I dragged myself hand over hand up the beach, I found that with each shallow breath I tasted more and more oxygen. My lungs were getting used to the dry air.

I collapsed again, this time at the edge of the rocks near some tussocks of silky grass growing off a small overhang. I felt pebbles pressing against my chest and cheek but had little will to move to ease the discomfort.

I felt arid and desolate. I felt ravenous with thirst.

I forced myself into a sitting position on the black sand beach and assessed my body. My skin was moon pale, but that was no surprise considering that it had not seen the sun in so long.

How long?

I was aware of the passage of time, uncounted but still missed... like the eggs of a tame hen. I raked my hands back over my face to clear my eyes of hair, then twisted it into a knot at the nape of my neck. The need to move, to make my way... somewhere... rose within me like a raging storm.

From a crouch, I managed to get myself to standing, braced against the grassy outcrop. It took me longer than I expected to master the art of walking. This got easier when I learned to accept the slight swaying of my body, synchronised with the water lapping at the beach, and counteract it.

There was nothing for it but to practice.

I fell often.

I made faltering progress to the little village that I could see dimly on the horizon, but I persevered and found that each step was a little bit more firm. Here and there candles began to wink on in the distant windows which helped me to mark my way. They also spurred me on as they stole, piece by piece, some of the cloak of darkness that was serving to hide my nakedness.

By whom had I been returned?

For whom had I been broken?

To whom – *to what end* – had I been bound?

A tall and narrow figure swam into view before me, seeming to hurry toward me along the beach. The figure wove about in its haste, intermittently blocking the warm gaze of the window lights. I felt myself begin to weaken once more as the figure broke into a run.

Masculine. A loping stride.

I wanted to tell the figure that they needn't hurry, that there was within me an inexorable pull that would reel me in like a resigned fish. But I could not. Instead, I fell onto the...

No, into...

I tumbled into the clutching embrace of rocks that parted sullenly to accommodate the weight of my body where it fell.

I was aware of the gentle hand cupped against the base of my skull. I felt my head tipped carefully back to allow wind in and out of my lungs.

Nothing helps, I thought absently. *Return me to the waves.*

A touch at odds within itself; a calloused thumb drawn softly along the ridge of my brow, and I opened my eyes.

Familiar.

The dark eyes lashed in black and winged by sweeping brows. Raven hair, likely bound by morning, pulled loose in his haste.

Wulf.

A movement tugged at the corners of my mouth – a grimace that looked like a smile.

My eyes closed again.

* * *

Wulf slid his hand out from behind the waif's head. That was what she was now... a waif. Long strands of hair tangled about his arm, escaping from a clumsy knot at the base of her neck. It felt like spiderweb pulled carelessly loose from a bough, and it clung to itself just as much as to his skin.

He searched the swell and slope of her face, noting the lashes that – once night-dark – were now like white frost upon her chalky skin. His heart thudded in his chest, wishing the moment of waking closer. There was a longing inside his soul that was born of both his desire to see her beloved eyes once more and a need to see the end of this mad waiting.

He told himself again that he was right in breaking the vace. He told himself that he had compromised nothing in doing it now, rather than later. He told himself that he had broken the *right* vace.

None of his tellings gave him any real confidence.

"Haedi?" He asked after a long silence. He hated the question. Hated that he couldn't be sure. But the girl he held... whoever she was, was unrecognisable as any of the four girls who had endured the ritual.

Haedi, when last he had seen her, had been a pale beauty with thick black waves, strong shoulders, and powerful features. While the girl he now cradled (chest darting pigeon-quick) was undeniably pale, it was now more of a stricken translucence than a lack of sun. Her hair lay like strands of whitened wool across her shoulders and over her eyes. Wulf ran his thumb once more across her face, clearing some of the flaxen webbing, and tucking it behind her ear.

"Once," the waif replied. "I was Aidi once."

Aedi? The name caught in his ears. Stuck on his tongue. Lodged itself in his throat.

Had he misheard? He peered at the line of her nose, the curve of her jaw.

Haedi? Aidan?

Not Haedi.

Gods. Sweet, fickle gods.

Not Haedi.

He had been wrong. How had he been wrong?

He clenched his teeth. The urge to run, to turn and run for the sea cliffs, was so strong that it nearly had a taste.

He scolded himself. His body felt torn in two. He pulled himself together.

That I was wrong was no fault of yours, and I'll not fail you for it.

His thoughts were for himself, as much as for the girl.

"You are still," Wulf declared. "You are Aidan still, or I have been false in my promises to many people, not least of all you."

Aidan hummed quietly as she exhaled, either in assent or dismissal, or some other condemnation, and turned her head away. Her body followed, peeling away from his hands as she rolled onto her knees and made to stand once more.

Wulf startled, his stomach rolling at the thought that he had been careless enough to drop her.

"I need to keep going," Aidan murmured. The incessant pull.

"Going where?" Wulf asked, catching up to her easily and gently laying his cloak over her bare shoulders. Her nakedness did not startle him any more than her very countenance did, for the *perversity* of her did not stem from the fact that her body was without clothing. The otherness came from the lack of colour.

Of warmth. Of life.

"To the boat," she gasped. "I have to protect the boat."

Wulf's eyes flared suddenly wide as he realised his error. In thinking that he was waking Haedi, he had named the boat after her. He would have to change it immediately. The characters weren't so different. He could easily scratch a few strokes clean with his blade and daub the necessary amendments on with the ochre. She would never know of his mistake.

"We're a long way around the cusp of the bay," Wulf said, thinking quickly. "If you wait here, I'll run back and bring her to you."

Aidan shook her head foggily. "I can't. The need to move towards it is too great."

"I'll be bringing her to you, so you'll feel the closing of the distance. I promise it will be better soon. Just wait here for me."

The Jarl's son, clearly troubled, turned once again and fled back up the beach, sending black sand scattering out behind him in the wake of his footfalls. He was dimly aware of Aidan following resolutely, stumblingly behind him, but the distance between them grew with each of his bounds.

Not that he could be rid of her.

The urge to be violently sick reared threateningly, but as with all moments of violence, Wulf was able to master it, to banish the urge to be dealt with at another, later, more private moment.

He had made a mistake. A mistake that he would set to rights.

The birchwood craft swam out of the morning half-light, bobbing tauntingly on its mooring, teasingly brandishing its inscription: his error writ in paint the colour of old blood.

Haedi.

A second, more shameful wave of heat threatened to undo him, and, as with all moments of shame, Wulfric was very nearly overcome by it. Haedi's face filled his mind as blood rose from his shoulders deep into the hollows beneath his jaw, but he turned and spat its sour taste away, and resolutely got on with the task at hand. It was her old face that he imagined, now, anyway. Wulf pulled his dagger from where it lay at his hip and carefully pared away the thin layer of paint.

More speed, less haste, he told himself sternly. There was no point in moving quickly if the end result was blood on the white wood rather than rust pigment.

He finished with a second to spare. Wulf turned at the sound of a scuffle and a gasp to see Aidan crumple into a pile at his feet. He caught her and swept her easily into the boat which was now devoid of any clear markings.

Once in the boat, Aidan felt a slow sort of release move through her body. Her limbs, which moments before had been tightly coiled, had been urging her onward with all need, now unspooled. Her lungs, which had been tight in her chest, relinquished their grip on her air. Now, she found that she was able to breathe.

Able to think with more clarity.

As the pounding in her ears faded to a dull thump somewhat like a great bird beating its wings, Aidan found that thoughts came flooding up in its place. Unwanted thoughts. Difficult thoughts which led to difficult conversation.

Not yet. She was not ready to know, yet.

Aidan kept her eyes shut, revelling in the feeling of limbs and body once more, of being contained rather than confined. She felt her frame move subtly back and forth and, in the belly of the vessel, was unable (or unwilling) to discern if it was the boat, or her very fibres, which caused it.

She lay in the waist of a small boat – the likes of which she'd seen a hundred times – built of familiar silver birch, with lines that rhymed with every vessel she'd ever seen crafted before. Her brother had himself put hand and back to more than a few of them in his young life, gently drawing forth the angled planes of the boats like the sides of a boar, velvet to the touch.

Aidan sucked in a sharp breath, pinning in place the picture of her brother in her mind's eye. She determinedly imagined him lovingly at work over a birchwood bough, rather than allowing the screaming, ash-scented memories now threatening to break their levee to flood her face.

She was ready.

"Wulf," she said after a time. "Tell me..."

"How long?" Wulfric supplied after the silence made it clear that Aidan could not continue.

She nodded; a slight tilt of her chin that, had she been upright, could have easily been taken for defiance.

"Nearly five years gone," he said quietly, and her eyes snapped closed. How much had changed? How much had they managed to return to the way it was before? Before everything had been broken? She noticed now that his face, which she had taken at a hazy glance to be the smooth skin of a new buck, was in fact a hide wearing the beginnings of weathering, despite being recently scraped clean.

"Wulfric," she said, at last, trying to banish the fear and anger that had lapped idly at her insides from the moment that she had awoken. "I need you to tell me everything. I need you to tell me everything that has happened, every decision that you have made that has led you to this moment. And *me* to this moment. That is what I need from you now. After that I'm sure I will need something to eat, and something to drink. But now, I need to know. I need to know so that I can begin to understand my place in this world again."

Wulfric turned his body away and gazed out over the sea, where it seemed to fall away into nothingness that might have been either the edge of the water or the beginnings of the sky.

Aidan. Sharp-edged and feisty Aidan, useful despite her stature, was now laid out like a corpse, near helpless. Laid out in the belly of a boat that was built to avenge the very act of war that had left her *so* soft, and *so* sad... and she was asking him to tell her truths that he would just as rather banish to the depths.

I can spare her, he thought, his gaze flicking momentarily back to her prostrate form. *I can spare her the enduring of more pain.*

Wulf noticed that the frayed edge of his cloak had fallen askance, baring a round white shoulder to the wind's teeth. He smoothed it gently back into place and felt the sharp bones lurking just beneath the girl's skin where they grazed against his palm.

"Part of me says that you've endured enough," he murmured, absently rubbing palm to palm to ease away the memory of her frame. "That you should be spared this. But the terrible truth is that, now that I've broken your vace into the waves... although you once might have waited out time on its very periphery, you're now once again embroiled in it. So, I had best help you find your feet. Do you remember the ritual?"

Images chased each other behind her eyes: four girls, dressed in white. An altar, hewn from stone. The blood; theirs, and that of their kin. Words; spoken and sung and screamed until the blade, white as birchwood, drew her into what she was told would be sleep, but instead, was an agonising stillness that had seemed without end.

"Yes," she said.

Wulf nodded, as though he had been visited by his own recollections of girls ritualistically slaughtered, their souls caught in glass bottles like dead moths.

Perhaps he had terrible visions of his own, she thought. She did not yet know how these five years had passed for him, and until she did, she had best not judge him for them. No, she would reserve judgement and justice for those who earned it.

"Are you cold?" Wulf asked, trying to delay the moment. She was not shivering, particularly, but her lack of colour spoke of a lack of warmth that chilled him, too.

"Does the ocean feel cold? Only to those outside of it, who don't share its ebbs and flows." Unbidden, the memory blossomed in her mind like milk into water. The sight of her blood joining the swell of the sea. She might not feel the cold anymore, but neither should she feel warmth. She admonished him. "*You* don't know me, Wulfric Ravenson. You share nothing with me. Any friendship that we have is on behalf of my brother, and he is not here. And you are beholden to me, I would believe, even though you might have one day been my Jarl, had your father not ordered the priestess to slit my throat for an altar of stone. So, give me as I ask. Tell me everything."

If Wulf had thought that the sight of her had left him numbed, it was nothing compared to the icy wave that washed over him in the wake of her words. He found himself numbed and shocked into speech in equal turns. It gave him a candour that he would otherwise have lacked.

"The day they came, the enemy; you remember that day. And the days that followed. You remember *those* days, too. And the day of the sacrifice. But after, once the four vaces had been interred into the altar: of this, I will tell you. The revenge we hoped to gain on the enemy would answer blood for blood. But they are greater than us, and more powerful. So, we drew on the black sorcery of our ancestors, which we had left behind when we came to the bay. Each of you; yourself, Isevelt, Sylvi and... Haedi. Four of you, each one bound in blood and sacrifice to a vessel crafted and dedicated to you, as protectors, that would give us an advantage over our enemies. With just four arcane boats, we would overcome the enemy, and ensure a safety and peace bred from destruction that would last for our people beyond peace promised by accord."

"All of this I know," Aidan said impatiently. She made no effort to keep the frustration from her voice.

Wulf similarly spared no sympathy. "We failed."

"How?" Aidan tried to sit up. "Am I the last to be woken? Were the other vessels overcome?"

"No."

"Am I..." she faltered, hearing the gravel sound of her voice as her words turned about themselves.

"You are the first," Wulf murmured. "There is but one vessel; the other three have not been made." It was easier to say it quickly. Bluntly.

Easier for him.

"What power is there in one?" Aidan demanded, as she finally managed to pull herself up to a sitting position, her slight chest angled directly onto his. His shoulders slumped forward in defeat, filling the space made vacant by the thunderous set of her own.

Wulf buried his face in his hands and then drew his palms back to be linked around his neck, his own guilt laying heavy across his broad shoulders like a yoke.

"What power, indeed?" He cleared his throat to disguise the welling thickness of emotion there, managing only a strangled sob. "They burned the forest. The enemy. A mere week after the sacrifice. This is the only vessel to be built because there was only enough salvageable wood for one."

Aidan hardly heard the rest of his words once Wulf had spoken of the forest. Her head whipped around; her eyes were wide in horror at the obvious sight that she had somehow overlooked. In the early morning light, the lack of trees might well have been obscured by the pearly clouds, but now, upon true sunrise, the empty horizon lay desolate and blackened in a long sweep behind the low houses of the village.

"Does nothing remain?" Aidan whispered. She stood up slightly in the boat in an attempt to see past the houses.

"A little around the bay there is a stand of young trees. But even then, there are fewer than there should be, now that this boat is complete."

Aidan sat slowly back down in the boat. She allowed herself a moment of fear, before carefully folding up the feeling and tucking it away for later attention.

"After they burned the birchwood," she prompted him, "what happened then?"

"General uproar," Wulf replied, shrugging. "Half of the people wanted to rush out with sharpened swords and demand a reckoning."

"And the other half?"

"Wanted to flee. Just as our grandfathers did when they came here all those years ago."

"Who triumphed?"

"Sober minds."

Aidan felt her face twitch in surprise. "Can I ask who helmed each initiative?"

"Murdech wanted to fight; Alna wanted to flee." He paused. "I preached sobriety. My father heard each of our arguments and decreed that I had made the best case."

"You've changed in the last five years."

"So have you."

"Yes, but my change happened without my being aware of it. I simply awoke and here I am."

Wulf glanced at her from underneath his lashes. "It is no different for me," he said quietly.

"You convinced the people to wait, but what for? Why have you awoken me now, before the others?"

"I finished the boat this morning, so I had to bind one of you to it quickly or risk losing the chance." He licked his lips, tasting the lie before he served it. A half-truth. "I did not know that it was your vace. But I did know that the people would need some gesture of appeasement to make the wait seem fruitful."

"Where are they? I would have expected more of an audience."

He frowned. "They uh... That is, I didn't tell anyone of my intentions."

Not a lie.

The frown was returned with interest. "And beyond returning me, what *are* your intentions?"

Wulf thought quickly and spoke slowly. It was a talent he had long possessed but only recently honed. "The people are without protection. Whether we strike out, or simply remain at home, the people are vulnerable and afraid. It was a costly magic that led us to this situation, but not one that can be wasted in any good conscience."

"So, you mean to parade me around in front of the people, to convince them that they lie safely in wait?"

"I mean to feed you first. But then, yes, I will take you to the people. But only to remind them of the power that they have, just beyond their grasp."

Aidan's next words, whatever they might have been, were pulled from her lungs in the wake of a shocked gasp. She pointed over Wulf's shoulder, causing him to squint quickly back the way he'd come. Another figure was making its way toward them from the village along the line where the water met the sand. From this distance Aidan was unable to make out the face, however, she would have put her guess at another young male, due to the breadth of the shoulders, and the easy pace at which they moved nearer them, along the sand.

"I don't believe it," Wulf muttered, turning a deep shade of scarlet across his forehead. At the same moment, the figure broke into a hurried run, and Aidan herself moved to scramble out of the longboat, recognising him.

"Leir!" she cried, her thin voice barely carrying through the distance between them as she ran, stumbling, but with all haste towards her brother. "Leir, I'm alive!"

Chapter 2

Salt

Captain Crow was a man of little patience.

Determination, yes. Perseverance, yes. Tolerance, even. But in the virtue of patience, he was severely lacking. Truth be told, the regard that he was bestowing upon the portly goodsman was nothing short of severe.

"You're touted as being the best," Crow growled, leaning towards the goodsman in an attempt to physically close out the other captains with his generous shoulders. "The best at procuring certain... things. And then, the best at running an auction fair like. With equal opportunity."

The goodsman (a polite name for the piratical version of a tax collector) squirmed under the heavy gaze of the eight assembled pirates and spread his glistening palms in the waxy lamplight.

"Sirs," he pleaded. "Sirs, you must appreciate the stress you've put me under. Two bottles, and so many of you intent on procuring at least one of them. Not only am I worried that... hostility... may erupt between your good selves, but also..." he licked his top lip and darted his eyes from beard to beard around the circle. "I normally enjoy the opportunity to... sample my wares—"

"I'm sure you do," came one quiet rumble.

"But in this case," the goodsman pressed on, eyes closed, "I've no such luxury. What happens if neither of these bottles... or only one – what if there has been a mistake?"

"We get our money's worth or we get our monies back," stated one of the captains, his face obscured by the deep shadow of a heavy cowl. "Fair is fair."

"Fair," the others mumbled, leaning forward towards the spoils: two stiletto-sharp bottles made of thick greenish glass and filled to the impossibly stopped top with blood-red wine.

"Fair," Crow murmured, a second after the rest.

The room in which they stood was little more than a cabin, really, up the coast from the pirate port of Lincoln on the island of Dasheer. The windows had long been boarded up and while, at some occasions, Crow was sure the room was filled to its seams with the goodsman's investments, he had obviously felt it prudent to remove from it all but the items specific to the midnight auction.

The room was lit by a single oil lantern which seemed to persuade the darkness away rather than really push it back, and which did nothing to ease the thick stickiness of the swampy air. Crow sweated in his layers of impressive silk; *from the heat*, he told himself, *not nerves*.

Crow worried the knuckle of his little finger against the gold ring beside it, examining the two bottles in silence. That he would be boarding his ship, the *Silver Witch*, with one of the bottles in his possession... of that he had no doubt. But he did not yet know which he should claim.

The bottles were both of a size. Nearly identical, in fact, but for the slight etchings on the glass that adorned their breasts. They rested on their sides upon the murky countertop, as the bottoms of both vessels were softly rounded, forming a glass dome. And aged. Nothing in particular told of the many hundreds of years that had passed since their creation, other than the dim, weighted dullness of them that shimmered almost imperceptibly in the air around them.

Crow shifted his weight slightly so as to attempt to gain better access to the bottles. If these were, in fact, the mythical vaces that he hoped they were, then the writing on the labels might be very important. Very important indeed. He wondered how much the other buyers knew, or guessed at.

"Well, then, uh... gentlemen," the goodsman stuttered. "We will do this efficiently, honestly and... uh... promptly. Considering your uh... numbers, it is safe to say that this... these items are of high interest. I can assume that everyone here is serious about this auction?"

As the goodsman spoke, his hands hovered protectively over the table, just inches away from the glass bottles. Was he concerned for the price that he would achieve, Crow wondered, or was he somehow aware of the magic that they possessed?

If they are the vaces, at all, Crow chided himself. He had no proof; he wouldn't know until the time came for him to christen his ship.

Focus on the gamble, not the payoff.

"Well then," the goodsman said again. "Shall we begin? Captain Fortuna, what price do you name for this item?"

"Which one?" The man's voice was of a high timbre, but scratchy – like sun-bleached wood. The lightness of his voice was at odds with the heavy, squared weight of him.

"Ahoy?"

"Which item? There're two of 'em. Which one?"

"At this point, I will say either. We'll hash out who has which privilege when we get closer to the... uh... pointy end." The goodsman very carefully kept his gaze from the array of blades fastened seen and unseen upon the pirates' persons.

"I see. Then I name ten ingots."

The other captains all shifted and murmured at once, as though the hefty weight named by Fortuna had settled across their very shoulders.

"And you are good for this price?" The goodsman pressed, peeping quickly up at the large privateer.

"Aye."

"Blast," swore the one with the heavy cowl, stepping back from the circle. "He might be good for ten but I aren't. Even less so, eleven."

"Eleven, I can do."

"Eleven, aye."

"Thirteen," said the man to Crow's right, as the offers moved around the circle. At that, two of the other men stepped away from the greasy lamplight.

Crow counted his teeth with his tongue. He had well over fifty ingots to put to this purchase, and while he didn't want to put more money into the goodsman's pocket than needful, he also didn't want to advertise to the other captains just how fortunate the *Witch* had been that past season.

"Fifteen," he said finally, thinking that the number found the balance between showing the other captains his intent, while still remaining modest.

Around they went once more, and then once more again, until only Crow, Fortuna, and another with his face obscured by shadow remained in the bargain.

"Now, Goodsman," demanded the stranger, banging a fist against the countertop. "You've seen our gold. Now we three have the chance to observe the prize. Prize for price, eh?"

The goodsman pursed his lips, and Crow could easily imagine him drawing tight the cords on his wallet. With an almost pained expression, he slid the two bottles towards Fortuna, who lowered himself almost reverently before them. For the briefest moment, an emotion passed over Fortuna's face, warping his expression. He stood again, a muscle jumping in his jaw.

The goodsman slid the bottles carefully over to the stranger, who flicked back his hood to reveal a lock of red hair behind his shoulder as he snatched them both up in his bear-like hands. Crow drew breath sharply in through his teeth, feeling his eyes narrow and his composure slip.

Radley.

The goodsman let out a tiny squeak but composed himself under the burnished man's glare. Radley examined the two bottles, turning them slowly in the warm light. Suddenly, he let out a single yelp of satisfaction, and his eyes blazed at Captain Crow. Crow nodded. So, the fiend had known Crow the whole time. Lucky for Radley, he'd stayed silent – or Crow might have thrown it all away for a stab at his enemy.

"Well there it is, then," Radley said loudly. "I stake my claim."

Someone, the goodsman perhaps, had affixed a paper label to each of the bottles, translating the runes to letters. Crow did not need a translation. Scowling, Crow reached past Radley and closed his fingers carefully around the necks of the bottles. His ring made a tiny bell against the bottle on the left. He peered at the right, squinting, trying to make it out.

Haedi.

He rolled the name around on his tongue. Chewed its syllables, tested its texture. Swallowed, and turned his gaze to the bottle in his left hand. It was like swimming to the surface of salt water; the way the letters were skewed and distorted, before suddenly bursting into clarity.

Sylvi.

Small triumph bloomed white-hot in the base of his throat. Even a little victory had power. "You may stake your claim all you like," Crow growled quietly at Radley. "But the *Silver Witch* will have no liquor but this one."

He placed the other bottle, *Haedi*, back onto the countertop and rolled it carefully to the goodsman. Radley grit his teeth in what could have been a smile, but which Crow rightly took as menace.

"Your final price, gentlemen," the goodsman squeaked, obviously excited. The previous offers had been just shy of thirty ingots, and the final round of offers for the bottles would undoubtedly remove any of the anguish he had suffered at procuring them.

"Thirty-five ingots," Radley said finally, causing Fortuna to curse and step away from the table.

Crow felt his shoulders try to drop in relief but held them firmly in check. There was much still at stake.

"*Thirty-six*," Crow said softly as he tucked *Sylvi* into the pocket of his coat, tight against his side. He drew forth the pouch containing his gold and counted out each piece. The gentle thud of gold on wood laughed at the pounding gallop of his heart in his chest.

"Goodsman, a pleasure," Crow said as he swept his hat around to them all. "Gentlemen, a privilege."

They frowned at him, all empty-handed, bar Radley, who glowered despite the bottle that he slipped into his own pocket. Crow tapped his hat back onto his head and strode toward the narrow door.

"If you'll excuse me," he called over his shoulder, only dimly fearful of the threat of a sword in his back, "I need to go christen my *Witch*."

I will see to you soon, fiend, he thought, throwing his malice out behind him like a shield, buoyed onwards by the swirl of his cloak.

Chapter 3

Blood

August Anders had never been drunk a day in his life –
never touched the stuff – but earlier that evening, as his ship
(*his ship*) had lurched from her dry dock into the waiting arms
of the North Sea, he had felt it.

She surely slumbered now. The vast body tamed by time
and rivets no longer heaving amidst waves of her own making,
but rather, swaying with the ebb and flow of the water, like the
slow sighs of a sleeper.

August stretched his hands out flat, urging his fingers away
from his palms, trying in vain to ease the cramps that months
on months of wielding various tools and instruments had
brought to them. The thick muscles in his forearms groaned
in protest, but no amount of pressure would quiet them. Now
that he had begun to take stock of his aches, the list *had* to be
made – the order *had* to be answered.

Calves, knees, quadriceps.

All bunched and balled from overuse. Deep pain in his lower
back, mirrored in the muscles under his shoulder blades.

Biceps, neck. Angry.

And satisfied. For each of the twangs and stings stood tall
as a testament to the work that had been done.

"Nice to see you smiling."

August peered up from where his head hung over crossed arms (over cluttered table) to see his friend easing carefully past the half-open door and into the little office. August had toiled six days of seven for over two years alongside the crew building his ship, and Goose – Gustav Wainwright, to his mother (and August's mother, for that matter) – had been there for nearly all of them.

"No, I stand corrected. Now that I look at you, I see plain you wear a grimace, and not a smile." Goose himself smiled, a warm kind of thing that called creases to the corners of his blue eyes and split his clean-shaven face nearly in half.

"Will the softness ever return to my skin, do you think?" August wondered, running a rasping palm over the underside of his forearm.

"I don't believe you'll ever go back to the life you had before, no," Goose replied, answering a question that hadn't been asked. "Not that you'd want to."

"No. Not that I'd want to."

"Took real strength – *real* strength, if you ask me, to climb out from under the wrath of..."

"Yes."

August wasn't meaning to be rude. It just didn't need to be said.

Goose reached out a hand just as brown as August's own, gripped the proffered forearm, and heaved until both of them were upright. Gustav was at least two inches taller than him, which was an achievement, considering that August himself was rangy at over six feet. August swayed a little where he stood, bone tired. There simply wasn't room enough for the two of them in August's office. By unspoken agreement borne of a lifetime of anticipating each other, they made their careful yet carefree way out of the little office where it hid upstairs at the Viking Co. Yard, down the heavy wooden stairs, and out into the soft breeze of the evening.

They stopped, silently staring long and hard at the great hull of the ship rising up in front of them. They both knew intimately the ins, and outs, the softness, and hardness of her insides, hidden away behind the perfect lines of her white and blue skin.

"She had a decent debut," Goose said, throwing an arm quickly over August's shoulders as they gazed up at the ship's great and ghostly expanse rising up out of the water, "but I think she needs more dancing."

"I don't think I could dance even if I *could* dance," August sighed. But he followed Goose's retreating back, nevertheless.

"A glass of milk, then."

"Don't mock me."

"I'll only mock you if I see you dance."

"You won't see me dance."

"You won't see me mock you. I always do it when you're not looking."

"I dance when you're not looking."

"The two of us. Taking turns to dance and mock. You so clumsy, myself so uncanny, that the passers-by can't tell which of us is doing it on purpose."

"For all you know I'm a bonafide professional, but purposefully do it wrong to make *you* look ridiculous."

"You often make me look ridiculous."

August was about to retort but was taken by surprise by a jaw-popping yawn.

"Case in point."

The public house that they frequented was a favourite of many of the workers for Viking. Both Goose and August were welcome company, having paid their dues with their sweat in the building of the ship. As welcome as the wet tonic that August sipped, resting his bones and his brain in the company of men as tired, and as satisfied, as he was. Was he content, in that moment? As content as he'd ever been.

* * *

August was unsure of how he managed to return to his little office at the top of the Viking building, so tired, was he. He was even less sure of why he went there rather than his own bed in the tiny attic that he rented, which was closer to the pub than the shipyard was. Or to the big house, where his family lived, which was considerably more comfortable.

Perhaps he had not yet adjusted to the notion that the work was more or less complete, and so, *home*, wherever that may be, had become an acceptable destination at the close of a day. He had hoped to avoid his father, but August's busy little office was exactly where Nils Anders happened to be that night.

"Drowning your sorrows, son?" Nils asked, straightening slowly from where the plans of a ship – *his ship* – had been stretched out and weighted down at the corners in a way that August felt was bordering on obscene. His father's Yorkshire accent drew long vowels from the beginning of some words and squashed others flat in the middle. So different a voice from his own.

"No, Sir."

"Didn't get much of a to-do." *Mooch uhv a ta-doo.*

August swallowed the bitter taste rising on the back of his tongue.

"Nothing like the... bloody "transatlantic floating hotel" from the other blokes, christened by the Duchess of *La-di-da* herself, no less."

August heard the softened edges of his father's words and knew that they'd been soaked in drink. His father must have had a lot of it, for it to even begin to show. "It's difficult to christen a ship without a name to it," he said.

"Utter ridiculousness. The madness is mine, in letting you run this disaster... but not having a name for her? Even now, when she sits just outside your window like a foundling? You're a fool."

"You can't name a child before it's born. You know nothing of either the child or the world you're dragging them into."

"N-amed you 'fore you were born." Nils' head sunk low on the table, coming to rest gently atop the white skeleton drawings that sailed across the blue sea of the ship's plans.

"And what would you name me, now, I wonder?" August murmured, as he moved to stand carefully behind the now sleeping old man, gazing lovingly over the bowed shoulders to the inner workings of the great vessel.

And what should he name *her*?

The Anders' shipping company, the Viking Line, dealt mostly with cargo and freight. The company had started with August's grandfather Erik Anders in the early 1800s, run out of the north of England, helping the queen to cling tightly to the supremacy of the British Empire with the claws of trade. Three years ago, though, 1911 – the year before all those poor souls had met their icy doom – the considerably aged Grandfather Erik had convinced his own son, Nils, to allow August to helm a project that would begin a fleet of passenger liners, thus taking the Viking Line "back to where our family started – ferrying strong men and beautiful women across the seas."

August smoothed down the curling corner of the plans, soothing his own ire in the process. The Anders family with their auburn hair and golden beards looked the part. But in truth, their name was Andrews, the red hair was Scottish, and they were, the lot of them, about as Norse as the queen herself.

So, what should he name his ship? Nils and Erik would want something Scandinavian and flowery. August had three sisters – Ingrid, Astrid, and Eryn. Should he name his ship after one of them?

The ship was a beauty – 750 feet in length with eight decks and room for two thousand souls, not including the hundreds of people who would be employed to keep her afloat. Where the *floating hotel*, as Nils referred to the competition, was walled with dark wood and marble, his ship was light and clean. She called to mind an image of the top of the world, the north of Europe, covered in snow but with the cold kept at bay by simple luxuries.

Goose had been his right-hand man in the fit-out; the six hundred staterooms of varying classes had all been dressed in subtle furnishings and finishes, the staircases and new elevators had been banistered and screened in wrought brass, and the floors moved seamlessly from wood parquetry to thick carpet in a way that set your feet without your eyes ever knowing. There was a vast heated swimming pool, tiled in white, so that it would feel like floating amidst the glaciers of Norway in a hot spring. The promenade decks were decorated with twisted metal sconces designed to look like torches of fire. The library and writing rooms – one for the men and one for the women – had actual piles of bear fur on the sofas and settees.

So, what was her name? The luxurious sisters made by the *other blokes* were named after ancient cities. The ill-fated other family were named for the gods. *His* ship should have something out of time, too. A name that whispered of ages past. That said *I have always been here, and always I will remain.*

August spared one more glance for the old man now snoring low in the back of his throat, looked proudly once more at the shape of the ship drawn to painstaking perfection on the thick blue paper, and then carefully eased the building keys from where they were clipped to his father's belt. He slipped away.

The aesthetic of the great Viking passenger liner was an echo of the inside of the Anders' building. Goose had done well

in that regard, basing his orders for wood and fabric and adorn-
ments off of the choices already made by those in charge.

"Clean quality," he had said more than once. "Your family
likes things of the highest quality, in its most simplistic form."

That was true of most of the place. True of their home, too.
While his mother, Jane Anders, preferred the dark wood and
busy patterns of her contemporaries, Nils would only allow it
in her personal sitting room.

August often wondered if his mother took her decorating to
its violent extent as a kind of *so there* to the men in her life.
Her parlour was so nonsensically bedecked with cushions, and
textiles, and little oil paintings that shone dully in the light of
thick candles, that one could hardly sit down.

He paused on the landing at the top of the squared-off
staircase, rolling the ring of keys ponderously through his fingers. His old wristwatch read two in the morning. In a matter of
hours, he would need to be back at the office, in a clean suit.
He was already swaying on his feet. What good would he be to
anyone, turning up to the yard dead tired, even *with* a name in
his head?

With deft fingers well used to manoeuvring round rivets
within steel hide, August quickly slid a single ornate key free
from the bunch and tucked it into his pocket for another night.
Creeping back up the stairs to where his father slept in the
half-light, he eased the bunch back in place on Nils' belt.

The keys were easy to replace.

Affection, endearment, pride... less so.

* * *

August had managed to find sleep, eventually. He'd even
managed to find a new, crisp white shirt to pair with the silver-
grey suit he still wore, despite the fact that it was nearing
evening, again. The days slipped by like... no. Not slipped. The
days were spent; eked out like sand into cement, trowel after

trowel, with such regularity that it was almost a surprise when the bag was done, and the wall was standing.

"There's no need for you to work alongside the builders, now," Goose reassured him. "The building is done. Get down to your shirt sleeves and shovel coal, if it pleases you, but the rivets are set. The steel bent to your will."

"My will?"

"No one's will but yours. I've never before met a man who could defy their father by faultlessly following his instructions."

"I've never defied my father once in my life," August said.

They were standing in the first-class dining room which would eventually be filled with furniture, but which was now a great expanse of opulence smelling faintly of sunlight and new paint. The moulding on the ceilings was subtle, worked to seem like snaking vines of budding leaves around a hundred electric suns. Once the great ship set sail, this room would be where August belonged. But even now, alone but for his greatest friend in the world, he wanted nothing more than to quietly descend to the depths of the ship's belly, down to where the fires would blaze in the vast innards of the boilers.

There *was* still work to do.

Goose caught his attention by walking slowly over to the bright windows that opened out over one of the promenades.

"I've never defied my father," August pressed, suddenly annoyed at his friend's ability to start a fight and then walk away from it.

Goose shrugged, patted down his pockets, retrieved a single cigarette, and lit it in a puff of blue-grey smoke.

"Smoking room is down on *C*," August admonished.

Goose smirked and stubbed out the glowing end on the base of his matches. "Sorry. Wouldn't want to defy your father."

August felt his jaw clench, twice, before he deliberately opened his teeth behind tightly closed lips. He knew that his friend was ribbing him. Knew that he took himself, and his work, and *everything* too seriously. But he didn't want to *chase* Goose, didn't want to ask *again* for his friend to validate him; he shouldn't need Goose to confirm that he'd done nothing wrong.

He looked down. The carpet was a deep black colour, like nothing August had ever seen before. The pile was thick without being fluffy, closely woven, so that as he walked on it, he felt as though his shoes slipped softly atop a stretch of fine sand. He bounced his heels on it once, twice.

"August," Goose chuckled. "Your father demanded that you follow his footsteps in the family business."

"Which I did," August replied in clipped tones, leaning close to a wall to inspect the finish of the paint.

"Which you did." Goose's quick agreement was a gift. "You apprenticed in every department of his company. Excelled in every discipline."

August hummed, recalling the hours. The blisters. The effort.

"Your father asked you to oversee the building of a passenger ship."

"Which I *did*," August said again.

"You did not."

Goose's words made August turn sharply around, but the bemused smile made him hesitate.

"You did not *oversee* the building of a passenger ship," Goose urged, joining him at the alcove. "You bloody well *owned* it. I would wager there's not a single part of this ship that you didn't touch, one way or another." There was pity behind the warmth of his regard. His voice turned to a murmur. Would the observation hurt or heal? "I imagine it's made your father furious, seeing you exceed his own expectations and abilities in every way." Goose must have sensed the way that August's pride was warring with his humility. He pivoted away; hands clasped pompously behind his back. "Not here, though," he called over his shoulder, "I imagine you painted this wall, here. Terrible job. Brushstrokes everywhere."

"Thank you," said August quietly. He might have said more, but the entrance of about half a dozen new men stopped his words.

"There you are, Sir," said the one at the front – Burns – his glasses perched pince-nez style atop his aquiline nose. "Beautiful job, Sir, just beautiful. She's a marvel. And still no name? How odd. I mean, novel. We're hoping to have an article printed, out for the weekend paper, drum up some interest? Written by Mr. Murphy, here..." Burns pulled a portly fellow out from amidst the clutch of well-dressed men and set him solidly before August. "How long do you think until we begin time trials?"

August began by addressing Burns until he noticed that the reporter – Murphy – was scribbling notes on a ratty paper pad with a brand-new pencil. He turned his face to the reporter, let his pride show bright in his face as he spoke of the ship, their hopes and dreams for breaking out into the market of people and not just cargo, and the oddity ("novelty", Goose corrected with a wink) of a ship with no name.

"There's not all that much more to do, is there, before taking her out to sea?" Goose asked, watching as Burns led the reporter and the rest of the retinue out of the dining room and towards the main staircase, chatting enthusiastically.

Burns had long been a fixture of his life and had helped August to make the transition from child to adult less painful. It had been Burns, in fact, who gifted August with his wristwatch on his last birthday. He'd said, *"I don't have a son of my own, and I know you could buy yourself one new. But this was my father's, and it's been well-loved if not well-kept. A bit like you, my boy"*.

The watch was nearly a hundred years old when August inherited it at twenty-five. He planned to give it to his own grandson when the time came.

"Not much," August agreed, turning his attention deliberately to Goose and away from memory. "She'll need to have her fit-out finished, furniture bolted down. We won't bother with plate or stock until after we've logged a time, though."

"Are you hoping that she'll be fast?"

August shrugged and turned toward the promenade. He wanted fresh air on his cheeks. "I hope that she'll be constant. Reliable."

"What every man wants in a woman."

August allowed himself a snort. Goose had been making such jokes for at least the past two years. There had been no time for girls, in amongst his six workdays a week. For Goose, definitely, but August had not managed to balance the two demands on his time, so he had instead poured all of his focus onto the one.

"And who is your constant and reliable this week?" August sighed.

Goose leaned his lanky frame over the edge of the railing. They were on the port side, and so had the distinct pleasure of gazing out dreamily over the grey expanse of shipyard, knowing that the deep endlessness of the ocean was to their backs.

"Her name is Sadie, and I love her."

"To Sadie," August said, raising an invisible glass to the sky.

"And Caroline," Goose agreed, raising his own hand.

"Caroline?" August swivelled around to stare at Goose, incredulous.

"Always Caroline."

"What does Caroline mean?"

"Oh, you remember her, don't you? Brown hair and a bosom that—"

"Yes, thank you. I require the meaning of the name."

Goose let his hands fall back to the railing from where they had been about to grasp a memory. He squinted into the weakening sun and scratched his head.

"It's the feminine of Charles, isn't it? Charles means masculine, so it's... feminine masculine? That's confusing."

"No, that won't do," August murmured, rubbing his chin.

"Oh, now, if you're going to name this girl," he swept gentle hands along the top of her rounded railing, "I encourage you most enthusiastically to look beyond the bounds of my exploits."

"Not bad advice."

"Unless you like Ursula. I have my eye on *her*."

"Not right."

"For me? Correct. No, not at all."

August closed his eyes and pinched the bridge of his nose. "Goose?"

"Yes?"

"I might need..."

"For me to go away?"

August smiled sheepishly. "I thought more that *I* should go away. I have an idea for where I might find inspiration on a name. But it involves a measure of quiet and... stealth." His hand brushed the shape of the key in his pocket.

"Then you had most definitely leave me behind," Goose agreed, letting his long chin show his submission.

"I'll tell you the moment that I am victorious."

"And I shall do the same. Oh, Sadie!" Goose sang, turning away with a wink. August watched him stride off along the length of the promenade until both his back and his whistling had faded from him.

August had slept the night before, for a few hours, but still, his body ached. He hadn't had any more than tonic water at the pub, but still, his thoughts fizzed at the edges. He took a long breath in through his nose, tasting the balmy air on the back of his tongue the way that he had seen his father do with wine, at the beginning of an evening. By the end of it, there was no tasting. Just consumption, and being consumed. When he watched his father slide into nothingness, August knew full well why the term used for those who had had too much to drink was drunk.

Chapter 4

Ash

Wulfric stared sourly at his cup, tipping it slowly clockwise so that the amber liquid inside engulfed the eddies of foam that clung to the edges, fighting right up until the moment of release. This time yesterday he had been a catastrophe of nervous vigour – hells, he had been shaking even mere hours before he set out on the beach. But now, he couldn't tell if he felt like a heap of lead, or like nothing at all.

He turned his cup the other way. *One has weight and one doesn't*, it occurred to him. *Which am I?* He lifted and let drop his shoulders, tilted his head ear to ear.

Definitely heavy. But with what? Fear? Disappointment? Guilt?

Yes. All three.

He looked over to where Aidan sat with her brother. Hands clasped, heads bowed. He wasn't trying to listen, but there was only so much room in the wooden house, and so he heard the passing of their parents' names back and forth between them, like a talisman.

He was disappointed.

No, that word is not enough. Dismayed.

Devastated.

Wulf was devastated at having woken Aidan when everything in his plan had been incumbent on raising Haedi. Haedi had the mettle. Haedi had the fire. But more than that, Haedi had his heart. While last night he had been sure of their impending reunion, because of his mistake, Haedi was still in stasis, and Aidan was returned.

His fault. It was all his fault. He felt shame flood his cheeks, prick the corners of his eyes, and curl his fingers around his sweating palms.

Would Aidan be enough? Would her brother convince her to rise or to return to an impotent slumber?

They had appeared quite similar, once; Aidan and Leir. With the typical dark hair and pale skin. But now, Aidan was even more pale than the foam that clung to his cup. And her hair, though still long enough to graze her elbows, was light and fine as silver gossamer. She looked like an ethereal thing; almost ghostlike. But to say that she was just a shadow of her former self would be an untruth.

This embodiment of Aidan was unapologetic where she had once been timid, and decisive where she had once dithered.

She might have the strength that they all required.

But she was not Haedi.

Wulf stood sluggishly, warring with his desire to lay his head on his arms, and moved to the little table where Aidan and Leir were seated.

"Aidan," he began, not quite meeting her eye. "I need to know, before we present you to the people, if you're willing to fight. If you're willing to..." he put the cup down and dragged his gaze over to the window. "If you're willing to join me in rousing them... to revenge."

Aidan leaned back on the dark wooden bench to better peer up at his face. Her features remained impassive, which perhaps made the cold quiet of her voice all the more threatening. "If you had lost anyone on that day... in the blood... then you would not be asking me this question. If you had, you would know that I do not mean to gain revenge on the enemy. I mean to make a reckoning. I mean to avenge my mother's death, and to call in the enemy's debts. Every. One."

Leir shifted back in his seat and stared at his sister as though he had never seen her before. What had happened to her in the vace, these past five years? Surely it had not been like being asleep, as they had been promised. Unless the sleep had been restless. Filled with horrific dreams.

Aidan caught her brother's regard and met his concern with icy steel. The blue eyes, once black, held nothing of softness or mercy.

"I mean to make a reckoning," she repeated, enunciating each word. "And I mean to make the people join me."

* * *

Wulf had managed, at least, to steal away and warn the priestess of his grave error before she beheld it with her own eyes. Leaving Aidan with Leir in the longhouse to reunite, or reconnect, or rediscover each other, Wulf was now sitting at Gnarsa's dull workbench with his eyes streaming and his head dipped low beneath his heaving shoulders.

Gnarsa almost had trouble being furious with him, as pitiful as he was in the immediate throes of grief and regret. Almost.

She understood a little bit of what he was feeling. After all, hadn't she made sacrifices, expecting to see the fruit of them grow in her belly, only to be left with a fickle and empty womb? Wasn't she disappointed, and confused, and feeling impotent in the face of foolish hope?

Here is the problem with hope, she thought, finally reaching her limit of his sniffling, and sweeping around to where the young heir sobbed into his sleeves. *It does nothing more than expand your capacity for failure.*

"Enough," she commanded in clipped tones. "Nothing that we have done can be undone. We are in no position to question the will of the gods."

"What position are we in, then?" Wulf's voice sounded thick with crying.

"We are in the position to prove to the people that the magic worked – that will renew their faith in the gods. We will test the limits of Aidan's gifts, and then we will make a plan to destroy the enemy. We will harvest more birchwood; we will make more boats. We will wake those who remain. And we will be impervious."

"To what?"

"Everything."

Wulf nodded decisively and rubbed his eyes. He was easily managed. Gnarsa dismissed yet another momentary frustration at having to be the one to manage him; Haedi had always been particularly skilled in that regard.

No matter. Perhaps Aidan would prove to be just as able; to take the burden from her. *After all, I have what I need of the boy.*

"Are we going to the people now?" Wulf asked, blinking in the harsh swathe of light from the newly open door, where it cut unapologetically through the dimness of the house.

"No." *Stupid boy.* "You are bringing her to me." *As you should have done before you made this mess, so I could have checked your choice and fixed your error.*

In the quiet of the empty house, in the quiet before the boy returned with her creation, Gnarsa allowed herself a tiny, silent moment to feel pleased.

It had been a gamble of the costliest kind; the sacrifice. A wish and a prayer spun out of years of gathered whispers and stories, but never any surety, never any proof. Just a suggestion; a hope from Isevelt's pleading, her own determination and an acceptance that, should she fail, she would die.

A timid answer to her own demand of blood.

When she tried to recall the weeks leading up to the ritual, all of Gnarsa's memories amounted to frustration. At Valder, for denying her insistence for so long. At the gods, for withholding their gifts even in the face of the peoples' humble obeisance. The years since, however, had flavoured the memory with a certain fear. Fear that she had been wrong.

But now, with the boy's story of the girl returning to the waves, with his description of her cold fire... Gnarsa was not only justified – she was vindicated.

Blameless.

True, the ritual had not yet delivered the people any pregnancies. But perhaps... perhaps the very return of the girls proved that the ritual had not yet been complete. Maybe only now could it begin.

Gnarsa stood and prepared herself at the quiet scuffle that heralded Wulf's return. Greeting people was a fine art, and one that she had long been refining. For the girl, Gnarsa intended a subtly solemn, eminent welcome; as though Aidan were a favoured friend returning home to the hall of a queen.

Gnarsa lowered her shoulders and lifted her neck, schooling her features to a regal passivity that exuded calm, contentedness, and control. She saved this particular tilt of her chin and set of her mouth for those moments when she needed to remind others of their place.

Gnarsa moved quickly until she was nestled just behind the door; just out of view to anyone still outside the cottage. The many beads and bangles on her arms and neck were silently muffled within the folds of her cowl. She set her chin and shoulders once more and waited, ready for the wonderment and reverence.

It hit her like a double wave, breaking like a heartbeat over her expectations in a one-two swell and suction that left her without breath, without words, without a spine to hold herself upright. The girl swept into her cottage and over to the wooden table to rest her palms atop its surface. As though she were a monarch marking a map. Gnarsa slipped sideways and slid into the only woven chair in the room, landing in a jingling puddle, able to do nothing more than gasp and vex.

"You have a lot of explaining to do," Aidan said shrewdly. Her long arms were bowed where they braced against the top of the table. "I tried asking Wulf, but I think we can both agree that he's of little use at the moment."

Gnarsa felt her bottom lip pop out from where it had been tightly trapped under the envelope of the upper with an audible snap. There was a certain familiarity in the heart shape of the face, but that was where any feeling of kinship ended. Gnarsa had never seen a person with skin that pale – not even the heir who had washed up on the beach with the incriminating arrows through his swollen skin. Even the hair was eldritch; white like the moon, but without the rough texture of age. There was a power there; Gnarsa knew it in her bones that there was a power lurking in this girl like a treacherous tide.

"Wulf," Aidan said, "go and tell your father to gather the people. Don't tell him why. But suggest it."

So imperious. Gnarsa tried to snatch the moment back through the thick atmosphere of the cottage with her own fumbled command. "Wulf, tell him that I am also coming."

To even her own ears, Gnarsa's words were thin and timid. Not as timid as the boy, however, who scurried off into the blessedly thin, cold morning outside. The two women (one quartz, one ebony) watched him go. Gnarsa's eyes returned to the dim room long after Aidan's did.

"Now," Aidan said again, raising her chin. "Explain."

Chapter 5

Salt

Crow had been the image of confidence from the moment that he walked out of the goodsman's wooden hut with *Sylvi* in his pocket, right up until the moment that he had smashed the bottle to pieces against the *Silver Witch's* hull.

He had every reason to be confident. He'd thoroughly prepared; an easy feat, considering the aid he was given by his ship's bursar, Smith. Smith was a kind of cousin to Crow. They even shared the same name, in truth, when the captain was at home with his mother. But more than just the ship's finance, Smith controlled the ship's knowledge.

Where captains like Fortuna and Radley were intent on procuring treasure that didn't start its journey in their hands, the *Witch* and her crew operated more as mercenaries of the defensive kind, rather than as aggressors. But that didn't mean they were any less in the business of collecting. Crow ferried information from one side of the sea to the other. Books. Maps. Recipes. Words. And not always written down. Sometimes the thing that he deigned to freight was the story held inside a person – and it was *that* story that Smith was required to acquire and catalogue.

The *Witch* had become a veritable library upon the waves. The crew itself had an oral tradition to rival even the people that Smith claimed were ancestors to himself and Crow: the people of the wave and wing. So, in truth, he had every reason to be confident. But as the wine spilled from the shattered glass, looking much too much like blood running down the planks of wood from where the bottle had broken upon the ship's body, his confidence eked and dissipated, as wine would, in the waves.

Luckily Smith kept his head. He leaped forward, into the water by the port jetty, with no regard for his clothing or his comfort. Crow lost sight of his cousin's head for a few moments as the water churned and things wrestled just below the surface, like an angry school of fish. He saw the pale ghost of Smith's hand reach out and grab something even more pale and ghostly, then watched, frozen, as his cousin's head broke the water to gasp for air and mutter a series of unintelligible words.

Crow became aware of the presence of his crew as Smith reached the edge of the jetty. The arm that the sodden bursar threw up and over the edge for purchase was grabbed by two sailors who rushed forward from behind. A third man grabbed Smith's legs and dragged him up out of the turbulent water. It fell to Crow to reach down and grab the ghost by her arm and pull her up into the air.

He noticed her bedraggledness before he noticed that she was naked. Before he could stoop to sweep his oil cloak from his own shoulders, however, one of the boys from his crew slipped in front to wrap the thing in his own cast-off coat. Crow recognised the light brown hair and broad shoulders of William. The lad was new to the *Witch*'s crew, but he seemed willing, and he was certainly able.

The two erupted in a flurry of limbs and Crow cried out, thinking at first that Will was the aggressor. A second glance, however, revealed the truth: the girl had come from the water fighting. Her limbs were twig-thin, but she flung out and flailed with clear abandon, spitting what sounded like curses - if an angry cat could curse.

Will endured it all for a moment, seemingly not wanting to harm her, but in the end, self-preservation took over and he deftly wrapped the coat once more over her shoulders, twisting and gripping the arms in front so that her own were pinned to her sides.

"We could use a scrapper like that, next time we come up against Radley," Smith murmured. His shoulders were stiff, and his jaw was set in trepidation.

Crow turned his attention once more to the girl. She seemed positively ill. She had the sort of creamy white complexion not uncommon to bodies pulled from three weeks in the water. If she hadn't been so slim, so unblemished – and if he hadn't seen her draw blood from his sailor's cheeks – then her colouring alone might have made him guess at whether she was indeed just a corpse all but forgotten.

There was a certain energy to her, also. As though some kind of feral instinct lurked just underneath the surface; for although she was swaying slightly with each breath, every single muscle in her lithe body was tense and poised. And there was such alertness in her eyes. Colourless eyes, like a stormy sea before the storm arrives. The moment that her arms were unbound, she would fight.

Or flee.

Smith motioned deliberately with his chin towards the girl, and Crow took his meaning. He gently lifted William by the elbow and the boy moved gracefully aside, surreptitiously dabbing at his cheeks with his sleeve. The girl watched him go with a certain sort of gratitude, as though she'd marked him in a moment of need. She peered with the same expression at Captain Crow's proffered hand, approximating the weight of her decision to either take it and rise, or stand on her own. Her eyes darted every way, her lips pulled tight over teeth she chose not to bear. The knotted sleeves fell open slightly.

She took his hand and allowed him to pull her to standing. *She* allowed it. Crow found to his utter shock that he was terrified of her.

"I imagine that this is a fearful time for you, lady," he said eventually, bestowing the title upon her more as a reaction to the way she regarded him than from any real esteem for that kind of honorific. He watched as her brow furrowed, as she checked. Something was wrong, and she had only just realised.

She glanced around frantically, bird-furtive in the face of a wind she neither knew nor cared for. The smell was not of home, and more than that, there was not even the promise of being blown in the right direction. He tried again.

"You need not be afraid of us. We are so glad of you. You've no idea. We're so glad."

Crow spoke in a muted mutter. He had no desire for his crew to hear the exchange, but he'd been a lad who rode horses – more than that, he'd been the son of a man who tamed them – so the quietly flattering welcome was more natural than breathing in the face of the sylph before him. But much like the mares of his youth, Crow could guess by both the shuffling footsteps of the girl and in the worried purse of her full lips that although the low tone of his voice soothed her, the words themselves meant next to nothing. She turned her body towards the *Witch*'s hull almost longingly, but there was still a confusion in her that rooted her fine little feet to the rough wood of the wharf.

He reached slowly and deliberately around, never breaking eye contact, to grasp the sleeves of William's coat where they sat still knotted loosely against her navel. At the same moment that he pulled the sleeves towards him, he took a smooth and deliberate step away which she mirrored without thinking. He spoke to her the whole time; and although no understanding bloomed in her face like he imagined a pretty blush might, the panic in her eyes was held just at bay.

"Who knows what you find familiar," he muttered. "Certainly no face, not a friend amongst the lot of us. That'll change right soon enough, though, just you wait. Good bunch of men and boys. For the most."

He wasn't sure why he was speaking to her so, beyond a distant comprehension that such a tone was comforting. Smith, when first he had found the legend of the lost raven waifs, near ten years before, had said that their purpose was to lend a certain protection to the ship and her crew. In the years that they'd searched – first for evidence, then for proof – Crow had built up in his mind an image of a screaming siren, standing sword-straight at the front of his ship, fearlessly facing and frightening enemies in equal measure.

All that had been obliterated, though, in the seconds that saw her pulled, sodden, and all of twenty years – if that – from the sea. It well may be that she would offer him and his *Witch* some measure of protection.

But first, she needed his.

Chapter 6

Blood

August hadn't seen his father since he left him asleep atop his draft table in the early hours. Most likely, he'd woken at some point before the dawn, slunk into his own office, and changed into one of the suits he kept pressed and hung behind the door, meant for occasions when he had worked himself to the bone but, in reality, used for occasions when he'd drunk himself into a stupor. His mother wouldn't ask any questions, and Nils wouldn't volunteer any answers. Ignorance was their commodity – a currency independently valued and traded exclusively within their marriage.

It was unlikely that his father would be at home.

August had in mind a way to discover the name of the ship, but it involved letting himself into the big library at the house on the far side of the city with the pilfered key that he had slipped from one pocket into another before he left his attic apartment that morning. His father always kept the door to the library locked and, although August had seen what was being kept in there, he couldn't grasp how it merited such careful keeping.

As he contemplated unblinkingly the windows of the offices, blazing a burnt orange in the wake of the setting sun, August was sure that he saw movement in his father's window. A twitch like a disturbed curtain, or an angered eye. August felt himself shrink back from the many glazed faces of the windows and slink away like a guilty cat, keeping to the shadow of the wall, hoping to go unnoticed.

Nils had inherited his own father's distinct fascination with their fabled Viking ancestry. It had been Grandfather Erik who had changed the spelling of his own name from Eric Andrews to Erik Anders, after beginning his collection of literature and research into Norse mythology and history. Surely, within that collection, August would find some story about a great Norse goddess worthy of giving her name to the ship?

The streets were dotted with traffic: horse-drawns marching smartly up and down, their occupants concealed in deep-set seats behind narrow windows; road cars full to bursting, or else nearly empty, clanging happily along the tracks built fast into the middle of the stones; well-to-do on foot, with coats on against the lengthening shadows. The docks were always busy, with markets on the doorsteps of offices and all manner of people coming and going from all manner of places, even now, getting on into the deep of the afternoon.

August would normally hop on a road car if he was going to the family home, for dinner or the like, but today he had his bicycle.

His mother had been beside herself with worry when he moved into the tiny little attic that he rented now but, as he'd told her, it was closer to the shipyard. And, as he hadn't told her... it was further from his upbringing.

More than once as he sped through the city, August had to clamp his hand down to keep his flat cap solidly on his head. It wasn't that the wind had picked up, particularly, but rather more that flat caps were not made for bicycling. As he rode, August formulated a plan. He needed to get into the library unseen, but that would mean getting into the house unseen.

Could he manage it? He'd need an accomplice.

Ingrid would most definitely rat him out, the traitor. Eryn was too young, at seventeen, to be of any use to him at all. Astrid, though, if she were at home, might be valuable.

August swung one leg over the body of the bicycle as he rounded the corner into Beech Street, stepping easily from the pedals in a quick one-two in front of the house on the corner. Made of tall sandstone like all of the places on Beech, this one had recently been turned into a lodging house for some of the more affluent dockers and builders who had followed the shipping industry down the estuary.

A sharp glance told him that no one was watching. August easily lifted the frame of the bicycle over the iron gate of the lodging house, disguising its silver metal skeleton with a few artfully bent bushes. Still the slinking cat, he darted toward the back of the big house that sat further down the street – the one where he had grown up. It was not very wide but made up for its breadth with an imposing kind of height, made all the more sinister by the heavy guttering that trimmed the edges of the eaves like a pirate's sodden hat.

Overcome by a sudden desire to return to his youth – if not the setting of it – August found himself retracing the escape route he had frequented as a boy, but in reverse. Onto the roof of the wooden outbuilding where it butted up against the lane, across the bough of the aged oak tree (it was lucky he had grown, as the oak had too, and if they'd not managed to do it in tandem then he doubted that he would have reached even the lowest limb), back onto the pitched roof of the sitting room, across (ironically) the roof of the library, and –

Face to face with Eryn.

His youngest sister had apparently watched his entire journey in silence from where she sat upon his old bedroom windowsill, her stockinged but shoeless feet dangling carelessly above the slate tiles. Her hair – more honey than flame – had come loose from yesterday's pins and sprawled like the seeking arms of an octopus over her shoulders and down her back.

"What are you doing?" He asked her, his shock making him sound rude.

"Says the boy climbing up to my window."

As with each of her four children, Mrs. Jane Anders had ensured that Eryn had a perfect London accent, and at that moment, as his little sister sassed him in clipped tones, August felt closer to her than ever before in his life.

"Is it *your* window now?" he asked, motioning for her to shuffle sideways so that he could fit beside her in the casement. It was a tight squeeze, and his height didn't make it any easier.

"Once I've moved all of your nonsense out of it. What on earth is that odd brass contraption on your desk? Looks like something you'd core an apple with."

"It's a sextant," he replied, grinning. "To help you navigate at sea."

"And core apples, hopefully."

"Hopefully. Do they let you on the wards, looking like that?" August asked, flipping one of the golden tendrils across Eryn's eyes. "I know you've got special favours there, what with studying under Aunt Anne, but surely they make you pin your hair back?"

Eryn's face darkened under a petulant glower. "They certainly *do* make me pin it back, and I by no means get special favours from the *Matron*. If anything, it's worse. She had me scrubbing linen for hours yesterday, and I'm not even an orderly!"

The sun was near to disappearing, leaving long shadows where there was space between rooftops. August sat in one of the last remaining slivers of golden light, but Eryn shivered in the encroaching gloom. And, perhaps, under the oppression of the remembered linens and the formidable Matron, their mother's sister, Anne.

"Let's sneak back in," August suggested, pivoting around onto the slate tiles so that Eryn could tumble comically back onto the awful peach rug. Matching her, August attempted a clumsy forward roll which resulted in him being wedged half upside-down between the wall and the heavy bed frame, one foot up in the air. Eryn giggled.

"Now I know why you couldn't use the front door," she quipped. "Needed more of an entrance."

"You're not going to ask why I didn't?" August asked, setting himself to rights.

Eryn made a disgusted face, as though she had little patience for him. "Why else? Whatever it is you came for, it's not people."

August reached pensively into the secret pocket sewn within the breast of his jacket, nudged aside the brass library key, and found what he knew to be candied orange peel wrapped in parchment paper. "I believe that I have gravely misjudged you," he said, offering his sister the candy.

"No, you made the right choice. I was a pill." She chewed thoughtfully on the sweet citrus, gazing into nothingness and years gone by. "It just so happens that I've changed a bit, while you weren't paying attention."

"Huh."

"Yes. You still need to watch out for Ingrid, though. She's..."

"Yes."

It didn't need to be said.

Even as the sun winked out for everyone but those standing where they could see the horizon, the new fixtures on the papered walls sputtered into life. Somewhere, deep in the bowels of the big house, a servant had turned on the electric lamps.

A marvel, thought August. He realised that he'd spoken aloud when Eryn answered him.

"Much like your ship," she said.

He was pleased. "She *is* a marvel. Viking has nothing else like it."

"I'm sure it's lovely," Eryn said, flapping her hands dismissively, "but I was speaking of the fact that father allowed you to build it. Mother says that he truly hasn't taken control back from you?"

"Does she?" Eryn had clearly meant it as a question, which he tried to ignore by posing his own. "What else does she say?"

"That Grandfather has more money than he knows what to do with, but that he recognises you've at least the equal in raw talent to his raw coin."

August gaped at his little sister, a sound much like a splutter threatening to rise in his throat.

"She also says that Father tried to take control of the build, but that Grandfather said *not going to happen*, and that's why Father is so angry with you these days. He thinks you're entitled because you've allowed Grandfather to give you an impossible task and not asked why you deserve it. And that the fact that you've managed it, perfectly, even though no one can understand *how* you managed it, means that he'll hate you forever, but that Grandfather feels vindicated."

August opened and closed his mouth several times, sifting through different phrases that floated to the surface of his mind in series, only to be turned away as either useless or terrifying.

"Mother said this to you?" he asked finally.

"No. But she still said it. Any more of that candied peel?"

He flicked another piece at her which she failed to catch. They both chuckled as she ferreted around next to the bed frame, and when she couldn't find it, he conceded that it was his fault, and gave her the lot. The momentous revelations remained between them, bubbling, but not boiling.

"So, do I get to know the plan, or just be part of it?" Eryn asked, carefully selecting a piece of candy through apparently meticulous criteria that he couldn't discern. The moment had comfortably passed.

"What plan?"

"The one where you sneak about and then sneak away."

"I just want to get into the library," he said.

"No good, it's locked."

He produced the key.

Eryn's eyebrows rode high on her forehead, and she surveilled him appraisingly. "I believe *I* have underestimated *you*," she said happily.

They made the plan. Eryn would scout out the occupants of the house and, when the coast was clear, August would let himself into the library.

"But let me have the key," Eryn said smartly. "Once you're in, I'll lock the door. There's only one key, so if Father were to come home and try to get in, you'd be safe. At least until he tortures me, and I tell him all of your secrets."

"What sort of a seventeen-year-old speaks so of torture?"

Eryn made a face at him. "The sort that was abandoned here by her only sane sibling."

"Ah."

"Listen for my whistle," Eryn called over her shoulder, as she threw herself over the curved bannister – one leg on either side – and began to slide away, whistling quietly in a downward pitch that matched her descent.

Chuckling might have given him away, tucked in behind an oriental vase on the second-floor landing, so he pressed the back of his hand to his lips to suppress it. The library was down below him and around a corner. The attic and the maid's room were on the third floor, but the stairs to that part of the house were hidden elsewhere – in a false wall near the kitchen.

A low whistle wafted up from below, and August stepped forward onto the deep green of the runner that traced down the steps. He paused, smiled, and then flicked himself up onto the rail, sliding down with as much speed as had Eryn before him. The thump at the bottom was a testament to his lack of practice – and increase in height – since last he had tried the manoeuvre. Eryn scolded him with her eyes, peering up from around the height of his ribs, and shoved him roughly sideways by the shoulder blade so that he completed a lame, slow pirouette into the door of the library.

The brass post found its home in near silence, which was odd, considering how much August's hands were shaking. The latch snicked free, and he stepped reverently inside.

"Key!" Eryn hissed, reaching in, slipping the metal from his palm with sharp fingers and snapping the door shut, so that August found himself alone with the books, and the books, and the books.

*

It was quiet in the library. Sound was muffled by the softness of the mustard velvet couch, and the great patterned carpet, and the walls of stacked books, and shelves of rolled papers, dotted here and there with curios collected by Nils and Erik over time and stored in the inevitable obscurity of abundance.

August slipped his jacket off of his shoulders so that he was standing in just his shirt sleeves. After a moment, he stepped carefully out of his shoes. He had loved this room for as long as he had known that it existed, taking more than one lump for the indiscretion of creeping in when no one was in there to take a tome down from the shelf and curl around its words like a cat seeking sunlight that it can't comprehend, but can still feel warmed by. It seemed right to pad over to the back wall in his socks, hardly making a sound, almost holding his breath.

He was sure that the answer lay somewhere in this room.

He glanced at his wristwatch. Seven in the evening.

He ran a fingertip along the spines of some books, glancing at the gold and black lettering, searching for the right subject. He decided on a burgundy leather and eased it carefully from between its neighbours. The skin of the pages along the un-bound edges was foxed with age: spotted and blistered, but still, somehow, smelling like secrets. The pages fell easily open, revealing the guts of an academic essay on the study of geol-ogy particular to the Vesuvius region of Italy. August read for longer than he should have, considering the precious pressure of time under which he operated.

"I'll be back for you," he whispered. He bit his lip against the guilt that rang in the echo of the very words he had whispered against Eryn's braids, the first night that he had left for the apartment. It seemed that she had forgiven him the lie.

Vowing to be much more about the business, August leafed through several cloth and board offerings, a handwritten note-book, and one book bound in what seemed to be satin, with no reward. When he did chance upon a thing of importance, there was no grandeur. No suggestion of gravity or greatness. It was a dark blue cloth specimen about as big as his palm. It was full of poetry, most verses concerned with the sea. On the inside cover, written in a spidery hand, was what seemed like a late addition:

Sea fill the sea, salt filleth me
Salt wilt I be
To Blood break me free...

August felt his lips form the shape of the words, but they left a taste in his mouth, not unlike the iron of regret that flowed from a bitten tongue. He closed the cover quietly, not finishing the verse. The book slipped easily back into the gap in the shelf, but somehow managed to still stick out... to draw his eye. He went stubbornly to a different wall, sternly scolding himself for the compulsion that rose in him, even as he moved away, to slide the thing into his hidden pocket.

He pored over the shelves, plagued by a creeping panic. He chided himself for allowing anxiousness to colour his mood. It was an odd sensation, as though his conviction that the library held his answers was unnatural. Almost from outside of himself. Even the notion – *answers* – felt strange in his mind. After all, he was hoping for a name, not asking a question.

He stepped lightly toward the huge cherry wood desk, sat squarely in the middle of the room. As his eyes raked over the fountain pens, odd receipts, and smoking paraphernalia that his father had left about in either haphazard haste or careless abandon, August caught himself wondering at the strange predicament in which he waded. Eryn's words whispered in his mind, threatening to catch his attention.

Grandfather had given him an impossible task, and his father hated him for completing it.

"They gave me a Herculean task," he muttered, gently gathering and moving a stack of heavy papers to a clear area of desk, exposing a volume beneath them. "*Herculea...*"

The name fell from his lips and was not gathered up again. It wasn't right, anyway. But he was getting closer.

Underneath the papers was a book bound in black leather, with a grain so fine it felt like velvet sand. The papers were bleached white like the face of the moon. It was in no way pristine, however; many of the pages had been dog-eared and, as he flicked quickly from the front to back, written on. With his eyes glued to the pages, August pulled the leather wingchair out from behind the desk (carelessly, leaving half the job undone; he had to contort his tall frame in order to wrest his way between desk and chair), and sat.

Names and stories swam before him, familiar at once, significant immediately: these had been his fairy tales. *Freya, Nerthus, Embla.*

Valkyrie. Women gods who fought for Odin and carried the dead away from the battlefield. There was a certain poetry in the Valkyrie conveying souls. Was that the name of his ship?

A page at the back of the book snagged on his thumb due to the way that it had been torn at the corner, rather than folded. A whole page was taken up by what seemed like old wood cutting illustrations: a mess of indiscernible lines and smudged ink. He read:

...the Gods demanded the last and required that it be freely given. However, the people believed that an offering made in earnest would be met in kind, and that gift of life thus returned to the people as a means of maritime protection. As the people of the Wave and the Wing (roughly translated) were, on the whole, a seafaring people throughout their history, the promise of supernatural safeguarding seemed a reasonable trade for freedom, in many cases, and for their children, in some.

August pushed the book away from himself, feeling the beginnings of disgust settle low in his throat. The passage didn't say it in as many words, but it seemed to be suggesting some kind of pagan sacrifice ritual. He reluctantly pulled the book back toward himself and peered more closely at the illustrations, squinting, his face now quite close to the page. All at once the meaning of the sequence became clear.

In the first panel, a group of white-robed women waded waist-deep into the waves. Their hair was unbound and worked with deep lines of black into the page. The artist had apparently had a rather limited skillset, as each of the four women were all but identical.

In the second panel, a fifth woman (dressed in black) raised a curved dagger high above her own head, while the four women in white seemed to tilt their heads back, exposing their throats in readiness. There was an odd brown mark on the paper, smudged across the illustration of the blade, smeared as though someone had tried to wipe it away. Like a tear. Or a shameful stain.

The third image contained no more than a crude rendering of the ocean waves, although, now they moved in an almost unnatural way, like curling tendrils of black hair dispersing out into nothingness.

He felt almost ill. He couldn't remember ever hearing about human sacrifice as part of the heritage that his family so determinedly claimed. There was a pen mark on the final illustration which showed a bare-breasted woman cupping a medallion of some sort to her sternum. The word *vace* had been scrawled in a newly familiar, spidery hand, along the woman's collarbone.

He only realised that he had been staring at the page when he was interrupted by a sharp knock and slip of the key into the door. "Father is home," whispered Eryn, "and Grandfather is with him."

"Grandfather?"

"Yes, he's feeling ill. But no matter – quick! Are you staying or going?"

"Going, I think," he said. "I have something that I need to do."

She threw the little key at him. It arced through the air, and he caught it easily in one hand. His heart was pounding. Had he been holding his breath? He rearranged the papers as best he could, tucked the little key underneath one of them (with its curled plate just showing), and hurriedly stepped back into his jacket and shoes.

"You were successful, then?" Her eyes shone brightly in the hall's half-light.

"Perhaps. I'll let you know."

"Do, please, if that means that you'll come back soon," she said, helping him to straighten the lapels where they were tucked underneath themselves. She hugged him quickly but fiercely about the middle. She was gone in an instant, leaving

August to hurry quietly out the front door. If she had felt the rigid outline of the little black book in his secret pocket, she made no mention of it.

At the last moment, August turned back and whistled. It was the same pitched note that had accompanied Eryn's descent down the bannister, and it swam sweetly after her, calling her back from the darkness of the house. She appeared like a ghost out of the shadows, her blue eyes swimming like vast pools of hope atop the rise of her cheeks.

"Come with me for this," he said. "I..."

He sifted through the phrases on offer aboard his tongue. *I enjoyed your company. I want you to see this. I don't want to be alone.* But it seemed that Eryn didn't need the reason.

"Gladly," she said. Her raised finger was a stern proviso. "But I'm not getting in the motor with you."

"Deal," agreed August, trying and failing to conceal a wicked grin.

They weren't seen, although at one point he did spy his mother, with her black hair pulled into a tight bun at the nape of her neck, as she scolded someone unseen for something unknown. He felt a pang at not stopping to talk to her – was he wrong to distance himself from his family, so? He made a silent promise to visit them, properly, at the weekend. There was really no excuse now that the ship – *the Valkyrie?* – was all but built. If Eryn felt similar pangs, she said nothing.

She was not silent, however, when they reached the end of the row, and Eryn saw the bicycle.

It was harder to retrieve the bicycle than it had been to conceal it, but August managed it in the end. The ride back to the offices was easy, despite Eryn's near-constant stream of curses and prayer from where she perched atop the handlebars before him. These he largely ignored, as August had his mind fixed on one thing: father kept his alcohol in his office. Father was at the house. And August needed to christen his ship.

Eryn, instructed to wait patiently on the docks in the moon-shadow of the huge ship, was too intrigued by the adventure to complain of the mystery. Besides, August was as quick about it as he had promised he would be.

As he stood before the little cupboard, laden row upon row with his father's liquor, August realised that he was looking upon something that he hated. He was awash with dismay; thwarted in his goal so close to the prize. He detested the thought of one of these bottles being used in honour of what he had achieved. In his imagination he saw the bottles swept from the shelves to be shattered, the vile syrups soaking into the carpet. He almost did it. He readied his body to respond to a series of silent commands so that he was nothing more or less than a taut bowstring, poised to destroy every single bottle to crystalline shards with nought but his bare hands.

No. He wanted none of these. But he didn't want to have to clean up the mess, either.

Was he thwarted? Surely, there were places to look other than his father's tarnished trove. There must be. For the ship was waiting just beyond the building; a *nameless orphan in a salt sea*, huge and pregnant with the promise of days to come, but equally nothingness; nothingness.

The Anders men each had an office in the building. August had a repurposed drafts' room, which suited him, as all he ever really needed was the light, the table, and his tools. Nils' office was designed for lurking in; much like the library, there was more than one option for sitting and waiting and sleeping and...

Erik used his room mostly for storage. For keeping the history of the company – the hundred, hundred manifests and logs of their vessels – for they did not just make them, but operated them on the shipping routes between the continent and the New World (now not so new, now that they had broken away and set up government for themselves). It was in *this* office that August found what he was searching for.

Its very appeal lay in the fact that it sat on the shelf in solitude. Grandfather kept drink for marking special occasions, not for ruining them. The bottle was about the length of his stretched palm – tip of index finger to wrist. The bottom of it was a flattened sphere on which it would refuse to balance, were it so tested. The sides of it drew upward and in to form a dagger-sharp point. August knew too little of wine to pick the grape or vintage – but he guessed it would be something special, just by the peculiar form of the bottle. It was made of what seemed to be a deep green sea glass, but it was hard to be sure for the wine within was such a dark, thick red. He marvelled at the way the bottle was not stoppered at all, but rather finished of itself: a finite vessel that may have been breathed into being around its own essence, made by magic, for some sort of god. It was a beautiful, cruel thing, and he was loath to destroy it.

But as all of the bottles in his father's cache drew ire from the pit of his stomach, and as he wanted desperately to christen the ship now, for himself, before anyone could comment on the name, and as this beautiful bottle did not leave him with disgust, but rather a quiet kinship; an awe-filled affinity, there seemed but one clear solution in his mind. Sometimes, beautiful things needed to be broken in order to achieve an even more beautiful end.

He meant to leave his jacket draped over Grandfather's desk, as the air was again lovely and cool despite the northern latitude of the city, now that he had grown used to the lack of sun. They often got long periods of balmy weather interspersed throughout the rain and wind. But at the last minute, he put the jacket back on. It was the middle of autumn, after all.

The sky was clear, and he could see a number of stars through the mire and mess of the smog and fug that gathered near the estuary, where the chimney stacks seemed never to sleep, but rather, to belch incessantly into the air above. The ship cut an imposing figure, towering up through the late evening. The perfect white of her hull flared out on either side of the stern, seeming almost like a pair of spread wings. He walked quickly to the bow; the green bottle clutched tightly under his arm. It felt odd and uncomfortable to carry the swirling drink; perhaps it was that alcohol had a viscosity dissimilar enough from other liquid, for it to slosh in such a displeasing and unfamiliar way.

Men were moving about the yard but none close enough to see what they were doing, and none familiar enough to care to know, even if they could make out the shapes in the dim. Eryn peeked cautiously at the curve of his forearm, narrowing her eyes suspiciously as the bottle caught the glinting light of the moon.

"She needs a name," August said simply, by way of explanation. He turned to give his words to the ship, and Eryn instinctively stepped back; a witness, she was there to be there.

"I know that this is much more proper a thing when done with champagne," he said, hefting the bottle by its short, sharp neck, and attempting to square up his angle of attack. "And also timelier at the moment of launch, not a few days after. But I'm a slow man, and don't do anything without thinking. So, here goes."

He tried the bottle in the shell of his palm again, again, raising and lowering his shoulders. He shrugged off his jacket, which was chafing him. A deep breath, and a swing.

"*Valkyrie*," he said clearly, as the end of the bottle connected with the hull, cracking open at once and sending the thick red insides trickling down into the ocean waves.

It was all wrong.

August gaped in horror at the sight of his ship seemingly streaming with blood. He wanted desperately at that moment to wash it clean. His palms sprung open in shock, and the green glass toppled into the water with a heavy sound. Staring at the wounded smear of crimson on the hull, brought words that he had read in the library back to him in part. Whether he muttered them aloud or merely thought them loud, he did not know. "Salt wilt thou be, 'til Blood break thee free..."

Somewhere beside him, or perhaps behind him, he heard a woman scream. His words were stopped quick in his throat through sudden breathlessness and thick emotion as, at that moment, August became a liar.

Because his eyes caught sight of a body in the water, and he jumped in after it, without thinking.

* * *

Something shifted

S t r e t c h e d . . .

sang

In the great expanse that was she

(that she was)

That was Isevelt.

Gathered and grew and **groaned** and

was silence

and silent

Until
                    ...ever this vace...
it
                    ...ever this vace be pressed to my skin...
was
                    ...let death be without...

not.

Ever this vace be pressed to my skin

Let death be without

And life be within.

* * *

And then it was rushing in my ears like a torrent of blood flowing from the wicked smile that my throat had become, and I was being pulled this way and that and how had I managed to find the vace? The foot of the vessel? Because the feet are what keep you here – if you're not on the ground then you're floating away but my fingertips (I have fingertips?) grazed the ragged edge of the dome and it was lucky that the glass had broken so roughly because I was able to use the catches to dig the vace into my sternum and it hurt (oh gods it hurt, thank the gods I *felt* it) –

And then my head was above the water. For a moment I thought that I was drowning. But I had no fear of death – not anymore. Instead, I revelled in the burning, clawing pain scraping itself down my nostrils and into my lungs; the deep ache that thumped violently into the back of my head at the nape of my neck.

I rolled onto my back, to assist whoever was keeping me afloat, and spat out a lump of seawater. It tasted wrong, the ocean. And the air. Something was wrong.

Perhaps once one died, there was no going back to life.

Perhaps everything would be wrong, now.

Perhaps *I* was wrong.

My back butted roughly up against a surface that was all at once solid and slippery, and the water jostled and sucked at my skin. It was as dark as night, but the water was so often in my eyes that I couldn't tell from the edge of the horizon whether it was true night.

Out of the black unknown, a firm hand grasped me where my arm met my chest and heaved me out of the swell. As my body gained weight and fought against leaving the lull of the water I could have cried out with joy. I was becoming myself again – where I had been emptied and then had been nothing, nothing – not even a husk, but *stuff* to fill a void – I was now returned.

I had been nothing for millennia. Ages. Forever and a day. I had slept and woken and dreamed – and I had died, and floated, suspended, for no more than a second – but which was the lie? The death or the dreaming? I was a child, and I was a crone. I was a shell, and I was the ocean that filled it. A pure ocean lacking any grit – no sand to wear my edges smooth.

With my mind still separate from the vessel that had become my body, I thought of the world to which I would open my eyes, and I was afraid. *How am I supposed to live in a world where my father doesn't?*

I was lying on my back with the breeze tracing a line over the length of my body, and I was cold. I longed to go back into the water; I was naked, and the water had been a cloak of safety and obscurity.

The other person was a tall man; he was tall even where he knelt beside me, shivering, and clearly torn between moving toward me and keeping safely away. He looked like a wounded animal, like a wolf, which was odd, because *I* was the one who had died.

I lifted up onto one elbow, peering around in the darkness to find someone – or something – that I recognised. Where was Gnarsa? The priestess had explained how it all was going to unfold. What would occur while we were envaced. But not once we returned.

We.

Where were the others?

I turned and spat the question at the stranger. "Where are they? Am I the first?"

The man seemed even more alarmed at the sound of my voice. His nose was long and thin but thrown into an odd shape by the spread of his nostrils as he sucked in breath. His clothes, though sodden, were strange, and impossibly white.

"Where?" I barked again, and this time he moved closer, palms displayed in the wordless sign of peace.

I glanced up from his bared palms (here were hands that I recognised: calloused and browned and bent with use). At the moment his outstretched palms were a balm and a blessing that held me fast to my here-and-now without ever once trying to touch me. The thin moonlight shifted and sliced across his head where his beard and hair curled; at best a dark brown, and nothing near the familiar black.

His palms forgotten, I reared back and threw myself away from the enemy, who I had surely last seen as he pursued my mother – mine or someone else's – as they fled across the black sand of my home.

Mother.

My last conscious thought was that I'd been captured, that the power of the gods had fallen somehow into the hands of the enemy and that, already, without ever having been tested, I'd failed.

* * *

"Goose, thank God, you're here."

Although the *Valkyrie* was wired through and through – long coils of fibre wound and stretched under the metal of her skin like arteries and veins – August hadn't wanted to flood the ship with light, in the middle of the night, encumbered as he was with a naked and sodden girl who was awake enough to panic but not strong enough to fight. Even as close as his attic apartment was, Eryn had deemed it more sensical somehow to get the girl onto the ship rather than lead her up the external stairs.

"I can't say I could possibly have declined your invitation," Goose said, roguishly flicking open a fold of thick paper and reading from it. "*Meet me at the ship. Urgent. Bring dress.* Not your handwriting...?"

He raised one eyebrow in anticipation, feigned or authentic, who could tell, but August merely snatched the folds of cotton from Goose's other hand and hurried back into the labyrinth of bare passages, Goose close on his heels.

"Is the dress for you, or for me...?" Goose called ahead of them, but August brushed straight past it, unwilling in his alarm to be drawn into jocularity.

August found the way easily in the darkness. He had selected his private stateroom on the day that he had finished the *Valkyrie*'s plans, and it was there that his feet and fear now lead them. Tucked away on D level, close enough to the heart of the ship but not near enough to other passengers to be called on by them, the indulgence was a modestly appointed, yet still unfurnished cabin. It currently contained an apparition wrapped in a curtain, along with (he hoped) his sister.

August knocked twice, inched the door open, shoved the dress inside, and then snapped the door shut once more. In the dancing glow of the first fire ever lit in a *Valkyrie* grate (perilous, considering all but the one in the smoking-room were for show), Goose had caught sight of grey eyes swimming in white skin rimmed in dark circles and pain. He gasped.

"August Anders, what did you *do*?" Goose demanded roughly, shoving August by the shoulder.

August thought this was a bit rich, considering Goose's long history with the fairer sex, but decided to let it stand on merit, as the girl did look, truly, shocking.

"I pulled her from the water," he answered, hoping that his friend was startled enough by that particular revelation to ask after others, unmentioned. August didn't understand enough of what had transpired that night to answer for it.

"Has she said anything? Do you know anything?" Goose was white as a sheet. "I can only imagine she is the victim of something... sinister," he finished darkly.

"Nothing that I could understand."

"Should we tell the constabulary?"

August shook his head. "I don't know," he said. "I don't know".

Goose peered searchingly up and down the empty corridor, worrying a thumbnail against his front teeth. "I think—"

Whatever Goose thought remained unsaid, as the door opened once more to reveal the girl, expertly dressed by Eryn now, and significantly less waterlogged than when August had last seen her.

She looked from Goose to August, hissed something unintelligible and shoved August hard in the chest, before grabbing Goose's hand and attempting to drag him down the corridor in the wrong direction.

"Wait, stop – no—" Goose spluttered, stumbling until he managed to pull her up. They were a flurry of slapping and grasping hands and forearms for a moment before Goose managed to pin her arms down at her sides. "Friend," he gasped at last. "Safe."

She didn't slump or even truly relax, but she did turn her head slightly toward August, warily taking stock of his features. She sneered, baring her even teeth.

"Perhaps she thinks that you're the one who hurt her?" Goose asked, as she continued to mutter angrily in August's direction.

August shrugged, utterly perplexed. The girl shifted her muttering towards the walls and ceiling as she seemingly noted her surroundings anew. Eventually, she shrugged Goose's hands off her arms and gestured expansively around, sobbed once, and clutched her own forearms tightly with pale hands.

Eryn chose that moment to appear, sliding gently into the circle of the sodden girl's confidence, curling her fingers lightly around the girl's elbow and muttering something soft as featherdown.

The pale girl didn't seem hale, but she certainly wasn't unlovely. The dress – Sadie's or Caroline's or Ursula's – was ill-fitting, and the cloth-covered buttons were misaligned, but that did nothing to hide the straight lines of her collarbones or the smooth sweep of her neck, tucked away under long hair the colour and texture of bleached spider silk.

Her eyes narrowed as they fixed on Goose's lips. She said something to him again; demanded, and then waited. She repeated the word.

"I'm sorry, I don't understand you," Goose said helplessly.

Still glaring at his mouth, the girl repeated, "Sorry. I don't understand you."

Her voice retained its deep honey quality and turned the words into molasses spread over newspaper. There was a sweetness, but a distinct crackle and tear underneath it, too. Sticky, ripped paper. She clearly had an accent – but August couldn't place it.

"Are you from England?" Goose asked.

She repeated him again, concentrating desperately on the shape and sound of his words.

"Is she mocking you or trying to learn the language?" August asked quietly. She didn't mimic his speech, but rather, shot another disgusted glance in his direction.

"I think the latter," Goose said, and the rest of his words were obscured by her voice, saying them a second after he did. "Quick, recite something for her."

"God save the King?"

"Something else," said Eryn. She didn't break eye contact with the other girl, even though the other girl wasn't watching. It was as though Eryn was determined to be there, waiting; a place of safety should the girl think to search after it.

"I can't think of anything else," August snapped.

They were still standing in the empty hallway, lit from the side by the fireplace in August's empty room.

"You know heaps of poetry," Goose challenged, panicked now as she stepped inquisitively closer, matching his inflection.

"I used to, I don't right now!"

"Will you think of something, *please*?"

"Theenk of something, *pleece*," the girl said.

August quickly walked his palms from his waist to his shoulders before he realised what he was searching for. The little black book had been in the coat which he had *blessedly*, unthinkingly taken from his shoulders, before breaking the bottle; removed from his body before he jumped into the water.

There had been poetry in that book, surely, and if not, words enough. August ducked into the stateroom, pawed about in the half-dark until his fingers found his jacket, and, gaining the corridor once more, ferreted in the fabric until he found the secret pocket. In his haste, he had trouble easing the corners of the book through the little opening, and so to fill the moment, he mumbled the only words that offered themselves to teeth and tongue and other mechanical parts that made words.

"Salt fill the sea, salt filleth me... salt fill the sea, salt filleth me..." he said.

She regarded him warily, and although she didn't repeat his words, her mouth worked in a way that told of the taste of them, the weight of them.

The book came free, and August clutched it in both hands as the discarded jacket fell to the floor, no longer important.

"Friend?" The girl asked carefully, raising one finger, and tapping it firmly on August's sternum. *"Friend?"* she insisted again when he made no response.

"August!" Eryn prompted.

"Yes, yes, friend!" August stammered. If his own face was anything like Goose's, he must have looked afraid. Afraid of this ghost-like creature, nearing the height of his chin, leaving bruises on his chest with a single, insistent touch.

The girl narrowed her eyes again and reached out to lift the black book from August's grip. He let it go and she took it easily, letting the pages fall open. They lighted on the wood-carved illustrations, which, if it were at all possible, leeched her face of even more colour. She glared into August's eyes, desperately, for a long time. August was reluctant to break the silence.

"Friend," she said again, and clutched the book to her chest. August nodded, swallowed drily.

She turned as if in a dream back to the fire, slipped inside, shut the door. Goose and August and Eryn remained in the darkness, their features barely lit by the strip of warmth eking out from under the door.

"Eryn," August said finally, with a note of finality. "Eryn, I'll take you back home tomorrow."

And he slid his back down the wall until he sat on the carpet runner, his head in his hands, and his mind full of whirling concern.

* * *

I was aware of the way that my fingers trembled as they travelled over the deep black lines on the ancient page, but despite all of the weight my existence had gathered since the stranger pulled me from the water, seeing my own death stole all of it away.

Who had made the carvings?

It must have been someone who witnessed it. The details were disturbingly personal. I could tell which of the featureless figures were Haedi and Sylvi, because of the way that they stood with their hands touching. Aidan was clearly the one next to Gnarsa (the artist had managed to include the strings of shells and beads around the witch's throat), second to die, and so sure of it. So, then, I was the one on the furthest edge. Last to die.

Indistinct except for my place in the line.

As I allowed the sudden, hot tears in my eyes to settle and recede like an angry tide, more things swam out of the illustration and into my understanding. The nuance of the carving was deeply unsettling.

There was the wicked knife, with the suggestion of the wing and the wave worked into the hilt under Gnarsa's hand. The urns sat carefully on a rock rising up out of the water, ready to be taken back to the stone altar once they were given our blood.

Why did the stranger have this in his possession? Was he really a friend? The dark-haired man seemed to trust him. And the girl.

Think like a thinker, I scolded myself, sternly re-spooling my fearful thoughts around firm logic. *Diagnose the illness from the symptoms, not the other way around.*

I knew more about the ritual than the others had, so was best prepared to deal with whatever had gone wrong. Because something had clearly gone wrong.

I closed the book of memories and laid it gently aside, turning my attention to the strangely furnished room around me. I was curiously grateful for the abundance of unfamiliarity, as it was *that* alone which preserved my sanity. Had I found but a trace of my life... a skerrick of sameness...

But as it was I found nothing. From the feeling of the fibres in the textiles to the shape of the room around me; nothing that I felt or beheld connected with *me*, as *Isevelt*.

So, I was able to hold my own sadness at bay along with my fear. But while I managed to close the door on it, I could still sense it in the hallways of my heart, hear the rush of it as it coursed through my veins.

Time enough, once you know what you're dealing with, I told myself firmly.

I walked once, slowly, around the room. There was a strong smell that burned like pine needles, but with none of the honey that travelled on the back of that particular aroma. The room was perfectly square, with lofty ceilings unmarked by wooden beams or soot smoke. The fireplace was nowhere near big enough.

You're either dead, and this is what happens after... or you're dreaming... or this is somehow true.

I dashed the heel of my hand across my forehead as if to dismiss the thought. It didn't matter, because knowing could not have changed it. The pain in my bones was real enough. The ache in my heart. Real or not real, I would have to bear it.

The white skin of my hand caught my attention. The lines of my body were familiar to my eyes, but the sensation of existing within its bounds was completely foreign.

I raised my hand and rested the palm against the press of my lips, testing, again, the strange taste and texture of my new language. Although the sounds had echoed uncomfortably in my ears when first I had heard the people speaking, they had quickly settled to meaningful words and phrases – I imagined – by the magic, which rendered my understanding of this new master a necessity. I clenched my fist and pictured my parents. I tried to say their names in my mother tongue. It didn't sound right to my new ears; my mouth missed the vowels.

I was so tired. And remote.

I had never possessed friends of the sort that I had seen in others my age, in the village. As I curled up on the bare rug in the light of the dying fire, hurting in my very bones as though I had grown them that day out of nothingness, I longed for a companion. Should I call out for the pretty girl?

No.

It was easier to be silent, and alone.

The strange, burnished man had left his coat in the impossibly perfect room. As I draped the expanse of it over my thin shoulders, there crept from the folds and creases a smell that I found to be just as familiar and comforting as his calloused hands had been. The first familiar thing that I had found was not the taste of the sea, or the shape of a room, or the set of a sun, but rather... the smell of an honest man.

* * *

Goose had been right, as usual. At Goose's insistence, he and Eryn had returned to the big house in the night for a different dress (and the remains of the candied orange), and so this morning, Eryn had managed not only to dress the girl in clothes that fit and flattered her, but she also had her name and her trust.

"August, meet Isevelt," Eryn said gently, gesturing.

August bowed quickly, noting the lavender cotton blouse that draped over deftly worked lace, its matching skirt falling like a flute to the floor. The white-blonde hair had been wrapped around itself into a braid, caught up in a knot at the base of her neck. She still looked sad, but now she seemed less scared.

"Isevelt," August said, and the ghost of a smile had visited one corner of her full mouth.

There were practicalities to attend to, even in the midst of the magical. The *Valkyrie* was overdue to start her sea trials (delayed by August's hesitation to gift the ship with a name), and so her decks were intermittently filled with workers, sailors, and inspectors. The girl – Isevelt – could not stay in August's stateroom. Isevelt (speaking hesitantly but determinedly) made it clear that she wanted to remain near to the water, and so, with the added propriety of Eryn's company, the couch was made up in the attic apartment. August was to move into his office, albeit quietly.

Isevelt remained wary of him. She asked Eryn many questions: about the world, about the weather, about people. But she would not answer any of her own. She was often in his sight, though. In his orbit, but never in his way. But she occupied his thoughts, as much as his attic, remaining a mystery that he turned over and over in his mind like a worry stone.

Chapter 7

Ash

I realised upon walking into the main hall to find Valder and Xeva seated on their thrones that Gnarsa and Wulf had most likely planned this moment *long* before they had ruined it by waking me.

I knew that my return had been a mistake. Even though I hadn't been able to bring Wulf to say it, even though I knew that Gnarsa would never admit fault or failing with her mouth (but always with her features, always with her frame), I knew that I had not been their first choice.

I, the least faithful. I, the least willing. Until the beginning of the end.

But they didn't know me; now that I had died and woken up again at the hands of the gods. The most faithful. The most willing. Our relationship with the gods was give and take; I believed that now.

It was easier, I found, to walk now than when I first woke up. The pushing and pulling sway of the tide had settled to a mere suggestion of breath that I felt within the movement of my blood, more than in my body. The pull to the little boat also had abated, nearly as soon as I'd collapsed into its belly. The connection was still there, but I no longer *needed* to be near to it. No more than I needed to be in my own company; I simply *was*.

The two seated on the thrones at the top of the room received a single glance from me and, as I was feeling generous, a small dip of my chin. Upon the people in the rest of the room, I bestowed my attention. Faces that I had known in my past life, more weathered now. Ashen. Perhaps the flames that had raged here had taken with them, at their death, all of the people's fire. All of our heat.

I was the new burning.

The time would come for me to speak with the priestess; to ask her of her paltry little plans. They paled in comparison to the crimson heat of my own intention. The depth and the breadth of my own convictions, writ in scarlet. My call to war, sealed with the searing spill of my own sanguinity.

I spared a glance for the long, low, oil and smoke-stained ceiling of the hall. The once-silver beams of the roof were slick with soot, reflecting a pale kind of moonlight that danced with the golden throw of the central fireplace. I strode around the circle of grey stones, feeling the people shrink back from my form as I drew nearer to them in necessity.

I wondered why they were so perturbed. Surely with the fire casting its light on my skin, I looked more alive? I saw one girl – woman now – who had been just older than me before I died – what had been her name? She grasped the plait that hung over her shoulder, thick as a rope, in two claw-like hands.

It's not the skin at all, I thought, suddenly realizing. *It's the hair. The eyes.*

I stopped at the base of the single stair that raised the Jarl and his wife an essential and equally inconsequential foot above the rest of us. They gaped, faces like gutted fish, waiting for either death or release. I turned my back on them, held the pose that the priestess had attempted earlier when I entered her hut, and then stepped easily back up the slight step so that I stood equal to them, facing the people.

Gnarsa had given me new clothes. I had wryly agreed that the cloak of the Jarl's son wasn't fitting attire – and sent altogether the wrong message. Instead, I stood before the people dressed in grey wool that draped and gathered about my small frame, highlighting the white of my hair and giving my skin a soft glow. I wore no adornment, save the vace that was pressed, even now, and always, into the delicate layers of the skin on my breastbone.

I had never seen the vace in its virgin state. Impossible, I guessed. To see yourself from without, being that we are, by nature, within. But Gnarsa must have had them, empty and ready. Beurd – the glass man – he died before we did.

How did she know the right amount to make? I cupped the glass dome on my chest like a mewling pup. Like comfort.

I wondered how it did not fill with blood.

Perhaps I had none.

"We have lost," I said, simply, and my voice carried through the long hall, buoyed on its way by whispers like breeze in the grass. Was it evidence of dismay that I saw, on the faces of the people? Did they think that I was admitting defeat? "We have lost many, and we have lost much. But although we have been beaten, we have not been broken."

Another ripple of sound. The shifting of feet and the setting of shoulders. There need not be the shushing of children, for we had none. This promise was what many of them had hoped to hear. But not all. I noted more than one closed face, more than one pair of crossed arms. I would change their minds.

I would soften their hearts.

"The fathers of our fathers set out, once, from the home that they loved, to escape the enemy. Not just the threat of the enemy – but the wrath, and the storm, and the fury of the enemy. Our history was marked by the spill of our blood on the open flame. Our people chose *this* place. Here, we have lived our lives. Farewelled our dead. But always, living and dying under the silent threat of the enemy."

I couldn't say if I had composed this speech while I waited. If I had artfully arranged the words in the darkness of my death. But they arrived upon my lips, now, an instant before I spoke them: perfect, and powerful. As I spoke, I felt my own convictions grow. Felt more and more assured of the path that the people must take. The road for revenge, and for freedom from fear.

"No longer will we live beneath the threat of violence brought upon us *only* by our past. No longer will we be beholden to an ancient grudge that wears no name and bears no cause."

"How?"

The question came from behind me, from the Jarl. I turned toward him; a half turn, to include the people in our conversation. The time for truth was not yet nigh. I gave him bones, and he took them like a tired dog.

"We will sail out, and we will find their home, and we will destroy it."

There was a quiet clamour. A triumphant roar tempered with a tremulous wail. So, I hadn't managed to convince them all.

"How?" This time the question was from the people. A man who looked like Beurd, the glassblower. Couldn't be, though. I had seen him die, on the beach. "How? We don't have any boats."

At this point, Wulf cleared his throat and stepped forward. He seemed even more tall and thin than usual; although he bowed his head, he still loomed above me. Although he stood level with the people, I reached his shoulder with the crown of my head.

"Maz, hear me. I finished a silver birchwood boat, from the young trees, just this morning. The only way that Aidan is here is because I broke her vace against the side of the craft."

Again, the hissed outcry.

"That is *Aidan*?"

I felt the wonder being worn on my face but couldn't do anything to quiet it. Not wonder. Wound. For sores often weep, and it was surely the sting of weeping that sat, salt, behind my eyes, behind my nose. In the ashen pit of my throat. How could they not have known me? Did they know me for any one of the four who died? Or had they just thought me an apparition? A ghost?

Don't plead. Don't beg.

"The gods kept my life in a secret place," I said. "Waiting for this moment. They have returned me, as the priestess said they would, to protect you. To fight for *you*. I am yours just as surely as you are theirs. I tell you; *no longer* must you live as though under a debt that may at any moment be called in."

I gazed around the hall. Nearly all had their faces, their bodies, turned to me in trust. Nearly all.

"But you are *not* the mark of a promise fulfilled," sobbed one woman with tears in her eyes and a chill in her voice. "The gods took you, the last, but they have not given us any new children. How many more do we need to give? Who else needs to die before they grant us children again?"

I shrugged. The issue of children was not my concern. Why bother birthing babies under threat of butchering?

"Perhaps we shall give the enemy's children to the gods," I said.

"But one boat?" asked a man of fighting age over the shocked gasp of the crying woman. "How are we to triumph with just one boat?"

I nodded. I turned to Valder.

"Fashion another two crafts out of wood from the spruce and pines that grow along the coast. Promise twenty to each, to build them, and then to sail them by the next full dark. That gives you time enough. They will not accept another vace; we will have to wait for the birchwood to mature. But I can protect sixty men."

"Are you sure?" The Jarl's wife reached out to grab my fingers, then seemed to think better of it. "Are you sure?"

I turned once more to the gathering of people.

"The gods returned me for this moment. They needed me. They took my blood, and now, they are giving it back with a promise. This is the end. We are the last who will sleep and wake in fear. We are the last who will wear the swords of an enemy we have no quarrel with, beyond the *memory* of a sword, and a quarrel. We serve the gods, and they keep their promises."

Chapter 8

Salt

The waif, as the book had named her, became more or less a ghost in the weeks that followed. She was scarcely seen about the ship, preferring instead to keep to the little room that Smith had so readily given for her use. The bursar himself was hardly seen either, as he stayed with her in the room – giving every effort to the teaching of language. Smith had remarked to Crow that he was *sure* that the girl understood him, but that she seemed unwilling to bend her mouthparts to the speaking.

Crow felt conflicted, but his lack of certainty was a thing that he kept for himself. The crew had worked tirelessly for months trying to hunt down the vace – what they needed now was some kind of payoff. Some little reward to confirm that their efforts had not been for nought.

But even about that Crow had his reservations.

They needed to witness the full measure of her magic, but Crow himself didn't know what it was. So, what risk would he be running, to invite any measure of danger into their lives, not knowing her capabilities? He needed to talk to Smith; he needed to find out what the little man had learned, and then make a plan to use it.

He cornered his cousin one night, as Smith crept from his old cabin to the pile of blankets at the stern, that he had taken to using as his bed – while ever the weather permitted.

"Tell me at least, man, that she is what we thought?"

Smith removed the family spectacles from the bridge of his nose and rubbed them with the corner of his once-white shirt. The fabric had stood the test of time, but like all things so tried, it showed wear for it. Smith shook his head slowly while he worked away at the lens: a habit that Crow had long ago learned was a way to stall for time when he wanted to make sure that his next words were a well-chosen, comfortable fit.

"In truth, I'm not quite sure what she is. She's *something*, though." Smith paused and squinted at the captain, then pressed his spectacles back into place on his nose. He led with a cocked shoulder, a conspiratorial turn of his head. "Will you walk with me?"

The two moved casually from the stern of the ship, along her curved belly, and towards the rear railing. The few crew that they came across were content to nod respectfully in the captain's direction and carry on with their night work.

Crow allowed the silence, taking the time, as was his way, to visit with the existence of his favourite things in life, like a comfortable, old aunt: the way the stars stretched overhead, unending, winking over the sky as though made of light that crept through the weave of a well-worn blanket. The hush and sigh of the sea as it worked around the feet of the *Witch* like waves of molten, black glass. And the subtle creak and groan that her ribs made as they breathed with the very effort of simply sailing. He added *that* one to the list as a matter of personal determination. It was a sound that scared him and thrilled him in equal measure.

And that, he thought, *is something to love.*

"Tell me, cousin," Crow said again, as they stood with their arms resting against the moonbeam railing at the tail end of the ship. "Tell me that we didn't waste our time, or our gold."

Smith sighed and squinted off into the direction that they'd come from. "I don't think you wasted our time, or our gold," he said finally. "If only to have saved her from the fate that she had known for centuries."

"And what fate is that?" Crow asked, sharply.

Smith shrugged. "Being without existing."

"For centuries?" Crow asked quickly.

"Or thereabouts."

Crow frowned at the ribbons that the ship worked into the surface of the water as the wind pushed them forward, through it. He was not ignorant of the preservation and salvation of souls – his father had spoken often about the importance of safeguarding that immortal piece of a person's puzzle. But all that being true, Crow had the life of a pirate now. The things that got in his way were put out of it. People included. Did he value a single life at the weight of nearly the whole ship's fortune? He worked his tongue against the sharp edge of a molar – a relic from a tavern brawl, several years before.

There was a secret, there. One so grievous that he didn't dare form the words in his head. Refused even to call to mind her face. Her name slipped across his teeth like silk.

No. The captain roused himself from thoughts that teetered dangerously close to admission, turning once more to Smith.

"She remembers the time?" Crow asked. "She has spoken of this to you?"

"In a manner of speaking. I am still using a mixture of sounds, drawings, and flailing, as she will only nod *yes* or shake her head *no*. She is quite stubborn, but still, somehow... quite candid. Like a child."

Crow's eyes widened. "You tell me that she is innocent? How can an innocent protect us from anything?"

Smith's negation was swift but gentle. "I spoke of her having a child's candour. You've obviously never had a child, yourself, or raised another man's, to assume that any one of them is innocent."

Crow felt gall rise up in him like the wave that heralds a devastating storm and turned his countenance away for solitude as he slid dangerously down the face of it. If there was pain in his voice when he managed to speak, Smith made no mention of it. If Smith realised his offence, he made no mention of it. Crow kept his voice even. "What do you mean, then?"

Smith thought for a moment. "A child will announce their thoughts, without thinking about their implications. And if their implications offend you, they will not apologise for them."

"That's terrifying."

"You sound shocked."

"You're telling me that this slip of a girl is all but a child. How could she prove to be any sort of a force to be reckoned with?"

Smith chuckled. "Again, spoken like a man who has never raised a daughter. She is a force, alright. But it will need to be some sort of magic that bends her to any will but her own."

* * *

Inside the little wooden cabin, I frowned at the back of my hand. I was sure that I'd had a scar there, stretching from the junction of my first and middle finger down to where my thumb met my wrist.

I was sure not in the way that people are sometimes ingratiatingly pleading for something to be so. Rather, I was (quite simply) quite sure. So, the sudden lack of the little mark on the back of my hand was quite unsettling. I wondered what other hallmarks of my life were now missing from my person. I wondered if I still bore the marks of having my throat pared open by a sharpened shard of glass. Or the scratches from the enemy's fingernails, where they had ripped at my back. Perhaps I ought to ask Smith when next the strange little man returned.

I probably wouldn't.

It didn't really matter.

Whatever stuff my body was made of, it didn't matter.

Haedi often accused me of being one to feel feelings that I couldn't explain, or, if I *could* explain them, that I didn't particularly like. But this was more even than that. What I felt in the cabin, staring at the unblemished back of my too-pale hand, was the overwhelming experience of being at once perfectly contained, and completely at sea.

The little man would be back soon. With his gestures and his babbling, and that look in his dark eyes that seemed to suggest there was something in me that he was waiting to observe.

I had nothing to offer him because I had nothing at all.

I forced myself to stand and shuffle across the small cabin to where the round porthole sat snug within the wooden walls, and where the dim, oval looking glass swayed with the movement of the ship atop the waves. The little man had seemed apologetic when he placed it there. He hadn't looked at me. Hadn't spoken of it. Just carefully slid the loop of twine over the nail in the wall.

If I took a slightly deeper breath; if I paused before glancing into the rust-spotted glass, then it was indiscernible. I didn't know it. However, as I locked eyes with my reflection, a wave of sadness formerly held at bay only by the bounds of my body now moved visibly over my skin: a rush of emotion that somehow left more of the quiet nothingness in its wake. It ached.

My neck *was* without blemish.

I wasn't sure if that made me glad or made me feel cheated. I remembered intimately the sensation of my skin parting ways with itself; the infinitesimally small separation between the ice-cold razor-edge of the witch's glass knife and the hot flow of blood that tumbled forth from my insides. I recalled vividly the way that I'd taken the time, even at that moment, to wonder at how my blood somehow had more heat than my whole did. How the heat of my own blood had managed to make me feel cold.

As I ran birch-white fingers up and down the length of my spectre's neck, I realized what I hadn't in the first place; that the blood had nothing to do with it, and everything to do with it. I had felt cold because I was dying.

Had I died? And Haedi? Had *she* died? The others? Were they still dead? Was *I* still dead?

I *looked* like a dead thing. Hair leached of all colour from its time in the waves. Eyes the deep grey nothingness of the seals that lived by the beach. All of me almost transparent; but more likely, just not *entirely* there.

On my breastbone was the shallow vace, about the size of my empty palm, the skin around it still raw. The water inside of it was so complete, so imbued, that any movement of it was indiscernible, even as I trembled. Even as I breathed. I hardly remembered saying the words, finishing the ritual. I scarcely believed that I had, or – given the choice over – that I would again.

The ship that surrounded me creaked constantly. Its belly groaned in the way that meant that good food was either not long done with, or too long in coming. But the noise that worked its way down through the walls to meet my ears was a smaller sound: the distressed wood-on-wood of a door that had never sat plumb. A chair complaining of its occupant's weight. The twist of foot on stair.

The little man was back again.

Smith. But this time he had the big man there with him, his coat flapping around him like dark wings, waiting for the rain when their oil could be useful. The big man: the one who had pulled me from the water.

As he entered the room, I felt a nameless affinity. Almost like what I had felt for my father, but with much less affection. They had spoken in the same soothing way, the two big men, at different points in my life... as though I were a bird poised to fly away, but lulled into staying put by the promise of safety. The assurance of something sweet. This man had been kind to me, I was sure, even though I had no mind for the words that he had said, being unable to recall the sounds.

Smith began talking at me again, slowly annunciating vocal sounds that seemed like they could almost have been the drunken cousins of my own people's speech.

He gestured widely and slowly, smiling as he stepped towards me, but the meaning of the movements was lost in their very exaggeration. I understood everything that he said when he spoke in his own language; our hours of one-sided conversation had built a flimsy bridge of timid comprehension that allowed for understanding. The sounds were not the language of my own people, but my new ears caught them and sorted them with ease. I simply had no desire to speak back - especially not when Smith attempted to converse in my own language.

I felt as though I swam in a sea of abstruseness. Of sky-wide isolation. Within me, there was nothing much at all. Mild concern, perhaps, because part of me understood that the memories even now playing behind my eyes, memories of my own death, the death of the others, aroused little more in me than a quiet regret, and knew that it was not enough. I blinked once to banish the memories and turned my eyes back to the two men, as my gaze had drifted off of them to rest on the sleeve of the borrowed cloak. They were still talking at me. Still gesturing expansively. Or, rather, Smith was. The big man remained still, frowning at me from underneath his considerable eyebrows.

"Where is my sister?" I asked, interrupting the little man's dance. The two glanced at each other, and then back at me.

Smith cocked his head in the same way that an unfortunate seal had once when I had been a naughty child and he had been on the receiving end of my throwing practice.

"I don't know. I'm sorry. We don't know where you came from, or even how you happen to be here; only that we sought you, and then that we broke you." The bigger man. He spoke in a much more comfortable manner; his cadences rose and fell with all the familiarity of a predictable tide. He went on in a voice that was little more than a mutter... a scraping of butter on black bread. "But if we're being honest, I think it's fair to say that somebody else got there first."

Although his voice when he spoke was all of comfort, the face from whence it came was *so* full of sadness that his words slid over my skin – driftwood without anything to weigh it down. His was a sadness defined only by what it was missing.

I gave the smallest of shrugs. The smallest of apologetic grimaces. It was all I had to spare. And then I turned away from the both of them, curled into myself, and wished not for the first time in what felt like a hundred, hundred years, that sleep would come and claim me.

Chapter 9

Blood

The *Valkyrie's* first flight was set for the next morning, but I couldn't have been more discontented. August Anders had tried to move me into his attic house (but who would live that far above the level of the street?) yet still I kept finding my way back to the little room that had hidden me, the night that I returned to flesh and blood from salt and ashes. The little room with the soot stains just beginning to creep up the edges of the hearth that the sister, Eryn, had agreed was *truly good for nothing*.

The truth was that I couldn't bring myself to be away from the vast ship to which I was tethered. I knew the ritual. And that meant that, despite all else, when the sun rose, the ship would finally sail, and I might be needful.

I spent a long time staring over the ship's railing for the slight swell of the wharf-side waves but had trouble seeing through the thick fog that wrapped itself around the ship. I had perfect solitude; the other workers were taking refuge inside from the opaque air and the impending storm that rode the back of the gathering breeze, throwing out the scent of dry lightning before it.

I was truly hoping to see the slip of naked skin beneath the waves that would herald the arrival of a sister in my sacrifice... Aiden, or perhaps Sylvi. However, I couldn't even see the water, and so had little earnest hope of seeing anything hidden within it. If I were honest with myself (which was difficult, but necessary), the earnestness of my hope was limited by my belief that I had been lost, little cared for... and now, was alone.

* * *

"You're never around anymore."

The words were paper thin and rough as a cat's tongue – but it was the sort of sandpaper that one could endure, knowing that its purpose was to set the fur to rights.

"I know, Grandfather, I'm sorry. With the trials coming up tomorrow..."

August heard his feeble words as though from afar. He stopped and looked at Erik – actually *looked* – and what he saw was worse than thin sandpaper. The old man was clearly ill.

The whites of his eyes were a dull cream at best – and not the sort to keep a cat happy. The tenor of his skin was spoiled, as though he had been sitting underneath a green sun. August wondered whether he had permission to acknowledge the old man's health, then remembered that he was sitting at the old man's bedside, that one of them was still wearing pyjamas, and that he had been summoned by his mother in the early hours of the morning on the office telephone. Grandfather looked so tired. So *tired*. Eryn's constant presence in the house, despite her regular hours at the hospital with Aunt Anne, despite the desperate intrigue of Isevelt living in his flat, suddenly made perfect sense.

Erik knew that he was declining.

It was the reason for their meeting. Refusing to acknowledge it would just be wasting time... it needed to be said.

"Is it serious?"

Erik shrugged, coughed. "It's my liver. So, your father had better watch out, because he's hardly taken decent care of his own to begin with."

"How long?"

It was a question with two answers, and August let Erik decide which he was willing – ready – to give.

"I held it off for a few months. Caught up with me once the mad dash for the *Valkyrie* finished up. Like my insides had the time to stop and realise that they'd been left behind, and that's when they started shouting about it."

"You like the name?" August asked. It had sounded right, in his grandfather's voice.

"It's perfect. All of it... perfect." August felt himself glow as Erik rested his eyes for a moment, before pushing on. "I can't thank you yet, though, my boy... as there is still one more thing that I require of you."

"Name it," August breathed, picturing himself journeying to the ends of the earth in search of whatever magic his grandfather required. Perhaps there *was* something arcane at work, for the magic that August thought of now was exactly what Erik asked for.

"I need you... to go into my office... and retrieve for me... a little green bottle, filled with blood." He coughed lightly. Apologetically. "I need to see it."

In the silence that followed the stopping of August's heart, he heard the breath whistling in Erik's lungs. Heard the scratch and sweep of the man's nails on the woven blanket. Heard the bell from downstairs as someone called to be let in. Heard the hairs on the back of his arms grow infinitesimally.

"A... what?" August choked out. *No.*

"I need to tell you a secret, before it's too late. I need to... to tell you."

"Grandfather, I can't– I don't..."

"Please..."

Erik's voice fell from his lips in a steady hush, like a waterfall of grain that turned into a rhythmic rush of sleep breathing.

When August finally stood, tearing his eyes from the hollow cheeks and flyaway hair, he did so carefully. Quietly. Ponderously.

What was he to do? It was gone.

Or was it?

Was the *thing* at the centre of his thoughts... at the centre of his *life*... not a mystery at all, but a *secret*?

His grandfather wouldn't sleep long. But August would have – *should* have – enough time to go and make it back. To bring back the thing that he needed.

"Eryn!" She appeared so quickly that August wondered where she had been hiding, and how much she had heard. "Will you come?"

August didn't have his bicycle, which pleased Eryn greatly. He didn't think he could manage on a streetcar. He needed quiet, and calm. Luckily, Nils' vanity had a streak of luxury in it. August ducked furtively around the back of the house and slid into the seat of the motor. Eryn slammed the heavy door on the other side, exhaling with the effort. She seemed more inclined to let him drive after the experience with the bicycle.

"What's happening? Where are we going? Is it Isevelt?"

August pursed his lips. "You saw what happened, in the water, didn't you?"

Eryn nodded quickly and breathed her words in a rush. How long had she been holding it?

"It was magic. I know we haven't spoken of it, and I didn't want to push it, because I *know* that you think I'm a ninny–"

"I don't think you're a ninny." August sighed deeply. "Unless you feel bold enough to call grandfather a ninny, too."

Eryn's shock was an audible gasp and giggle. The thought was ridiculous and dangerous in equal measure.

"Explain," she demanded.

August pondered, choosing his words with care. Driving the motor through the streets, his mind turning over and over again the phrases that he might need – might want – to say, felt like manoeuvring a great horse through an ocean. Peaceful, but somehow full of danger and fear. Having led the thing into the waves, the fact of the danger was inescapable. But because it had been a choice, the danger was met with resignation.

It was simple. The bottle no longer existed. But that didn't mean that he had to return to his grandfather empty-handed.

Because didn't he believe, didn't he *know* (in the place in his heart that was deep enough to be missed by shame) what his eyes had seen, but his brain refused to put words to?

A credit to her patience, Eryn did not press him to speak. Perhaps the permission of her presence was enough of an assurance that she would find out, soon enough.

"Wait here," August said. "I might need your help convincing her to get in."

He left the motor turning over, purring like a great exotic feline, and leapt up the stairs that were built against the side of Mrs. Caulfer's building, where he seldom lived. He took them two at a time. He had scarcely called on Isevelt since he had ensconced her there, and so found himself – despite his leaps – unsure of how to broach the portal and ask after her company. Besides, there was every chance that she was silently sequestered on the far side of his own locked door, deep inside the belly of the *Valkyrie*.

In the end, he knocked twice and eased open the door which had been left unlocked, presumably by Isevelt, when she last left the place.

His room was empty. Neat, and clean, and unbothered. But immediately upon opening the door, August was aware not only of the empty hollowness that adorns a room lacking the warmth of a body, and also the quiet dim of a place that at one point held a woman, and now, was distinctly without. The room felt, to him, as though it had once held a bright bouquet of flowers, and now, all that remained was a watermark on the table. And a basin half-full of water.

How long had it been since she had been there last? He couldn't know. *Probably only minutes*, he assured himself, but within him, there was a panic that promised him she had been gone for days. He wanted to weep. What could he give his grandfather now?

August surveyed the square space, allowing his eyes to rest in turn upon the perfectly made bed, upon the sitting chair surrounded by hard-backed books (a collection that he had started well before, in his youth), and finally upon the newly gathered bundles of flowers and roots, laid out like loaves of bread, tied with rough brown twine. As he stared at the bundles of flowers (lifted one, rested it upon his lips, breathed deep the English lavender that was somehow salty like the sea), his thoughts returned to the books.

He searched the pile quickly and methodically for the little black book, knew almost immediately that it wasn't there, and just as quickly decided to look for it in his stateroom aboard the *Valkyrie*, as that was the last time and place that he could recall beholding it.

Leaving the door just as unlocked as when he had found it, August hurried down the stairs, his thoughts on turning off the motor. His intentions were arrested, however, by the welcome sight of Isevelt walking carefully into view around the corner from the direction of the dock. She had a basket slung over one forearm, in the manner of someone who had been so accoutred before, her chin turned instinctively up to the sun where it stalked behind the veil of overcast clouds. There was no sign in the sky of the storm from the night before.

In the basket were more dirty roots, a single rose, and some manner of reeded grass plant that August had either never seen, or had never bothered to notice before.

"Isevelt," he called out, and she stopped. "Please... my grandfather is very sick."

August didn't know why he said those words to her. Of all of the phrases that he had practised, that had not been one of them. Instinct, perhaps, just as sure as that which had bid her turn her lovely cheeks to the sun, told him that just as surely, *here* was someone who would help. Whose desire would be to help.

"Please," he said again, as he held up the single stem of lavender, still firmly in his fingers, as both offering and thanks.

Would she soften? Would she come?

* * *

I gazed upon the purple flower and felt a calmness settle over me, from the roots of my hair down, like water, to pool about the soles of my feet in unfamiliar shoes.

The priestess Gnarsa had explained it all to me... explained it all in harried and hurried whispers that scared me more than the wicked blade had... and I had believed all of it with even my last breath.

But since the moment that I had felt this man's arms close about my chest, nothing had been... I had not managed to reconcile *anything* of this second life with what I was promised in the first. But if August's family was sick, and I could help him... then it had not all been for nothing. The loneliness. The crushing burden of countless years. The loss of life and limb and love and *self*...

All I had ever wanted was to be useful.

"Take me to him," I said, and I gently plucked the stem from August's hand, just as I had done the day before when I had parted the sprig from its tree with the tips of my first two fingers.

I hesitated when August directed me into the shell of the waiting machine before he hurried away into the depths of the huge, white ship; I grew in courage when I saw his sister's young face peeking out at me from behind the glass.

I had never seen such perfect glass. I pressed the flat of my palm against the wide, flawless expanse of it... leaned in and let my breath fog up the cold, clear pane... and remembered my father. His words came to me through the aeons of time and space, deep in the back of my skull.

You can make this choice.

August returned, tucking something deep into the front of his jacket, seemingly frustrated that I hadn't moved any closer to the shell of metal before me. Its purring did nothing to alleviate the low panic hovering around my sternum like bees on salted lavender. But August was patient as he explained how the thing moved, like a boat, on the sealed rivers called roads. How the oars were all but invisible. Any frustration that he had worn on his face when he returned from our ship disappeared the moment that he saw my fear. He spoke to me gently. I knew that there must have remained in his mind a deep concern for his grandfather, but he didn't place that above the here and now of my fear.

"Do you remember the first time you stepped into a little boat?" August asked me softly. "The first time you let it take your weight, how it wobbled until you sat down still? How you were only afraid until you let yourself trust it? This will be the same. Close your eyes."

My whole life now felt like I was simply floating. So, it wasn't strange that, once we were moving, if I closed my eyes... it felt more normal than when I tried to walk on solid ground. I felt the hard seat below me, I felt the press of Eryn's side, and the firm grip of her hand against my own.

"We're only afraid of things until we decide not to be," August murmured from the dim nothingness beside me. I didn't speak, but I didn't contradict him. Didn't *I* know that, better than anyone?

Part of my aching heart longed for the strange lulling journey to never cease, but the other was oddly soothed when August bade me open my eyes and follow Eryn up into the house.

The house was a new kind of monstrosity, sat close beside two other similar redbrick squares, with tangled vines creeping softly up its face like an unkempt beard on a weather-beaten old man. It was dark and quiet inside.

The old man who reclined carefully in the white room up the stairs, while weather-beaten, was far from unkempt. It was clear to me, by the quality of the linen that draped his frame, and the soft white fall of his newly washed hair, that this man was revered... even loved. I looked upon him, and I thought of my father and mother.

There blossomed within me a deep, exquisite ache that felt like a bad tooth, except that it was all over my body. A thousand things occurred to me to say, but all I managed was a mournful hum. Unbidden, unexpected, August's fingers curled around my own for a single comforting moment, so quickly that I wasn't sure it had happened. I turned to him, my mouth open to thank him, but all I managed was to catch the sight of his back as he left me.

As he left the room.

I turned back around at the sound of the old man slowly waking in the sun-strewn sheets beside the window. He hadn't seen me yet; he hadn't known to look for me yet. I perched carefully on the spindly wooden chair that had been drawn up by the bed on some previous visit, and let my eyes rove over his stirring form, taking note as I had seen Gnarsa do.

The men in my village all wore their hair long and carefully braided back. When our hair did turn to snow, it was a fine grey the colour of a whetted sword. When it happened by age, that is, and not by magic. August's grandfather had hair the same colour and consistency of spider silk. Like mine. Except that, as he had so little of it, it floated in the air above his deeply lined and darkly spotted skin, like a cloud of dreams and wishes.

Underneath the thin skin of his fluttering eyelids, the bulbs of the man's eyes roved left and right as though searching for something. His chapped lips were slightly parted, but the breath that escaped from between his teeth was undoubtedly sweet. Below the curve of his jaw, dusted now with salt and pepper flecks where yesterday it would have been clean-shaven, his pulse beat purple in a pattern that was steady – but altogether too quick; too quick.

I pushed the few strands of hair that had escaped from my own careful braid behind my ears and slipped my fingers into the waiting shell of his own. His palms were dry and soft, but not smooth. Like August's, these were the hands of a man who had known hard days. Honest days.

I felt a quiet resignation settle across the line of my shoulders like a yoke. August was right; his grandfather ailed. But it seemed to me as though he suffered from aught but old age. There was a pallor to his skin – in a younger man who knew the sun more intimately, it may have seemed like the kiss of its warmth – but in this one, it seemed like the sickness of a failing body.

A wound I could bind. A burn I could soothe. Old age would be neither bound, nor quieted. It would march ever on toward its end, and it was up to us to either meet it gracefully or flee foolishly.

Does that count for my death, too?

"You know a bit of nursing," said Eryn, reminding me suddenly of her company. "Healing," she added, when I appeared confused.

I spared myself the necessity of an answer, as the sudden tightening of my fingers had called the man at last to full consciousness. His irises were the same cool blue as his grandson's: like a spring sky when the air isn't quite yet sure if it should commit to the warmer weather, or if it has one or two more frosts to deal out. As he stared at me, the roundness of his eyes was matched by an equally wide, equally shocked mouth which formed an "*oh!*" of awe and wonderment.

"Who are *you?*" he asked. His voice was as dry and soft and hard-edged as his palms. I imagined that if a great owl could ever talk, it would ask to borrow this man's voice.

My smile was interrupted by the door as it swung softly open, pushed inward by the blunt knock of August's shoulder against the deep wood. His hands were full, holding a great silver tray bedecked with all manner of beautifully blown glass vessels; some were empty, some were full of a fine white sand, another large decanter held a thin liquid the colour of tree amber.

August sat the assortment carefully atop a waiting table, and for a moment abandoned all care for it as he hurried over to the old man's bedside. I noted his shock, and then contentment, as August bent down to fold his grandfather into a warm embrace that was devoid of all self-consciousness.

"You're awake," August noted. "Tea?"

My people brewed a tisane made from the catkins of the silver birchwood tree. When taken by mouth, it induces a deep sleep devoid of dreams. It was suggested that we girls imbibe the tea before the ritual, to spare us the terror of our own deaths – but Gnarsa said that it was not allowed, as the power of our sacrifice lay in our intention. I had thought since that the power was born instead of the terror itself. A measure of that terror touched me then, at August's blithe offer, and I shrank back into the bars of the worked wooden chair, gripping its handles like anchors.

I saw the old man's awe turn to concern, and perhaps August did too, for he introduced us. In a manner of speaking.

"Grandfather... this..." he faltered and turned his eyes back to me. "Isevelt, this is my grandfather, Mr. Erik Anders. He asked to see you."

The concern was once again replaced by awe, and swiftly. Erik Anders lurched bolt-upright in his bed, pillows discarded, and old age forgotten.

"August, you lie to me," he said. The soft wisdom of his owl-voice became immediately the edge of a talon and the hard regard of a yellow eye. August stood firm in the face of both.

"I do not deny that I have wronged you, Grandfather, but I swear that I do not lie to you."

The old man's lips pursed like an avian beak.

No mouse, I spoke.

"How could you have asked to see me, when a phase ago I did not exist?" I asked them both.

"It's true, Grandfather," said Eryn, and they both startled. What manner of ignorance led people to forget this girl so consistently? "It's true. I saw it."

The fight and the fury eked out of Erik, who lowered himself back to reclining on the full pillows. He peered longingly at August, who nodded, and I watched as a tear slipped unchecked from the outer corner of each eye to slide through the spring forest of his new beard. "Is-ev-elt," he whispered, saying my name as though he were reading the runes.

"Tea?" August asked again.

Chapter 10

Salt

"You told me that she was a force to be reckoned with," Crow stormed, striding towards the stern of the ship like a man who was unaware that the ship was only so long.

Smith sighed. "I meant it," he replied. "I can't promise that she has any desire to reckon *with you*, though. And I can't know unless she tells me if that's because she won't ever be forced again, or if that's just me filling her silence with my own fears."

"Forced again?"

"You think she went willingly into that vace?" Smith's smooth, gentleman's hands alighted upon the wooden rail like a clean white napkin at a ladies' lunch. How long had it been since Smith had last seen them, chittering like hens, moving like swans? The meringue-like memory clashed horribly with visions of blood, struggle, and sacrifice, as he thought of the girl. *Sylvi.* The force to be reckoned with, should she care to attend a reckoning. "You think it's an easy thing? Fitting a whole person inside a bottle?"

"I would imagine certain things need to get left behind," Crow allowed, joining Smith at the side of the ship. His feet were planted firmly at shoulders' width, allowing his hips to sway easily with the up and down of the *Witch* as she forged her way east, away from the sun, and towards a port on Dasheer. Not Lincoln, again. Crow had quite carefully put several weeks' worth of distance between the *Witch* and the business of the midnight auction. Couldn't be helped, though, that those several weeks had depleted their stores of food and liquor. So, they'd taken the long way around the south of the island, to make their landing at the forgotten little village that was called "Browning" by its inhabitants, and much worse by its visitors.

* * *

As the *Witch* carved through the waves at my feet the salted sprays scattered, catching the edge of the sunset. Although the encroaching shade brought with it the lie of a sudden chill in the air, the afternoon remained stalwartly, stickily warm. It would be yet another hot night.

I had learned, from my listening, that although it was not essential for Crow to lead the *Witch* to anchor in the darkness, it *was* customary. He liked the way the bleached wood gleamed in the moonlight. Like bones. It was a rare enough thing, to have a ship built nearly entirely of silver birchwood (let alone in the hot centre of the seas), so having her hull swim silently out of the dimness of evening was often enough to keep her and her crew safe. Whispers went before her, and wariness followed behind.

It was strange to be surrounded by so much of the timber; more than I'd ever seen worked together in one place, but it was also oddly comforting.

I wondered if my colourless skin allowed me to blend into the wood of the hull if my limbs were thin enough to seem in the night air like railings; for the two men – Smith and Crow – appeared, again... and they spoke of me.

"You keep speaking of the girl as though she has a spine, but so far, I've yet to see anything more than stubbornness," Crow growled, spitting something black into the deep of the water below.

"Perhaps what needs to be made clear is your expectations of the magic. You expected a warrior–"

"Because that's what you promised me."

"–Which is what the accounts suggested. But perhaps it is our interpretation that has been lacking, rather than the girl, or her magic."

"Nearly the entirety of the *Witch's* gold, we gave for the girl."

"Yes."

"And for what?"

Smith regarded his captain for a long while, as though it was uncharacteristic for Crow to demand so many answers without offering solutions in hand. Perhaps his anxiety stemmed from a fear greater than the gold?

"What lies in your heart, Captain?" Smith asked, running the palms of his hands atop each other with a sound like cotton over the hush and hush of the waves. "From where comes this worry?"

"I seek the protection of my own. That is all."

Smith pursed his lips but was prevented from speaking further by the quiet and polite arrival of William, the young hand who, according to Smith, had come recommended so highly.

Something... no, not *longed*... more like *caught* within me, like a thread that pulls and bunches a cloth so that it's out of shape. Even the wind stilled, so that although I stood up above them on the second balcony, even my white hair did not give me away.

"Forgive me, Sirs, but I wondered whether it would be worth inviting the... the lady up to deck, to perhaps rouse her spirit with the sight of dry? And steady?"

Smith raised an eyebrow at Crow. "It might at that. It's been days since she's seen the sun, at least."

I felt as alone as I had in the water. But worse, because I was not hidden. I was just unseen. The crew had taken to treating me like any other piece of their historical cargo. I was a curiosity, and any wonder that they'd felt at my mysterious introduction had faded to a state of hesitant disbelief. I was hardly even noticed, let alone remarked upon anymore. I had never in my past life been celebrated – but neither had I ever watched myself become such a profound disappointment. Perhaps they were all still upset at the marks from my claws.

I moved quickly, slipping down through the timber slats and around into the corridor that led to the lower decks, Crow's voice lapping up over the barrier like a careless spill of oil.

"He can invite her, what good it will do."

I hesitated, peeked back over, hurting. Aching. Numb. What did I *want*? To go back to the water? I had never been so alone as now. Without my other half. Haedi.

Smith and William turned to the hatch, but Crow caught the bursar by his collarbone. "Stay within earshot, though, if not arm's length."

Smith nodded once and followed behind the careful young sailor. I kept to the shadows, lurking, with no goal other than to *see*.

The young man slipped neatly down the stretch of the hatch ladder, youth and confidence making the rungs unnecessary. Smith seemed quietly pleased, however, by the way the younger man waited patiently at the bottom and gestured for Smith to go on ahead to my quarters.

Smith frowned, popped his head back up the ladder, whispered to Crow: "*He might be confident, but he's not eager. And that's something to be mindful of, when it comes to a young man's interest in a girl he's seen unclothed and helpless-looking.*"

It was that, perhaps, and nothing else, that settled Smith's mind, and caused him to gesture William on ahead of him, instead.

I saw William sweep the honey-hued hair from his brow, knock twice, and duck into the room under a low hanging bar that didn't exist.

Smith leaned lightly against the dim, waxy wood of the gangway, alert, yet he didn't see me duck into the room after William.

* * *

Will didn't see the girl at first, sitting on the bench that served as a bed, nestled behind the door, until he had entered, thought the cabin empty, and turned to leave. Her limbs were wrapped around themselves, giving her the appearance of a sculpture carved, or merely imagined, from the roots of a tree. Her head was turned away from him, exposing the long line of perfect skin between shoulder and jawline.

"I'm so sorry," he faltered, clearing his throat, and starting again. "I'm so sorry to disturb you. But the sun is setting, and we're making for the port of Browning, and should be there in the matter of an hour. Only, I thought you might want to join me on deck, to have the sun wash the sea from your back as your face turns for land. It's a trick my father taught me when I was young. I'm not sure quite how it works, but there's nothing better for finding your land legs, it seems."

As he spoke, Will edged cautiously forward until he was standing in the middle of the room. It occurred to him as she turned to meet his gaze that he didn't actually know whether or not she understood English, and he felt like a fool. He flushed red, and then flushed again as he realised that she might mistake his colour for boyish nerves. He found her pretty; in truth, he found her breathtaking. But his interest in her lay in the mystery and wonder of her, rather than the inarguable truth of her beauty. There was something arcane, and ethereal, in her. A quiet power that at once thrilled and cautioned him.

Just as he was about to devolve into some kind of desperate mime designed to get his meaning across the language divide, the girl spoke. Her voice was deeper than he expected, and throaty, like a warbling bird. As though, perhaps, the language of her heart was much more melodious than his own, and so was struggling with the atonal crispness of its words.

"My father used to recommend warmed liquor," she said simply. He weighed her words, forming them with his own tongue and cheeks within the bell jar of his lips. It sounded like *my forther. Wormed leeqor.*

"I'm sure that it can be arranged, if that's what you desire."

She shrugged and looked away, but glanced back, furtively. While her eyes remained averted, her shoulders twisted imperceptibly until her posture was less defensive, less closed, even though her face was turned away.

Will found that (despite the stubbornly lingering crimson of his cheeks) he felt quite at ease in her presence. He felt a sudden sadness at the thought of her, so lonely, so set apart, and found that he wanted to comfort her, somehow. To make her know that she *could* belong.

"You mentioned your father," he hedged, perching carefully so that his back was to the grimy porthole. She shrugged again.

He noted the way that the linen shirt she wore managed to seem a shade of its original white. He was as fastidious as the next sailor on Crow's *Silver Witch*, but still, his shirt had dimmed from its original clean white to the greyish hint of a cloth used often to polish silver. He imagined it was somewhat due to the saltwater that it was washed in, and was at least happy to himself be clean, if not exactly gleaming. He wondered if Crow or Smith had chosen the clothes, or if they'd found a dress somewhere in the depths of the hold, and at least given her a choice.

"You probably don't remember what it's like to make a choice," he murmured. She said nothing, and he guessed that she hadn't heard him. *Just as well*, he thought, and clenched his fingers into fists to give them something to do.

"I would really like to speak with you," he said slowly, pushing off the wall so that he was standing once more. "If you would like to speak with me, which would be a great pleasure. But if you would not, I won't trouble you again."

She bit her bottom lip and worried it there, back and forth, like the teeth of a saw set against timber, but didn't make to move her body. He hesitated a moment longer, nodded to himself as though committing to something, and ducked back out of the door. Nothing good would come of forcing her. In the end, he'd only be pleasing himself.

Will was shocked to see Smith standing there, still, in the hallway. Not that he'd expected the bursar to leave; rather, he'd forgotten that they'd approached together. There was a strange expression on Smith's face. Wariness and excitement in one knot of expression.

"Did she speak with you?" Smith asked quietly.

"A little." Will pulled himself quickly back up through the hatch. "Not much."

Smith was longer in appearing, his weightless white hair catching the breeze as he worked his way up the ladder. "What did she say?"

Will reached down to pull the older man up by his forearm. "Just that her father recommended warm liquor for staving off sea legs." *Wormed leeqor.*

"That so?"

Will pushed his lips together, jutted his lower jaw. "Yes."

The golden light of the sun was long spent, now just a candle flame, and far across from the red horizon, heavy stars were being strung like lanterns across the sky. Will was looking forward to an evening off the ship. He was a sailor born; as a child, he'd learned to walk against the rolling swell of waves under wood. But any man could feel joy at the stillness and space that came hand-in-hand with the corner of a taproom and a long pull of something cold, and the colour of caramel.

Crow was still standing at the side where they'd left him. His broad shoulders were cloaked in layers of his jet-black hair – unmarked by any grey – which somehow smoothed the heavy lines of his face. Smith knew his age, having spent a portion of their childhood together, rollicking on the lush green lawns of his uncle's vast estate. Playing pirates with swords. Bringing back "treasures" for their mothers: lengths of lace and sparkling pins that they'd rescued from the very boxes that they belonged in, and which were quietly returned there after the boys had fallen, spent, into their beds.

And now? What of this latest treasure? Did it have any more value than the fact that it belonged, somehow, in their family box? Was there any point in prolonging the game of plunder? Smith slipped his spectacles from his short, straight nose and gently rubbed circles with the cuff of his sleeve. He shook his head, pressed them back into the dent they had made. There was no use in guessing the point of the game without first having been told the rules. It was time for some truths.

* * *

The taproom on the wharves of Browning was everything that Will had hoped for, right down to the slow slip of amber-coloured alcohol down the length of his tongue. They always had reserves of rum on the ship, to warm them when they got unexpectedly cold, or unexpectedly morose. But there was something transcendent about the ice-cold crispness of an ale kept in a cold cellar, in a close room warmed by fire and talk.

The girl hadn't emerged from her cabin. He'd been disappointed, but it was alleviated a little by the spark in Crow's regard when Smith told the captain of their conversation. The captain had paid particular care to his retelling of the trick about the warm alcohol. Nodding slowly. Smiling, just. Some good had come of it, even if Will didn't understand it.

The two older men sat talking together, now, hunched over, and whispering. Growling, even, as men with years so plenty often did, forgetting how to set their teeth to anything quieter than a thrum. Every now and then one would stab a finger into the table, *thud thud,* like a startled heart, and the other would nod or shake his head in response. Will narrowed his eyes and urged his concentration out towards them, but couldn't make out the meat of their conversation. He sipped his drink and turned his mind to other things.

Smith, however, would not be distracted.

"I understand the pull of the legend. I don't fault you for sinking so much—" Smith said.

"Sinking?"

"—Time and gold into procuring the vace," Smith persevered, shaking his head slightly to ward off the interruption, "but perhaps the time has come for you to tell me whatever part of the plan you have still in your head, but you've not seen fit to share."

Crow flicked some crumbs from the surface of the table, as though scattering Smith's words away. "I want protection for my own, that is all."

Smith jabbed the table sharply. "That is *not* all, and I'll thank you not to try *that* again. Ten years we've been about this business, and you swore honesty to me when you turned up at my door as a cousin, begging a family favour." He glanced from beneath his brow, remembering Crow's unannounced arrival, a decade before. Haggard, and hurting. But also, hoping. "You asked me, that day, if I still knew the language of the ancestors. As true as that day, I tell you, I have read the writings. I am as sure as I can be sure. But there's a nuance in it, because there's a nuance in *her*."

Smith waited for Crow to interrupt again, but he merely glared. Smith sighed.

"The truth *may well be* that the *only* magic that exists in this girl is the desperate treachery that paused her existence for a few hundred years. I don't understand it, but there's at least evidence of her being... called, or some such, at the breaking of the bottle. We've seen nothing – *nothing* – of any sort of arcane ability. She is a scared, lost little girl."

"She is not."

"Not what?"

Crow harrumphed and shifted in his seat. "A little girl."

"But scared and lost."

Crow scratched the hair behind his ear roughly and squinted at the oily black beams overhead. "Confused, I'll give you."

Smith's offended expression softened to the resigned pallor of wilted cream. Had any of them any fight left? After all they'd seen? After the burning flames? Could any of them possibly stay hot for that long? He snapped his mouth shut, pursed his lips, and tried a softer tack.

"Cousin, this is madness. It's been weeks, and nothing. You can't keep her in that cabin forever. For nothing. Just sailing around Dasheer and pulling into port whenever supplies are low." Smith's voice dropped deep and quiet, edged with a satin pleading. "At the very least, we'll go broke."

Crow stood suddenly, offended at the talk of gold.

The taproom experienced a moment of taut silence, while drinkers and carousers took the measure of the man towering and glowering over his companion.

It took no more than a breath for the most weary and least wary of them to note that his fingers were unclenched (and nowhere near his sword), his eyes were more sad than angry, and the companion leaned back rather than forward in the face of his regard. Voices babbled back to life, but silence stretched out between the two old friends.

"How can you expect me to help you, if you won't tell me of your plans?" Smith asked quietly.

Crow was just as gentle in his reply, but much more final. "I do not need you to help me, cousin," he said. "I need you to trust me."

And with a whirl of his opulent cloak, he left.

* * *

On the *Witch*, I was alone in the moonlight.

Talking with the boy had been nice. A moment of comfort in the midst of so much sadness. It was clear that the world in which I had died was dead. The people spoke differently, they dressed differently. Their boats were all but floating houses. And I knew not one of the faces that filled the warm air around me – not even my own.

I guessed that one of the men, Crow or Smith, would be able to answer some of my questions if I felt inclined to ask them, but I did not feel so inclined.

I did not feel much at all.

The long railing on the side of the ship stretched out at rib height, or just above. Circled around the whole of the vessel and back to where my hands rested, one under the other, in the pale light of the moon. My fingers twitched slightly as I thought of my father's sword.

With a start that pushed a little gasp out of my lungs, I remembered the sword. I clenched my eyes tight shut and dug the heels of my palms deep into the hollows above my cheeks, willing myself to remember, to see. To know.

In the hours after father died, cut down by the flame-haired enemy, we had attended to his body, and the ritual of a final goodbye, but left his sword driven down into the black sand, to rust and dull from ash, salt, and blood. Had anyone cleaned the sword? Had *I*? So much of who I was had drained from me, even the certainty that I had done my duty to my father. Surely, I would not have gone to my death before doing that small thing?

I shoved my body roughly away from the side of the ship, where I'd been looking-without-seeing toward the warm glow of firelight in the town at the edge of the waves.

My gaze fell to the base of the *nest*, the tower that the men climbed to see to the other side of the sun. Empty now, the ropes waved in the cool air like spent streamers on fair day. My eyes tracked upwards until I was staring at the wooden basket.

The sudden desire to *do* something eclipsed all others, and in three sure strides, I had tied the tails of my shirt high on my waist and grasped hold of the lowest knot on the rope ladder that led up to the top. Maybe if I reconnected with the fear... maybe then I would remember.

The rope burned almost immediately, and I quickly had to trust to the twist of my ankles to hold my weight. There was certainly a great fear in me, that knotted my stomach and sheened my palms almost immediately in sweat, as I heaved myself further and further away from the deck. I was panting by the time I reached the top, half from terror and half from exertion. I slid my body through the narrow gap in the basket rather than pulling myself over the top – an easy task, as I had wasted away to near-nothingness in the water or the weeks of self-inflicted starvation since.

I hadn't prepared for the way that the basket churned seemingly on its own, tossed around exponentially more by the ebbs and flurries of water nearly unnoticeable when down on the deck. I felt almost drunk, like I had the night of the Baker wedding, the year before.

No. Not the year before. A life before.

The tavern town seemed tiny from my great height. I'd scarcely been worried by heights, and this one was surely not any more than the sea cliffs. But the vast expanse of the sea around me on three sides was nigh on overwhelming. That (and the fear that my own strength wouldn't be enough) kept my muscles rigid and my teeth set.

I backed myself up to the wooden stem in the centre of the basket, bracing the soles of my feet and the bones of my back opposed to each other, giving myself some small sense of security. My breath came in little puffs, evening out after the exertion of the climb, as well as from the thrill of the view.

As I sat there, wedged tight in the small space of the nest, one hundred feet in the air, I thought of all that I remembered, and all that I knew I would soon forget, and I wept.

I wept until I was dry inside.

By the time the tears had turned to salt on my cheeks, I had hiccupped myself into silence, and then, to sleep.

Chapter 11

Ash

"She certainly is a force," Valder said to his wife.

Xeva, where once she had been slim, and then slight, was now a mere sliver of a person, like a moon hiding from her sun. Her palms went constantly to the flat plane of her belly, smoothing down garments and skin and memories of swirling babes arching their backs beneath the membrane of time.

"You sound so surprised," Xeva whispered, but not loud enough for Valder to hear. She pressed on, for herself alone. "You always sound so surprised, these days, when you encounter a woman with a spine."

"And I've never seen the people work so quickly, building the boats. So many hands making such light work."

"Mmm."

The arrival of Gnarsa stole the Jarl's attention. It was a simple theft, as of a toy that long ago had lost its lustre.

"The people seem united," Valder commented. "It seems as though your magic has truly done its work, Witch."

Gnarsa clenched her teeth and raised her chin. "I have asked you before not to call me *witch*."

Valder brushed her words away with a careless palm. The years had taken his warmth. Or he had given it to them. "You cannot tell me that what I see is less than magic. It seems that I have *you* to thank for your bloodless remedy to a bloody problem."

"Am I to understand that you doubted me, these last five years?"

"Don't suggest that you didn't doubt yourself."

"Don't suggest that the Jarl can change his mind," Xeva whispered. She stood, looked slowly and sadly upon her husband, and then left. To seek the shelter of the sea cliffs. To grasp the ribbons of sharp grass against her palm and slowly... *pull.*

Gnarsa spared a glance for the wasted wife of the Jarl as the wan woman left. Seeing as much as she did, all the time, Gnarsa was able to spare a single glance.

"Truly, I am grateful," Valder pressed on. He dipped his hands into a big stone bowl and rolled them about together, cleansing them of whatever had occupied his mind before her entrance. "You gave me an impossible choice, and then saved me from its consequences."

"You are referring to the choice between your own remaining son, and the children of your people?" Gnarsa asked lightly, as she offered him a soft cloth to dry his fingers with.

Valder's eyes flicked almost to her own, alighted like a moth upon the rise of her cheeks, and then darted off and away to the dim of the windows.

"There still remains the question of the babies," Valder said lightly.

"Which question is that?"

"Why there are still none." He lowered himself easily into the carved chair near the vast bed.

Gnarsa remained standing, despite the other, empty chair. She had no desire to sit beside him.

His beard, once black and soft, had gone to wire shot with silver. Where once his eyes had creased in kindness, they rested atop loose pouches of bruised skin. The creases all gathered between his eyes, now. He had lost a tooth, in the last five years. Lost it, for she had not pulled it. Only a genuine smile or a sneering guffaw revealed its empty grave. The latter drew it forth.

"A week ago, I thought that we were all fools; that nothing of your promises would ever arrive on our doors. Now, though... having seen her, spoken with her... heard of her passion for the gods who yesteryear would have seemed so far away... now it seems as though we are seeing first fruits."

"None of this is anything that I have not said to you."

"Yes, but now there's *proof*. Now I can bite into the skin of the thing and taste that it is tart. Not yet sweet," he barked, pointing a warning finger at the place between her breasts. "Not yet sweet. But, given another summer... like nectar."

"Very poetic."

Valder twiddled his thumbs around and around each other, each turn like an hour in a suffocating room. "You think the babies will come?"

Gnarsa felt the muscles in her shoulders spasm as her instinct lifted her palms to rest atop her hidden belly, but at the last moment, she silenced them, so that the only movement that escaped her mind down the channels of her muscles was the smallest of shrugs. "Yes."

"Do you think that the girl has childbearing capabilities?"

The look that he shot at her was hawk-like, and greasy, curious for the sake of spectacle rather than any real kind of victory.

"No." Where her *yes* had held decades and galaxies of possibility, her *no* was a closed door.

Gnarsa wanted to leave. To follow the Jarl's wife out from under the suffocating presence of her husband. Her original intention had been to invite the Jarl out to see the boats, which were all but finished, but now all she wanted was to leave this self-satisfied shadow of a king to preen his ragged plumage alone in the half-light. Let him see her triumph as it sailed away from him; let him feel no pride in that which he had not done.

"Pity," Valder said to himself, long after the witch had left. He languished in the wooden chair, dabbling his fingertips in the cool of the stone bowl. His thoughts had slipped easily from the soft, hollow husk of his wife to the fierce, cold alabaster of the gift of the gods. "Pity."

* * *

I knew, even as I stood in the shallows of the bay (even as I raised my outstretched hands to the sky above the people gathered there) that, even though the thing that I was about to ask them to do was madness, and treacherous, and full of peril, they would do it.

For the gods demanded the last. And *I* was the gods made sinew and bone.

The black sand of the bay was just as I had remembered it, but to me, it was completely different. Everything was completely different to me. And not just because the birchwood forest that once grew like columns of stone around the edges of my home was now no more than a mouth full of charred and broken teeth. Not just because so many of the people and faces that I had known had either aged or died. Not just because the very body in which I lived was a mere simulacrum of feminine youth (let alone any real or knowable effigy of *me*). It was because there had been, within me, a fundamental *shift*.

I had always doubted the promise of the gods giving back even a tenth of what they received – never mind tenfold. What business did an uncountable group of immeasurable power have in concert with a finite, grasping clutch of people, huddled in fear and the ashes of a village which was not even the place of the initial covenant?

My eyes had seen. Not much – but more than they had before death.

My body had drained away and been made more. Not much – but more than I had been in life.

I had yet to try the breadth of my abilities. I had plumbed the depths of Gnarsa's guesses, or hopes, in a quiet conversation that had not unfolded according to her intentions. I had learned that the crux of the power was water. I could *engage* with water; stronger, and *more*, in proximity to a body of it. Stronger, and more, in proximity to the gods. They had taken all of my blood and given me back what they had in abundance to spare. It was my task to figure out what that truly could mean.

But first: madness. And treachery. And peril.

"Push the last boat out into the bay, past the waves," I commanded. "It is for the gods."

The twenty fighters who had been promised to the boat fussed and jostled, trying to get their shoulders behind that of their neighbour. They thought that I meant for them to be in it when it floundered.

"Don't let the water pass your waist," I amended, and they complied. *Still unbelieving*, I thought. *That will change. After all, hadn't I needed the firmest proof?*

There was a collective gasp and hiss as the water found its way up past ankles, snaking around calves and knees and thighs. The waves broke soft and small, as a tongue curling gently for a missed drop of milk at the corner of a mouth is soft and small. When the water reached the waist of the smallest woman, I held up my hand to halt them.

I gathered my will and then let it unspool. It felt like draining an abscess. Bitter; bitter. But then, release.

The boat surged forwards out of their grasp, pulled away by my urging into the middle of the bay. With a great shout, they snatched back hands and bodies, not wanting to be drawn along with it.

It was a quick thing. Quick and unimpressive. One moment there was a newly made vessel, crafted from creamy yellow timber in freshly planed lines, rising and falling on the smallest of swells, seeming like a wooden pendant that rose and fell on the breaths of a deep blue chest.

And then it was gone.

Bitterly released.

Swallowed up by a great blanket of water, covered over by a wave that rose and wrapped tightly around, like a blanket heavy enough to crack its ribs, soak its fibres, and take it without sound to the bottom.

The people saw neither a whisper nor a sliver of the boat; I made sure of that. Pinned it down to the black sand with the sheer weight of water atop it; slid it further out and away into the waiting grasp of the ocean.

"You have given the last to the gods," I said simply. "They have returned your fighters to you. I need only forty."

Arms found each other. Palms found faces. Kisses found cheeks. It was a reprieve. How long had it been since they had gone out to seek a fight? It had been at least the five years since any of the people's swords had smelled a battle, let alone tasted blood. Those who were spared were grateful. Those who were *not* were given a new confidence. The gods gave back.

"Make your preparations," I said clearly as I walked away from them, back through the people and up along the stretch of sand which clung to my damp skin, like armour. "Our moment comes tonight."

I locked eyes with Leir and held them as I walked past him. I sensed my brother follow in my wake and felt comfort. It wasn't until I led him back to the door of our parents' house that I realised Wulf had come, too. Did that relieve me, somehow? I dismissed the thought. They followed me in, and I closed the door firmly behind them.

Leir had clearly been living here, alone, in the years since my death. Where in the past the two little rooms had been taken up by our beds, and by the low table that my father had turned with his own hands from a single, huge tree stump, I now couldn't discern in the depths of the place where my brother had been sleeping. But there were signs of his life, and of his living, all over.

A half-finished block carving on the windowsill. A basket of vegetables that had been carefully brushed and dusted clean. A fireplace swept carefully of its ash, all the more conspicuous for the pile of driftwood stacked neatly, but precariously, in the shadows beside it.

"I need to speak with you, before tonight," I said to Leir.

He joined me at the windowsill, relieved my hands of the half-finished carving. "I'm glad."

"What do you need to say?" Wulf asked. When he stood with us at the window it was clear that there wasn't enough room. *Too close.* I shrugged away, sitting tightly at the roughly shaped but lovingly smoothed table. They joined me again, and this time we fit comfortably.

"I don't need to say anything," I replied. "I just wish to speak with you."

Leir sighed contentedly and placed the carving firmly on the tabletop. At this angle, I could see the beginnings of myself. Or of one of the others. The twisting sweep of an impossibly white robe. The soft beginnings of lines, of ocean waves worked carefully into the flat plane of the square block. It would mean more, in relief, once it had the ink applied like blood, once it was pressed to the yielding face of cloth like a newly sealed promise. But now, unfinished, I could see the beginnings of myself. Leir followed my gaze to the carving.

"We spoke, in the days after you died, of working your likenesses into the front of great warships, hoping that would draw you back to us. Capture you in vessels bigger than all of the vaces that Gnarsa had hidden, along with any real hope. I was going to do it. I knew your face the best. The others could just be versions of you."

"That wouldn't be fair," I said quietly, and gripped his hands with my own. "Anything you made would have been beautiful, but that wouldn't have been fair. We are, each of us, our own. It's better that you didn't."

"It would have helped me feel close to you."

"It was Haedi's mother's idea," Wulf said through choked tears. I watched as he discerned his distress with his own ears and registered it as shameful. The emotions slipped across the parchment of his face like a too-sharpened pen. He cleared his throat. "Before she died, when Locx had only just... she found my mother, one day, standing atop the cliffs and just... staring... into the waves. She told of a custom of her first people, to bury their dead, and lay a likeness of stone atop the place as a marker. A reminder."

"So many dead," I murmured. I squeezed Leir's hand and set it gently on the table. We were dangerously close to despair, and that was unhelpful. "Do you have a drink?"

Wulf turned and fetched a set of earthenware cups while Leir found an old bottle of honeyed beer. I wondered how many days had passed with the two of them here, together, mourning their families and finding solace in each other's company. In the absence of family, it was good to find a friend. I suppressed a hot wave of jealousy and envy. Jealousy of my brother. *Mine*. Envy of Wulf.

With a measure of golden mead in each of our hands, which was turned to silt against the deep red of the cup, we recited the names of those we had lost, in a circle, one after the other.

Parents. Siblings. Lovers. Friends. All named.

"Valder," said Wulf, after a time, and sipped.

"Your father?" I challenged. "He was there just this morning! He didn't die?"

"Part of him did," Wulf whispered. "It must have."

"There has been a deep and... worrying change in the Jarl since the sacrifice," Leir explained. "There has been a change in all of us."

"What do you mean?" I asked.

Leir flicked his hair out of eyes. His face had taken on a quiet but panicked caste, like a cow backed into an unfamiliar barn. "Something broke in us all, I think, that day."

"The day of the sacrifice?"

They both nodded silently.

"What do you mean?"

They shared a glance. Had they spoken of this before?

"What do you remember of the ritual? Of that day?" Wulf asked.

I refused to let the images flash in the darkness of my mind.

"We went willingly, we died peacefully, and we waited patiently," I said softly. "That is all I remember."

"Well, it was significantly different for those watching," Leir grumbled. "To me, you were led to a silent death that was, somehow, the most violent thing I have ever seen. And I say that as someone who watched our mother choke on her own blood."

His voice cracked. We raised our glasses wordlessly.

I will not remember it.

"Then you may need to adjust your memories to marry with mine," I suggested. It did no good for him, for any of them, to hold on to the fear of not knowing, when I was here, proof, of the gods' return. That was why the nearing raid was so important. So crucial. The priestess did not give her answers readily, but she gave them, nonetheless.

"It is so strange to hear you speak so," Leir wondered aloud, his face suddenly spitting into a wide grin that washed over us both. "Do you remember the day on the shore, when we salvaged Locx's boat, and I teased you about the small potatoes?"

Wulf and I both laughed in fond remembering. It felt like an embrace. "I was so embarrassed," I admitted.

"I was so confused," Wulf conceded sheepishly. "Until you left, and I pestered Leir, and he eventually told me everything."

"You untrusting peon," muttered Leir, tutting in my direction. "Now look at you. Weapon of the gods."

We lapsed into wordlessness again. The air grew warmer with every silence, as though each pause were an exhaled breath in a closed space. I felt the room darkening around me once more but realised when Leir moved to strike up a fire that it was more to do with the going down of the sun than the fading of happy memory.

"*Are* you a weapon of the gods?" Leir asked.

I tilted my head to the side, measuring my brother's words, waiting to see if he had more of them.

"Has the priestess said that you are? That is..." his words trailed off and his cheeks flushed burgundy, his embarrassment just as emboldening as the mead. His next words tumbled out of him, tumultuous as a clutch of stones taking the plunge over a wild waterfall. "Have the gods ever actually made their desires known, beyond that we need to give them things?"

I frowned at him, hoping in that instant to cover my unbidden, fraying certainty with a placid patience. I had seen the stone altar since I had returned. The blood that pooled in the cracks of its face may well have been infinitesimally mine, but in the years since the ritual many other rabbits, and birds, and fish had bled out over the edges and down into the ribbon grass that grew like a moat around the altar's feet.

"We can ask for things," I said. "We have a right to desire, and a means to manage it. What more?"

I made a chore of drinking the mead remaining in my cup, using the time to gather together the torn edges of my assurance.

"Do you know where the enemy is?" Leir asked eventually.

"Gnarsa will have told her," Wulf replied. Leir raised his eyebrows in consternation.

"*Will she?*"

"Yes. Gnarsa knows." The finality in Wulf's words spoke of lengthy conversations; of secrets spilled and stories told. He twitched when he said her name.

"She *has* told me," I admitted. "She found them after the death of Wulf's brother."

"How soon after?" Leir asked quickly. "Did she find them before the sacrifice?"

"Why does that matter?" Asked Wulf.

Leir worried pointedly at a knot in the wood of the table, rhythmically snapping the nail of his thumb against the imperfection, speaking to Wulf but not looking at him. "I've said it all along, brother; I don't trust her."

"Well, you'll have your perfect proof by dawn," I said with crystal finality. Leir moved to pour another measure into my cup, but I rested my palm across the mouth of it, concealing the last mouthful. "Clear heads tonight."

Leir gazed longingly at the bottle, shrugged, and pushed the stopper deep into its neck. *So, he's willing to take orders*, I thought, and then shamefully silenced both the words and the feeling that they evoked in the pit of my stomach.

"We sail with forty fighters, under your guidance, to find the enemy sleeping. Then what?"

I closed my eyes, imagined it, just as I had done a hundred times before. I swallowed once to make sure that my voice did not falter. I could tell them now.

"We will find them up a wide river, behind a bend that wears a single black tree. Their only water source is a spring that is birthed in the middle of their houses. We will poison it. They won't know; not until the last of them dies. Drowns on the bile from their own stomachs. Perhaps even then they will not know, but only ever guess at the power of the gods. For they will never see our swords, never see our hand, never see it coming."

Wulf's face wore lines of deep discomfort, but he nodded. Had he known? "A truly bloodless victory."

"Then why have forty of our own bodies there? Why risk it?"

I explained, even though I wanted to wave away his words in my impatience. It would help to have them convinced before the moment came to hold the people back.

"Witnesses," I said, "are useful when they are our own."

"And if you *are* seen? By chance? By people *not* ours?"

Now I did shrug. "Then I have fighters to protect me. But I wager that I am also able to protect myself. Besides, the wide river flows swiftly to the sea. We will have the advantage of speed, as well as surprise."

Leir wound his fingers around my own. "I believe you simply because you are so sure. I trust you simply because you are mine."

I tightened my fingers in what could have seemed like comfort, hearing the distinction between Leir's offered belief, and trust.

Chapter 12

Blood

August really had no business being on the *Valkyrie* that morning as she steamed away, having been set free from her dock like a new babe, birthed on a wave of saltwater and sent out into the wide unknown. His role in her creation was well and truly spent; he had already overstayed his welcome with the amount of meddling and fussing that he had bestowed upon her whelping.

He might have been a particularly talented upstart, but an upstart he remained, relying on the weight of his family name and the good graces of the workers to pay his passage into the many inner workings that he had somehow been made privy to.

Generally, August would have had the honour of drawing up the plans and giving her a name. He'd done that. But he'd also driven thousands of rivets, and watched as huge fan blades were fitted to her vast underbelly, and hounded Goose's workers as they fitted wood and painted walls, and all that even *after* Goose had washed his hands of it.

August loved the ship. Loved it in a way that could only really happen when something was borne on one's back and birthed of one's mind.

And today she was taking her first steps – so, *damned* if he was going to remain ashore in his office, or worse, back at home.

That was the attitude that he tried to adopt as he stood with his feet apart and arms akimbo on the bridge as she nosed out of the estuary and made for the open fields of the North Sea for her first real engine test.

"Very convincing; you don't look presumptuous at all," said a friendly voice from behind him.

Goose was climbing the narrow stairs that led to the little glass navigation room. He was there at August's behest and seemed to be genuinely thrilled by it.

August wavered in his firm resolve to be stalwart as a thousand revelations presented themselves as fodder for conversation. He desperately wanted to tell Goose the truth that he had learned of Isevelt, and of the ancient magic and the bloody sacrifice, and all of the other wondrous and terrible nonsense that his grandfather had told him the night before.

After all, Goose had been there in the beginning... but now that August had the moment, the words failed him. Because while it was daring and romantic and macabre in his head (like a fairy-tale out of Germany or Russia), he knew that the moment it appeared in the space between them, as uttered words, it would sound simply ridiculous.

And he felt ridiculous enough, standing like a king when he felt like a pageboy.

"I *feel* presumptuous, if I'm honest," August said instead. "I need to be careful. Have you heard what they're doing in Europe to dictators?"

Goose wrinkled his nose in distaste. "Assassination? How perfectly medieval. No, I think that if the little people were as distressed as all that, we'd have heard the rumblings." Goose gestured expansively out at the edges of the ship, including all of the necessary sailors and engineers and stokers in his remarks.

August let his hands fall from his hips, and his shoulders joined them. "Rumbling is the word for it. Do you think it will come to war?"

Goose scratched his eyebrow thoughtfully. "I think it has to."

"It has to?"

"Unfortunately. Bullies don't listen to reason; they listen to a punch in the nose. They speak the language of blood."

August bit his tongue. He thought of girls with slit necks, and men with swords, and of suffering. He swallowed down his distaste for it. "Don't we all, in the end?"

* * *

The first tiny thump of rain onto the back of my hand made me jump, but far more from pleasure than from shock. It didn't feel cold to me. I brought my hand up close to my face so as to see the little raindrop on my skin and know, for the first time in what felt like weeks, just how dry I felt. With the tip of a finger, I broke the surface tension of the raindrop and rubbed the water in gentle circles until it was gone.

I shouldn't have been on the ship; not officially. August knew now – whether he understood it or not – the pull I felt toward the *Valkyrie*. Surely, after all he'd heard, August couldn't have expected me to stay on dry land while they climbed up over the horizon and disappeared?

I'd seen him earlier that day, before the sun topped the hill of the afternoon, talking to his friend Goose up on the bridge, but I hadn't spoken to them. Instead, I had listened.

Listened to the great heavy rush of the water breaking before the stern of the ship. Listened to the whip of ropes and the thump of feet on polished boards. Listened to the chatter of men and, underneath it all, but so much more potent, listened to the creak and strain and strength of the great ship as she stretched her sinews and felt her viscera pop and crack, free from the narrow confines of canal and moorage. I took a deep breath in through my parted lips and tasted the moisture filling the air.

It tasted of freedom.

On a sudden, glorious whim I turned and hurried, my bare feet making low thuds on the wooden deck, towards the back of the ship. As I ran, I felt a few more drops hit me, but there were still not enough to show up on the deck in the dull light. I wanted to stretch my own legs.

Throwing a quick glance back over my shoulder to be sure that I was alone (although who else would be out here in the burgeoning rain?) I clambered up to the roof of the second deck, where it jutted up like a single, wizened tooth. It had taken me all of a day to learn the intricacies of the ship; left alone by the one who brought me here to go and do as I pleased, the huge expansive map of her was worked into the fabric of my thoughts. As soon as I reached the summit, I stripped off my coat and shoes, unpinned my hair, and waited for the deluge promised to me by the sweetness of the air in the encroaching cloud.

It did not take long.

Before I had space to yearn there was water all around me, falling so thick and fast that I might have been back in the ocean. It was a strange thing, to stand in rain so familiar, when nothing else was vaguely akin to anything I had ever known. My body thirstily drank the water in through my pores, and I could feel my skin becoming dewy... swelling to a plump soft fullness that I had so lacked since I returned. I tipped back my head and let the water run down my face in rivulets, tracing lines down my neck to get lost in the fabric of my clothes.

There must have been something about the solitude of my perch (coupled with the deafening rain) that allowed me to forget about the world and simply *think*. The day was so old and golden, but the cover of clouds meant that it could be dawn as much as dusk. What did time become, after a thousand years? Just the rain.

I felt at once magnified and brought low, having recently sat beneath the desperate satisfaction of August's grandfather. There was nothing of my flesh and blood that remained to me. But my conviction that *usefulness is akin to beauty* was the ground on which my bones were raised. And truly, Erik thought that I had a purpose.

Could I marvel with him, though, in his view that my purpose was to protect *his* family, even in the devastating loss of my own?

My musings were cut short by a sharp, violent stab of fear and pain that emanated from somewhere below me, and what felt like a lurch of sound and space. I immediately and instinctively threw myself flat to the floor and pressed my cheek against the wood, concentrating on the direction of the calling.

I knew this ship like I knew my own skin: not as one who had been in any way involved in its making, but as one who was fundamentally linked to its living. And so, it didn't take me long to imagine the route that I would need to take to the person who needed me. For the first time since I said the words, and returned to life, I was truly needed. I was searching for someone else, yes, but at that moment... I finally had hope of finding myself.

I threw my body over the railing and down onto the boat deck, landed hard, and retraced my steps back inside the ship, knowing that I had to make my way down, down into her very belly. I pulled open a set of double doors and nearly wrenched my shoulder joints in the process, aiming straight for the great staircase. I'd no time for the *elevators*, nor the explanations for using them, in my haste.

My bare, wet feet slipped and slid on the polished floor of the steps as I hurried down, my palm grabbing and sticking slightly on the silver, polished wood of the bannister. Every few seconds I felt a renewed wave of fear and pain but was distantly buoyed when I realised that the waves were growing stronger, rather than waning. He was holding on. He was waiting for me.

As I wrapped my hand around the pole that stuck straight up from the bannister at the first landing, I threw out my weight and used it to pivot on one foot to get around. My hair whipped out from my shoulders like a great fan of white feathers. My breath was coming in heaves and spurts as I sent my feet out before me, down and down the floors.

The staircase was miraculously empty on my flight down, but it was immediately clear that there were more people on this level. They all seemed busy with charts and tools and so I moved quickly through the doors, wound around the tables, and made it safely out the other side without making contact with any of them. So much closer to the cry for help that I felt the pull that much more potently.

Gaining the far doors, it was a small matter for me to make my way through the scullery and various adjoining rooms until I was clear; down yet more stairs, hatches, and passageways, until I began to feel the smothering heat of the stokehold on the orlop deck.

The wall of heat was like the pathetic little grate fire from my first night, magnified by a hundredfold. My village had always been cold and slightly damp, and a lifetime of knowing the feeling of cold was so innate within me that the total and inescapable dry warmth of this place was an assault to my very being. I felt my lungs threaten to close in protest and, immediately, a wave of heat burned its way up my nose and down my throat like the worst salt scourge an angry wave had ever dealt.

Despite this, my senses and my focus guided me further into the blazing dungeon, to a knot of men lit by a ruddy glow, covered in sweat and grime and wearing smudged clothing and grim expressions. In their midst was another man, laid out on his back, the right side of his face clearly burned, and the cloth of his shirt melted away to reveal the furious skin beneath.

By some unknown consent, the men all parted at the sight of me, perhaps knowing from the cool of my calm in the face of obvious disaster that I was the best chance their friend had. He was truly close to death.

Were he groaning or clutching at his wounds I might have been more reassured, but as it was, he was lying completely still, surrendered to the pain, the only movement of his body the tiny gasping breaths he managed to pull in past scorched lips.

I fell softly to my knees beside him and, firmly but gently, tipped his chin back to clear his airways.

"Do you have water?" I asked his companions.

"We used it all. Someone went to get more..." One of them managed to choke out a response despite the tension that was clearly wiring most of their jaws shut tight. Fear had rendered them useless. Their fear, were I to allow it in, would render *me* useless.

"Burns need running water," I said again, recalling from an age before, the words of the priestess one day near the smoker's hut, where she had shown me how to pour water out evenly over the flesh without soaking it. I fought to stay above the panic bubbling up from the pit of my own inexperience.

The same man spoke again. I was impressed by his mettle, there in that place, surrounded by the stink of charred flesh.

"I will get you water," the man choked.

"No." I turned from them, knowing even as he offered that it would take too long, and that if they had enough water close enough at hand then, surely, they would have already retrieved it. The situation was too immediate to wait. It took me only a moment to make my decision. My duty was to the ship and her people, not to myself and my own preservation.

Even if they're not your people? Even if it's not your ship? The little voice spoke in an insidious hiss.

"Move back," I instructed quietly, and felt them all obey in the rustle of clothing and the sudden emptiness in the space around me.

I was afraid.

"What is his name?" I asked as I carefully probed the burn, noting how recent it was, along with how deep the heat went, where it travelled down his neck onto his chest and hand. My fingers were deft and sure, working gently, gently, as I had seen Gnarsa do so many times before.

"Rafe."

As though swimming out at me from behind a curtain of reed, I reconciled the sweaty and blackened face of the speaker with August's friend, Goose.

"That's a strong name," I murmured, as I schooled myself to concentration. I dismissed the question of why an upper decks man was wearing such a veil of smoke and sweat. It wasn't worth thinking of now.

I held one hand, fingers splayed, just above Rafe's face. I hesitated half from fear... and half from uncertainty. With the other hand, I reached inside my collar to the vace on my chest, that dome of rounded green glass the size of my palm and my faith, and carefully, carefully, peeled one edge away from my skin. I concentrated with all of my might on channelling the current of water out through my fingertips as my body strove to be unmade.

It hurt.

Like the heady swell of a wave unravelled by a riptide, the vace wrenched away from the core of who I was.

There was a sound like a sleep sigh from Rafe as the unquestionably magical saltwater poured out of me and cascaded over his angry skin. I slowly passed my hand down over his body, tracing the burns once, twice, three times for luck.

Gnarsa never taught me this, I thought. But I hadn't needed her to.

I knew when it was done.

I sat back on my feet and murmured for the second time in my life the vace spell, fastening it once more to my body. Rafe stirred in the firelight, sweat mixing with water on his mottled skin.

"How did you do that?" Goose asked in a brave whisper.

I sat in silence with my eyes closed, my hands clasped softly in my lap, as the men lifted Rafe into a sitting position, ostensibly surveying my work. Marvelling.

I was so, so tired.

I slowly picked myself back up off the floor. "Take him to the infirmary," I directed them. It would be staffed; it would be foolish not to once the boilers were lit. I waited to see Goose nod in acquiescence and then turned to retrace my steps – slower this time – to the main parts of the ship.

As I climbed once more into the light, I had to shield my eyes at the brightness of the electric lamps. I glanced down and saw for the first time just how conspicuous I looked: wet to the bone and covered in bloodstains, with my hair plastered to my forehead and shoulders, bare feet hidden by a long but sodden hem. I sighed with exhaustion and resignation. If any of the men marked my passing, they did not do so to me.

I paused for a moment to rest my head against the smooth black door to August's private room, my hand resting lamely about the handle. My skin felt clammy. I could not reconcile the gravity of what I had just achieved with the light-headed hysteria threatening to spill up to the surface of my thoughts. A sob escaped my lips, shocking me.

But not as much as the hand that descended upon my shoulder, fingers like talons and nails like claws where they dug into my skin, urgency straining in every muscle.

"Isevelt!" growled a deep male voice. "How did you do that?"

*

I stared up in astonishment at the face of August Anders. His eyes were wide open, bright blue irises burning into mine. His eyebrows were arched high in concern, mouth thin and downturned. I felt liquid in comparison to his stern rigidity.

What right did he have, demanding explanations of me, when it was entirely *his* doing that I was there? Something akin to anger flashed hot in my chest. In a quick movement, I shoved his hand off my arm and whirled into his stateroom, snapping the door shut behind me. There was a dull thud just on the other side of the door as if a fist had collided with the timber.

"Saints, Isevelt!" his voice was muffled, but close to the latch. "What the hell happened down there?"

He must have seen, but not understood. Surely after hearing his grandfather speak of the sacrifice, speak of the magic, he would accept it?

"Isevelt, come out. Please. I need to understand."

Emotion again, clearly anger this time, shot through me like a dangerous current. I spun back to the door so that he could hear my voice, even at a whisper.

"*You* need to understand?" I hissed through my teeth; lips pressed up against the door jamb. "What right do *you* have to understand?"

"What I saw down there..." he trailed off into a choked gasp. "I saw... Lord. We were all working, stoking the coals. The *Valkyrie* needs to make the crossing faster than the damn *floating hotel*, or there's no way we'll be allowed to play in the Atlantic game. We... we worked the ovens too hard. We needed to get her really sailing for the first time, we wanted to get her ready and warmed.

"Rafe's young, this is his first ship. It's dangerous as hell down there. He should have been paying more attention; closed the grate. There must have been some kind of impurity in the coal he shovelled in; something popped. It's so hot in those flames, Isevelt. He must have... reached in. All of a sudden, he was screaming; he was on the floor. We shut our grates and rushed over, all of us. Marshall and Goose got him on his back, but he was thrashing. There was yelling, we should have known what to do but... Then he stopped. I went to get water... burns need water. I came back, and for some reason, *I* stopped, I just stared at them; a tableau. And then... you were there.

"I saw you walking in through the dimness, like a ghost. As you stepped into the firelight it was like you caught fire... There was all of this steam coming off your skin, your dress caught in a breeze that didn't exist. It was... unreal. And then you knelt, and the mien of your face. You seemed so – so young."

I found, from the sharp ache in my bones, that I had slipped down onto my knees, my fingers pressed into the carved curve of the closed door. I waited in silence for him to go on.

"And then your face changed. It was like you aged a thousand years in a moment. And then you touched your heart, and you sighed. And water streamed out through your fingertips, and the heat went out of every one of Rafe's burns as the water touched it. And no one else seemed to care that you were soothing Rafe with water from nowhere, or that you were turning grey...

"I couldn't move. I just watched. And then Goose asked you..."

I couldn't speak. The silence that followed was the longest yet. When his voice finally came it was pleading.

"What are you?" The handle of the door rattled softly.

My thoughts rolled sluggishly back to the little room in his family's home, where Erik Anders had held my hands and wept. August had stayed away, his back pressed against the wall, trying so quietly to... to...

"I thought when I pulled you from the water that it was just chance, and that you'd been injured somehow," he said, "but I couldn't bring myself to involve the police, because it just didn't... but there's something here that I don't understand. Something about the bottle of blood. Something... arcane. Isn't there?"

The words in my head were merely echoes of the night before. Erik had told him. *Greater than magic, my boy. Rituals worked with sacrifice.* He needed to hear *me* say it.

I didn't answer then, and I didn't answer now. I didn't know how long he waited outside my door, for he didn't speak again, and I couldn't gather the courage required to look out onto the hallway to check. I sat all night with my back pressed against the door, my bloodstained clothes drying on my skin, my hair turning to wool on my shoulders. The dress was ruined, irrevocably.

Eventually, I slept. My dreams were filled with Rafe and fire, and again and again the question: *what are you?* When, finally, I rose, I felt the ship come to life around me. I heard the people working, the metal groans, and I knew the shape of the feeling inside of me. And I was able to put it to words.

As Gnarsa had promised, I felt akin to the master of the ship, and, like him or not, would aid him and any of his people without question, without pause to consider the cost to myself. But where that had been a noble answer to a needful problem (when my master was a man of my own people), it was pointless now.

Knowing the problem did nothing to alleviate it.

I knew that I needed to wash my body, change my clothes, and gather my wits about me before I could face the new day.

After finding a basin for water I stripped layers of clothing from my skin. I winced as I peeled the bloodstained fabric from my stomach where it had dried and stuck to me.

What are you?

I felt ill. A sound that was part gasp, part choke, part sob escaped my lips, as I gathered up a double handful of the water and splashed it carelessly over my face and neck.

"Isevelt? Are you awake?" August's voice through the closed door was muffled and sleepy, but it was expectant, too. "May I speak with you?"

I tapped uselessly at the exposed stretch of skin across my chest and stomach, knowing instinctively that I needed to clothe myself without my conscious brain having the chance to understand.

"Isevelt?"

"Yes, wait," I called, finally reconciling the ruined pile of silk at which I stared with the idea of a dress. I eased the expanse of it back onto my frame but didn't bother with the buttons. My arms were too aggrieved to manage them.

The door slicked open with hardly a touch; I realised that August could easily have entered last night but must have chosen not to. He fell into the room now – he must have been leaning his weight against the door. There was a slight pressure mark on his forehead which made me imagine him bent at the door, as if in prayer. Not shocking. For a man without faith, the truths that he'd heard and seen must have seemed positively divine.

He peered up at me first in wonder, and then in concern.

"Are you alright?" he asked, quickly gaining his feet but still hanging back. "You look terrible."

"I feel terrible," I admitted. My head was throbbing, my tongue felt like sand in my mouth. There was an ache across my shoulders that sang of an entire evening crouched over an open wound, neck bent at an odd angle in order to allow the candlelight to catch the rise of the neat stitches made one after the other, all in a row, while Gnarsa chided me for inattention that was truly just drowsiness. I frowned at him as I felt myself sway. "Did you sleep in the hallway?"

"For a time," August shrugged. "I was with Rafe, the young stover, for a few hours. He's going to be okay; I've organised for him to leave the ship when we return back to home. He'll be looked after there. We'll be back in the estuary within the hour."

I sighed in relief as some of the ache eked out of my bones.

"He should be dead," August said baldly. "He should be dying. But he's getting better every minute."

I nodded dumbly and turned toward the small but lovely room. Strange, to know a room is lovely despite its bareness. I tried to put a word to the feeling of the place. Impossible, as I was so unwell that I could barely give name to myself.

August caught me gently as I fell into a soft chair. Had he been standing that close? "From all that I've come to understand about you... *you* should be dead," he murmured.

"I think I am, to be honest."

I felt the gentle press of fingertips at the pulse point in my wrist.

"Your heart is beating," he said.

I tried to wrench both of my eyes open, but truly only managed one. "You sound surprised."

He shifted half out of his crouch beside the chair, thought better of it, and rested once more on his haunches. He opened his mouth as if to speak, thought better of it, and closed it with an audible snap. "No, I won't say it."

"Say what?" I tried to ask, but my question was interrupted by an awful fit of dry coughing that doubled the pounding in my head and caused me to gasp and retch.

August left my side for a moment, and when he returned, he held a plain cup filled with water. He raised it to my lips, and I took it from him. It was such relief.

"Do you... do you need more?" August asked.

I can't say how much water I drank. It was too sweet, but it was wet, and it was enough.

"How did you know to come down to the boiler room?" August asked. He sat with his back against the closed wooden door.

"I heard him cry out. I think."

"With your ears?"

I frowned. *Yes...* "No. Maybe. It was different to sound."

August ran the plains of his palms along the smooth stretch of his forearms. "I didn't even know you were aboard. I mean, I might have guessed, but..."

I was met for a moment by the image of my mother: her beautiful, soft face wearing such worry even as I spoke harshly to her. Every time I passed a glass window, I touched it and thought of my father. All I had left to remember my mother was the bitter taste of regret. What had I ever gained from speaking ungently to her?

What had I ever gained by remaining silent?

I tested the weight of my words, sifted, and then redistributed them.

"August, I have little choice. The spell that prolonged my life could only work while ever it bound me to the life of another. I must be near the source of that life, or I will wane."

The poor young man was stricken. His face took on an ashen grey caste and his blue eyes bulged as though from a sudden rise in pressure behind them. "Your life is... bound to *mine?*" he gasped.

"No," I corrected quickly. There are certain truths whose power rests behind a shield of sophistry. "To the *Valkyrie.*"

Reprieve showed in his face, but something else, too.

"How does that work, then? Grandfather said yesterday that it was like a figurehead? As though your spirit goes through the ship and... protects it? Could you save the ship from disaster? An iceberg, maybe?"

I shook my head in quick denial. "I don't think that I have any ability beyond my own power. I am exhausted as soon as I am exhausted. But I have the power to exhaust myself... and I have the compulsion to exhaust myself, if that is what is required."

"The flowing water," he said. I hummed in agreement. "Anything else?"

"Perhaps. I won't know until I try. But I don't know *what* to try."

Something wicked sparked merrily in August's eyes. "I wonder if you could speed the *Valkyrie's* progress, when it comes time for full trials."

I shook my head, but I smiled. I liked the companionship of conversation. Perhaps August could be a friend. Perhaps.

"What were you saying, before? About my heartbeat?"

He was saved the need for reply by the sharp rapping of knuckles on the hall-side of the door. August flung himself forward so that his back was no longer braced against the wood. Goose appeared, his face a strange mask-like version of August's, back in that brief moment when he had believed that my life was bound to his.

"What is it?" August demanded quietly.

Goose shook his head, glanced at me, shook his head again.

"If it's to do with the ship, you've no worry in saying it here. Isevelt is for us." August drew himself up to his full, considerable height as he spoke. He clenched his jaw and braced his shoulders, clearly preparing for the worst.

"It's war," Goose said simply. "War has come to England."

"No!" August's voice was choked by the tension in his throat.

Goose nodded sadly. He looked over at me, and August's eyes eventually followed suit. I found that I was standing, leaning forward in readiness, seeming to have made the leap before they did. Of course, *I* had realised. Who knew better than I?

War meant ships.

"So, the *Valkyrie* is going to war," I said simply.

There is a certain look that crosses a brave person's face, as they realise that they will have need of their bravery. It visited both August and Goose at that moment, souring and setting atop their features like the skin on day-old cream.

If you're not paying attention, regret tastes a lot like grief.

Chapter 13

Salt

The *Witch* was well out to sea by the time disaster struck.

Even further from land when Crow realised just how much danger he had put the ship, and each of her souls, in the way of.

Storms in that part of the world, near the equator, were fast-forming and ferocious. A captain of Crow's years and experience would know when and where they would gather, and to either lash tight to friendly moorings, or else, manage to sail safely around the outside of its fury.

But Crow had used his wisdom to fly straight into one.

He'd known what to search for. The bruised smudge of clouds low on the horizon; a deep, wounded grey-red that was in people a remnant of either passion or punishment. He felt the pull of the great, waxen sails as they gasped and strained like lovers in throe, and though instinct told him to turn away (find land, find calm), desperation, and a deep need to prove that *none of it* had been wasted (the gold, the time, the dream; *none*), saw him hold the tiller steady, shout down Smith and Boron and whichever other man felt game enough to voice their protests, and steer straight into the belly of the weather-beast. And now, on the edge of it (in truth too far gone to turn her safely around), the *Witch* had begun to roll and keel and strain against herself as the waves whipped her sails one way, and the wind pushed her belly another.

Crow had begun to shout his orders: a sure sign that he was feeling far from confident, and even further, still, from contentment. The men, too, were moving with a surefooted determination that told of their fear more than any outward panic ever could.

At least the rain hadn't hit them yet.

Where was the girl? Surely the danger to the *Witch* was real enough that she should have been drawn from her quarters by now?

This is a grave mistake, Crow scolded himself, as he gnashed his teeth against the tension of his forearms, *and one that will surely lead you there.*

Crow grasped the top of the wheel with both hands and reefed it down with all the force he could muster, sending it spinning like a pinwheel in a garden bed. The image opened the door to memories that tasted of childhood and toffee which fought with the salt in the back of his throat, as imagined lace petticoats flicked and flung where the sails should have snapped in the gathering dark. Crow caught the wheel sharply with the flesh above his knee and used his now free hands to grab Will's shoulder as the lad hurried by.

"Have you seen the girl on deck today?" Crow growled, using the boy to keep his balance as he braced against the wooden wheel.

"In truth, Captain, I haven't seen her since before we called in to Browning last night."

"She's in her quarters, then?"

"No, Sir, not as far as I can tell. Shall I see again?"

The boy's eyes were showing white around the iris, like a horse second-guessing a jump. Crow felt poorly for the lad. He must have known enough of the sea to guess that their present danger was Crow's choice. Crow's fault, or folly. *Which is worse?* Even though Will would have known better, the call of below decks was probably a comfort to him, if only to escape the terrible noise of the howling wind and growling thunder.

The rain hadn't hit yet.

"Aye, see again," Crow snarled, rescuing the wheel from the brutality of his knee. The boy hurried off at once, leaving Crow to call after him. "And ask if any have seen her since last night on your way!"

The waves had picked up in height. Crow could tell, not from any kind of swell that he could see, but rather, the way the *Witch* seemed to take a longer sort of *breath* in between her rhythmic swaying. The rise was bigger this time.

The pause.

And then...

The plummet.

Seemingly sliding sideways down the slope of the wave, like the face of a mountain giving way to an avalanche. The *Witch* didn't slip down the surface of the wave; no, rather, the wave itself surrendered – let go – and, grasping the wooden beams of her belly like a comfort, took the ship with it.

At least the rain hadn't hit.

Smith's face loomed in the sudden dun light of the storm, brandishing a rope, like the one tied about his own waist. Where had he anchored himself? Smith's words were snatched from his lips as they were spoken, as though they were never said. Crow's eyes followed the tail of the rope, found it, finally, tied to the vast trunk of the nest.

Crow was afraid. They were too far gone; he had led them to their deaths.

He thought quickly. Tie the rope around his waist, and risk getting pulled to the depths by the weight of the *Witch* herself. Remain, and risk being swept from the safety of her decks by the sea. The wind whipping across his cheeks stung, turning the black tendrils of his hair to lashes. He feared that he had earned every one.

The Witch *is a woman*, he thought harshly, grinding his teeth with the strain of the keel. *A woman like any other. Sailing where she is bidden; hiding all of her fury and power until the moment the reckoning comes. Then, refusing to answer.*

The rain hit.

In the same moment that a crack of thunder rent the swollen clouds, a deluge of water cold and sweet fell atop the world like a blanket. And now the wind had a plaything. The sleety drops of ice-cold water sliced first at their cheeks one way, then at their backs another. All of the ropes grew suddenly sodden: in an instant, they were too thick and stuck to work the sails. Crow abandoned the tiller and threw himself toward the nest, grabbing Smith and the empty rope on his way past.

A glance around suggested that he was the last to tie himself fast. It was hard to know in the glowing haze, but Crow felt almost sure that none had tethered themselves to a cannon, like the last time. No coming back from *that*. As he tied the length of rope around his middle, fingers working deftly at the sailor's knots he knew so well, Crow found himself sadly glad that the girl had seemingly left them at Browning, for at least she had been spared this.

He began to say his prayers.

A hand landed like a vice around Crow's forearm. Will, the lad, his brown hair plastered in a lattice across his forehead. The *Witch* keeled over toward the east as the mighty storm continued to gather its fury about their heads.

It took Crow but a moment and his knots were untied. A moment more, and the rope was fast around Will's waist. The slippery deck threatened to steal Crow's footing, but both Will and Smith grasped tight around his arms and shoulders, keeping him steady. Twice more the *Witch* shook and spit, bobbing erratically like a broken cork in a wasted bottle. Twice more they managed to hold him, and then came the third. Three times proved to be too many. It was not that the men let go; rather, he simply slipped from their grasp and into the arms of the ocean below.

* * *

Crow was surprised by how much more peaceful it was, down in the jaws of the sea. He pitied his brothers tied tight to the bones of the *Witch*, surely already dead. She would start to split soon. There was no world in which a vessel could withstand that much pulling and twisting.

What a fool he was, to have put so much store in legends.

But no, he thought, rolling onto his back to let the pellets of frozen rain assault his face in penance, the waves tugging insistently at his hair. *It was* hope *that I invested in. The legend was just the receipt.*

Even over the horrific cacophony of the storm, Crow heard the splitting shriek of fabric as one of the *Witch's* sails rent free from its beam and danced, like a grotesque circus contortionist, away into the unseen reaches of the wind. His own gasp was lost to the sound of the storm. Or, perhaps, it never actually left his lungs. For there, revealed by the ripping of the sail, was Hope.

She stood as though suspended, leaning out over the rail of the nest, staring down the barrel of the storm with thunder between her brows. If the tempest had gathered to a greatness, it was nothing when compared to the greatness of the silver girl who faced it down fearlessly and, in her own power, found an answer to its challenge.

"Praises," Crow gasped, but his words were stopped by the harsh slap of a wave over his face. He spluttered and struggled, trying to get his body back around so that he could see the girl in all of her glory, atop the *Silver Witch*, fighting down the storm.

He thought he saw her lips move, but that may have been the effect of her exertions on her breathing. She raised her arms as though she were lifting a heavy object over her head. The thunder rolled and lightning still struck, but the rain did not fall atop the deck of the *Witch*. The ocean in which Crow struggled still tossed him about and turned him around, but the *Witch* grew gradually still until the waves began to part and glide far away from her hull, which was still – blessedly – gloriously – intact.

So, *this* was the measure of her magic. She could, indeed, calm the storm. Or, rather, spare the *Witch* from it. Crow could hear the amazement from the men on the deck, hastily untying themselves and wiping blood and salt from their brows. He made to strike out toward the ship but felt himself borne mercilessly – again and again – backward in the swell. He could not breach the invisible edge of her protection.

The wind still roared, the rain still ripped at his face, and his limbs grew more languid by the moment. He tried to roll once more onto his back, but his legs were like logs, pulling him downward.

As his face slipped beneath the waves, Crow swore that he saw the girl dive, like a swan, from the height of the nest, to disappear with him into the deep below. But he felt no despair. The *Witch* was safe, and it would remain so.

His silent exhale was relief.

* * *

I hardly came down from the basket atop the nest in the days after rescuing Crow from the storm. Now that I had learned the way of my magic I slept in the nest, rather than in the hold. The decks were always dry.

The crew were more or less in awe of me, calling up to me, or else waving as they moved underneath my tower like insects on a rock. Sometimes I acknowledged them.

Crow had not sought me out atop my perch. Perhaps he had no need of me, yet. Or, perhaps, the sheer fury in my face when I had deposited him on the decks of the becalmed *Witch* was warning enough that, should he value his safety, he should not attempt to ask anything of me anytime soon.

We had moved out into the vast open expanse of the ocean. All terror and motivation had abandoned the men, turning the important tasks of mending sails and fixing fastenings into summertime pleasures, accompanied by a thirty-man-strong chorus of whistles, shanties, and laughter. I felt the full hundred feet apart from it all.

The colours here were unlike any I had ever seen. My mother had saved a piece of silken cloth from her lost childhood, dyed nearly the same deep blue-green of this ocean where it caught the light. The flecks of gold I saw in my memory now were the like of the gilding of the sun on the peaks of the waves. Haedi had scoffed, once, at the cloth, wondering why someone would have spun it so thin, so useless. Our mother had chided her gently, promising that there were, indeed, places in the world warm enough to wear silk such as hers and be happy.

I clutched my own bare shoulders, stripped down to gather in the golden warmth of the afternoon, warding off the cold and grey ache of remembering my mother. Merta was dead to the world. This I knew, as surely as I had cleaned the rushes of my mother's blood with my own two hands. But Haedi was not guaranteed dead.

Haedi had been split at the throat and left to drain into a vat, like a doe. But so had I. And yet, here I sat, clutching my own shoulders as I shivered in the sweltering sun, tears drying even as they welled against the rise of my cheeks. *What am I, that I have become here, and this?*

A voice called out from below, but much closer than any other had in the passing days. It was young – not the voice of Smith or Crow, but still, it was nervous. I inched my head out through the bars of the wooden cage, and my silver braid slipped over my shoulder like a rope or an invitation.

The open and earnest face of Will peered up at me, his features unsure even as his arms and legs held confidently to the rope ladder where it swayed and danced in the breeze.

"You encroach at a time where my mood is already sour, despite the sweetness of the air up here," I warned him, but I moved my body for him to climb through, nevertheless.

"I'm sorry to add to it, then. I'm not here to encroach upon your solitude – although it seems to me as though you have the best position of all of us."

"Then why are you here?"

"I'm here at Smith's secret behest."

I sat back against the ribs of the basket, wedging my shoulder blades between two vertical planks, and bracing with the ball of one foot on the other side. There was room enough for Will to do the same, but he instead remained near the portal to the rope ladder, legs crossed against his chest, and arms locked around them to keep them there.

"You show your cards easily for someone who has been sent in secret."

Will pursed his lips, glanced away, smiled. "I am of the opinion that keeping secrets from *you* will only ever end in loss."

"You are wise."

"And what of you?" Will pinched a long-discarded strand of rope between his fingers and rolled it idly back and forth. "What are you?"

"I am wiser."

"Than me?"

"Than before."

The basket, being so many feet up in the air, moved in a way that sent the stomach a certain shade of drunk. It didn't reach me at all, anymore, but I imagined that Will would feel the beginnings of it creeping up over his wits, presently.

"You are not inclined to trust people," he suggested.

"I did that once. It left me dead."

I wasn't sure why I spoke to the young sailor so freely. Perhaps it was because he didn't seem to fear me, and so I needn't worry about preserving his opinion of me. Perhaps it was another reason.

"What do you mean?" Will asked.

Visions danced before my open eyes, harsh against the crystalline sharpness of the sea flickering out around me, as though I were a sharp knife driven into virgin ice.

Cold stone glistening with blood in the darkness. A blade made of glass pulled from the ocean, which lapped hungrily at the hem of the witch's robe, turning my bare feet an unearthly shade of pale.

"I trusted a witch with my life, and she took it from me."

I watched Will desperately fight with his features, focusing on the feeling of the frayed rope between his fingers. "Why did you give it to her?"

Faces. Voices.

"My people were in danger. They had disregarded the gods, and the gods had abandoned them. We were apologies. Sorry-gifts. We were willing to be useful because we were promised that we would have our lives returned to us."

"The witch lied."

"No. I misunderstood."

The rope slipped from his fingers. "What? How?"

I spoke a sour truth that had been fermenting in my heart, clouding my thoughts and slowing my limbs. "I believe that she meant for us to have our lives. The witch promised that

I would have my life returned to me. And, in truth, I am no longer dead. I think. So, therefore, she spoke in earnest."

"However..."

"However, although I am *not* dead, I also don't have my life anymore. All that I was is lost. But I can't ever know how much of her promise was a half-truth."

"So, you're... as though..." Will struggled to fit words to his meaning, without allowing insult to intrude. "You're alive, but dead."

"Like Death, or like I'm dead?" I asked, my voice barely a whisper, knowing even as I spoke and leaned forward that *this* was a moment into which I had entered, once before.

"Well, you can't be Death, because you saved us all. I think Crow *was* right about you, whatever it is that he was right about."

"Hmm." Where I had been leaning forward like a stalking cat, I let go my shoulders and relaxed once more against the planks. I refused to be dismayed. Life moves on in a line. You can't circle back.

Will closed his eyes against the swaying of the basket. "I imagine you're inclined not to trust Crow with your life, seeing as how it seems as though he was so intent to end it."

"I miss your meaning."

Will shrugged, eyes still closed. "Any sailor with a week on a ship knows the smell of a storm. Any sailor with a head on his shoulders knows that Crow knew that storm, and sailed straight on into it, anyway."

He waited out the silence for as long as he could, finally peeking out with one eye to see me staring at him, straight on.

"So, if you think he did that," Will continued, shutting his eye again, "you need to decide whether Crow is empty-headed, or bull-headed."

"How so?"

"What reason could he have for jeopardising the *Witch* and all of the crew? And himself? I know that you want nothing of them, but... perhaps it would be worth asking questions, because either Crow, or Smith maybe, might just have answers. They know something. And *you* know nothing. So, there's only gain in asking about it."

He turned as he spoke, rolling his body out of the gap in the basket and wrapping a forearm around the top rung of the rope ladder. "And there is only loss in me staying up here. Loss of my drink. I'm sorry. Please, think on it. You owe yourself answers. They *owe* you answers. But only you can ask."

* * *

Should I ask? Could I? I thought on it all day, laying spread out in the sun with the central post of the nest putting firm and constant pressure against my back.

Crow obviously had a plan for me. At the very least, some kind of expectation. There was no guarantee that he'd know any kind of truth, or that he'd be able to offer any insight into the ritual performed by Gnarsa so long ago. But perhaps he could explain to me how *I* featured into *his* understanding.

As the sun slunk low on the horizon, beckoning us on to the inevitable crest of the ocean, and the next nameless port that lay beyond, I slipped over the side of the nest and down the ladder, before sidling up to Crow where he stood at the front of the *Witch*, watching the night encroach.

He knew of my presence even before my arm brushed against the fabric of his coat, but he made no mark of it beyond the subtle straightening of his back. Instead, he continued to gaze out into the depths of the blue expanse that was his world. Sea and sky. Sky and sea.

I joined him, uninvited, but clearly welcome in the silent regard of the sea. The waves, denied the slanting shafts of sunlight that sometimes cut through the water, were ink-dark and cloudy, keeping their secrets. Would Crow keep his?

"You watch the sunset," I remarked eventually. "Stern, or bow, or even side if we're sailing north or south. You watch the sunset."

"You know a lot of me."

"Only what I see. You have *told* me nothing."

If he heard it for the rebuke that it was, he did not acknowledge it. "Thank you for saving the *Witch*," he said, instead.

"I had no choice."

"That is very selfless."

"I find that I am without self, yes." My voice was cold. I set my teeth. "You may thank me, but I curse you for making it necessary. That was a dangerous game that you played."

He made no effort to break the silence that stretched out behind my accusation. I was dimly aware of one of Crow's men approaching, but the man turned at the last moment and went elsewhere. Here and there a new star winked into existence, mirrored in the glassy expanse of the sea below.

"Will prying reveal a treasure? Or a plaster fresco that flakes away?" he wondered.

"I don't understand."

"What do you know?" He asked, finally. Quietly.

I frowned, finding comfort in the feeling of my furrowed brow. *What did I know? Nothing. I know what I feel. Nothing.*

"I know now that it is better to clean a sword of rust, than of blood," I spat.

Crow's eyes were wide when he turned towards me. Perhaps his intent was to ask me what I knew of his game, as my answer seemed to intrigue him. I stood with my back rod straight, my hands folded gently on the waxed wooden bannister. The shirt that I still wore bunched and caught slightly in the pull of the breeze.

"How is *that* lesson learned?" he asked me.

"I asked my sister, once. When I was cleaning my father's sword. If it was better to clean a sword of rust and know that it is dissatisfied because it is unused, or to clean it of blood, and know that it is angry, and in its anger, insatiable. I know now. Better to leave a sword dissatisfied."

"I must say that I agree with you."

"I must reply that I am shocked." The conversation fell upon my ears like a song played in the wrong key. Forming the sounds with the instrument of my mouth felt like I played the harp with all the knowledge of a drum. My phrases were oddly formal and left me sounding sterile, and staid.

"You say that you are shocked?" He glanced at my serene composure, as though challenging the truth of my words. Or, perhaps, hoping to reveal the steel beneath them.

"You seem a rather determined man, Captain. As though you will have your way, even if it means satisfying your sword."

Crow looked profoundly uncomfortable at the turn our talk had taken, showing his unease in both the sudden sweat on his palms (which he rubbed away) and whatever feeling it was that must have been in the pit of his belly, to have left him as pale as I was. Crow tried boldly to turn the tenor of our conversation, painting me once more into the picture of girlhood that he seemed to hold in his mind.

"Our next port is a day away. It's bigger than any we've been to, yet. A city, to be fair. With a harbour. When we arrive, would you like me to purchase you a new dress?"

"No."

His knuckles jumped where they nestled together. "No? Ah. I thought–"

"It means nothing," I replied simply. "Dress or shirt. It means nothing."

I left him, as satisfied as a rust-free sword, and climbed back up my tower. Safe from all manner of sea monsters.

* * *

The next port was, indeed, no less than a city.

The water broke straight onto rock walls, barrelling head-long atop unseen beaches to crash and flurry about the pylons of jetties that struck out into the sweeping swell. There were more ships than I had ever seen in my life anchored there, swaying like drunkards, and lit in the already evening light by candles from the inevitable taverns that decorated the rocky shore, like so many pearls on a lady's throat. I had grown tired of taverns, dotted as they were around the mouth of every har-bour like rotting teeth.

As I sat once again atop the shoulders of the *Silver Witch* (this time on the main mast rest, rather than the cramped basket), I tried to hush the memories in my mind of ships rolling and heaving in another distant, sinister swell, shattered together until their bones were strewn on the black sand beach for all to see. The memories of the last weeks of my life had become persistent in their petition.

It doesn't matter what manner of creature; one should never see its insides exposed, I thought.

Crow had made the decision that the crew should wait for morning to find their land legs but thoughtfully sent ashore for ten bottles of rum, to warm the waiting sailors as they of-fered their cheeks longingly to the beckoning glow of firelight.

"Better to wait 'til morning," he had said, sternly. "I've *real* business to make here, and business is made better when it's not being chased out of parts by consequence."

I did not care to know the nature of his business. Instead, I had resigned myself to compose a set of questions, designed to reach the bottom of my own business.

I was both pleased and surprised when Will joined me, again, atop the mast.

"Not so high, this one," he explained when I questioned him. And then, when I questioned him further, with his tongue poking out from the side of his teeth, and with a crude model made from his own, perpendicular palms, "See, the further away from the pivot point we are, the more obscene our reaction to each movement. If we're only halfway as high up, then we only get halfway as sick."

"You'll grow sick on *that*, if not the basket," I said, gesturing to the brown bottle tucked under his arms with my jutted chin.

"Oh, this?" He asked, seeming to realise anew that it was there. "No, this is for you. Warmed liquor. Like your father used to recommend; for finding your land legs."

I felt myself flush, hot and sharp with sadness and sweetness, and turned half around. He must have seen many things in my face, for he hurried to try to ease them away.

"Oh, I'm sorry. Truly. I meant it as comfort, I swear it..."

"I *am* comforted," I conceded quietly, offering my face to the stars, where I'm sure it caught the reflection of the heavens in the tracks of my tears. "But sometimes, when I am not comforted, I forget that I am sad, at all. And then comfort reminds me."

"I wonder if I feel a little of what you feel," Will said, still looking at me.

"Bound by sacrifice to a man you don't know, burdened with power you do not understand, filled with questions and longing that will never be satisfied? Aching for revenge but held fast to a sense of duty to souls you neither know nor–"

"Alone," he interjected.

I shut my teeth with a snap.

Watching him carefully, I reached out and grasped the neck of the brown bottle. Delicately, I removed the cork with my teeth and let the rum touch the tip of my tongue. It was indeed warm, and *that* alone was enough to dry my sudden, shameful tears. Had I ever cried in life as much as I had these past weeks, in death?

"How did you manage it?" I eventually demanded, incredulous. Crow allowed no fire aboard the *Witch* – not even to cook with.

"As surely as my honour, I'll never tell you."

"Crow will have you thrown to the sea."

"He will never know."

I sipped again, warmed from the inside.

"It was already warm from the sun," he said simply, giving out without any fight. "When I touched it and felt its heat, I thought to bring it to you."

I laughed once. It was sharp, but it was easy. It hurt and it healed. "Then you have no honour. You told me."

"I believe I have honour."

"The proof, as they say, is in the rum." I handed it back to him.

"Do they say that?" He squinted at it, scratched his chin, and rested it, undrunk, on the plank of wood on which we sat. "Did you get your answers from Crow?"

"I did not ask my questions."

Will sighed and appraised me for a long time. "I do not know why, but my very bones tell me that you should. Because I cannot believe that he has been as he is with no purpose. And I fear that his end is impending."

"What do *you* know of this man? He treats you like nothing more than a sailor, yet you revere him as a father."

"He is my captain."

It was so simple. The dull tattoo of *knowing* in between my shoulder blades that spoke of an urge to keep the *Witch* and her men near, and safe, like little hens, contained in the eggshell of a single word: *captain*.

"How can knowing help me?" I asked, letting my bare feet dangle out over the expanse of the deck, where men lazed and sat in pockets of happy company, sharing Crow's gift of drink.

"How can not knowing help? Tonight, sleep, and tomorrow, go ashore with Crow. See what you see. Know what you know."

I glanced again at the warm bottle, then at Will, and finally at the stars. "I already know what I don't know," I muttered, "and that doesn't scare me. The truth is... the truth is that I am much more afraid of what I *do* know."

Chapter 14

Blood

August's hands shook even as they gripped the smooth railing of the bridge – so hard that his knuckles turned the dry white of bone. If he stood to his full height, my head would barely graze the underside of his chin. But where he stooped now, his head hung down over the decks below, his whole self – had I stood near enough – would have barely reached my chest.

I had been right in my guess; not only had the war come to England, but it would be taking the *Valkyrie* back out with it.

August had received no consolation from Goose's assurances that the rival ships, the floating hotels, were to be requisitioned too. All he could do was lament the loss of this dream that he had come so close to grasping, as the very workmen who had built her, truly, from the ground up, were now employed to skin the *Valkyrie* like a rabbit, casting all of the beautiful skin and viscera off and into the fire of fickle industry. August stooped now because he couldn't bear to watch as the precious ship was torn apart. But, by equal measure, and by his own admission, he couldn't possibly have been anywhere else while it happened.

I hovered a ways behind him, watching as armfuls of appointments became barrow-loads of furniture and finishing, which were walked carefully down gangways to become cart-loads of trappings that would never be used, never beheld, never enjoyed. I imagined it was like finding the box that held a child's first teeth and casting it away without time or place for either ceremony or sadness.

The awful extent of the bad news had come even as the *Valkyrie* had slid, triumphant, back into her lodgings at the Viking yard's dock; of the hundreds of ships that constituted the British Merchant Navy, the machine of war required still more ships, and more again. Any sailing vessel would be conscripted and put to use, according to its size and shape.

And the *Valkyrie*, as big and strong and as fast as she was, had been called up to carry hundreds and hundreds of men across oceans to fight on the fields of battle, and, perhaps, bring pieces of them back again.

Of course, I understood that this was not war as I had seen it.

Or, rather, it was... but on such a scale of distance and time and cost that I could not fathom it for the imagining. Surely, this was the deep of despair that I felt. Surely, this sudden loss of the shape of my life, in the mere moments after I had gathered the shape of my body, was equal to the breathless, crushing death of drowning.

"Mr. Anders...?" My own thoughts were interrupted by a quiet voice.

August and I looked up at the same time, as though choreographed and rehearsed in a dance. The words were uttered as an offer rolled up inside of a question. Neither of the tones reassured. I watched as August braced his shoulders and leaned back, away from Burns, who stood before him with his hat in his hands and a tremor in his tightly clenched jaw.

"What is it, Burns?" August rasped. "I've already lost the *Valkyrie*; what else could you say to me that could cause that tremble in you?"

Burns worked his jaw back and forth, glanced at me, but remained silent. August saw the direction of Burns' gaze and turned to look at me, too. I realised that the man's hesitation may well lie in the fact that I was a stranger, and so I stepped carefully back into the cool shadow of the doorway.

"Please, Isevelt, stay," August said clearly. His voice had raised itself above a rasp, and he tipped his chin up to match. Perhaps August's use of my name convinced Burns to speak before me. Perhaps the older man simply wanted to take advantage of the distraction of August's steel-sharp attention.

Whatever his thoughts, his words were clumsy and cruel. But in the face of their meaning, in the glare of them, and the desperate silhouette of the emptiness that they left behind, I think that August forgave him both clumsiness and cruelty.

"He died, August," Burns said in a rush. "Erik. Just this morning."

I knew by instinct and in the rush of the current of my blood that August needed my comfort, and so in two swift steps, I was firmly beside him, beside and just behind. Unseeingly, he groped in the grief that surrounded him for my hand and caught it up fast. He held my small hand in both of his so that I was no longer behind him at all.

"I'm sorry," Burns intoned, apologising perhaps for the gaucherie, or for the words themselves, and August nodded tightly. I felt the high-pitched whine of his sadness building in the depths of his body like a stringed instrument that had been abused. Did Burns hear it? Did August?

The night when Erik had spoken with me – had it been only two days since? That night, the old man had given me a gift of words that leant me a certain kind of fixedness in the midst of my loose-ribboned fate. In a moment I was back in the sick room, face to face with the old man who had hoped for me.

"*It's odd that you say* returned, *my dear.*"

"*That is the word that the priestess used as part of the ritual, when she promised us life after death.*"

Erik had coughed and waved his hand dismissively at my explanation. As I thought of the conversation in the light of day, and in light of Erik's passing, I wondered if he had actually been dismissing the handkerchief that I offered him, rather than my words.

"*No, no, you misunderstand me. Poetically, I grasp perfectly well what you mean. I merely wonder if... perhaps... you should christen your existence with a new word... one that takes into bearing the fact that you have... returned... to nothing at all, but rather, have been thrust into a time and place and people who bear no familiarity to you in the least.*"

I had resisted, telling him that the ship was familiar to me. That the need for me to be merely one amongst many, united for a cause, was familiar to me. But he would not hear it. Insisted, even.

I had not returned at all.

I had arrived.

"*We may think that we control our lives, or our deaths... but the truth remains that we have little say over either of them. What we* do *bear is an ability to work within the bounds of where we exist.*"

I hadn't realised that I'd spoken aloud until Burns nodded his head. His balding pate glistened with the leavings of a fine fog, sending his dark grey beard a darker shade of iron, and dappling his spectacles like so much morning dew.

"If I'd seen it written down, I'd've sworn the words were composed by Mr. Erik himself," Burns said. "I've brought the motor, to take you back to the big house, if you've a mind..."

Burns swung his body away from us, as though beckoning and inviting us through an invisible door all at once.

Since I had returned to this place... arrived in this place... I had felt, apart from my conscious needs, a quiet submission to the many insanities that I simply could not understand. And I was thankful for that, for it meant that I could tuck away in a velvet box my rage at my own death, and my terror at the immeasurable time that was no more than a second of silence, and my horror at knowing that my parents' bones had probably turned to clay in a decaying bay of black sand that I would most likely never again find, even if I had leave for looking... and my disdain for the sensation of this language on my tongue, and the infinitesimal moment that existed between the hearing of the toneless utterings before they arranged themselves into intelligible speech within my comprehension...

All of it could be tucked away in a box devoid of sharp edges, with little light... so that they could sleep, undisturbed, and allow me to simply *be,* outside of my control or comfort.

But in my heart, I knew this to be a mere shade of the truth. For as the *Valkyrie* had first eked out of the estuary and into the open arms of the ocean, I had felt unspooling within me a surety, a *surety*, that I belonged not just *within* the ship but *to* the ship. Even as I had walked through the rooms hardly furnished but lovingly finished, even as I had trailed my hand softly along the smooth stretches of what *must* be birchwood, feeling a shiver and shudder trade places along my spine, I had known full peace and not only mild calm.

So, could I leave the ship now? I had no fear of beholding the dead. I had done so in life, and the many mirrors in August's life meant that I had also done so in death.

No, I feared that perhaps I could not bear to leave the *Valkyrie.*

But perhaps, if August's need was greater than my own?

"You should go to your family," I said quietly. I spoke for August, and no one else.

"Please, will you come?" he asked. His pale face had taken on the shape of a heart, where his auburn hair had fallen forwards in one desperate lock. Floating above the surface of his skin was a flotsam of freckles that stood out all the more against the wan expanse of his cheeks.

"Yes," I breathed. "Of course." And, simply, despite the intricacy of my worrying, I did.

* * *

The funeral service had, in the end, been held on the same day that the *Valkyrie* had left the estuary to make her way to Southampton, where she would collect her first hundred, hundred souls.

It was fitting.

Erik's funeral had been strange to everyone present. His family were unnerved by the inclusion of several Viking customs specified in his instructions. I was nonplussed by it all – neither the stuffed birds nor the heavy incense bore any resemblance to any ceremony that I'd ever seen. The faces of the mourners were familiar. People turn a certain shade of grey when they're in the presence of death.

Goose was there. He'd apparently been granted special dispensation to arrive at the infantry training camp a day late, however, he did attend the service dressed in his officer's uniform, and he left shortly after.

As with nearly all of August's important conversations those last few days, I was present for the one on the station platform, where Goose and August said goodbye. August seemed and sounded completely bereft. His empty palms and lack of bags when juxtaposed with Goose's heavy khaki satchel served only to further prove the point. Goose remedied the problem by filling August's hands with both of his own.

"We've always seen eye to eye on this," Goose said gently. "You and I both know the difference between right and wrong. And even if your father didn't manage to live that for you, Erik did."

August tightened his bottom lip over the top edge of his teeth and nodded. "You be safe," he said, pulling Goose into a tight embrace.

"I'll be brave, and I'll be humble. But that's the best I can offer you."

"What if you end up on a hospital ship?" August asked suddenly.

Goose wrinkled his nose as he thought.

"Well... best place to be, isn't it?" He asked with a sardonic smile. "They don't pick you up if you're too dead. And if you're not dead enough, then they make you go and try again tomorrow."

August laughed a single bark, like a satisfied wolf, and clapped Goose on the back. I dimly registered the sight of a black stain drawn like a line of blood along the bottom of August's palm, but then they stepped apart, and as the palm in question found my own, I ceased to think of it.

Somewhere close, and yet also far away, a long alarm like a whale song split the air. Goose (and many others besides) took this as a signal and stepped quickly up into the doorways of yet another great, hulking machine – a train – to be swallowed up and carried off into the unknown.

"I'll see you soon," Goose called as his face grew smaller. August raised his free hand in reply.

"What does he mean, he'll see you soon?" I asked, stepping around so that I was face to face with August, who exhaled slowly through his nose but remained silent in his regard of me.

August glanced at the face of the bracelet on his wrist, and then pulled me over to a bench worked from regularly fitted slats of white-painted wood. People moved about us like fish in frightened schools. Everywhere people embraced, and from further away again the sad whale made her warning call. But for me, all that existed was the two of us.

"What does he mean, he'll see you soon?" I asked again. August still held my left hand, and now he gently took up my right as well.

"I know the difference between right and wrong," he said sadly. "So, I'm going to follow Goose, to fight in the war."

"On the *Valkyrie*?" My voice sounded thin even to my own ears. He shook his head.

"It's not for me to choose. She doesn't belong to me, anymore. Not that she ever did. In the same way that, in giving her over, I am not the master of her fate... when I give myself over to my country, to fight—"

"You're not the master of your own fate, either," I finished for him. "I can't go with you."

August's eyes were sad. Perhaps, like me, he had felt the warmth that came from easy company. And perhaps, like me, he felt it would be a shame to lose it.

"No," he said, finally. "You can't."

I took my hands back into my own lap. "What will I do?"

"You may go to the *Valkyrie*. I might not have any measure of control, but my Aunt Anne does. I spoke to Eryn at the service – Anne has arranged for Eryn to serve on the *Valkyrie* as a junior nurse. Eryn begged her – mother and father said no, but it turns out that Aunt Anne is made of sterner stuff that any of us ever realised. It's been arranged for you to go, too."

I fought down the sudden heady rush of tears as I resigned myself to his words.

"Only if you want to," August said hastily. He moved his face around until his eyes fell naturally into the place where my gaze rested. "If it is not your desire, then I can have the papers put into your name at Mrs. Caulfer's flat. I just thought..."

"No, you're right."

"I just thought you would want to be with the ship."

"Yes."

"Helping people, if you could."

"Yes."

"You look so sad," he said, and he smiled like an uncle sympathising with a tired child.

"Aren't you?"

His shoulders fell, but the warm smile remained.

"Yes," he said. "Yes, I am. There are so many questions I would have asked you. Tried to understand, to know. But instead, like an idiot, I've taken it all for granted and wasted you. But it was the same of angels and idiots in the Bible. Who am I to think I'd be any more selfless or aware than Abraham himself?"

I didn't understand his words, but I gathered his meaning sure enough. "Who indeed?"

August stood and offered me his hand again. We walked slowly through the thronging crowds, who seemed to part easily around us, as though we were sharks. Or kings. The sunlight was spearing golden through the afternoon, lighting upon edges of the day and gilding it with molten fire.

"Will you leave today?" I asked, peeking up at his profile. He gleamed in the sunlight like a statue worked already in his own honour.

"No."

"Then you may ask your questions tonight."

His hand twitched in mine, and we locked eyes for a moment. And then looked away.

* * *

It seemed strange that they should be having the conversation in August's old bedroom – recently Eryn's – rather than in his stateroom aboard the *Valkyrie*. But as the ship was halfway to Egypt by now, meeting in *that* place was far from possible.

They sat like a tableau: Isevelt in the window, Eryn with her legs crossed, childlike, beneath her on the bed, and August once again on the carpeted floor, his back pressed against the door, lest any other family members should see fit to try to enter. When Isevelt had requested his sister's presence, August had been disappointed, but he couldn't say why. Wouldn't.

"Will you tell us, again, what happened to you?" Eryn asked, and Isevelt turned her head to look long out the window and across the sea of rooftops. The sun was gone now, but the moon had yet to rise to its peak. The moon was late in her visits.

"My mother and father..." Isevelt began, but she faltered. She took a breath, swallowed, and spoke again. "I was the last child to be born in my village. The priestess took me under her wing... taught me that my value could lay beyond my mother's fear, and be in overcoming my own. One of her tasks – beyond advising the Jarl and healing the needy – was honouring the gods."

"How did you do that?" August asked, and his hand lifted almost without thought to rest against the breast of his jacket.

"The gods required the last," Isevelt said. She closed her eyes, remembering. "If all that they gave was good, and if we knew that we would always receive, there was no agony or fear in giving back to them the last of what we received. Chickens born of eggs, eggs that bore no fowl. Stretches of smooth-spun wool. We gave them back last measures of everything. But for one gift."

"What did you keep?" Eryn asked in a whisper.

"We kept our children."

Both of the Anders siblings reacted in shock, faces aghast.

"You said to grandfather that your death was a sacrifice," August said. "Is that what you mean? You were the last, and so your death put the gods to rights again?"

"That's sick," Eryn spat. "I think that witch took you in, just so that she could use you."

"My father used to call her *witch*, too," Isevelt murmured. "But she didn't manipulate me. She didn't ask me to do it until after the other girls had offered. And that was after my parents died."

"Which others?" He asked. He hadn't seen her so pale since the night that he had spilled her blood into the sea.

Saying their names felt like a balm. "Aiden. Haedi. Sylvi."

"Beautiful names."

"Haedi is Astrid's middle name, do you remember?" August prompted Eryn. "I wonder how much of this grandfather knew. If he told father."

"If I were father, and I knew all of this, I'd probably be driven to drink, too," Eryn observed baldly. August looked unwell.

"Haedi was meant to marry the Jarl's son. She understood the power of sacrifice for the good of the people. It was her idea to do it... but of the four of us, Aiden and Sylvi and I are... were younger, so without the three of us dying, too, Haedi's offer would solve nothing."

"But... you're not *dead*, are you?"

Isevelt shook her head and leaned her cheek back against the cold pane of the glass window. "No. *That* was my idea."

"What do you mean?"

"I argued with Gnarsa – the priestess – that as long as our people had *had* lore, we'd known that the gods give back what they receive with a measure of reward, so there *must* have been a way to harness that goodwill through magic. This is what we devised."

"For you to be tethered to a passenger liner hundreds of years later?" The quality of Eryn's voice made her question sound pugnacious but, in truth, it was merely angry scepticism that coloured her words.

"No."

"What did you think would happen, then?" August asked. He had his legs stretched out before him, making a triangle with the side of the bed.

"My people were under attack from our enemy. It was the retribution of the gods, and in their anger, they gave good fortune to the invaders. We four were to be bound to our own boats, and our own people, to protect them and aid them in setting things back to rights."

"But what happened? How could you have gone from that, to wasting away in a bottle on Erik Anders' shelf?"

Isevelt slid from her place on the windowsill and onto the floor. Her feet did not quite reach August's. She tucked them away under her body.

"I don't know," Isevelt admitted. "I'll never know. It tears me to pieces and leaves me bloody, but I'll never know."

"Unless you die in this life and wake up to find out it was all a dream," Eryn supplied.

"That is a cruel curse," Isevelt said, shaking her head and flicking her fingers as if to ward off the words. "The worst thing that I could endure would be to learn that it had all been for nothing."

"Watch your words, Eryn," August cautioned.

"No, it is alright," Isevelt said. "Truly, I have lost nothing in submitting to the priestess' knife. My father and mother were killed before then, and I had no friend."

"That's so sad."

Isevelt shrugged. "If it is all you know, you don't think to miss it. Once you've felt love, though..."

"That's when it aches." August's voice was deep with emotion.

"Goose will be fine," Eryn assured him, but August didn't appear comforted. Instead, he held Isevelt's gaze, unblinking, feeling the silence spool out like an anchor tethered to a delicate ribbon.

Eryn yawned suddenly, throwing her arms out in an expansive stretch that caused enough havoc for the ribbon to snap. "I'm exhausted," she said. "Shall I call for tea?"

"No one will be up, at this hour," August said. "Surely you wouldn't wake them just for that?"

"You're right," Eryn agreed. "I'll make it myself."

She nudged August aside with a stockinged toe until he moved to the adjacent wall, then she eased the door open a crack, and slipped out into the hall. August realised, once the door closed, that the wall adjacent to the door was the one against which Isevelt leaned.

August knew that he was going to war. He knew that the romantic notions of the American civil conflict, or the Indian campaigns of grandfather's time, were lies told to keep boys enlisting and throwing their bodies at the enemy. But even his pragmatic understanding of the hardships that he might face paled in comparison to the thrill of fear that he felt in that moment, realising that he was alone with this creature who he did not understand, yet could not put from his mind.

Realising that he might never see her again.

Knowing, now, all that she had endured.

Isevelt did not seem so afraid. She regarded him levelly, her mouth impassive, her delicate fingers curled in the folds of her skirt. It was odd, to see a woman with such white hair, such pale lashes, but he had stopped being shocked by it, and instead saw beauty in her frost-like features. And such warmth in the nearness of her hand.

He glanced out the window. The moon had made her appearance, and the light that washed in, onto Isevelt's braided hair, was like new milk.

"I will miss you," the woman said quietly. Her daring, even now, was such an endearment.

What man it would take, he wondered, to walk beside that kind of power in wartime, let alone in peace? August felt his own daring rise up inside of him, found that he was now on his knees before her, reaching out his hand and pulling her up so that her chin was almost level with his own, their eyes each able to bore through the other, their hands clasped once again. Did he dare to ask her to consider him, if he managed to make it to the next year alive? When the business of peace was won?

He was close enough to her that he could see the swell of moisture in the corners of her eyes. Did she cry for those she had already lost? Or those who she would lose next?

No. It was not fair to ask someone such a thing. How selfish of him to ask her to give anything of herself to him, to keep as his own – even a promise of affection.

Instead, swallowing the mad compulsion he felt deep in his chest to lean forward and sweep his lower lip along the beginnings of her tears, he gently pressed his mouth to the back of her hand and rose them both up to standing.

"I will miss you, too," August said.

And, kissing her hand once more, he left.

Chapter 15

Salt

In the city the next day, Sylvi rescued three chickens and declared eggs.

It had been half a millennium since she had walked through a marketplace, and although some quiet compulsion bade her remain close to Crow at all times, there was no fear in her.

The chickens had been a sort of compulsion, too. The group of sailors, with Crow and Sylvi in the middle of them, had rounded a cobbled corner and happened upon the strutting and scolding mass of feathers and feet. Sylvi had found herself squarely back by Haedi's side, in the middle of the village, trading the newly married Sorrell a plump brown chicken for a bushel of dried fish.

"I need these," Sylvi said to Crow.

He peered down at his own sleeve, where Sylvi's little white hand clutched and tugged at the fabric with all the insistence of a five-year-old. He felt a sudden rush of wordless warmth toward the cold girl who was illuminated for the first time since the storm, from within, with a fierce determination that demanded action.

"And what will we do with these?" Crow asked, bemused by the gruff patience in his own voice. "I need to see Carson, not buy chickens."

"Eggs," Sylvi said. "We will have eggs."

He chuckled, sounding more like a clucking hen than he liked. She mistook his hesitation for reluctance and rolled her eyes.

"Fine, then, give me the gold for the dress," she said.

"You'll just use it to buy the chickens," he laughed.

"Yes." She held out her hand.

He laughed again, louder this time. He was dimly aware of a group of men from another vessel glancing furtively at himself and the girl and waved them down apologetically. They frowned and disappeared into the flowing crowd. Sylvi brandished her palm at him again, but she was still gazing happily, desperately, at the chickens.

"Alright, alright," he said, shaking his head in disbelief. "Just make sure you get them a basket."

"They can have mine!" she called, flopping down onto her knees to peer happily into the shuffling mess of feathers.

Crow found that he was still shaking his head happily as the coins and the chickens changed hands.

"Take these back to the *Witch*, Gideon," Crow said to one of his men, and the sailor gently gathered the clucking wicker basket from Sylvi's arms. "We'll return in the hour – once I've spoken to my contact about the case."

The stout and browned sailor, Gideon, nodded meaningfully, leaving the corner place with an attitude that lent him grace, even despite the busy rustling of the basket.

"Who is your acquaintance?' Sylvi asked, "What is the case?" She immediately clamped her jaws shut, regretting the wastefulness of her frivolous questions.

"The *Witch* is not a pirate vessel in the way that you might know of," Crow began, not realising that Sylvi knew nothing of pirate ships at all. "In fact, we're really quite legitimate. Paid the right price, we move cargo safely across the seas – rather than stealing cargo that belongs to others."

"What is the right price?" she asked.

They were moving easily through the press of people. Unlike the port of Browning that she had not deigned to enter, this city was clean and squared and well built. The people wore fresh clothes, and the smells from the markets were inviting – or at least, inoffensive.

They all moved in tandem, their shoulders brushing over the crowd who parted like the sea, before the sailor at the front of the pack.

Did the men prepare for this, she thought, *or was it a natural instinct to gather around the captain?*

"The right price depends on the cargo," Crow said, looking easily around. It was clear that he had been that way before. "Sometimes it is a story, or a book, or a map."

"Or a bag of gold?" she hedged.

He laughed again, as he had when she had pressed him on the chickens. "Or a bag of gold."

"What is the cargo this time? Tell me, and perhaps I will guess the price."

"A box of old monk-made manuscripts."

"Simple. One of the books is incredibly rare, and you want it for your collection."

"Actually, the box itself is a beautiful walnut piece that would be at home in my cabin."

"Of course."

A tall, whitewashed building swam into view at the end of the street, its hand-painted wooden sign looking almost picturesque in the morning sea breeze. Crow raised his eyebrows in its direction, and the party turned their chests toward it.

"And what of me?" Sylvi asked, as they reached the heavy, dark door, and Crow raised his fist to knock upon it. "Was I the cargo, or the price?"

The shock on his face, verging on comical, was made all the more satisfying by the way his hand hung, suspended, upon the iron ring of the door knocker.

The heavy door swung inwards into the cool darkness of the large house's insides, and Sylvi pushed past Crow easily. She felt immediately uncomfortable.

"I don't like it here," she said quietly, narrowing her eyes in the gloom. "We're going to leave, now."

"We'll leave as soon as I have my crate," Crow corrected her, walking to the bottom of a sweeping staircase and peering up into the gloom of the second floor. "Carson, it's Crow!"

Something thumped in one of the upstairs rooms, and Crow's posture changed immediately. He silently caught the eye of one of the other men. They fanned out across the bottom of the staircase, weathered hands resting on the hilts and handles of various pristine weapons. Sylvi found herself pushed gently back to the door by Boron, one of the *Witch's* boatswains.

"You'll be best out here, where you can run, should things sour," Boron muttered to her, watching carefully as first Crow, and then the other three men with him, stepped lightly onto the stairs and up into the darkness.

A second thumping sound was joined by a sharp scrape as something heavy was dragged across the wooden upper floor. The last of Crow's men disappeared onto the landing as Sylvi held her breath. She felt less unsettled out on the front step, but that was in no way a comfort, for the sense of impending danger grew only stronger as Crow moved further and further away from her, up into the darkness of the house.

"I'd best be in there, should things sour," Sylvi said to the boatswain, making to move past him as she had ducked by Crow, mere minutes before.

"Captain charged me with your safety," Boron countered. It was a refusal.

"I have no regard for my own safety," Sylvi said, knowing the lie even as she said it. She made to push past him again, but he blocked her with his hip.

A sudden, loud, and sharply stifled yell erupted from the room at the top of the stairs, and Boron's momentary distraction was enough for Sylvi to slide past him, drawing his sword in one smooth motion. Although he hesitated in shock as she leapt up the stairs, two at a time, Boron was close behind her, and then beside her. In the flurry, he seemed not to have noticed that he no longer carried his own sword.

They barrelled through the door, both sinking almost immediately into a defensive crouch. Boron groped once for his weapon, but, spotting it in Sylvi's double grip, quickly flicked a second knife from his opposite hip and held it, ready, before him.

The bound man in the corner under the window must be Carson. She glanced around the room, counting. The ornate crate in the opposite corner was unopened. So *that* wasn't what the trouble was about. Crow, Boron, three other *Witch* men, and Sylvi. The strangers themselves numbered four, grouped siege-like behind the crate in the sudden rush of Crow's men. Ten in one small room was a promise of blood.

"There she is!" one of the strangers yelled, and the other three moved swiftly out from behind the crate.

"Back outside, girl!" Crow called. "If we bandy blades in here, we all end up in ribbons."

Sylvi hesitated, half-turned.

"There's a line between a sword satisfied and a glut," Crow called again, narrowing his eyes and dropping his chin to his chest so that his words took on a darkly significant meaning.

Everyone moved at once. Sylvi turned and slipped down the bannister, mindful of the edge of the blade thrown out sideways for balance. She flew off the end of the polished railing and landed, cat-like, on the grey boards of the hallway. Boron's sword skittered out of her grip, chiming as it rung and warbled against the doorframe. She cursed and chased after it, scooping the sword up by the handle as she turned to face the strangers now tumbling out into the street.

The entire company, bar the seemingly still-tied-up Carson, spilled onto the stones and spread out. The people of the city moved out of their way, but with more chagrin than panic.

"Pirates," one of them spat tiredly. And then, to someone else as they rounded the corner, "Don't bother going that way, there's a skirmish of some sorts. Fetch the watch."

Sylvi hefted the sword in her hand, rolling one shoulder against its weight. The weeks of climbing had left her upper body stronger than when last she had wielded a sword. The past still resonated, however.

The bright flame of hair under one of the other men's hoods was nauseatingly similar to one of the men she had killed, before. The one who had killed her father first.

Her breath came in gasps as though she were drowning.

Satisfy the sword, or leave it angry?

One of the other men faked around behind her in a sudden burst but was met with a stunning blow from one of the *Witch's* sailors. It was clear that the strangers were after her, but their hesitation suggested that they wanted her unharmed. The two groups were in a standoff; one which the strangers seemed at once equally eager and reluctant to break. Crow, in the end, made the move.

"You'll not have her," he cried, stepping forward and swinging his sword up toward the chin of one of the other men. "Satisfy!"

The stranger jumped out of the way of the blade but quickly brought his own long sword down to meet the rigid steel. The noise was deafening as each of the men engaged, Boron once again keeping back in Sylvi's orbit. One of the men (friend or foe?) cried out loudly, the sound eking off into a guttural sob that she declined to seek the source of.

The stranger with the bright red hair skidded along the ground, drawing blood from his knees on the rough cobbles of the street, and made to grab Sylvi around the middle.

She brought the rounded handle of the sword down on the man's forearm, feeling something crack and splinter beneath the weight of the iron and her own downward force combined. The man cried out and doubled over in pain. Sylvi made to strike out again, but the battle was aborted before it truly began, as Crow strode over to them, scooped Sylvi up easily where the other man hadn't, and marched back out of the street toward the corner where they'd bought the chickens. Sylvi threw Boron's sword back to him, allowing herself to be swept along in Crow's wake.

The feeling of danger had all but abated now that they were leaving Carson's house. The muscles around her ribs ached from the impact of Crow's arms, but she was otherwise unharmed. Boron and Crow were moving easily. It seemed as though the skirmish were more of a threat of altercation than an engagement itself.

Crow did not speak as they all but fled back to the *Witch*, and he seemed completely uncaring of his lack of books. However, there was a deep storminess across his brow, and the muscles in his neck and shoulders bunched menacingly. He was more than unsettled. He was angry.

They got back to the *Witch* unhindered, far more quickly than she had expected. When Crow ushered Sylvi ahead of him up the rope ladder it was with a gentleness that he must have needed to strive for against the adrenaline of the fight. When she glanced back, Crow was still waving each of the men ahead of himself, peering feverishly around as he scanned the docks and decks of other ships.

When Crow himself finally began the ladder climb, he used his left hand to grip, but would only wrap the crook of his right elbow around the rungs. Sylvi realised with a start that he must have injured his palm in some way. Or, had had it injured *for* him.

"Haul anchor," Crow yelled as he rolled over the side of the ship and shoved himself up off the deck. And, when the crew who had remained on deck did not move fast enough, "*Seadragon.*"

* * *

The men leapt into action, rushing back and forth across the decks as they worked sails and heaved on ropes. They glared darkly at each other as they worked, some muttering, some shaking their heads and baring their teeth. Crow himself disappeared into his cabin, at the stern, under the quarterdeck. I scampered after him, trying to keep out of the way of the bustling men.

I had never before been inside Crow's cabin, and so, I was surprised to find how homely and familiar it felt. It was modest, barely lit, and perfectly ordered. I was reminded of my own home, by the beach. A bed draped with the fur of a black bear. An upright wooden chair; clearly turned by a loving hand. The scrubbed wooden table, big enough for four.

Big enough for Crow, who, now dragging the table and one of the turned chairs across the floor and into the bright light of the vast glass windows at the tail end of the *Witch*, drew me through the memories and years, back to the present. He was using his left hand to grip the tabletop, his right curled protectively against his chest. I moved to help him, and immediately the dull scraping sound grew less as the task grew easier.

"You're injured," I observed, staring pointedly at Crow's curled hand.

He opened it out, fingers unfurling like the petals of a bruised flower. There was indeed a long, neat gash across the flat of his palm, the trailing blood now drying over his fingers and wrist.

"I can clean that for you," I said, turning his hand gently one way and then another in the light. "Was this a knife, or a sword?"

"An ungodly combination of the two," Crow growled darkly. "The weight of a sword but the size of a knife."

"It's not deep."

"It often doesn't need to be, with a cut like this. It's the swelling sickness that turns you."

"Where do you keep the linen?"

"Try the drawer in the table built into the wall."

I padded lightly over to the table and felt carefully with my fingers, bracing the seam of the wood with one hand as I gently pulled the handle with the other. The drawer slid noiselessly from its housing, but its contents rattled slightly.

There was indeed a length of wrapped linen, pristine white against the deep colour of the velvet lining. There was also a thin silver knife, a lock of golden hair tied with a pink ribbon, and a single, black feather the length of my forearm. I examined the curios for as long as I dared, and then slid the drawer home.

"Isevelt would most likely do a better job of this than me," I admitted, retrieving Crow's injured hand once more from its protective cradle.

"Who is Isevelt?"

"One of the other girls in my village. She assisted the witch who killed us both. Her father made glass. I believe that he made the bottles our blood was kept in."

"Good God." Crow hissed through his teeth but did not make to pull away. I frowned (more in consternation for myself than concentration on the task, having once again uttered a delicate truth with no care) and bent lower over the work.

"I was told that the gods did think it good. It was their wish that we be killed, after all."

Crow shook his head resolutely back and forth, while he scrubbed his eyes with the back of his uninjured hand. "To what end?"

"Protection."

"For *you* to protect the gods, or for *them* to protect you?"

I sucked the sides of my cheeks against my back teeth but did not answer. I felt within me again the wordless rage that came from the hopelessness of my existence, but I refrained from directing it at Crow. I needed answers, and in order to get them, I needed him to listen to my questions. I lightened my voice. Gave it a sweeter cadence.

"I had hoped that *you* could answer that. Am I here to offer you my protection, or to benefit from yours?"

Not sweet enough, it seemed. Twice in the one day I had offered him a binary, and each time he had reeled back as though he felt the force of both blows, as though he hadn't been spoken to with such self-assured acid in years, and found it still raised his hackles.

"It would seem I have bought myself a bit of both," he growled. "For although you protected the *Witch* from one storm, today, I protected you from another. And paid for it."

I probed the edges of linen across his hand, reprimanded but satisfied. "So, I *was* the prize."

"Yes, you were," Crow murmured, taking his hand back and flexing it gently. "After a long and dangerous race."

"How long?"

Crow stood and turned his great body so that he was looking out over the stretch of rocky coast where the city still perched, watching it get smaller and smaller as the wind pulled us back out to sea. "About ten years."

"That's half my life," I said, and Crow turned quickly to stare at me. I could discern no emotion in his expression.

"I have just realised what ten years can do for a girl," he whispered, "and it has given me a profound sadness."

His sadness was not my concern. "Why do you crawl from port to port? Why not just make yourself a good home on land?"

I ran a single finger along the grain of the wooden table at which I still sat. It smelled of leather and paper in the captain's quarters – none of the briny fish smells that had filled my own home. Yet still, I could have been sitting at my own family table, asking my own father questions that I knew very well he might not deign to answer.

Had I not had my throat cut.

"I had a home, once. A big one. Lots of land. Full of people." He sighed. "But it doesn't satisfy."

"What *does* satisfy?" I asked.

Crow turned around, grinning. "Eggs."

I smiled back, turned away once again. "Thank you."

"You gave me no choice."

"It seems I shouldn't be trusted with those, either."

"It was your choice? To die?" Crow made to move back to the table but must have thought better of it. He turned back towards the thick glass window.

I weighed the answer in my chest before allowing it to rise up my throat. "It was my choice to remain with those I loved. Those who were left to me."

"But you lost them?"

"Or I was lost. I do not know."

To my shame, I sobbed suddenly and buried my head in my crossed arms. Not knowing was agony. What of Haedi? The others? Would I find my people one day, settled on a stretch of black sand in the shade of a forest of silver birchwood? Waiting for those of us that they lost? Or were *they* lost, like me, to time? I faltered, and then gathered, and said as much to Crow.

"There are yet legends of your people, if nothing else. That I can promise you."

"How?"

Crow shrugged, quickly glancing at me but, perhaps, sensing that the fragility of the moment was like spun sugar, which, too warm, would melt away, and so he did not let his gaze linger. "They led me to you."

I clenched my fists, managing in a whisper, "Please tell me."

Crow moved over to the wall where I had found the linen, popped open a different hidden compartment, and retrieved two goblets and a dark green bottle.

I flinched as he set it gently on the table. It made a sound like bone on bone, and the liquid inside seemed too thick against the glass. Like blood. Measuring me with his eyes, Crow eased the stopper out of the mouth of the bottle and slipped it into his pocket. He tipped the bottle over the face of each goblet, and wiped the last drop with the fine edge of his sleeve. One cup he slid over until it grazed my balled knuckles, the other, he raised slowly to my health.

"Not rum?" I asked, tipping the glass by its delicate stem so that the liquid bathed the surface inside.

"You're not a pirate," he said, taking a shallow sip, which I mirrored. It was wine, pressed from red grapes, and it warmed me in a way that Will's rum hadn't. The rum had dried me, but the wine warmed.

"Neither are you."

"You speak the truth."

"I don't know what *I* am," I admitted.

"You're a waif," Crow said. "At least, that's the name given to you by legend. A young woman whose essence is captured in a glass vessel through ancient magic. The story says that, and Smith knows it better than me, if the glass vessel - or vase - is broken over the stern of a ship, the right words are said, and the magic is called upon, your *essence* will protect the ship and all of its souls in times of need."

"That's near enough to the story that I was told."

"It is?"

"Yes. Although, it is said... *vace.*" I gulped, swallowing another mouthful of wine. Tilting my head back on my neck, I nudged the ragged edge of my borrowed shirt aside, bared the dome of the vace where it clutched the stretch of my skin.

Crow recoiled, which pleased me.

"Except that my expectation was to be bound to a ship built by my people, so that I could protect them from ever facing the wrath of the gods again." *That was a lie. I did not die for them. I died for Haedi.* "How long has it been since the time of my people? How many years? Everything is different. Nothing is familiar except me. And even then... not even that."

"What does the wrath of the gods look like?"

I shrugged. "What does it always look like? Death."

He cursed again, devastated by the pragmatism in my voice.

"How many years?" I asked again, pleased that it came out with the same, cool calm.

"...Hundreds."

I cursed back, calling the wrath of the gods upon the spirit of the witch, in my own tongue. Crow would not know the meaning of my words, but he would have felt their poison in his ears. My pride at the calm of my voice burned away in the wake of my rage.

"You entered into it willingly, to offer protection to your people," Crow ventured, perhaps hoping to offer some kind of comfort. If not that, then perhaps some measure of power that I could wield on my own account.

"...Yes."

If he sensed my hesitation, he did not let on. Rather, he tipped the green bottle once more into our cups, first one, then the other. When they were full, and the wine back on the table, he spoke. "You are a worthy captain, then. For that is what it takes."

"You put yourself in danger in order to use me to protect your ship?"

"Doesn't seem as noble, now that you're a person."

Am I, though?

"How well known is this legend?" I asked, sipping again.

"It wasn't, at all. Smith came across it, years ago – he's a sort of cousin of mine, you know, in the family history. And then, we chanced upon a different story that spoke of the vaces, and so we set our minds to it." He said it more like the original tongue, this time. *Vay-ces.*

"Show me." It was a demand, and I did not apologise for it.

Crow washed away the words waiting on his tongue with the wine, swishing its silken length to measure the flavour. He returned to the wall of drawers and plucked a book, bound in fine black leather, from its place. The page was torn, and so he found it easily.

I looked long upon pictures drawn in thick lines. The face of the witch was not the face of the witch. But the curve of the knife was its own.

"You knew the words of the spell?" I spat, glaring still at the knife on the page that somehow swam in an ocean of red in my mind, taking into itself channels of blood that stained its face, as surely as it stained the freezing water in which we had drowned.

"Smith knew. Smith knows."

272 ～ K. D. KIND

"But others know, it seems. Otherwise why did the red-haired man and his men try to take me?"

"Radley's men. He is the greatest enemy I have."

"What makes him your enemy?"

"He took something of mine."

"What did he ta– wait, did you say *vaces*?" I asked suddenly. I pushed the goblet away from me roughly, angry that I had nearly missed something so important, careless of the spot of wine that pooled on the page, exactly on the point of the knife. I dashed it away, leaving a smear of blood-red across the page. "How many are there?"

The whites of Crow's eyes glowed bright as he dealt with my sudden fervour. "We found two. I bought one."

"And the other?" I cried, standing and bracing against the table. "What was her name?"

Crow stared up at me, his mouth agape, showing squared teeth. He maybe realised for the first time the reality of the other vace. The other waif.

"*Haedi*," he whispered, and the name sounded like a gasp of breath.

I slammed my fists onto the table, filled with fire at odds with my colourless face. "Where is she? Who bought her?"

His mouth hung open like a silent scream. When he finally admitted the truth, his voice was barely a murmur.

"*Radley*."

I drew myself up until I was as straight as a birchwood bough, my voice as cold as my regard. "Your enemy?"

Crow lowered his own head to his hands. "Yes."

I laughed once – a cold, biting bark – and threw the last of my wine back into my throat. "He has something that belongs to each of us, then. We are united."

"Haedi belongs to you?"

"She is my sister."

"Your sister in the sacrifice."

"No. Yes. My sister in blood, in memory, and in life. There is not a memory I have that she is not in. For even my life aboard your *Witch* has been coloured by thoughts of her."

"And she gave herself, too?"

I picked up my empty goblet and assessed the cut edges in the light. "She gave herself first. I followed her. But they killed her, first. The Witch. And Aidan. And Isevelt."

"We'll get her back. From Radley. From the *Seadragon*. I'll claim the ship as my own, and then she will be with you."

I looked at him for a long time; whatever turmoil lurked beneath my surface remained hidden under my serenity.

"What does Radley have of mine?" Crow puzzled.

"He is keeping your revenge from you."

Crow nodded slowly, the blazing light in his eyes a counterpoint to my ice.

"You'll need your sword cleaned of blood," I said finally, reaching out a single hand like an offering and a beckoning all at once. As I took the hilt of his sword in my palm, I defiantly raised the cup once more to my lips, tipped back my head and, to be sure, drained every last drop for myself.

Chapter 16

Ash

The single black tree that had been promised to us seemed more like a charred skeleton than any kind of living thing, where it towered over us in the light of the shy moon. There had been a moment, as we reached the place where the wide river spilled into the waiting arms of the sea, where the people's quiet confidence had faltered; but then I had changed the direction of the water, turned its feet until it flowed inexorably back the way it had come, taking our two little boats with it, and they had returned to reverent silence.

To say *little* boats is misleading. Each of the vast crafts – one silver, one golden – held twenty adults with broad shoulders and broadswords. I had not hesitated when the time had come, claiming my seat in the birchwood boat.

I had been to only two places in my life. The first, the village in which I was born. The second... death. To have arrived in the silent, wind-barren village of the enemy in the hallowed hours before dawn, to find it completely unfamiliar but, at the same time, in the same moment, so perfectly predictable, was like dying all over again. There was nothing remarkable about it.

Up until the point that disaster struck, there was absolutely nothing about our raid that a single person could have re-

274

marked upon. I turned the tide, we flowed upstream. In the centre of the spring, I dropped the glass vial containing the priestess' poison, and then I moved the water counter wise once more with the flat of my palm and the press of my will.

I watched the glass shatter where it hit the sharp corner of a black volcanic stone, felt something fray inside of me, and dismissed it. Darned the shredding fabric of my substance with the knowledge that not a single light had winked on, not a single rush had been disturbed by a wakened foot. Not a single sword had been drawn against us by the time we reached the mouth of the river; by the time disaster struck.

The people's swords offered no protection from the threat at hand: the river flowing far too rapidly, the boats gathering too much speed. I heard a cry from the other boat, the golden one, and cast my will and my attention out towards it.

Owning both of the vessels with my power, I flung out a net of intention, over the edges of the two boats and everyone in them, and willed the water to slow and the boats to be calm. At once the thrill that filled my nose and lungs and pulled at the roots of my hair and the folds of my clothes quieted to a lull as the water beneath us slowed to a honey pace.

But I breathed easily a heartbeat too soon. Because a cry rent the cold night air once more, like the first tendrils of sunlight that promised to peek at us over the far edge of the horizon in mere moments. The other boat had not slowed. Beneath its hull was a vast gathering of water, turbulent and washed with white foam, even as it slapped and bit at the delicate balance of the boat.

I flung my power out again, and this time *felt* the wall of resistance that bullied me back, like a malevolent and solid wind that froze; a wind that denied me purchase on the skin and bones of the golden boat.

"They are *mine*," I growled to the wind, and flung my will out once again.

The wall was even more solid this time, even more insistent, and, as an answer to my insult, I felt the wall roil and roll and heave at the curved underside of the golden boat, flinging the thing over onto its cheek with such force that all twenty of its occupants were thrown like debris from their benches as oars flew like dying birds through the air.

"Turn around! Turn around!" I yelled, spinning in the bow of the silver boat to better see the shapes in the water. Leir was in the golden boat. He was in charge of it. Master of it. And I had lost sight of him in the frantic throe.

The combination of my willing the boat to slip easily through the water with the determined work of the people at the oars meant that we reunited with the golden boat in truly no time at all. Seconds.

"Count them," I ordered one of the faceless, bearded men as I shoved past him, pushing myself in beside Wulf at the edge of the silver hull. "Twenty."

The people were pulled easily from the water, one after the other, as they were counted. Many were shivering; one was retching. Another was calling for her lost sword. I had no thought to spare for any of them. Nineteen.

"Where is he? Where is Leir?" I demanded of Wulfric, as we both peered into the darkness of the now quiet water. The mirror-smooth water.

I forced my power down into the depths like searching fingers, willing the water to find and return him to me. Like with the wall of resistance, I felt what could only be described as a slap, and quickly withdrew into the safety of my own mind. I felt numb with shock. Outraged at the offence. In my powerlessness, I was rendered useless.

"There!" Wulf cried. He tore the outer layers of his clothing from his arms, pointed once more so that I could be sure of where he was going, and dived headfirst, in a perfect arc, into the murky depths.

I watched as the white cloud of his unbleached shirt dissolved into the dimness, counted the breaths after the bubbles disappeared, kept my eyes rooted firmly to the spot that Wulf had pointed to. I hadn't seen Leir – hadn't seen any suggestion of him below the water – but Wulf had been sure. Sure enough to jump.

I managed to gather my courage and search out into the water again, wary of another blow from the power at odds with my own. Instead, I felt my will clutched in a vice-like grip that wrenched me bodily from the dry safety of the silver boat and down, down, into the sodden fathoms below.

I understood as soon as my eyes picked out the white cloud what was wrong. Wulf had found Leir and was trying to swim him up to the surface, but Leir's useless weight was too much for him, and they were both sinking at an alarming rate.

As soon as I reached them I grasped the place where Wulfric's hand clutched Leir's arm. There was a thin ribbon of black blood that somehow caught the light of the moon, where it escaped from a deep split in Leir's temple. He needed to get to the surface immediately; they both did. I could feel in my own chest the deep, deep need in Wulf's lungs for air.

The moments that followed, even as they occurred to me, took on the same strange, oily, dream-like quality that the sacrifice had, in my mind. Apart from myself, as though witnessing a poorly constructed puppet performing one of my chores, I watched as one of my hands grasped Wulf's arm, and the other Leir's, so that I was the conduit holding them together.

I watched – I didn't feel – I watched as the hand holding my brother, holding Leir, simply... *let go.*

As I swam easily back up to the surface, precisely where I had entered minutes before, away from the ghostly face of my drowning brother, each of the puppet strings snapped.

One. By. One.

I broke the surface screaming.

Chapter 17

Salt

Crow's wine was still swimming in my head as I stood in the darkness of the deck that night. Or, rather, my head was still swimming in the wine. I still reeled cold from my choice not to leave any drink in the cup for the gods. But how could I be punished more than I already was?

No, I corrected myself sternly. *How could I possibly have anything left owing?*

Haedi.

I breathed it out like a whisper, and I felt in my own breath warmth, and comfort, that draped over my shoulders like a blanket.

"Haedi." Her name on my lips was a salve.

I was not alone, as I had thought. Did my sister know that we two were in this place, bound by magic that we did not understand? I thought of our own bond, the one that had always alerted me to Haedi's presence the moment she entered a room. The one that carried our wordless thoughts across quiet and conversation, both, so that we each knew what the other was thinking and feeling without ever needing to speak.

I closed my eyes, concentrating on the feeling of the ocean breeze as it pillowed around my body and cheeks, and gathered it to myself. I breathed deep, and then pushed outwards, sending what felt like my consciousness seeking out over the waves, searching for the familiar feeling of my sister.

I could find nothing.

I closed my eyes tighter, willed my thoughts further, not even sure that what I was trying to do would work. I pushed so far that I forgot myself; forgot the ship on which I stood and the course that it now charted back around the far side of the city that we had left that morning, to find and engage in what would surely be a bloody battle with Radley's men. If Haedi was indeed with the *Seadragon*, I would surely feel her presence. I pushed again.

There... a pull... a whisper... a word...

Was that her?

A hand clapping heavily onto my shoulder wrenched me unceremoniously back to the deck of the *Witch*, leaving me frightened and gasping and ready to fight.

"I'm sorry!" cried Will, out of the darkness, raising both hands in apology.

"No," I breathed, shaking my cloudy head slowly back and forth. Despite the instinct that called me to arms, my arms themselves had risen sluggishly from my sides, and my balance had been a long time coming. "I wasn't paying attention."

"Weren't you?" He asked, stepping up beside me like one approaching a wounded animal. "*I've* been paying attention. I've noticed how hard you work to be at the edges of the ship. If you're not up in the sails, you're leaning over the edge, like you're thinking about going back into the water."

I glanced at him without turning my head. Will had his head tipped back on his shoulders so that his neck took none of the weight of his thoughts. Locks of his boyish hair had escaped the tie at the nape of his neck and moved delicately in the breeze that never stilled.

"That may be," I conceded, realising for the first time that there *had* been such a motivation within me. If what I had felt was a link to my sister, then nothing would stop us from being reunited – sea or sky or man or whim. "But it's different now. I'm at the edge of the ship so that I can be closer to where I'm going."

"Where is it that we're going?" Will asked, squinting, and rubbing his brow. "None of these past weeks have had any purpose. No direction. And now it seems as though we're doubling back on ourselves, but at half pace. The sails are trimmed."

"Crow has something to collect."

As do I.

Will scoffed. "Always."

His derisive laugh sent a puff of air towards me that swam above the salt smell of the ocean. No, rather, it sank beneath it, revoltingly sweet and cloying: alcohol.

I made to turn away, a habit that had long granted me protection, but Will clumsily caught my wrist. "No, stay."

"I don't want to." I pulled my elbow firmly, gently, down toward my hip, so that his fingers fell free.

"Please. Stay. I fear we will lose you soon. I have not yet had all of you I would wish."

I frowned, unsettled by his words. "You may have nothing of me, for I am neither inclined nor free to give you aught."

"Because you're bound to the captain," Will said, pointing at me as though discovering me in some kind of indiscretion. He smiled, but there was hurt rather than light in his eyes.

"No."

"The captain's ship, then." He took a step toward me, then away. He leaned dangerously far out over the railing, teetering on the balance point of his hips. He spoke to the waves, his words tumbling up onto the deck as they were borne on the back of the buffeting breeze. "If I were the captain, you could aid me. I have a need for your protection."

I clenched my jaw and backed away from the place where we stood, but Will swung back up to standing and advanced on me.

"I fear for my very life," he whispered, and his eyes gleamed white and scared in the light of the moon. "Truly I fear it."

"What danger threatens you?" I asked in a whisper, torn between feeling, and fleeing.

"Anyone aboard a pirate ship is threatened by something," he said. "Why else leave the safety and comfort of land?"

"Perhaps safety and comfort don't satisfy," I replied, glancing surreptitiously around. Were there any others about on decks? Surely.

He turned towards me again, took two steps closer. He was just too close. I could feel his warmth and smell the bitter honey on his breath. "The most important thing is to be satisfied," he agreed, and he seemed so solemn that it would have been comical, had my instincts not been screaming in my head.

I turned my head away again, thinking furiously. Will was the closest thing I'd had to a friend since I died. I remembered times when I would speak to Haedi just as Will was speaking to me now: scattered, unsure. Saying thoughts aloud just to heft the weight of them on my tongue, to sift for meaning. He spoke of danger, and threats. And needing my protection. But who, and how, could I protect?

"I think what would satisfy you is your bed," I said finally, and made to turn away.

His hands latched once more to both of my upper arms, and he drew me in close, as though to embrace me.

In an instant I had my hands up between us, my palms flat against his face. He moved closer, gripping me so tightly that I imagined bruises blooming on my skin.

"No," I whispered, but even *I* barely heard the word. Behind my closed eyes, Will morphed into an ugly man with bright red hair. The deck of the ship became the black sand of the bay. The damage that the ugly man had done to my first body was undone by the ritual of the sacrifice. All of my scars and brokenness were gone. I couldn't let that damage be done to me again.

"*No*," I said again, and I flung my will out from within myself, focusing on the pressure of every single fingertip on the rough and smooth of his skin. As I wrenched my body around, I felt a nearly imperceptible twist of the vace.

Water flowed immediately from my nailbeds, driving into his mouth and nose and eyes and every part of him that I could reach.

He spluttered and turned his head, let go, but the grip of my hands held him steady. He fell to his knees, and still, I held on, now because I could not bring *myself* to let go. As water cascaded violently over his face, I felt all of my heat and energy flow out of myself, weakening by the moment.

I was going to die again, and take him with me.

I'm sorry I'm sorry I'm sorry I'm...

My knees hit the deck with a dreadful thud. As I felt myself begin to evanesce into the nothingness that had claimed me for the long sleep, I thought of Haedi.

*

Two strong arms grabbed me about the middle and wrenched me away, flinging me across the deck.

"What happened?" demanded Boron, taking in the sight of the gagging and blinded Will alongside my bedraggled and retching frame.

"I don't know," I whispered, trembling. "I don't know."

Someone else lifted Will by his sodden shoulders, tucking themselves each under one of his limp arms, and leading him away into the elsewhere. Boron seemed unwilling to touch me in any similar way, and so settled for finding a thick, itchy blanket and wrapping it *just* too tight around my arms.

"Are you... hurt?" Boron asked, taking to one knee beside me, braced with a forearm on the wood of the *Witch* above my head. "Fetch Smith," he called softly over his shoulder.

Someone else ran off into the darkness, and I felt myself being raised and led by the front of the blanket, as I had been led so many weeks before by the sleeves of Will's coat.

I found myself in Smith's quarters, as I had so many weeks before, empty and confused, and feeling transparent and cold.

The bursar appeared like a grandfather, shock and concern made more obvious by the twitch of his wispy white hair, uncombed in his haste.

"Dear, dear, dear," he tsked, deftly removing the stiff blanket and replacing it with a much softer one. I was soaked through to the skin, shivering, and silent.

I was dimly aware of Smith lowering me to the pillow and shuffling out of the room.

He was gone for some time.

He returned, hopefully, with something warm to drink. Rum. Will must have told him. I refused it. He left again.

Had I killed him? Was Will drowned?

Smith returned, this time with Crow, and yet another pitcher of liquid. "Drink, drink," Smith cajoled, the force of his offering almost laughable against the gentleness of his voice. The two of them together seemed too big for the little room. Crow perched on the bed. Smith hovered. The pitcher was full of seawater and, surprisingly, when I drank it, it helped.

"Is he dead?" I asked, examining the corner of the blanket.

"Does he deserve to be?" Crow asked. His voice was deep and full, but sharp, too; like velvet dragging sand across a glass surface.

"No."

Crow leaned back, nodded. He exchanged a glance with Smith, who stood quietly and crept out of the room. I heard his little footsteps fade away up the ladder.

"I'm glad of it," said Crow, and he sounded it. "Will is of my family, like Smith. I took him on when he ran into trouble at home. Got on the wrong side of a particularly volatile uncle. Story quite similar to mine, it turns out. I'm glad that he doesn't deserve to die."

I continued to stare, resolute, at the blanket.

"But I don't know what he does deserve."

"Not me nearly killing him," I whispered. My eyes felt rounder than the shape should have permitted, my lips surely nearly invisible between clenched teeth. My body shook.

"And taking yourself along, too," Crow replied. "What did you do?"

I shrugged, but spoke, as though saying the words were nothing to me, and his to fill with meaning as meaning allowed. "I drowned him."

"With what?"

I barked a laugh. "My soul?"

Crow sighed and rubbed flat palms along the length of his thighs.

"How can you find your sister if you lose yourself?"

I closed my eyes, felt myself drifting toward sleep like foam on the waves. "How can I be lost if I find my sister?" I asked.

I held out the pitcher of water, motioning for Crow to take it from me. I was agonised. I was spent. I slid down on the bench, gathering the soft blanket around my chin.

"I've half a mind to ban rum on my ship," Crow muttered, and I laughed, and then I knew no more, only mild fear, as I sunk into the depths of the sort of sleep that only ever brought healing or nightmare.

* * *

When I finally woke, parched and aching, there was no sign of either the port city, or of Will.

He had disappeared at some point in the night, and no one had any word of him.

Any of the happiness that I had gathered about myself since breaking free from the vace had drained out of me, replaced by a singular determination: to find Haedi, and be reunited with her.

I would not be assuaged. The *Witch* would seek out Haedi and the *Seadragon*.

Crow sent scouts into the port city, but the *Seadragon* and all of Radley's men – bar the one cut down by Crow – had sailed on, with no word of their heading.

I took to the nest again – empty of chickens, for a steady rain of feathers and droppings from on high had satisfied no one – and came down only to demand an account of our progress from Crow.

There was a new sadness in Crow in the wake of Will's disappearance, and what seemed like a disappointed coldness toward me that I avoided, out of fear of having my suspicions confirmed.

Days wheeled overhead. Perfect days, or else, clouded days, where rain and thunder fought raging battles just outside the reach of my protective shield, disappearing as it broached the outward edge of my energy. Every now and then I let the rain in so that the men could drink and wash. The men, *and* the chickens.

The most that I could manage, though, was to keep the weather at bay. I'd tried, the day after Will disappeared, to call upon the *Witch* the sort of deluge that could maybe wash away my disappointment, my sadness and guilt and regret at acting out of fear more than true threat. But it had taken a full hour of straining and sobbing to gather the thunderous clouds to myself, let alone cause them to open up and join me in my sorrow.

It was the first time that Crow ever joined me in the tower when he did come, and it was the most generous he had ever been to me. Not just because he gave me a precious gift, but also because he gave me a precious pardon. I had been working a net out of spindly rope, bending and weaving a single bone hook about in endless spirals.

"What were you trying to do?" Crow asked. He had removed his great big velvet coat in order to fit inside the nest, revealing a precious silk shirt in a soft lemon yellow that I had always taken to be one of stained white cotton.

"I tried to gather a storm."

"Why?"

I shrugged. "To feel better. To give my thoughts some direction. To find an answer to a purpose, without having to wait. And wait. And wait."

Crow regarded me for a long time, waiting patiently until I was able to return his gaze. Once he had my attention, he tucked his hand into a pocket and pulled out a long slip of fabric the colour of deep, red ink. More silk.

"For you."

It was all of a colour – no thread shot through it to give it texture or depth – but it was the softest liquid material that I had ever felt. Softer, even, than the pooling blood that it resembled. For a moment I was clutching my mother's scarf. The next instant it was red again, instead of blue.

I stared at Crow, struggling for words. I knew the admission that I needed to make, the mistake that I needed to confess. But it shamed me more than the perceived transgression had.

"He misunderstood," I said finally. "William. When he asked me, what would... s-satisfy, and I suggested his bed, he misunderstood. It was an honest mistake."

Crow's glow dipped; gaze softened. "A hopeful mistake, I think, on his part."

"A fearful one, on mine." I thought of telling Crow of the man on the sand, but the words stuck in my teeth. "He will never return because he hates me," I said flatly, instead.

"He will spend some time away because he is fond of you, I think," Crow corrected, "and he is sad. And he is regretful. It is easier, I think, to push things away, than to gather them to yourself."

Desperate to say something... *anything*... I held out the newly made net like a plea.

"For you," I said simply.

"What is it for?" Crow held the net up between us, letting the loops stretch open like a map. "For wishes or fishes?"

My smile was small, but genuine.

"Yes," I agreed.

He lowered the net to his lap so that all that remained between us was a tender kindness. Crow raised the knuckle of his first finger to his lips, and I saw how he worried the fourth against a little golden ring that sat around the fifth. The kiss that he bestowed upon his knuckle was silent, as was the graze of it drawn gently across my forehead.

He left me then and did not try to join me or coax me down in the long days that followed. But he had left me the scarf and taken my net, and I had spent hours alone, letting the silk spill over my hands and catch the breeze, like blood.

Chapter 18

Blood

All around me there were yells and cries and gasping but, between Eryn and I, there was silence. I had expected that she would teach me the healing practices of *her* time, and help me to put them to work, but the truth was that the two of us became a "well-oiled machine", as one of the doctors had said.

It was lucky that the two of us were so preternaturally gifted, as the medical officers who were in authority aboard the *Valkyrie* had realised within a day or two that Eryn was only seventeen, while I was – for all intents and purposes – all but nineteen. This they chose to overlook, as we proved to be equally stalwart, equally intuitive. And resources grew more scarce every day.

It was a bloody war.

The crew of the *Valkyrie* swept across the stretch of the seas, pulling soldiers and sailors from the water and caring for them as best we could, while speeding back with all haste to the new hospital in Southampton. Before turning about and doing it all again.

We had held and beheld many dying boys in the months of our labour and, in truth, I had supernaturally saved more than a few. But, to our equally silent sorrow, neither had we seen nor heard aught of Goose or August since they had left us. We did not say their names. Not outside the quiet of our hearts. But I knew, just as well as Eryn must have known, how desperately we searched for their voices and faces in the vast sea of khaki that flowed like spilled sick-water through the rooms and halls of the gutted ship.

We knew much of each other's mind, without speaking it.

Which made the moments of companionable conversation all the more sweet. I'd never had a friend, before. Someone whose interest in me was equal to their care of me, whose attitude towards me was as constant and warm as the light of the midday sun – held tight and close and contented, forever.

I had been right when I told August that I would gain the measure of my abilities once I had need of them. I had not tried to unmake myself since the hell of the boiler room when I had sated the heat of the young stover's burns with the waters of my soul. Instead, I found that I had sway over the current of the men's blood. I could slow or speed the rate of its flow through their veins, depending on what was needed. I found that I could desiccate a wound – even just the borders of it – so that it dried, keeping seeping and infection at bay. I found that I could raise or lower a body's temperature – which was exceedingly useful, with all of the boys that we pulled, freezing, from the water. And in the days that followed; all of the boys raging with the fire of infection – the disease that stalks a mortal wound.

I found that I retained much of my natural compassion.

And although the lack of August's presence was like a long, yearning string that pulled constantly at the corners of my consciousness, from it I could almost convince myself that I knew in my soul where he was, and *that* he was, just by the direction from which I felt the pull.

The first few days were difficult, when Eryn and I were bundled into a long room on C Deck with a dozen or so other nurses and orderlies, lined with beds, and looking nothing at all like the stateroom that felt like home on D Deck, with its immodestly stained fireplace.

Perhaps the hardest moment for me had been the first time that I saw the windows. The beautiful, clear, perfect windows... slicked over in a thick black paint, as was regulation for ships such as ours. I realised the moment that I saw it, what the mysterious streaks of black had been on August's hands on the day of the funeral. He had helped, even amidst all of the horror of losing both Erik, and the *Valkyrie*, to blind her windows with mourning colours. I wondered if it had cleared his head or clouded his heart, to obscure the ship, so.

The days that followed were the worst, when we picked up our first lot of wounded men. Harder, I think, for Eryn – as the slaughter of my parents and people had prepared me, a little, for the odd colour and texture of flayed skin; "*like a new rose bud*," Eryn had remarked hollowly.

But now it was nothing. Now, as overwhelmed as we had been with the constant journey of the dead and dying to Southampton, and the subsequent, silent return to the front of the battle, it was not the endless loss that left its mark. Rather, we felt all of the victories – minuscule and magnificent – as drops of rain bringing soothing and softening to our stinging skin.

Eryn and I worked in silence over the young Lieutenant laid out on the stretcher between us, while on either side, once-white uniforms wheeled like geese over the sea of sodden green and brown. The young soldier had suffered a tearing shrapnel wound to his outer thigh. I had learned months ago what shrapnel was, along with the tell-tale shapes that it tore into a person. Eryn was holding either side of the wound taut while I concentrated my will on backing the blood away and sealing the edges of the gash. I had to constantly admonish myself as the need to rock my hips, to adjust my seat, rose, unbidden, to the front of my mind. *Focus. Ignore your discomfort.* It was working perfectly, right up until the moment that the soldier came to consciousness.

He didn't scream, exactly. In fact, I think that his exhausted, child-like gasp cut at my heart with more fervour than an outright scream would have done.

"Where am I?" he panted, the whites of his eyes showing as he tried to twist and turn, getting panicked bearings and overwhelming the best efforts of both Eryn and myself to keep him still.

By instinct I caught once more at the flow of his blood, stopping the panic from flowing too far from where it began.

"You are officially aboard His Majesty's Hospital Ship *Valkyrie*," I said, hoping to calm him, as I gently laid a cool hand along the line of his face. They always reacted well to that. To a gentle touch. In those moments, I was a mother. Or a sister. Or a sweetheart. All three. And I became so willingly.

"One of the lucky ones," he whispered.

"How do you mean?" Eryn engaged the soldier in conversation, but the meaningful stare that she offered me over the top of his attention told me to carry on with the work.

"It's just... someone told me once, that the best place to be is on a hospital ship."

"Why?"

He shrugged, then hissed fiercely through his clenched teeth at my probing touch, before schooling himself once more to soldier stillness. "It's just that... well, they don't pick you up if you're too dead. And if you're not dead enough... then they make you try again tomorrow."

"Who told you that?" I asked sharply. I knew that it sounded like a reprimand, but it was the first sign of him that I'd had since August and I put him on the train. That been Goose's reply when August asked him.

"A... friend."

292 ~ K. D. KIND

"Oh no," I said. I held the soldier's hands tightly, as Eryn took up the work around his wound. "What happened?"

The man closed his eyes as if to sleep away the weariness that made up his entire world. The pause in his reply spoke volumes. "What always happens? He died."

I bit my bottom lip so hard that I tasted blood. *Don't panic.*

Could I slow the rate of my own heart? August had been surprised that it still beat. Why was that? He never did say. And now he might be dead. Dead like Goose, if my terrible suspicions were correct.

No. I could still feel the pull.

"How?"

Eyes still closed. Mouth held tighter, though. Beneath the paper-thin lids, his eyes roved erratically back and forth while the short lashes quivered atop the swell of his cheeks like little caterpillars. The soldier had dark hair that had, at some point, been close-cropped, and now stood up at odd angles, full of mud, and gods knew what else.

"Quickly."

I glanced up to see Eryn staring hard at me, clearly attuned to my fear, but not knowing the direction from which it came, or what had set it in motion. She seemed poised on the cusp of genuine panic, waiting only for my indication that we should jump together.

"What was his name?" I asked the soldier, holding Eryn's eyes with my own and carefully exaggerating the slow rise and fall of my chest.

"We all called him Frenchie."

At that moment I was nearly sick from sudden sheer relief. I silently scolded myself for the stupidity of my quick assumptions. I smiled and slumped my shoulders, showing Eryn that all was well.

"He was French," I prompted the soldier.

"No, Yorkie. Had a French name, though."

"York?"

"Yes, North England, like. Had a real passion for tree wood. Kept talking about how timber warms a room, when we was freezing cold at night. I told him, yeah, in a fire."

I hardly heard the humour.

So, it *was* Goose. *Gustav.* It must have been.

Gone.

I smiled benignly and nodded along, keeping my chest filling, and emptying, filling, and emptying. Eryn seemed not to have realised.

I did not want to tell her.

"Well, I suspect you *are* one of the lucky ones, soldier," I told him, tying a final stitch. Then, as I did with all of them, dead or alive, I pressed a soft kiss into the centre of his forehead, before standing and signalling to the orderly that he could be moved from triage into a makeshift ward.

The orderlies never hesitated to move one of my boys on. They knew by now that if I had worked on someone, and given them the all clear, there was nothing to be gained by keeping me from another one.

This time, though, I couldn't bear the thought or sight of another one.

Still smiling tightly, I cupped Eryn's round cheek with my palm, just as I had done with the soldier mere moments before.

"I need a moment," I said, and she nodded in understanding. We all needed time and space and air to breathe, sometimes. "I won't be long."

But where could I go?

There would likely be nurses sleeping in the room that we all shared. Every inch of the deck was crammed with stretchers, or soldiers laid out on nothing but thin blankets, or rows upon rows of tightly packed bodies draped in bleached sheets.

I knew where I *wanted* to go. I hadn't even been past the door these many months, busy as I was with the work, and sad as I was at the separation. I didn't even know who was living there, if anyone. Perhaps they had filled the stateroom with bedding, or bandages. Well, I would know soon.

My feet followed the familiar path. It was perhaps only the familiarity that kept the keening wail of my soul trapped tightly beneath my tongue. Poor Goose. At least it was quick. I didn't wonder for a moment if he'd been brave, or humble. Of course he had.

I stood for a long while with my head pressed to the door, as if in prayer. I didn't hear any sound, but that may well have been because the room was devoid of its occupant, or the occupant was sleeping. I knew how easily the door snicked free of its latch, were it unlocked. The slight pressure of my hand was all it took, and the door swung open easily on contented hinges.

The room was untouched. The bed was made, as it had been when last I left it. There was within the room not a single item that I did not recognise, and in fact, there was such a uniform layer of dust atop the surfaces that I believed wholeheartedly that it had not been visited since the *Valkyrie* had been commissioned.

Silently, I swept inside and shut the door. Unthinkingly, I thanked the gods.

And then, kneeling with my head bowed before the little fireplace, still stained from the fire of my first night, I cried. And cried. And cried.

I cried for Goose, and for August, and for Eryn. I cried for me, and for my parents, and for the other girls who, like me, like every single soldier whose insides and outsides I had seen, had given so much... for such little gain.

My shoulders ached. My stomach rumbled and churned; I did not know when last I had eaten. I did not have water or salt to spare for tears or sweat, yet still, I wept. I stared at the back of my hand, remembering the press of August's lips to the skin there, knowing that each kiss I pressed to a stranger's forehead was meant for him.

Finally, feeling the wrenching, tart sensation of despair dissolve in my chest, I drew a bloodstained fingertip along the lashes of one eye and swept it across the soot stain coating the little fireplace. It revealed a streak of the white marble beneath; stark, like my own skin.

It seemed right that I draw the little line of ash, salt, and blood, carefully across the sleeve of my uniform where it buttoned at the wrist: a token, and a trophy. And a talisman, against the next loss, and the next loss. For I wore my loss on my sleeve, just as surely as the price that I had paid to win it.

Chapter 19

Ash

"He was all I had left!" I gasped, holding desperately closed the gaping hole where my heart and my faith and my hope had once been.

Gnarsa bowed her head in solemn piety. "He was the price the gods required for your success. The gods demand the last."

I abandoned the abyss where my life used to be and grasped one of the glass bottles that sat atop the witch's table. I threw it with all of my might straight at the place where her head had been, moments before, but instead of cleaving her chin from her neck, I was rewarded by the sound of the thousand thousand shards splintering from themselves and sprinkling dangerously throughout the rushes that lined the floor. The whole room would need to be re-threshed.

"Success?" I screamed, and the edges of my throat tore apart, turning my mouth into an open wound. "What success?"

Gnarsa still did not move, save to step once more out of the path of the stone that I threw at her. "You are an instrument of the gods," she scolded. "Bend your will to their desires."

"Their whims," I growled, baring my teeth. "Their conceit!"

"They let you bring his body home," she said pointedly, as though revealing a reward. "You would do well to honour that with a good, honest sea-burial."

"*I honour them not.*"

The fight and the fury left me as quickly as the sun winking out at the horizon. I had awoken, a mere week before, loving the gods. Their champion. But they had not *let me* do anything. It was Maz who had dived deep down into the black water to retrieve my brother. To salvage his corpse.

How foolish they were to have wronged *me*. Wronged me to the point where I had nothing left to lose.

"You honour them not?"

"They will have *nothing* of me, save my last breath."

Gnarsa's face was hard as she tentatively cradled her own middle, as though she felt even an echo of the chasm that was my wretched hope. "There is every chance that your last breath is exactly the price they wish for."

"How can you say these things?" I croaked. "You must fix this. *Please!*"

Her top lip curled into a sneer. "I see nothing amiss."

I stepped toward her, arms outstretched, searching for comfort, or solace. An answer. I had given everything I had, everything I was for the gods, and they had left me with nothing. *Nothing.*

They had left me as nothing.

"How can you see no wrong in this?" I whispered. "The gods didn't just let my brother die... they *took* him from me."

"They would not have done that."

"Gnarsa, I watched as they moved my hand. I felt as they used my fingers to pry Leir's gripping fingers loose, away from his own salvation."

Gnarsa turned her head slowly back and forth. "No, you are remembering it all wrong. Your eyes saw it wrongly, in the moment. This has nothing to do with you, or your brother."

298 ~ K. D. KIND

"What?"

She continued to shake her head, like a nag at a tether. "It isn't about you or Leir. It's about Wulf. The spell was to preserve the commander of the vessel. Your loyalty is to Wulf. And it was him, or your brother."

"Did you know that was the way of it, before you killed me?" I whimpered. I hated that I was pleading. But barren as I was, all I had left was to beg.

"There are many things I did not know," Gnarsa shrugged. "But what I lack in knowing I make up for in planning."

"I don't understand."

"No... you wouldn't." She leaned close, baring her teeth in a ghastly smile that mocked my own desperate grimace. "Who do you think sent the heir out to his death? Who knew where to find the enemy, drew them out of their wretched *peace* to tear our village to the ground? Who managed, finally, to draw forth from the Jarl the blood the gods demanded? *I. Did.*"

"Why would you do those things?" I gasped.

Gnarsa banged both of her fists on the table, splitting the skin on the outside of her palms. Spittle flecked at the corners of her pale lips and the whites of her eyes showed like the panic on a mare.

"Because they demanded it of me!" She cried. "Because they're given what they want, or they *take* it!"

I shrank back, back into the shadows that I imagined existed outside of the circle of her rage. I believed that she was finally, *finally*, spewing forth the secrets that she had spun about herself into cumbersome clothes.

"You would have done the same thing in my place," she growled, banging the table again and leaving smears of bright red blood across the wood. "You *have* done. And you will continue to do so, or you will find that you *do* have something left to give, and it will hurt all the more, this time, knowing that you won't escape it."

"Why did you let us live?" I breathed. "If all you needed was the blood, why bring us back at all?"

She advanced on me slowly, and I realised anew just how tall her slim figure was. She stood so close to me that her belly grazed mine. I wondered if she delighted in looking down at me.

"I didn't expect it to work," she shrugged, her voice oddly calm like the still after a slammed door. "I simply couldn't afford for you to resist."

In her sudden docility, I saw my chance. I turned on my heel and fled out of the dark little hut. I was distraught. Desperate with anger and grief and a deep, violent desire to burn the grey house and everything in it – witch included – to the ground.

I set my jaw and bared my teeth to the cold air, seeing again and again in my mind the face of my brother as he slipped away from me in the water, bubbles of air escaping from his nose and mouth in shock and fear and sudden sadness. His last thought must have been that I murdered him, and, in realising this final betrayal, he had stopped fighting for his own life. Let go of it.

I hadn't seen Wulf since we returned with the dawn and the dead. Rather, I'd come straight to the witch's house, seeking some kind of help... of healing, or relief. Where was he now? With Leir?

I stopped at the point where the worn foot-track branched into two separate directions and thought. I thought with all of my disciplined desperation. Teeth still bared; fists still balled.

This was not the first time that Wulf had had to burn a brother.

I spun on the ball of one foot and ran up and around the huge, sheer face of the first cliff where it cleaved itself out of the earth and strained, shameless, toward the sky. I knew that I would not sleep another moment. Would not eat, or drink, or in any other way be satisfied. Not until I had righted this most monstrous of wrongs and removed the stain of blood from my hands and my home.

Wulf would help me.

Wulf owed me.

He had claimed his own life in the place of my brother's.

Worse, he had claimed *my* life in the place of his own.

He was where I expected to find him, in a shallow cave formed from the weathered overhang of a sheer edge.

Sobbing.

I set my jaw and flicked the errant hair out of my eyes, banishing the disgust that rose like acid at the sight of him failing to face the world and his wrongs.

I slid easily over the edge of the earth and into the little hollow that held our despair, like a clutch of snake eggs under a hen. The rock was gritty beneath my fingers, but as the wind ceased pulling at the ropes of my hair and rustling the fabric of my clothes, I pushed it roughly from my mind as easily as brushing my palms against my thighs. It didn't matter.

"Gnarsa killed your brother," I panted, paying no heed to the tears and other mess streaming down Wulf's cheeks. "She told me."

"Why...?"

"Because the gods told her to."

"No... why did she *tell* you?" His mouth hung open in grief and pain, his teeth normally even and straight, now looking like a crooked gate. "She must have known that admitting that would mean her death."

"It will," I vowed, my abused voice lending the promise a bloody edge.

"Does my father know?" He made to stand up from his crouch. A shadow passed eerily over his features, pulling the anguish from them, and leaving a dry resolve in its wake. My sudden realisation of his indiscretion robbed my regard of any respect.

"Is this how Haedi managed you?" I asked.

"What?"

"Nothing. No. He doesn't know. Not unless she told him."

"I need to tell him. She needs to be brought to justice." He pushed past me and made to scramble up, out of the cave, and onto the bed of sweeping ribbon grass above.

"Wait, Wulfric!"

"Come with me," he commanded, and my hands and feet obeyed.

"Stop!" I cried. He slowed, paused. "You *can't* order me – it's not fair. I have no choice!"

His face paled as he gulped. "I'm sorry."

"Then make amends," I said. I strode towards him, feeling the grass grab and slice at the fabric of my skirt. "Make it right. Help me *end* this."

Now that we were up on top of the cliffs again the ferocious wind bit and snarled at our skin. It tried to snatch my words away, as though the very air served the gods who traded in blood, stealing any power that I had claimed through collusion. But there was their error: my power now came from the very bond that they had forced upon me.

Now, Wulf owed me a debt.

Chapter 20

Salt

I lay pressed into the corners of the basket, a hundred feet above the waves, feeling the ship around me rock like a child's hand-turned horse, wondering where all of my lost people had gone.

I wonder if Gnarsa got away with it, I thought to myself, trailing one hand over the hot, dry skin of my other arm. *Or, perhaps Valder killed her.*

There was a small satisfaction in that idea.

Did Gnarsa know what she was doing? I thought, examining the quality of my skin. *How much control did she have over the thing? Did she expect us to be truly alive again? Or was her hope for a set of spirits... of nothing more than energies?*

My attention was caught by a calling gull, gliding just outside of the scope of my vision. *I can certainly make choices. That would have been an inconvenience to her. Is that why I'm here? Now? Because I would have been too much trouble?*

I called to my mind a picture of Haedi, fierce and sure. The dark hair, framing a pale face. Onyx black eyes. *She won't look like that, now. She won't have the birthmark on her jaw. Will she know me? With most of myself stripped away by salt and sand? And time? And grief?*

A second gull called back, gliding overhead on a river of hot air.

How will she react, learning that she lost Wulf?

One of the sailors called out below, sounding like a third gull.

Perhaps I will be enough. I am hers. She is mine.

A realisation, sudden and sour, bloomed hot and quick somewhere in the cavity of my chest. Haedi was mine. But what, *or who*, had belonged to Crow?

I slipped easily over the edge of the basket, climbing effortlessly to the main deck by use of my hands alone.

"Where's Crow?" I demanded of a passing sailor, grabbing him by the sleeve.

I followed his jutted chin to the main tiller, where Crow stood, legs apart, working the massive wooden wheel alone. I stomped towards him, aware of the parting of people in my path even if I didn't see them.

"You said he took something of yours," I said, gripping the wheel and pulling it towards me. I felt the wheel stop in its turn as he tightened his own muscles against my insignificant strength. "Something? Or someone?"

"Gideon!" Crow called, directing another sailor to the tiller as he turned his back on me and marched toward the darkness of his cabin.

"Who does Radley have?" I asked again, hurrying to keep up with the captain's strides.

"In here," Crow responded, pushing aside the door and allowing me to enter past his open chest.

It was as dark as always in the cabin, and I realised as I marched towards the compound windows that there was no other light in the place. No hearth, no candles. Not a lamp in sight. Did the captain eke out his evenings bathed in no light but that of the moon and the wheeling stars?

"Well?" I demanded, turning from my thoughts, and crossing my arms. "Does it all come back to this?"

"All what?" Crow asked, sounding bone tired. His shoulders sagged.

"*This.*" I gestured expansively. "Your efforts to find the vaces. Sailing into that storm. Me."

He sighed. I noted distantly that, where I tipped my head back on tired shoulders, Crow's head hung forwards. The angle between frustration and defeat. I moved closer, three quick steps across the thick red rug rolled out atop the *Witch's* wood. There was a telling moisture at the corner of his eye.

I had only seen my father cry once in my life. It had been when the Jarl's son had died. The oldest one. Locx.

I had come home from walking along the sea cliffs with Haedi. Haedi had been all but obsessed with being out on the edges of the earth in those last days. We'd both known that something was wrong even as we approached the low stretch of our home. Everything about it had seemed normal: the cold grey smoke that spoke of a warm hearth fire; the heavy door flung open to let in the light; the quiet murmuring voices... but those quiet words had screamed of awful, terrible things. The next Jarl washed up on the black sand beach, with a broken boat and a broken sword and a broken body full of rents and rips.

Haedi had turned and fled immediately, off to find Wulf. But I had remained, stayed by our father's side, allowed him to cry and not even pretended that I didn't see.

Here, in this moment in the dark cabin, with the dark captain, reminded me of those minutes with my father. The tears leaking like fat drops of sap to creep slowly like ice into the wild beginnings of beard on his cheeks. And the desperate sadness of a head hung low.

"I know what it is," I reminded him quietly, "to follow someone into death and then to wake up alone."

Crow opened his eyes and peered into me, judging and weighing, with sight and faith. I had been a disappointment in the most unfair sense, in that, I had failed to live up to the desperate dream version that he had of me in his mind. I had been sullen, and fickle, and unpredictable, and nothing like the warrior of the waves that his hope had envisioned.

But perhaps he had been wrong about me.

Crow shuffled over to the clean wooden table at which we had taken our wine and lowered himself tiredly into a chair.

"I loved a woman, once," he said, blinking his eyes until they were dry.

"Only once?" I quipped and, despite himself, Crow smiled.

"Once is enough, when it's like mine was. Burned me up until there was nearly nothing left of me."

"So, Radley has your woman."

"No."

I raised my eyebrows. Crow breathed slowly in through his nose, hesitated. Like the pause before the fall down the far side of a swell.

"The woman was Radley's sister."

"I see," I said, untruthfully. And then, "*Was?*"

"She passed. A sweating sickness. It was quick. But there was a child."

"A child?"

"A daughter."

"*Your* daughter."

"Daughter of my heart, if not my body."

"You've done all of this for a child?"

He offered me a watery smile, along with open and apologetic palms. "What other reason could possibly justify half of what I've done?"

"I would do all of it, and more, if it meant having my sister," I admitted quietly.

"Then we need to come up with a plan." Crow pointed imperiously to the wall opposite, which was riddled with drawers, cupboards, and owl holes. "Fetch some paper, and a pen."

I rummaged, eventually finding a stretch of white paper that was blank on one side and decorated with tally marks on the other. "Will this do?"

"Yes, and the feather pen in the same drawer as the linen cloth."

I eased the familiar drawer open again, bracing the hard corner with the heel of my palm so that the wood on wood wouldn't cry out in its distress. There, next to the lock of hair, was the long black feather.

"How many of the things from this drawer are of your family?" I asked, bringing both the feather and the golden knot over in upturned palms. I offered them to Crow, and he took them both reverently.

"In a manner of speaking, all of them. Because what is family, if not a claim?" He reached blindly under the table and retrieved a little glass pot, the lid of which he carefully unscrewed.

"What was her name?" I asked, as Crow spun the lock back and forth in his fingers like a straw of hay.

"Cloette."

"Beautiful."

"Yes." He clutched the lock tightly in one fist, drew it protectively under his chin. With the other hand, he began to slowly draw what looked like a line of coast, complete with islands and inlets. "Radley has a kind of... terrible magic... of his own. A liquid fire that floats on top of the water, drawn to living things, or ghosts of living things. Bodies. Wooden ships. It latches onto anything it touches and burns and burns, and the only thing that can beat it is water on water, suffocating it. Ripping apart its fabric and denying it the right to breathe."

"That's quite a magic to possess."

"Yes. When my woman died, he demanded her body by right of blood. She and I had no law between us, only love, and so I had to give her to him." I wondered if Crow had ever told this story before, had ever given words to the pictures that swam like sea monsters before his staring eyes. "Radley did not ask after Cloette, and so I kept her with me. But Radley was jealous. *So* jealous. He couldn't stand the thought of me trying to get Daya's body back. So, he sent the fire after my ship, in his own grief and anguish. Making sure I couldn't follow."

I carefully gripped his clenched fingers, turning his fighting fist to a knot of comfort.

"But he did not ask after Cloette. Didn't think on her, count on her. And so, when she threw herself into the sea, to try to swim to her mother, he did not – I think – even realise the fate to which he sent his own niece."

"He doesn't know of your revenge?" I asked, shocked.

"He doesn't count on it. But he should. Now that I have you, his *Seadragon* will be worthless. I have bided my time. But now, he will pay."

"And Haedi will be free," I added.

"Yes." He sighed, squeezed my fingers, slapped his palms on the tabletop, a man of business, once more. "Smith will most likely be in his quarters at this time of day. You should speak with him, while I make our map. He has some knowledge of the *Seadragon*. And to get back our own, we're going to need knowledge, *as well* as magic."

* * *

"It seems as though the magic relies on blood," Smith suggested as he rifled through a big wooden box, seemingly looking for something.

"Are you truly just realising that now?" I involuntarily ran my fingers over my throat.

Smith paused in his ferreting, aghast.

"No, my dear, not in that – I mean, rather, that each of the parties involved in the... sacrifice, and the waking... need to be bound by *shared* blood. Lineage. You see?"

"Family."

"Generations."

"So, you are my relative?"

"Collateral descendent, is the most correct term."

"And Crow?"

"Yes, him too."

"How is he related to you?"

"Cousin, of some sort." Smith's words were muffled by the box that his head disappeared into. He promptly reappeared, having apparently found the thing for which he was searching. "Here."

Smith pressed a volume into my hands. It was covered in a dark blue cloth, and gilded simply, albeit beautifully.

"What is this?"

"Poetry. But that's not the appeal. I've written down, in the front there, the words that I learned for when you... the breaking..."

"The witch called it returning, if that helps."

"When you returned. Can you see?" He gently took the book from me, flipped the cover slightly, and then settled it back into my waiting palms. I stared at the shapes scrawled across the page but could discern no meaning from them. I shrugged and handed it back to him.

"Ah, of course, so sorry..." Smith perched his glasses on his nose and read in a tremulous voice. "*As the sea is filled, so am I filled. The salt of my blood will be sea water, until the blood of my Blood calls me to return* – oh! Yes, I see, it's right there, *return*!"

The words were not exactly the same. But they were close enough. The witch had made us all learn them by heart – saying that it wouldn't work, wouldn't be convincing to the gods, if we had to be prompted in our promises to them. But the detail was lost to me, amidst the memories that flooded back to drown me.

I was back in the bay, as I had been so many times before: washing my hair; cleaning a tool; talking with my sister. The water was cold where it lapped at my waist. I was wearing a white shift, which was not enough in the weather, but it hardly mattered, considering that I was about to die.

What concerned me more was the feeling of being exposed – watched – by so many desperate faces. The ones who longed for the return to relationship with the gods, blurred in agonised countenance with the ones who desperately wanted their children returned to them. Their faces moved as though they were wailing. I heard none, heard nothing; nothing but the rush, rush of the ebb and flow of blood in my throat, so close to my ears, as though I were already one with the ocean.

The witch's lips were moving. Isevelt was shaking, hesitating. Haedi gripped my hand, but had eyes for no one except Wulf, who had half stepped forward, mouthing something – the same thing – again and again – *promise promise promise promise prom* – and then Haedi was walking forwards, her head bowed. Gnarsa pointed at me – a command, to stay. Did she believe that the magic would work? That I would return? That if I returned, it would be for a purpose?

The only purpose that remained was Haedi.

Mother, father, gone.

I would follow Haedi anywhere. Even into death. And then, hopefully, life. I licked my lips, gathered the words. The knife was at Haedi's throat.

We would all say the words together. Four of us when Haedi died. Then three, when Aidan died. Two, for me. Isevelt spoke on her own. Poetry. We chanted together, a rhythm with no rhythm, like a heart full of fear, getting thinner and quieter as each girl was killed.

"Sea fill sea, salt fill me
Salt I be
To Blood break me free
Visceral vessel
Of ash, salt, and blood
Ever this vace be pressed to my skin
Let death be without
And life be within."

It took the pressure of Smith's heavy hand on my shoulder to return me to the little room in the depths of the ship. I blinked seawater from my eyes.

"Say it again, slowly," he whispered, unscrewing the top of a pen, and setting it above the scrawl in the book of poems.

I repeated it, shivering over certain phrases.

"I've altered it a bit," he admitted, "to make the rhythm more... modern. Get the tense right, you know. It's beautiful. In an ugly way."

"Sacrifice often is."

"Did your people have a long history of... sacrifice?" Our conversation felt stilted, due mostly to Smith's obvious desire to balance his thirst for information with the reality that I had experienced a very real, and very great sadness. Nevertheless, he pressed on. "Was this the first attempt? Only, you seem woefully uninformed..." Smith tugged on his ear and then reached for his spectacles. He seemed outraged and intrigued all at once. "What were you told would happen, once you... returned?"

I nodded passively, without thought, as though content in my ability to repeat a lesson rote learned. "The people were building a fleet of boats from the birchwood that circled the bay. When the boats were completed, we would be safely returned; bound to a boat and its captain, and then to war."

"Against the gods?" Smith sounded confused, but intent on keeping up with the narrative.

"No. With the flame people."

"Now, just wait a minute... who are the flame people?" His confusion was softened by intrigue.

"The enemy." I knew that I wasn't being particularly forthcoming. I knew that it was good to tell Smith these things. But I also knew the way that remembering it all stung my throat and scorched my eyes like the acrid smoke from a too-young bough, thrown in the fire before its time.

Smith stood up. He walked halfway to the little door, turned, and marched back. "I need a drink," he said.

"You don't. It doesn't matter."

"It might matter, though." Smith sat back down atop a precarious pile of papers and boxes. "What characterised the flame people?"

I shrugged. "Red hair. And death."

"Beyond that. *Think.*"

I flapped my hands impatiently. What did it matter? What weight did all of this have against the need of now? What could be gained by living it all again? "Tell me what you want to hear."

He regarded me pensively. "I think," he said eventually, "that we cannot discount the truth of magic that flows through the veins of your story. Of this legend. I *think*... I think that there is something eternal and inevitable... in the way that you are meeting your enemy, again, after five hundred years, and that *you share that same enemy with your captain*. We have meddled in things beyond our ken, but not managed to meddle at all, because of the sheer enormity of the thing."

"The eternal enemy?"

Smith nodded, his tongue sticking out from between his little teeth. "It is not *possible* for you to exist, and to not demand a reckoning from this enemy. You simply *cannot* mutually exist."

"And who is our enemy?"

"Radley. The captain of the *Seadragon*."

"That's ridiculous," I said dismissively. "Neither my people nor our squabbles warrant such cosmic preservation as you are suggesting. You've missed the meat of the matter."

"No, my dear, I think that perhaps *you* have," Smith corrected me. "What happens to rum while it sits in its vat?"

I tried my hand at dry wit. "I don't believe such a thing is possible – especially not on a ship captained by Crow."

Happily, he chortled. "No, sharp tongue. It grows more potent. Perhaps the original purpose to which you were put has expanded. Stretched? Solidified."

"My original purpose was to ensure that my sister's purpose was realised," I corrected him.

"How do you mean?" The question was quick and sharp. I half expected him to pick up a pen and write down my words.

"My sister was going to be the wife of the next Jarl. She believed that it was her duty to serve the people in any way that she could. But, alas, she was the firstborn."

"That is normally the more favourable position in which to be born, I think."

"Normally, yes," I sighed. "The gods constantly demand sacrifice. The gods require the last. The last cut of meat. The last draw of milk from a goat. And we were told our giving would leave us satisfied. But then, things started going wrong. People, children, started dying. And none new were being born." I paused, traced the inscrutable words of the book's cover with a white fingernail. "And there were other things... There were four of us who died. Haedi, and then Aidan, and then me, and then Isevelt. I think. I didn't see Isevelt die. We were the youngest in the village. The last."

"Good god," Smith said, the horror in his words strangely familiar. Someone had said that to me, recently.

"I wouldn't have agreed, except that Haedi volunteered. And I was... I *am*... younger than her, so if I didn't offer myself too, then her sacrifice would mean nothing."

Smith inched closer to me. While he cleaned the glass of his spectacles, he spoke, like an offering that I might choose to ignore, should I have wanted to.

"You say that Haedi was willing to give anything for the people," he said. His next words he punctuated with the press of his fingertips in the bowl of my palm. "And you were willing to give anything for Haedi. The question that we should ask those in power over us... to test them... is not necessarily what *we* are willing to *give*, but... what *they* are willing to *take*."

He allowed me a long stretch of silence. Smith was similar to my father, as Crow was, but in ways that complemented each other. My father would have made a cut and then waited for the blood to dry, just like Smith, before moving on to the next limb.

"Do you know why this ship is named the *Silver Witch*?" Smith asked.

I glanced around. "Because it's made of silver birchwood."

"Just so. And the *Seadragon*?"

"The magic flame."

Smith shook his head; a negation. "The men of the ship are all of a relation."

"Is that so?"

"Characterised by their *flaming red hair*."

My memory flashed with an image of the men that we had met in Carson's house. The burn of red hair, curling on a collar. I closed my eyes tightly as the group of men became a marauding band blazing through my village, dragging my mother out of our house by her golden braid.

"You say that without your death, your sister's sacrifice would mean nothing?" Smith asked, bringing me back.

"Yes."

Let the blood dry.

"I think that's a load of bilge water."

Move on to another limb.

I looked down at my hands. "Yes."

"Don't you see?" Smith asked, taking my hands, and lifting them up like a promise. "You're *supposed* to be here. You're supposed to meet the *Seadragon*. You're supposed to rescue your sister."

"And then?" I asked, feeling a tightening in my chest, which was still somehow preferable to an unravelling.

"*And then*, indeed, my dear."

Chapter 21

Blood

Our days had taken on a tumultuous rhythm that was as punishing as the most ferocious tide. Our journey began (over and over and over) in the same way, as we ferried screaming, stinking, dying men from the back lines of battle across the sea, to be divested like the most valuable treasure upon the shores of Southampton. And then, in what could only be described as the nearest thing to silence attainable amongst a hundred people, we made our way back again.

I hadn't told Eryn of my suspicions about Goose's death. I had managed to convince myself that it was impossible for anyone to ever be *truly* gone, while ever even one person still held out hope for their life. And while I didn't know whether Eryn and Goose had been particularly close, it was clear that she and August *were* – and so, Goose belonged to her by proxy.

I had let Eryn in on the secret of the undisturbed stateroom, and, in turn... in a generous display of confidantes... she had welcomed me into the secret of the hidden library.

I knew the ins and outs and backs and forths of the *Valkyrie*, but only as one might memorise the pattern and shape of caves underground. Laid out like a vascular map, I could only know of its accoutrements if I sought them out and saw them for myself. When the ship was being built, August had insisted on a display of precious books and maps in the first-class reading room. These had mostly been removed around the same time that the windows were painted black. But some of them had been hidden away in a tiny antechamber, behind a false wall, next to the reading room fireplace.

Eryn told me that this was the only true, working fireplace aboard the whole ship. That its function came only from the single flue that carried the exhaust and smoke up, up through the innards of the decks, and into the rear smokestack. The antechamber was originally for the pure mundanity of keeping firewood. Perhaps there was an element of humour in the decision to move the small library there; in a world run as mad as this one, it may be that the only beautiful use for a collection of pages was to keep the ignorant and bull-headed comfortably warm.

We sat in the secret antechamber sipping, from steaming and cracked mugs, the tea that we had brought with us from Southampton. It had cost a fortune, and we drank it black and unsweetened.

"Would you like for me to tell you my most precious memory?" I asked Eryn. My words crept lazily through the companionable silence, not as a way of interrupting it, but more as an accompaniment, like a low harmony coaxed from the throat of a woodwind instrument.

"I don't imagine you would expect me to say no," Eryn replied quickly, eager as always for a crumb of my history.

I blew across the top of my cup, delighting in the way that something as simple as my breath could cause the tendrils of steam to hurry and bluster out of my way, as though shepherded by someone terribly important.

"I have two," I said. "One from after I was born, and one from after I died."

"Tell me the one from your old life, first."

"It's a simple thing. I had a quarrel with my parents."

"And you treasure this memory?"

I could tell that Eryn was thinking of her own parents, who, from all I had observed, did nothing *but* quarrel, and I rushed to appease her.

"I do. I remember that I spent most of the last months of my life in a state of comfortable conflict with my parents. You see, they knew that I was the last child born to the people. The last child born to them. They were loath to let me out of their sight."

"They were overprotective?"

"I thought so at the time," I admitted, allowing a smile to form around the lip of my cup. "I think, now, though, that it was more likely because I was precious to them... no, not *me*. My *life* was precious to them. And for me to be away from them meant that I was living it out... without their company. They didn't want to miss out on a single moment of the life that they had gifted me with."

Eryn stood restlessly. She shuffled over to the wall lined with cleanly drawn maps. "Do you think they missed you?" she asked.

"They didn't get the chance to," I reminded her. "They died before I did."

Eryn reached up and traced a coast to the north of the map. "I'm sorry."

"Death is always abhorrent," I agreed, by way of passing the ill-spoken sentiment by, as one would cross to the other side of a path to lend decorum to a drunkard.

Eryn placed her empty cup atop a stack of encyclopedias and ran both palms across the dun-coloured continents on the wall. "We have travelled so far," she lamented. "So little to show for it."

"Where do you think I was born?" I wondered, placing my own cup, still half full, next to Eryn's. "Not England. The days don't feel the same. The sun walks a different path."

"Describe the day to me."

I closed my eyes. "The coldest day was nearly completely night," I said. "The warmest had no moon."

"That means you were either up here, or down there," Eryn said, encompassing the whole world in the stretch of space between her arms. "What was the land like?"

"We lived in a bay, entirely of black sand and black rocks. There was a sweeping forest that crept up to our gardens made of silver birchwood. The same wood that adorns most of this ship," I said. "The water was a deep, precious blue, almost the ink of a pen. The earth rose up behind the village along the coast in a great weeping arc, like sobs, and then fell away as though the stone had been pared off by a heavy sword, to land like shards in the water."

"It sounds beautiful. And terrible."

"It was," I agreed. And again, "It was. But I don't think that I realised, then, how terrible. It's only been with my hands soaked in the blood of war that I fully understand how often my hands were worked with blood, even before my own poured out into the sea."

Eryn let her hands fall to her sides. "God, it feels insane when you talk like that. I know that what you are saying is true, because I saw August pull you from the water. I *saw* the terror in your eyes as he wrapped his jacket around you, to hide your body that looked... lifeless. Like a dead thing. But... if your gods are able to do *that*... to give you life after death... where are they now?"

I worried a loose piece of skin from my lip with my tongue, trying to order my angry thoughts into words that would not sting my friend. "I don't think they ever really went away. I just think that people must have realised they weren't worth dying for."

"What do you mean?"

The skin came free, and I was left with the conundrum of what to do with it, hating the way it felt in my mouth. I swallowed it quickly, telling myself sternly that it was gone now, it was *gone*, so never mind how uncomfortable it had felt.

"We were told – we *believed* – that the power of sacrifice lies in death. The greatest gift of all. But I think that was a lie. Either the gods were wrong, or we were wrong to believe it." I could see that Eryn was still wrestling with words too sharp, words that threatened to cut. I hadn't made my meaning clear. "Imagine this. What power is there in a bolt of lightning that strikes once, and cleaves a bit of rock from a mountain? Only what constitutes it. Consider instead the power of an ocean that rolls, time and time again against the face of a rock, like a tongue wearing away at the rough of a tooth, until it is smooth. My death was not a sacrifice, it was a submission."

"Obedience, submission, sacrifice, gift," Eryn muttered, like a list.

"It's not just that the boys will run straight at the bullets – it's that they got on the boats, climbed up the hills, pulled themselves out of the holes. And again, and again, tomorrow, and tomorrow, until it is done."

"With no promise that there'll be a tomorrow," Eryn murmured.

"Exactly. I went to my death thinking that it was temporary, that it was no real loss. Where is the sacrifice in that?"

Eryn reached forward and gripped my hand. "The sacrifice is in what you're doing with your tomorrow, and your tomorrow."

"I–"

My words were suddenly choked by a fierce shuddering from beneath and all around us. Where we were, at the back of the ship, was directly above the auxiliary propellers, and something had just happened with them. Something important.

"Quick," I said, pulling Eryn along behind me as I plotted my mental path up to the promenade, where we might learn more about the strange shiver in the ship.

"Were we hit?" Eryn cried.

The *Valkyrie* had her green stripes painted onto a white field; she wore her humanitarian crosses like huge badges on both of her sides. If we'd been hit it was breaking the rules. But perhaps *we* had hit something, or the captain had ordered us to suddenly change course...

"No," I said confidently. *I would know.*

"I'll be there in a few," Eryn called as she veered away down a hallway toward the sleeping room.

I didn't bother to respond. There was a sudden urgency in me, made all the more elastic by my sharp, aching awareness of the pull that felt like August. Was he nearer? Was he hurt? Was this the sudden swell before the snap?

I gained the promenade, found the captain.

"Captain!" I cried, pulling myself up straight and saluting as befitted his authority. "Have we changed course?"

The ship's master looked the way every man in this war did. Tired. His uniform was well creased, but the threads were soft from wear. His eyes wore heavy bags of responsibility, and although he had clearly shaved that morning, there was a patch of stubble below his left ear that had evaded his attention.

"Nurse, how do you do?"

"As fine as the day, Sir," I replied.

"I say, are you quite well? Only, you're incredibly pale..."

"Fine, thank you, Sir. I was just wondering if our commission had changed?"

"From what?"

"From the back and forth."

The captain glanced at me sharply, and I read suspicion as it danced boldly across his features. It was not proper for me to be asking such questions. "I shan't be saying."

"Sir, with all respect, we need to go to wherever it is we're going to, *now.*"

"We are waiting until we are needed. The rules say that we must not interfere, must not engage."

The pull was like breathlessness.

"There is imminent danger," I said. I placed a hand on his arm.

The captain raised his bushy eyebrows. "My dear, we are at *war*. Of course there is imminent danger."

"Will there be changes to routine?" I asked. I concentrated on the place where we touched, focused on slowing his heart just enough that he felt calm. Safe. It worked on the dying.

Aren't we all, though?

"Possible," he sighed, frowning at me as he scratched the missed line of whisker beneath his ear. "We've been picking the boys up from a land campaign. We've just heard that the next offensive is sea-to-land. So, there might be more boys pulled from the water."

Again, the tug at my heart. *August.* I tightened my grip on his arm.

"We can't break the rules of the game," the captain repeated, but he seemed unsure. As though I could change his mind if I only gave him the right words.

"We don't need to break the rules," I whispered. I pleaded. "We just need to be close enough to pick up the pieces."

I begged.

Chapter 22

Salt

The crew of the *Silver Witch* were gathered in the moonlight, the planes and edges of their faces picked out like molten silver bones. The ocean breeze flicked and brushed incessantly at their clothes, and at the sails, which were trimmed tight while they waited to make their move.

Crow stood before them, a mountain of a man in deep black and red brocade. Men of his profession often wore such finery until it fell to rags. Rare were the men who wore the luxurious fabrics that they, themselves, had always owned, as most often the riches were pilfered. But Crow was a rare man, indeed.

He spoke and his voice hovered below the hiss of the wind, and above the low boom and creak of the *Witch's* hull: a sonorous hum that spoke of both passion and fear. He spoke to persuade and to pardon.

* * *

"You should tell them," I had suggested, as we took wine in his quarters earlier that day. "You should tell them for *what* they fight, and then you should allow them to choose to fight or flee."

"That is not how it's done," Crow replied. "They ask to join me, and they know that request means my protection and provision, and in return, they fight for me."

"You ask them to sacrifice their lives."

"Aye. It might come to that. We've had more than one contact with the *Seadragon*, and not once have we walked away without scathe."

"What you need from your men is to find courage in the face of their fear. And they *will* find fear. The power of sacrifice comes from a willingness. If they are not willing to die, they will not lay down their lives."

Crow was shrewd enough, or I was blatant enough, for my meaning to be clear.

"I cannot promise them life after death," he said.

"No, nor should you. You can give meaning to it, though."

* * *

"You know that we have long had quarrel with the *Seadragon*," Crow began, addressing the cresting waves rather than the expectant faces of the men. "Some of you may know my history. Some may..." he paused, pondered. Changed tack. "Radley killed my girl. Without thought. Without care. How many of you have lost life or limb to that dog? His ship is a weapon that he has no right to wield."

His eyes found Sylvi who perched carefully on the railing of the forecastle, where the crew were gathered like crabs in a net – all claws and tough exteriors. Sylvi herself wore the blood-red silk about her throat. She nodded to him, once.

"I ask you to board the *Seadragon* with me, and bring our revenge back to the *Witch*. If you wish not to do so, you may take the boats to the nearest port."

The men shifted and glanced at each other. They'd never been given such a choice. Boron, one of the boatswains, edged forward.

"If your daughter was killed by Radley and his lot, why have you not got them back before?" He asked.

"Hopeless," another sailor, Gideon, replied before Crow could speak. "You heard him say that Radley has that magic fire that ruins anything he sets it on. It'd be suicide."

"So, you're asking us for suicide?" Boron asked.

"No."

"It's her, isn't it?" asked Gideon, cocking his head toward Sylvi. "You know that she has some kind of magic that will protect you?"

"Protect all of us, I believe," said Smith softly, sidling out from behind one of the taller men. "What better remedy to magic fire than magic water?"

"So now it's just men on men?"

Crow nodded. "Men, and men, and revenge."

This bore consideration. The sailors shared furtive glances that grew boldly to shrugs.

"Do we know where they are?"

"We will find them," Sylvi said. Her voice was deep and mysterious but brokered no further questioning.

"And then? What then?"

Crow answered. "Man to man. We hook and leap onto the *Seadragon;* close quarters combat. If it suits, the waif will join us. She's more use with a sword than without one." He nodded at Sylvi. "We just need to find Radley, and once we have his hat and his compass, return to the *Witch*."

"What happens to the *Seadragon*?"

"It is ours. Staunchest man gets the wheel, hat and compass, under Crow," Gideon said, nodding slowly.

"And the crew?"

Smith answered. "That depends, as they say, on who has the rum."

Sylvi felt a pang of sadness deep in her chest. "Do they say that?"

"They also say that preparedness is the mother of success. So, let's away." Crow surveyed each one of his men. "I offer you leave. I implore you fight. I assure you my best protection."

Crow thumped quickly away toward his quarters, giving any men who wished to leave the honour of doing it without being watched by him. It was a generosity that showed that he truly meant the meat of his words.

* * *

"This is for you," Crow said, pressing a sword into my hand. "I cleaned the blade myself."

"Rust or blood?"

"Likely both."

The night was clear, like glass; the air could cut. Our lungs burned with anticipation and a swallow of liquid courage. Boron was at the tiller, following a heading that didn't exist. I stood at the prow of the *Witch*, an alabaster figurehead with shoulders back and chin forward, seeking out our fate and promising protection all at once. When I felt the pull shift and grow taut – that tether that connected not to my heart but somewhere deep behind it – when I felt that move, I would pace around the front of the ship until the line was soft again, and Boron would work the wheel until I stood once more like an anchoring knot at the middle of the middle of the bow.

A rarity since the terrible storm, we were far from open sea. Rather, we were making haste for a vast archipelago dotted with the warmth of lamps and windows, and the suggestion of ships in the hush of wind through canvas sails, somewhere near the equator.

"Not far, Captain," said one of the men, rushing up to Crow's elbow in the near-dark. "Gideon up in the nest says that he spied the *Seadragon's* wings just inside that yonder bay."

"Ready, then," said Crow, turning a great shoulder and making for the cluster of boats amidships. Not a single member of

326 ~ K. D. KIND

the *Witch's* crew had opted to leave when given the chance. It had been a blessing, as the *Seadragon's* anchor in the unnamed bay meant that any kind of direct approach would be useless. The *Witch* far outstripped the *Seadragon* in speed when it came to the open ocean, but sailing ships were not made for stealth.

Instead, the crew of the *Witch* were to disembark in the dark of the night, steal towards the *Seadragon* under cover of my own sorcerous silence, and take the enemy unawares in a rush.

It made the need for total victory, or else swift escape, all the more great.

I slipped easily down one of the ropes to the waiting rowboat below. Weeks of climbing the *Witch's* rigging had left my wasted body strong, if not at all browned. I still looked like a dead thing come to life, which (as I had pointed out when Crow had said the same) I was.

In my boat were men that I knew. Crow was with me, but Smith had been left on the *Witch*, a small and symbolic protection. He wore Crow's hat and clutched Crow's compass. If Crow fell in the coming fight, at least he would not default the *Witch* to Radley. They would need to find Smith for that.

I was tense beyond sound. Beyond breath. My whole body thrummed with anticipation. I was a lute ready to make harmonies with a lyre. And I was determined. Crow would be victorious, and Gideon as Crow's second man (or Boron, or whoever earned the stripe), would captain the *Seadragon* in Crow's name, so we could be together again.

Haedi would understand that being without Wulf, without the people we had loved, *all of it* could be made small in the wake of we sisters being together again.

I kept half of my heart focused on the pull of my sister, and the other I kept wrapped around the threads of energy that formed woven nets above the heads of the men as their little boats carved silently through the water. I felt something thicken and gather in the back of my throat, at the vace in my chest, the further we moved from the *Witch*. I shuffled closer to Crow, and the thickening eased, somewhat.

But not entirely, as part of the ill-feeling in my stomach came from the promise that I'd made to myself, after much cajoling from Crow, that once I had Haedi safe, I would tell her that I wouldn't wait on her to make my decisions anymore.

Safe first, then sound.

The *Seadragon* swam out of the evening ocean mist before us, her keel crafted of a deep brown, burgundy timber. All along the main deck were carvings of flame worked in wood; so well worked, in fact, that it seemed as though the fire truly danced and beckoned. I had been prepared for the trickery of the *Seadragon's* oily flames that claimed everything they touched. Crow thought that Radley's stores were running low, though, because the flames hadn't been used in years. The threat was enough to keep the enemy safe.

There grew within me a soft awareness that the thread connecting me with Haedi had dissolved. My throat flushed red with wonder. Surely, she was here. The distance had respooled. I had her, just beyond the reach of my desperate clutches. I was ready.

We rounded the bony, reaching fingers of the rocks and rowed into the cove proper. I searched the decks, peering up through the low light for signs of sentries or sailors. The *Seadragon* did not move beyond the slow bob and dance of a ship at anchor.

That is, not until it did.

Her sails unfurled with a snap that shocked me, left me reeling, until I realized with a sting that my protective barrier kept out all of the wind; wind which had blown up unnoticed, high above the choppy water.

They must have hauled the anchor on the other side of the vessel, for we had not seen it. Our only saving grace was that the *Seadragon* had not seen us. But it would spy the *Witch's* ghostly body in mere moments, with her cannons ready in their place, for if things should have gone awry when we boarded the *Seadragon*.

There was an irony as heavy as a cannonball in the fact that what had gone wrong were the very measures that we had taken for good measure.

Crow kept his head.

"All back, all back to the *Witch*!" he cried, working the oars on our little boat with the strength of a man half his age and twice his tenacity. "If you manage to reach the *Seadragon*, board her! This ends tonight!"

His long beard was wild with the exertion, and his eyes were bright with something similar. We caught the *Seadragon* with ease, aided by my own strange mastery of the waves. Crow sent a few of the little boats ahead to the *Witch*, to bolster Smith, and to keep guard.

When we came alongside the deep red belly of the *Seadragon* I gathered up the swell of the waves and lifted each of the little boats to near the height of the gangway. I heard the silken pull of metal on leather as thirty swords were drawn in unison, and then joined them in the collective pull of breath. Nodded once to Crow. Followed him over the side and onto the unfamiliar deck of the enemy's ship.

The alarm was raised before the first man even found his feet on the planks. Smith had been right – the men were all of a relation. Dressed in near the same manner as the men of the *Witch*, they all had hair of varying lengths and style and shade, but the same tone of red. Some had beards, some were clean-shaven. All wore expressions of sudden fear and fury, brought on by our threatening and unexpected arrival. I fought to ignore the dissonance. Why were they gathered so against us, and yet, clearly so surprised by our presence?

Like all good men, they all wore their blades, and so in mere heartbeats the air was full of the sound of weapons meeting in flurries that sounded (if you stopped paying attention) like a loud feast, rather than a battleground within the bounds of waist-high rails, already spilling precious parts upon the table.

Crow moved through the whirling and shouting throng like a hot knife through butter, drawing no undue consideration through his lack of fine aplomb. My sword – Crow's sword – got its first taste of blood when I drove it quickly through a sailor's chest. My wrist jarred as I grated against the bone. He fell, the blow that he had aimed at Crow's back never landing.

The *Seadragon* was much the same as the *Witch*, and yet still completely unfamiliar. I knew as I drove forward behind the wedge of Crow and Gideon's attack that I had never, and *would* never, belong here. Which told me nothing about the *Seadragon*, but afforded me a surprisingly sweet morsel about the *Witch*.

Crow was shouting something above the din of the fighting. I strained my ears, concentrating on the duck and slash of my own bout with yet another red sailor. He fell.

"RADLEY," roared Crow. "RADLEY! YOU HAVE SOME-THING OF MINE."

I lost sight of him behind a great flapping sheet of sail, torn free in the melee, and took my chance to go and find Haedi. If only I still had the tether, from her heart to mine. Then I would find her without looking.

My first thought was the nest. Was she anything like me? I darted around in the silver moonlight, finally spying the long rope ladder that they used to ascend. Praying that no bold sailor lay in wait, hiding above me, I flung myself quickly into the air, up and up, pausing on one of the cross beams before the summit.

From up on my perch, I surveyed the maelstrom below; it was now so fierce that the *Seadragon* had begun to whip about atop the waves as though it had fallen to its own madness. I scanned across the scene, noting the whirl and whip of men like dancers on the *Seadragon's* deck. Our men had indeed made it to the *Witch* – the ones that Crow had sent on, at least.

I saw no sign of Radley or Haedi below, but I did mark with a stifled sob that the number of heaped clothes on the deck was, friend or foe, a deep loss. Some of them had been spilled by my own hand.

I reached up sightlessly, expecting to wrap the thick, damp rope once more around my wrist. Instead, my fingers grasped a warm hand.

I screamed, and pulled my elbow down and backwards, trying to release myself from my unknown assailant.

"No, no, it's me!" cried a familiar voice, as Will tumbled precariously onto the round beam upon which I balanced. He grabbed onto the plank with both arms, wrapping as much of his body around it as he could.

I rushed forward and braced my legs on either side of the beam, heaving Will until he was safely astride as well.

"What are you *doing* here?" I demanded, hitting his shoulder roughly with my closed fist. And then, "I'm so sorry, I nearly killed you–"

"No," Will gasped. "Don't."

"Don't what? Apologise? But you were right – I talked with Crow, and Smith, and I *understand* now, not just about why he hunted me, but what *I* feel–"

I was speaking so quickly that even I wasn't sure of my words. But in my desperately anxious fear about the little time I had to find Haedi (to try to get *her* to understand), I needed... wanted Will to understand, too.

"Sylvi, stop, *please*," begged Will, and I snapped my mouth shut. There was an iron ring to his voice that scared me.

"Will... what is it?" I felt the fear showing in my face in the cold sting of the night air, touching too much of my eyes. I must have looked like a ghost, glowing in the moonlight, smeared with other men's blood.

"Sylvi... Haedi. I—"

I grabbed him by the front of his clothes, heedless of our height. Haedi. He knew where she was.

"Where is she, Will? Take me to her!"

But he moved his head slowly back and forth like I had seen old women do when they'd run out of things to say. His breath came in quaking gasps, and he peered down, measuring the drop.

"*Will*," I pleaded again. "You said once that you have honour. On that honour... *Where is she?*"

Will looked nothing like the boy that he had been. It had been mere weeks since he disappeared (since I had nearly drowned him), but in that time his cheeks had grown gaunt, his strong limbs thin, his honey hair lank and dull. I might have been a ghost, but he was a ghoul.

"I have no honour," he whispered. "I sold it."

Whatever words I might have managed were snatched from my mouth by a commotion below, beyond the cry and ring of the men fighting. Crow had reappeared, and he was duelling who could only be Radley, one-on-one. But Will was unaware of my inattention, for once he had begun his confession, he could not stop it.

"The night that... when I left the *Witch*, I swam to shore," he whispered. His eyes were squeezed shut; his knuckles were white where they gripped the rope knotted around the beam. I noticed absently that he had no weapon. "I found Radley, and bargained a berth on the *Seadragon*."

"What was your price?" I asked. I did not whisper.

"I told Radley that I knew of the magic needed to wake the waif in his vace, that I had seen it done, that I knew the way."

"Haedi!" I cried. "She's here? She's returned?"

I have to tell her that I love her, but that she doesn't live for me anymore, and I don't die for her.

"No." Will's shoulders shook.

My attention was snared once more by the sound of a deep, guttural cry from below. Had Crow been hit? I peered through the moonlight.

No, Crow was sound. But the *Witch*, where she waited a hundred yards away in the night, was in the direct path of a ribbon of what appeared to be dragon's breath, that had been unleashed from the *Seadragon*, and was now creeping its way over the waves towards her precious hull.

"No?" I demanded of Will. "Then give me the vace!"

"I can't," Will wailed. "I was too sure. I didn't tell them everything, because I didn't know everything."

Was it raining? Ice cold droplets appeared on my shoulders and began to trickle down my spine in rivulets of pure dread. No, the air was as dry as it had been moments ago, the sky just as empty of clouds. What I felt on my skin was a sheen of sweat, borne of terror, creeping over my flesh. I managed to speak through gritted teeth.

"Where. Is. My. Sister?"

"She's... *gone*."

I shoved him, hard, with two balled fists. I hadn't forgotten about the sword at my waist. I just didn't need it yet – I needed his answers before I needed his death.

"She *can't* be *gone!*" I snarled.

"Radley broke the vace against the hull of the *Seadragon*, just as I told him to do..."

Crow screaming again, from below. The men falling back from the *Seadragon's* deck, as cannon blasts began to sound from the *Witch's* decks. One found its mark and blasted a mast into thousands of useless shards.

"NO," I heard Crow crying, "THE SHIP IS MINE! I NEED HER INTACT!"

You do not. I turned my face once more towards Will, my mouth agape, my tongue dry, my eyes staring. He was still talking. Another cannonball, this one in slow motion.

"...and the blood down the hull, just like when you appeared, but it didn't pool together and take a shape... it just... dissipated."

Dissipated. Dissolved. Dead.

"We searched the water for any sign, but... none. She's... gone."

"When?" I demanded.

But I knew. I knew the moment that it had snapped.

He reached into his vest, groped. The vace... the bottom of the vace that should have held the saltwater against Haedi's chest, sat perfect and empty in the shell of Will's palm.

I stood slowly from where I had been crouching next to him, where I had been comforting him. I gazed down at him. I watched his lips form words, but I did not hear. Crow continued to shout over the disaster down below, but I did not hear. I shook my head, trying to clear out the strange, seething silence. Something final in Will's eyes died. A last little light went out.

What was it that he had asked me? What request had I denied?

I don't know if he let go, or if it was another cannon shot. I don't know. It was such a long way down... and so much longer, considering how the air had gotten so thick, and time was moving in slow motion. I watched his entire descent to the deck below. In the minutes the followed, his body was lost amidst the melee on deck.

The dragon flame had reached the place where the *Witch's* hull met the lapping waves, and already I could see the beginnings of scorching spread over her skin. The men had all made it back to the *Witch*, to die there. Even Crow. I could see him hoisting himself up on the ropes to join his men. Had he taken his revenge with him?

I saw the cannonball as it coursed towards my chest. I saw it early enough that I had time to decide. To decide to either dive or die.

The arc that I took through the air was perfect, like a gull in its final fall, way out in the middle of the sea. How many of them had I seen since I had awoken?

Enough.

The water broke over the tips of my fingers, but that didn't stop the harsh crash of the waves onto my cheeks, throwing water back into my throat and eyes. I was fast. I needed to be fast if I was going to get there in time.

I swam deep under the surface of the water, watching the lick and curl of the flames above. They couldn't touch me.

The swim was a hundred yards. One yard for every five years since I had died the first time. But the first time hadn't been my destruction, because I wasn't alone, then.

Haedi. Headstrong, passionate, damned Haedi. Wasted. Despite all of her plans, and her... all of it, for nothing. To eke out the final dregs of her existence at the hands of a brute on the hull of a beast. Minutes before I found her. Were we separated by minutes, or by millennia?

The *Witch* was well alight by the time I crawled over her side. All around me men were coughing and straining, trying to get water atop the blasted flames. I slid by them all.

Crow caught me as I reached the foot of the tower. *Haedi?* Asked his mouth, but my ears were closed. I shook my head, and he hung his. His embrace was dear and generous. He cupped the base of my head as though I were an infant, and for a moment, I was, curled into him like an answered question.

And then I stepped back, stepped away, and climbed.

I hardly felt the blisters erupting on my skin as I made my way up past the fluttering sails. My hair erupted in a halo of light as the wind whipped up around me, bringing with it embers and heat.

Behind my staring eyes, I saw a dream play out, in which Haedi's vace was broken, was shattered, and the dregs of my dearest one poured out to the waiting cup of the gods.

The basket was not high enough. Not if I wanted to reach to the edges of the *Witch*. I pulled myself even further up, up into the danger of the open air, atop the point of the mast, balancing somehow on shaking feet.

It would take forever to call a storm into a night as clear as this. I needed to do it now.

But even at that moment, knowing that everything that I held dear had been lost to me... I hesitated. Resisted.

The men of the *Witch* still worked below, refusing to give up on that which they loved so much.

Did they love the same as I did? Was their love for the *Witch*? For each other? For life itself?

Haedi no longer lived for me.

I no longer died for her.

So, for whom did I die?

Chapter 23

Blood

His Majesty's Hospital Ship *Valkyrie* waited in the quiet of the waters just out of sight of the place called Constantinople. The nurses, doctors and sailors lurked about her vast insides, either bravely staring square into the face of the man-made thunderstorm, watching as the sky was rent apart by vicious explosions and metallic screams that sent an artificial wind sweeping over their heads, or else, cowering behind blackened windows, praying and pleading and readying themselves for what was to come.

Isevelt had never felt in such danger before. Even the day when she had watched the priestess open her own throat had been less turbulent than this. More predictable. Isevelt had known without fail the moment of her own death.

As she stood at the railing of the *Valkyrie*, looking serenely out into the maelstrom of war just clear of the horizon, Isevelt wondered if she even *could* die. She'd done it, once; did one have leave to die over again? Given this choice, was she pleased with the second death? Had she even loved the first?

No. The first had been cold. And then dim. And then black.

This felt as hot as the fire and twice as unpredictable. Better to marry intention with chance, than chance with a promise.

The battle reached them in an instant.

Where was Eryn? There, by the dickie boats. The ship shuddered in anticipation as she came to life, woke from her slumber, and slipped ponderously forward, forward, carving through the swells of the ocean like a scythe desperate for threshing.

The smell changed. All around was the reek of combustible fuel; another ship must have met her match.

I hope not, Isevelt thought. For she had seen how the fuel floated on top of the water, how it called the flames towards it and, having caught them, jealously hoarded within the ring of its arms the men that they could never save.

Isevelt knew that there was a chain of command aboard the ship; knew that in times of quiet there were men who answered to each other, and women who answered to everyone who was not a woman. But as soon as the heat of battle reached a boil, each person's wits were equal, and equally valued.

In a moment, men were being heaved up onto the decks, triaged into the saloons and the ballrooms, and the chapel and the gutted quarters. Isevelt swept through them all, moving towards Eryn but keeping her hand pressed firmly to her middle, where she could feel the pull that was *August* tugging most insistently, like a child at a mother's skirt.

It was getting stronger.

She fell down next to Eryn, using her eyes and hands and questions to assess the first casualty. Eryn pressed her fingertips to the pulse point below his jaw, then crept her hand down beneath the neck of his shirt. She shook her head. Isevelt grit her teeth, kissed his head, and stood again, waving to the orderly.

The next was alive.

Sobbing.

He had a burn across his chest and the right side of his face. Isevelt pulled the heat of the burn from the edges in, gathered the water from his sodden clothes and poured it out over the angry skin. Eryn dressed the wounds expertly. Isevelt kissed his head, and they moved on.

The pull grew stronger.

* * *

Had it been minutes? Hours?

An amputated arm. Another dead man. Bullet wound to the cheek. Kiss. Kiss. Kiss.

Pull.

Near drowned. Isevelt drew the water from his lungs and stomach. Kiss.

Pull.

Another burn; across the back this time. He didn't sob. He swore and apologised. He made them laugh. Kiss.

Pull.

Her neck felt permanently bent at a sharp angle so that the muscles in the backs of her legs protested. Had it been minutes? Hours? Kiss.

The captain came past, all the formality of relaxed hours fled in the fury of the work.

"Have you got one of those kisses for me, my dear?" he asked, his eyes shining, above the once-white moustache, now tinged with foamy pink.

Isevelt stood (her legs screamed), laid a hand along his cheek so that the line of fugitive whiskers tickled her palm, and kissed his head.

Pull.

Snap.

No.

The tether was gone.

He can't be gone.

Isevelt prepared her mind for the inevitable, encroaching despair that welled up in her, knowing that it would commandeer her senses and render her useless, right there on the deck, in the midst of the dead and dying; knowing that it would take her, that she would do nothing to stop it.

She drew in a single, sweet breath.

"Have you got one of those kisses for *me*, my dear?"

The voice was cracked from use, or perhaps even exhaustion. The blue eyes had lost much of their lustre so that they now sat like worn sea glass atop cheeks dusted with more freckles than before. He had grown a full beard, and it was as bronze as his hair, which curled from the assault of the waves. He stood, clutching his middle, doubled over in pain.

Chapter 24

Salt

Crow watched, as if in a dream, as the waif heaved herself up, until she was standing, perched, atop the spear-point of the mast, silhouetted like an angel by the light of the moon and stars. It was all silver up there, and molten hell down in the waves.

His ship. He had claimed his revenge, but it was not sweet. It tasted like bile, like acrid smoke. She must have climbed so high to get away from the burning.

He told himself that he could see her face. See the strength there.

She turned her cheeks to the sky, gathered her arms tight to her chest, and flung them wide.

And then.

* * *

Blood

I ran across the slippery deck, throwing aside his hands to assess the wound in his stomach, but found none. He was hale. I gazed wonderingly into his eyes.

"Just a stitch, from swimming," he explained with a slow breath out. "The ship that I was on went down."

"August," I breathed, and I placed a hand on either side of his face.

He leaned his head down, as though in prayer. I pressed my lips to the soft skin in the middle of his forehead, to the tip of his nose, to his lips.

His arms came around me, a firm embrace. The pull was gone – for I was complete. Each of the little parts of me that had been broken shards of glass came back together.

So did his.

The first time I gave myself for another, it was for duty.

The second time, it was for love.

* * *

Salt

I felt myself burst, the bloody vace held tightly in my right hand, and I knew that my edges would go far enough. That I would be enough. The *Witch* would be covered in the soft mist that would drift down out of the night sky, drowning the flames.

I *knew* for a long time, just as I had known when the priestess had left me to float in the waves. Only this time, I was not gathered back together. I scattered, drifted, slipped apart from myself. Feeling the threads of my weave not just pull free, but age and turn to dust.

Had Haedi *known*, for this long?

Perhaps some part of me would find some part of her, in the great expanse of the ocean, in time.

As the *Witch* guttered and faded to a dull glow, the *Seadragon* dipped finally, battered and crushed, to disappear below the waves.

The first time, it had been for love.

It was the second time, too.

* * *

Chapter 25

Ash

They stood on either side of the stone altar; vessels of salt-water cradled in the curves of their outstretched arms. The blood had dried to rust-coloured pockmarks, as though the altar had endured some long-ago battle. As though it had been more than a passive slate upon which unknown generations had written their history of weak subservience. Written it in their own blood.

"Did you bring the flint?" Aidan asked the darkness.

Wulfric stood in the shadow of a tall birchwood tree, the light of the moon falling and pooling in the upmost edges of his ridges and whorls. His forearms strained with the weight of the ewer, and his straight shoulders bowed under the weight of recent days.

"I brought everything you asked of me."

"It's the only way," Aidan insisted.

Wulf nodded, but the tightness of his jaw made the movement into a shiver, rather than any real acknowledgement of truth.

They had talked for hours; first atop the sea cliffs, far away from the houses. Then, inside the low-roofed house that still smelled of their brother. They talked about the treachery. About the betrayal.

Gnarsa's, yes... *but more offensively*, said Aidan, *the perfidy of the gods themselves.*

Standing in the moonlight, seeming like skeletons beside a monument to the dead, Wulf longed to speak of it no more. He owed Aidan a debt. He owed.

So, let us do it and have done with it.

"Do you really believe this will work?" Wulf asked.

Let this be the end of it.

Aidan lifted her own urn and tipped it by its swollen belly, so that cold water, thin as tears, slipped in a sheet over the lip to cascade upon the flat surface of the stone. The water turned a repellent shade of pink as soon as it touched the altar, the turbulence of its spill leaving behind cold, grey rock, which was unmarked now by generations of jealous taxes.

"It must work," Aidan said. Her voice was a gravel path that cut through the sharp knell of the water striking the stone. "The gods have no real power, outside of the blood. We talk of balance... of the gods giving back what they receive. What we failed to understand is that they *have* only what they receive. We take away the blood... nothing remains."

The pitch of the pouring water changed as the depths reached their end. Aidan cast her ewer off to the side where it nestled somewhere in the pillowed undergrowth between the trees. She reached for the other vessel. Her palms glistened where they had been splashed and speckled with her labours.

Wulf shied suddenly away, clutching the heavy stone ewer tight to his chest. "Nothing?"

"Wulf, give me the water."

"Nothing remains?"

Aidan straightened her neck and ran her hands back over her hair. "Let us have done with it, Wulf. Let us settle it."

"What about the other vaces? Haedi? And the others?"

"Sylvi. Isevelt."

"What happens to them?"

Wulf still held the vast pitcher away, as a child with a threatened toy. As though he held a bargaining chip. As though there were any hands left to play. The infantile furrow in his brow softened Aidan's ire.

He doesn't understand.

Aidan breathed deeply to calm herself.

He would. Once he saw it all, he would understand. When she spoke, her voice was quiet. A hum on the back of a sigh. Like a raven on a gust of wind, way up in the expanse of the clouds.

"They *died*," Aidan said. "They already died."

"No." Wulf flicked his chin back and forth. A dismissal. A plea. "No. *You're* here. *You're* alive."

"What good is there being alive but not free?" she asked.

Aidan stood with her feet together and her hands clasped before her waist. She did not advance upon him, although her instinct cried out for her to abandon his understanding and simply complete the task herself. But no. She needed him, for the final step.

"There is no way for them to return themselves," Aidan explained. "They can never be free. Even now they slumber, dreaming of their heat and weight and... *imperium* draining out of them. When they wake all that will change is that they'll *feel* it, not just remember. They're already dead."

"But I'm listening to you." Wulf's voice wheedled, even as his arms held the water aloft. Away. "*I* could return them."

"You'll lose Haedi. She'll hate you. For what you've done."

Wulf gasped a strangled sob.

"There is no good that can come of it. Believe me. I have learned this lesson by flesh and bone and teeth and tongue. Serving any master that requires something of you is *no* service at all. That master is not serving you, and you're not serving it."

Wulf wrapped his body around the ewer so that his back bent and his skin pulled. It aged him a hundred years in a moment where the moonlight cut a harsh relief into the details of his face.

"No *god* should *need* anything from you for its own glory," Aidan pushed. "That's no god. It's an ominous parasite masquerading as worthy."

Her words were punctuated by the inconstant *drip drip* of water falling like the unpleasant echo of a heartbeat.

"Give me the water, Wulf," Aidan said once more.

He relented. Reached out with trembling arms, offered the ocean to the waif in his thrall, and hoped it was enough to wash himself clean of her blood. As he had stepped back in fear, the distance was too great for Aidan to reach the heavy urn without stepping towards him, and away from the altar. Sending her will out in a spiral, she gathered up the edges of the deep well of water and lifted it out of the vessel. A vast, rolling mass, it rose up out of the mouth of the ewer and hovered over the altar like a ghost.

Fighting the urge to simply burst the thing and wear the wrath of it, Aidan instead let it go in a steady, careful rill that bunched and smoothed, taking the last of the iron tithe with it back into the now sodden ground.

"Here is what we will do, now," she said quietly, gauging Wulf's eyes as he watched the flow of the water. "The gods are gone. Gnarsa is fled, and she will never return here on pain of death. All that remains are the people – in a hundred years even *they* will be gone – back to the sea, and gone."

Aidan allowed the water to spiral and swill, matching the cadence of her voice to the movement of the light across the stone. Lulling him away from his fear. His grief.

His guilt.

"Haedi. Sylvi. Isevelt," she intoned, as though their names were a poem. "All gone. We are going to put them to rest. Let them go. And then I will go. And it will be done. And you will live out your days."

"How?"

He whispered. It echoed.

How. How. How.

She answered the part of his question that she had leave to answer. Whatever Wulf had on his own horizon would be, in a matter of minutes, no longer her concern.

"Ever this vace be pressed to my skin, let death be without, and life be within," she recited. "We will break the vaces, and pour them out, and let them return to death, where they belong."

"And you?"

Aidan didn't hesitate. She had decided.

Have done with it.

"You will burn the boat, with me in it."

"*What?*"

"You owe me, Wulfric Ravenson. You owe me a life." Aidan spoke harshly, her teeth bared in a warrior snarl. "I could just as easily demand *yours* in payment, as demand mine."

"All of this for nothing," Wulf moaned. "*Haedi, I'm so sorry. I failed. I'm so sorry.*"

"Not nothing," Aidan corrected.

The water had stilled now, leaving the altar shining like a perfect, silver mirror. She drew him close to the stone, holding his trembling hands. Bid him look upon the water, see the truth of it. Their faces (equally ghostlike, equally bare) stared up at them, framed by the skeletal branches of the birchwoods behind them.

"Ash from the fire used to make the glass. Salt in the glass used to form the vaces. Blood from our bodies to fill it. Nothing of any of this was for anything."

"Except for eyes to be opened and the dream to end."

Aidan turned her gaze so that she could see Wulf's profile. "Yes."

"Do you know where the other vaces are hidden?" he asked. His voice shook. He was terrified.

"No."

"I do."

He placed his hands on the side of the altar, bent his head down low as if in prayer, and heaved with all his strength. The great stone came away from its base, toppled loudly to the wet ground and split cleanly in two. In the space below the slab was a dark hollow, empty but for three glass cylinders. Wulf had said that they were in the grove, but Aidan had never imagined that the altar itself would be as empty as the ritual for which it had stood.

Aidan reached down and gathered them into her arms. The glass was clear and perfect, with not even a streak of ash disturbing the smooth planes of the vace. Each end cut cleanly away in a perfectly rounded edge, exactly the shape of the dome even now boring a deep gouge into her breastbone. The pure liquid inside caught the moonlight and sparked sharp flashes of lightning across her skin where the reflections landed. She held one of them (she knew not who) up to the moonlight, watching as it danced and distorted through the swell of the glass.

"How comforting," Aidan whispered after a moment. "I don't feel anything."

"That doesn't mean it won't hurt."

"No." Aidan lowered the vace. "No, it doesn't."

She handed him one of the vaces and grasped the other two firmly in her freezing cold fingers. "Are you ready?"

A muscle flashed in Wulf's jaw as he lowered his eyes to the ground. "Are you?"

It was understandable for Wulf to be angry. She was forcing him to kill four girls.

Again.

Ah, she thought wryly as they picked their careful way through the stand of trees, down the natural ridgelines, towards the sea. *But this was always his lot.*

"We must break them on the rocks," Aidan said once her feet were fully in the freezing water. "If we break them on the boat then you'll have to burn them with me."

"You speak to me as though I've not done this before," Wulf spat. He glanced at his birchwood boat where it bobbed in the gently rippling waves.

"No," Aidan sighed. "I speak as someone who hasn't."

She weighed the vaces in her hands. They had a certain kind of symmetry to them. As though they were sisters. She crouched down so that the fabric of her dress gathered water right up to her waist, picked a place on the rock before her, closed her eyes, and swung with both arms.

The breaking glass sounded like the end of a frost. The sound of a morning grown just warm enough that the layer of ice over all of the petals and leaves broke free, fell to the earth, and revealed the fragile death that had so long been hidden behind brittle strength.

Beside her came the echoing ring of the third vace coming apart. When she opened her eyes Aidan could scarcely discern where the essence of her sisters had run into the waves.

"You need to burn me here, upon the water."

"You'll need to get in the boat, then."

Wulf appeared to be grappling with deep, unnamed emotions. His face was set into a kind of horrid grimace, and he rubbed his palms back and forth in the water, over and over, as though trying in vain to clean the skin right off.

The heavy skirts made clambering into the boat difficult, so Aidan slipped them off. Dressed once more in her clinging slip, Aidan prepared again to meet her death.

She laid back so that she could see the stars. Imagined the bodies of the others bearing her up, calling her down.

"I'm sorry," she thought she heard Wulf whisper, as the flames licked suddenly at the oil which had soaked completely through the white wood; oil which Aidan had poured by her own hands earlier that evening. "I'm sorry."

We were sisters.
If sisters were women who were bonded in blood.
Knowing that the others would endure the same trial
wasn't comfort enough.
It was knowing that the others were spared.
As the flames crept finally onto my damp skin
I clasped the vace on my chest with desperate fingers.
As the heat rose to a point beyond endurance,
as I felt myself meet the point of my own mettle,
I dug my nails down deep into the press
of my own flesh, pried the edge of the glass loose,
and pulled myself free.
The first time, it had been condemnation.
The second... Release.

***

Epilogue

"Do you know where the other vaces are hidden?" he asked.
His voice shook.
He was terrified.
"No."
He was relieved. "I do."

Acknowledgements

I wrote the first line of this book in 2013. Our second child was a few months old, and like our eldest before her, she had started to actually, finally, *sleep*. I felt like I was learning how to breathe again. I was Aidan clawing myself, hand over hand, back onto the beach of normality. It took me another child, a teaching degree, and a year of full-time employment before I picked up the threads of this story again, this time intending to finish it. I think this is a story about many things. But, at its heart, it's a celebration of women and the people who fill and shape their lives. This book would not have been possible without the support and contribution of my people.

To my husband Steve, thank you. Thank you for creating the cover for this book. It's perfect. Thank you for encouraging me to write it, rather than to finish it. You help me to remember that there is such beauty in *doing the thing*, as well as having it done. Your love and care of our family served as the inspiration for Isevelt's *good man*. It is truly an honour and a privilege to do life by your side. To our children, you are the most wonderful gifts that we have ever received.

To my wonderful editor and friend Laura Neggo, bless you. And thank you. For taming my errant punctuation, for paying such particular attention to detail, and for being genuinely excellent at many things. It has been such a pleasure refining this with you. Your belief in me and in this story is something that I will treasure, always.

To Emmalee, you were my first real reader. Without your enthusiasm for the characters in this story, and your demands that I keep writing them, this book would not exist. I cannot tell you how much I appreciate the conversations we've had. Maybe one day you'll get your anime adaptation.

Lauren and Hayden, I will forever hold dear your willingness to read this story in its infancy. Even more, your willingness not to kill me in mine. Lauren, you left a post-it in my kitchen years ago. Every day it tells me, "you've got this, it's going to be fine, I believe in you". Even though the post-it is showing wear after all of this time, your constant friendship endures. I adore you. Gar, you've been my creative sounding board for as long as I can remember. Thank you for acknowledging all of my neurotic emails without always feeling the need to indulge them. I could not have explored the difficulties and subtleties of the sibling relationships in this story without first having had the camaraderie and affection of our own. I cherish you both.

Mum and Dad, when I told you that I was going to be a writer, you believed me. When it took me a couple of decades to get there, you were patient. When I finally gave you the first draft, your passion for the project and your pride in me filled me with such joy. You've always been so good at that; filling your kids with joy. The adventures, the opportunities, the loving care. Thank you for all of it.

A special thank you to Zach and Abi. I had no business asking you to critique my work. That's a terrifying task, and one that's fraught with peril. Your generous and genuine notes helped me to make this story into the one that I wanted to tell. I cried with happiness when I read your reactions. I'm expecting a distinct mistiness from you, in return.

To Viv and Ali (and Laura), thank you for the very last-minute advice on the look of this book. I admire your intelligence, sophistication, knowledge, and opinions. You guys make the days better, and the job easier.

Thanks to Kristen Kieffer at well-storied.com. You don't know me. We've never spoken. But the quality and scope of the resources that you've created for writers is awe inspiring. Your newsletter helped me to remember why I love writing, many times, over many years – all the way back to the *She's Novel* days. If you're thinking about writing, I really recommend that you visit well-storied.com.

As a final thought (although, to be honest, this thought was the genesis for the concept of *The Iron Tithe*), I'd really like to talk about the problem with the paltry, nameless gods. Many of the characters in this story struggle with fear and satisfaction in their quest to serve the higher power. As Aidan says, "no god should need anything of you for its own glory". The God of the Bible is good, constant, and loving. His desire is for relationship with us, and He offers it freely. God, in his love, gave *himself* to death, rather than requiring it of us.

"For God so loved the world that He gave his one and only Son, that whoever believes in Him shall not perish but have eternal life" (John 3:16).

– Kate